WHA__
A
WEEK

OMNIBUS

BOOKS 1-3

Rosie Rushton lives in Moulton, Northamptonshire. She is a school governor of a new secondary school and in May 2004 was licensed as a Reader in the Church of England. Her hobbies include tracing her family history, travelling the world, being with her grandchildren, walking, theatre, reading and all things Indian. In the future she wants to write a TV drama for teenage audiences, visit Kathmandu, write the novel that has been pounding in her brain for years but has never quite got to the keyboard, and learn to slow down and smell the roses. Her many books for Piccadilly Press include *Break Point, Tell Me I'm OK, Really* and several series including Best Friends, The Girls and The Leehampton Quartet.

Already available from Piccadilly Press:

Book 7: What a Week to Take a Chance

Coming soon:

Book 8: What a Week to Get Real
Book 9: What a Week to Risk it All
What a Week Omnibus: Books 4–6 including:
What a Week to Make a Stand
What a Week to Play it Cool
What a Week to Make a Move

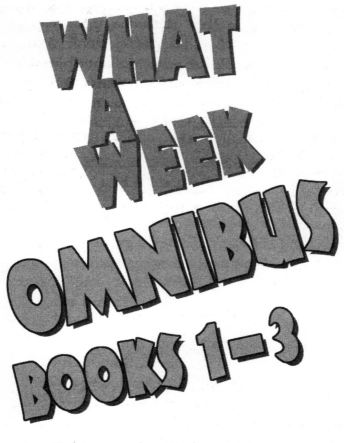

WHAT A WEEK OMNIBUS BOOKS 1-3

ROSIE RUSHTON

Piccadilly Press · London

First published in Great Britain in 2005
by Piccadilly Press Ltd,
5 Castle Road, London NW1 8PR
www.piccadillypress.co.uk

A catalogue record for this book is available from the British Library

ISBN: 1 85340 866 2 (trade paperback)

1 3 5 7 9 10 8 6 4 2

Printed and bound in Great Britain by Bookmarque Ltd
Text design by Louise Millar.
Cover illustration by Susan Hellard
Cover design by Fielding Design.
Set in Legacy.

WHAT
A
WEEK
TO
FALL
IN
LOVE

For the budding authors of Mereway Middle School,
who inspired more than they know!

MONDAY

7.00 a.m.
The Cedars, Weston Way, West Green, Dunchester.
Despairing of mothers

Monday mornings, thought Holly Vine, yawning and flicking her nutmeg-brown hair behind her ears, were bad enough without having to contend with a totally manic mother. Here she was, five days away from her fourteenth birthday, with lopsided boobs, a wardrobe full of clothes that everyone had seen a thousand times and the absolute certainty of getting a C-minus for her geography project, and she hadn't even got a normal mother to turn to in her hour of need.

Normal mothers took you shopping and said things like, 'You choose – I'll pay'. Holly's mother considered clothes as merely a way of preventing hypothermia. She also seemed unable to grasp the fact that Holly simply had to have some hipsters and a new pair of black boots, and even less able to appreciate that if Holly was ever going to get Scott Hamill back from the clutches of Ella Hankinson, her wardrobe needed some serious updating.

Normal mothers came into your room in the mornings with a cup of tea and perched on the end of your bed and asked how your life was. Holly's mother, who had spent all Saturday taking a coachload of mums and toddlers to Clacton and most of Sunday slapping paint on the walls of the crèche at the Lowdown Centre, was so caught up with sorting out other people's lives that she barely realised Holly had one, let alone found time to ask how it was progressing.

Holly grabbed her blue-and-white bathrobe and padded across the landing to the bathroom, thinking that it was grossly unfair that a woman who gained enormous satisfaction from forcing the parishioners of St Saviour's into attending strawberry teas in aid of the crumbling bell tower seemed totally devoid of any desire to deal with the crumbling social life of her only daughter.

This morning had been a case in point, she thought, peering in the mirror and scrutinising her ivory skin for any sign of a spot. Ten minutes earlier, her mother, dressed in an ancient, shapeless cord skirt and a sage-green jumper of uncertain age, had flung open Holly's door and crashed into the bottom of her bed, thereby rudely wakening her from a most satisfying dream featuring her, Scott Hamill in his rugby gear and a very romantic stretch of tropical seashore.

'Marker pens, sweetheart!' her mother had cried.

Before Holly had managed to prise open one reluctant eyelid, her mother had been rummaging through her drawers like a thing possessed.

'Mum!' Holly had protested as her mother tossed make-up brushes and pots of lip-gloss on to the bed. 'What *are* you doing?'

'Looking for your coloured markers,' she had repeated, slamming one drawer shut and wrenching open another. 'Half of mine have dried out and I'm in a tearing hurry.'

'*Good morning, Holly darling, and how did you sleep?*'

Holly had muttered sarcastically, sitting up in bed.

'What? Oh yes, sorry, sweetheart – sleep well?' her mother had responded distractedly, brushing a strand of greying hair from her eyes.

'Actually no,' admitted Holly. 'You see, I – '

'That's nice,' said her mother. 'Darling, where are those pens?'

Holly had sighed and raised her pewter-grey eyes heavenwards. 'In my school bag – what do you want them for anyway?'

'Posters, darling,' her mother had explained enthusiastically, casting an eye around the assorted debris littering Holly's pale-blue carpet in an attempt to locate the school bag.

'Oh yes?' said Holly. 'And what is it this time? Hands off our Hostel? No Superstore for Swan's Meadow?' she chanted, listing her mother's two most recent projects. 'Of course,' she added coaxingly, 'it could be that you are going to do a Come To Holly's Amazing Birthday Party poster.' She waited, more in hope than expectation.

'Here they are!' cried her mother triumphantly, totally ignoring Holly's pointed hint and pulling a packet of felt markers from the top of her daughter's kitbag. 'I'm doing a couple of posters for the nursery raffle.' And she headed for the door.

'Mum!' Holly had begun. Her mother had paused, hand on the doorknob, and eyed her daughter impatiently.

'What?'

'I need to talk to you,' Holly had begun.

Her mother had looked as astonished as if Holly had expressed a desire for them to go scuba-diving before breakfast.

'Darling, I've hardly time to breathe, never mind talk,' she gabbled. 'I've got these posters to drop off, and a committee meeting about the Michaelmas Fair and I haven't even looked at the agenda yet. Can't it wait?'

Holly shook her head adamantly. 'No, it's about Saturday,' she began, thinking that surely even her mother could see that Holly's birthday took precedence over discussions about bric-à-brac stalls.

Her mother clicked her tongue impatiently. 'Saturday? But that's days away!' she said. 'At the rate I'm going, it will be a miracle if I am still upright by Saturday.' She caught Holly's miffed expression and softened. 'Look, if it's anything important, darling, we'll talk about it tonight,' she promised. 'Truly really.'

She glanced at her watch. 'Now I really must get on and so must you.'

'But, Mum . . .'

It was too late. Her mother had shut the door and pounded down the stairs muttering, 'Tickets twenty-five pence each or five for one pound.'

That's typical of my mother, Holly thought now, standing under the trickle of tepid water that passed for a shower in their ancient bathroom, and eyeing her non-developing boob anxiously. If it's anything important, indeed! She had forgotten. She knew she had. She could remember posters for some poxy raffle, but her daughter's birthday meant nothing to her at all.

Sometimes, thought Holly crossly, I wonder whether I mean anything at all.

7.45 a.m.
3 Plough Cottages, Cattle Hill, West Green, Dunchester. Pondering over paternity

While Holly was busy considering her mother's shortcomings, around the corner on Cattle Hill, Tansy Meadows was attempting to discipline her badly behaved hair and thinking about her father. This exercise was complicated somewhat by the fact that she hadn't a clue who he was. Her mother, on whom Tansy had pressed the issue several times, admitted that she wasn't oversure either, although she thought she could narrow it down to a choice of two.

Tansy adored her mother and was well used to her tendency to vagueness, but lately this gap in her ancestry had been bothering her more and more. All her friends at West Green Upper School had fathers somewhere or other; even Jade Williams had a dead one and lots of photographs in silver frames which people looked at and exclaimed, 'My, aren't you like your dad!'

Tansy assumed that she too must resemble her unknown father. Certainly she didn't bear any likeness whatsoever to her mother. Tansy was small and wiry with sandy-coloured flyaway hair, eyes the colour of snail shells and a fiercely determined nature. Her mother, Clarity (who had been christened Kathleen but who changed her name when she got in with a group of New Age travellers at the age of seventeen, because she thought it made her sound ethereal), was solidly built with a mass of frizzy auburn curls, hazel eyes and a temperament so laid back as to be almost horizontal. She drifted through life expecting everything and everyone to turn out just fine. Had she been a bit more switched on, Tansy thought, she might just have managed to keep closer tabs on the parentage of her child.

'Tansy! Breakfast's ready!' Her mother's voice called up the stairwell.

'Coming,' Tansy called back, abandoning her attempts to make her hair look sleek and sophisticated. She wondered what her mother's idea of breakfast would be today. Clarity Meadows may well have forsaken the open road and returned to a more traditional lifestyle, but she still harboured pretty strong ideas about treating one's body as a temple. From time to time this led her to experiment with the most extraordinary diets and serve up platefuls of things that would have been much better left growing in a stretch of undisturbed woodland. It was supposed to be kids who had unconventional ideas, thought Tansy, clattering down the uncarpeted stairs and bashing her head against the wooden wind chimes which her mother insisted drew serenity into their living space. It seemed slightly unfair that when she only had one parent, she got landed with an eccentric one.

Tansy eyed the untidy sitting room with distaste. The floral covers on the two battered armchairs were faded and frayed. Three large wrought-iron candlesticks stood in one corner and a fat china Buddha grinned cheerfully from the fireplace. Piles of gardening magazines were stacked in every corner, whilst the coffee table was covered with seed catalogues and garden implements. Her mother referred to herself as a garden-design consultant. She spent most evenings drawing elaborate plans of patios and lily ponds, but her working day was spent mowing lawns, weeding borders and pruning rose bushes. Clarity loved her job because she said she could commune with nature all day. Unfortunately she didn't earn a great deal and while she repeatedly assured Tansy that money didn't buy you happiness, Tansy felt that it would be nice to have the opportunity of putting that theory to the test. Then they could have a big house with rag-rolled walls, thick carpets and a whirlpool bath. And her mother could get rid of her ancient and rusting van, which she insisted was ideal for her job, and the ownership of which Tansy said was so lacking in street cred as to be a punishable offence. She was sure her father, wherever he was, would not be driving such a disreputable vehicle.

Whenever she fantasised about her unknown father she imagined him as being well off, with a shock of sandy-coloured hair just like hers and a warm, all-encompassing smile. His shoes would be real leather and he would have a cashmere overcoat and a real pigskin wallet. Tansy liked beautiful things. And one day, whatever it took, she vowed she would have them.

'You're looking very thoughtful this morning,'

remarked her mother, kissing the top of Tansy's head and dumping a bowl of something utterly extraordinary on to the wobbly Formica-topped table in the kitchen.

'I was thinking about my father,' said Tansy, peering suspiciously at the contents, 'whoever he might be.'

'Oh, that again.' Her mother sighed. 'Darling, I've told you all I know.'

Tansy had, of course, on frequent occasions quizzed her mother about the two possible candidates for the role of father. One apparently was called Jordan and had spent a whole summer painting pebbles in a converted bus parked outside Glastonbury, before upping and leaving with a girl called October for a new life in the Faeroe Islands. The other had been called Pongo, which unfortunately for the detective in Tansy was not his real name, and he was an American university student from Illinois with whom her mother had had a brief fling in an attempt to get over the defection of the said Jordan.

On balance, Tansy thought Pongo sounded more promising, apart from the unfortunate name. After all, if he had a degree he could be a successful business tycoon by now, or a TV personality or a wealthy lawyer with a big house and who took holidays in Florida. That he could also be out of work, penniless or a total jerk, Tansy refused to consider. She had great ambitions for her future, and if she couldn't have a father on hand to help her achieve them, she could at least dream about one who had achieved a few of the things to which she so earnestly aspired.

'Yes, that again,' retorted Tansy. 'Mum, you must

know more than you've told me. I mean, you don't go having babies with people and not know something about them. At least, you shouldn't,' she added sharply.

Her mother sighed. 'You're right, sweetheart, of course you are,' she said. 'I was young, homesick, romantic, and very, very stupid. And in those days I wasn't a very good judge of men.'

Nothing's changed, thought Tansy. Her mother's latest boyfriend, Laurence Murrin, was a complete dork – a walking fashion disaster who considered himself to be a world authority on everything and could bore for England.

Clarity touched Tansy's shoulder. 'I'm sorry that you don't know your dad,' she whispered. 'I know it hasn't been easy for you – but it hasn't been a bed of roses for me either, you know.'

Tansy chewed her lip. 'Do you ever wish you hadn't gone ahead and had me?' she asked, scanning her mother's features.

'Darling, never!' cried her mother, hugging her close. 'I wouldn't be without you for the whole world.'

Tansy suddenly felt a great upsurge of love for her mum. 'I wouldn't be without you either,' she said. 'And anyway, who needs fathers?'

But still, one, somewhere, would be nice, she thought to herself, peering into her cereal bowl.

'What on earth is this?' she asked.

'It's a mixture of hazelnuts and wheatgerm and dried figs,' Charity said. 'I mixed it all up and added some wheat bran and then – '

'It's disgusting!' said Tansy, wrinkling her nose.

'Darling, it's brain food – I read up about it,' insisted her mother. 'Helps you concentrate. And now you're in Year Nine with all this new coursework, I thought . . .'

Clarity, who had spent most of her schooldays avoiding work, never failed to be amazed by her daughter's appetite for learning and information.

'Mum, it's no big deal – the work's easy.'

Tansy had found the first week of the new school year a doddle work-wise but something of a disappointment as far as romance was concerned. It wasn't that guys didn't ask her out, but she simply couldn't get excited over any of them. They were all so . . . ordinary. She wanted someone who was a total dish, with a wicked sense of humour, a functioning brain and loads of ambition, and that was a combination that was pretty thin on the ground at West Green Upper.

Just as Tansy was wondering if she could bring herself to swallow even one mouthful of her mother's idea of cereal, the telephone rang.

'Dunchester five-seven-seven-zero-seven-eight, Clarity Meadows speaking,' said her mother in her gardening-consultant-with-good-references voice.

'Oh, it's you, Cleo. Yes, yes, she's here – I'll hand you over.' She covered the mouthpiece and handed the receiver to Tansy. 'Cleo,' she said, 'sounding peeved. I'll go and try to persuade the van to start. And,' she added, gesturing to the bowl, 'eat.' Grabbing the car keys from a hook above the boiler, she kicked open the back door and disappeared.

'Hi, Cleo,' said Tansy, tipping the offending mixture into the pedal bin and grabbing a mango yogurt from the fridge. 'You are an angel. You have just saved me from the breakfast from hell.'

7.50 a.m.
6 Kestrel Close, West Green, Dunchester.
Otherwise known as Chaos City

'You don't know you're born,' Cleo told Tansy, switching the receiver into her left hand and ramming a finger into her right ear in an attempt to block out the shouts emanating from behind the closed kitchen door. 'You should try living here for a day.'

How, she wondered, could breakfast, or any other time for that matter, be hell when there's just you and your mum living together in peaceful harmony? Right now Portia, her sixteen-year-old sister, was having a blazing row with her mum in the kitchen, Lettie, who was ten going on four, was sitting on the stairs, head in hands, doing the dramatic sobbing bit and saying she couldn't go to school because everyone was horrid to her, while Peaseblossom the cat, yet another member of the family who had failed to escape Mrs Greenway's passion for Shakespeare, was doing something exceedingly unsavoury on the doormat with the remains of a small butterfly.

'You have to help me,' pleaded Cleo down the phone to Tansy, while peering at herself in the hall mirror and wishing she had stunning cheekbones and a sylphlike figure. 'I haven't done any of my geography homework and last term old Beetle said that if I handed in a single piece of work late this year, he would write to the parents. And that's all I need.'

'OK,' said Tansy cheerfully. 'You can look at mine when we get to school.'

'And your French?' asked Cleo tentatively, fiddling with a strand of crinkly blonde hair.

'Sure,' said Tansy, who always put work first as part of her campaign to become Somebody but who never minded sharing her endeavours with her friends. 'Er, what cool things were you doing this weekend that stopped you working?'

Cleo swallowed. She didn't want to admit that her mum and stepdad had had another row or Portia had stormed out and gone walkabout and Lettie had thrown up because Lettie always threw up in a crisis. She didn't want to let on that it had been left to her to cook lunch and make her mum some camomile tea and persuade Roy, her stepdad, to come in from the garden shed, or that her precious Sunday afternoon had been spent taking Lettie for a walk while her mother and Roy attempted to become mature adults again. She didn't want to admit to Tansy that after it was all over, her mum had spent ages cuddling Lettie and saying she was sorry and everything would be fine now, and Roy had sat down with Portia and spent ages helping her with her German coursework and all they had said to Cleo was that she was the sensible one and what a good thing she never lost her head. And most of all she didn't want all her friends to know just how often these rows happened. It was bad enough that her mum and real dad had got divorced, without people knowing that the whole horrid arguing and fighting bit was beginning over again between her mother and Roy.

'Oh, we had visitors and stuff,' she said airily.

'Who?' asked Tansy, whose experience of visitors was that you usually wanted to use homework as an excuse to escape the boring chat. 'Was it a boy?'

Tansy knew that given the choice between equations and a decent guy, Cleo would forsake the maths in an instant.

'No it wasn't!' exclaimed Cleo. 'But talking of boys – guess who I saw on Saturday?'

'Who?' asked Tansy, spooning the last of the yogurt into her mouth.

'Scott.'

'Holly's Scott?' queried Tansy.

'He's not Holly's Scott any more – he dumped her for Ella Hankinson, remember?'

'I know that,' said Tansy between bites of banana. 'But she reckons she can get him back. She's decided to throw this amazing party for her birthday and invite Scott and really lay it on. Ella's going to her grandparents' Ruby Wedding party in Norwich this weekend so she'll be out of the picture.'

'I don't actually think Ella is the only problem,' ventured Cleo. 'Oh, go away, Lettie,' she hissed as her sister tugged at her arm.

'What do you mean?' asked Tansy.

'I saw him on Saturday in Beckets Park.' She paused for effect.

'Yes?' urged Tansy.

'With Jade. And they weren't just admiring the view.'

'Jade? Jade Williams? With Scott?' gasped Tansy. 'I don't believe it.'

Jade never seemed remotely interested in guys. Or in anything else really. Of course, she had had a terrible time. But still. Jade with Scott.

'Got to go – Mum's about to leave,' said Tansy, sighing down the phone. 'I'll meet you at the gate and you can tell me everything.'

'OK, and whatever you do don't say anything to Holly,' urged Cleo.

'Course I won't,' said Tansy. 'What's that noise?' she added.

'Oh sugar!' said Cleo. 'Lettie's thrown up on the cat.'

8.15 a.m.
The Cedars. Feeling somewhat unwanted

Perhaps, thought Holly, ramming the geography homework that she hadn't done into her school bag and grabbing her hairbrush, my mother should never have had me.

Holly loved her mother dearly but she sometimes wondered whether she had been put out by the arrival of a daughter ten years after the birth of her second son. She knew that her conception had been something of a surprise to her parents. Her brothers, Thomas and Richard, were already ten and eleven when she arrived and her mother had decided to celebrate her imminent freedom from full-time child rearing by standing as prospective Labour candidate for Dunchester West. At a somewhat exclusive cheese and wine evening at Party headquarters, she had been smitten with a severe attack of nausea, which at the time she attributed to the rather dubious Wensleydale, but which turned out to be the beginnings of Holly.

Although Angela Vine had not been exactly overjoyed when Dr Penwithen beamed at her over his rimless spectacles and informed her, just four days after her fortieth birthday, that now there would be another little branch on the family Vine, she had rallied to the challenge with her normal fortitude, turning her attention from national politics to local issues, with the result that much of Holly's infancy was spent sleeping somewhat lopsidedly in a baby sling while her mother dished out chicken noodle soup at the local night shelter.

As Holly grew, and Mrs Vine decided that the playgrounds weren't safe enough, and that holiday playschemes weren't long enough, she began taking up the cause of the young; or, as Holly was prone to mutter to anyone who would listen, other people's young. For as long as she could remember Holly's parents had introduced her to their friends as 'Holly, our little afterthought' which made her feel like a PS at the end of a thank-you letter.

She brushed the tangles out of her shoulder-length hair and pounded downstairs to tackle her mother once again. But when she crashed through the kitchen door, nearly tripping over Naseby, her father's lilac Burmese cat who was playing the role of draught excluder, she found the paternal parent sitting at the table in his scarlet bathrobe, grey hair all awry, reading a copy of *History Today*. Of her mother there was no sign.

'She's gone to sort out a problem at the crèche,' said her father by way of explanation. 'She said to say goodbye.'

'Oh terrific,' muttered Holly, flicking a strand of hair out of her eyes. *'Have a nice day, Holly. Make a list for your birthday, Holly. Decide how you want to celebrate, Holly.* Maybe if I was two years old with hammer toes and a glue-sniffing father, she'd notice my existence.'

'She enjoys it, dear,' he said benignly, peering at her over the top of his reading glasses. 'Women need to express themselves in the wider community.'

It would be nice, thought Holly, if she would give me time to express myself in the narrower one.

'Dad,' she began. 'Can I have a word? It's about Saturday.'

'Just a minute, dear,' he said, holding up his hand. 'I just want to finish this article. Absolutely fascinating – "Cromwell – Saint or Sinner?", written by Doctor Entwhistle – you remember, he came for supper.'

Holly grunted non-committally and slotted two slices of bread into the toaster. So many strange people drifted in and out of their house that Holly tended to ignore all the ones that weren't male and under the age of twenty.

Her father, Rupert, was a historian who spent his days closeted in his study at the top of the house writing biographies of long-dead generals. When he wasn't writing, he lectured on the Civil War at a variety of universities and colleges and held forth at great length on late-night radio programmes, all of which was just about bearable; and by way of relaxation, he dressed up as a Roundhead and fought mock battles with the Sealed Knot Society, which most definitely was not. The year before, he had appeared at the local carnival wearing an authentic but totally ridiculous-looking helmet and waving a pikestaff with unrestrained enthusiasm. Nick Balfour, who was the loudmouth of Year Eight, had seen him and told all his mates that Holly's father was a nutter. She had wanted to lie down somewhere very dark and quietly die. Having a manic mother was bad enough but being lumbered with a sixty-year-old father who still played soldiers was more than any human being should be expected to bear.

Holly turned on the tap over the sink to fill the kettle. There were several loud clunks and the merest trickle of sandy-coloured water.

'Dad, the pipes are playing up again.' Holly sighed.

'What's that, dear?' murmured her father, not raising his eyes from the magazine.

'The pipes,' repeated Holly. 'Dad, you'll have to get the plumber. Mum will go spare.'

The other passion in Rupert Vine's life was the house, The Cedars. It was also a source of great disagreement between Holly's parents. Her mother wanted to move to a modern house with windows that fitted and radiators that didn't clank and ceilings that you could reach without first finding a three-metre ladder. Her father, who vastly preferred the past to the present, refused point blank to even consider the matter, saying that modern houses had no soul and that Vines had lived at The Cedars for over a hundred years which accounted for the sense of continuity and history which pervaded the place. To which Holly's mother replied that as far as she could see all that pervaded the place was a whole lot of dust, some rising damp and the occasional adventurous mouse.

Their house had been built by Holly's great-grandfather, Ambrose, who had loads of money. It had been handed down through the generations to Holly's dad, who didn't. Which was why three months earlier, after some very strongly worded letters from the bank, her dad had sold off most of the rambling back garden to a builder who assured him that the site would be perfect for a couple of executive homes of taste and discretion. Now there were earthmovers where the orchard used to be, with two almost finished houses on the far side of the newly erected back fence, and all the water was a sallow shade of orange.

Holly had been really cheesed off when the bulldozers moved in, but Cleo told her to look on the positive side.

'Just think,' she had said one day as they sat under the one remaining tree looking at the boy posters in *Heaven Sent* magazine, 'your destiny could lie in one of those houses.'

Holly had stared at her quizzically.

'Well,' Cleo had explained, 'for all you know some gorgeous guy might move in, catch sight of you and fall irretrievably in love with you. Then all your problems would be solved.'

Cleo was very keen on happy endings. She also knew how desperately Holly wanted to fall in love.

Holly's love life was an even greater worry to her than her mother's unreasonable behaviour or her disappointing figure. The awful truth was that she had only ever had one boyfriend. She'd been out with Scott Hamill for three weeks and two days, and stood on the touchline while he played rugby and cheered in all the right places, only to lose him to Ella Hankinson, who had baby blonde hair and a thrusting chest. Holly was sure it was the chest that had clinched it. She had pretended not to care. But she did. Dreadfully.

She buttered her toast, convinced there was something wrong with her; no one normal got to the age of fourteen without ever having been properly kissed. Scott had given her a couple of quick pecks on the lips but there had been nothing long and lingering and it was proving very difficult to take an active part in the lunch-hour discussions on passion when you had never experienced it at first hand.

Perhaps it was because she was tall. She had tried sagging at the knees when she thought Scott wanted to kiss her, but it got very uncomfortable waiting for it to happen. If only she was tiny like Tansy, she would probably be kissed to distraction.

Her only good points, she thought sadly, were her ivory skin and a decent-shaped mouth, but that was about it. In addition to the lopsided boobs, which meant wearing baggy sweaters and thinking up endless excuses to get out of swimming, she had thick ebony eyebrows which, unless she disciplined them regularly with tweezers, threatened to meet over her nose. Tansy said strong eyebrows were a sign of a deeply sensual and passionate nature. Holly said it would be nice to have the opportunity to put her dormant sensuality to the test. Preferably on the errant Scott.

And her birthday had to be it. If she could just get her mother to agree to a proper party, the works, the real biz, she was sure she would have a chance of getting him back. If only she could make the most of Ella's absence by getting Scott in a darkened room with some suitable smoochy music and the chat-up lines she had memorised from last month's *Cool Girl*, she could crack it, she knew she could.

'Well, I'd better take this upstairs and get started,' said her father, getting slowly to his feet. He was almost sixty and always joked that his knees were seventy-five.

'Dad,' said Holly quickly, deciding that in the absence of her mother she might at least try her tactics on her paternal parent. 'About Saturday . . .'

'Saturday?' Her father peered at her enquiringly. 'Oh yes, Saturday.' His face brightened. 'Big day. Looking forward to it.'

Holly's heart leaped. So they hadn't forgotten. Brilliant.

Go for it, Holly. Now.

'Can I invite loads of friends?' she added quickly.

'Friends?' For someone who had won the Hubbard Prize for Historical Biography he could be amazingly slow on the uptake.

'On Saturday,' Holly urged.

'Well, I suppose so, but . . .' Her father rubbed his stubbly chin and looked doubtful.

'We won't be any trouble,' she added earnestly. 'Please, Dad.'

'Well, yes, of course, if you really want to,' said her father, frowning slightly. 'But I thought – '

'Oh, great, Dad, thanks a million.' She flung her arms round his neck, a gesture which caused him to look even more astonished.

'Must dash,' she said, stuffing the remains of her toast into her mouth. 'I can't wait to tell the others.'

Her father watched as she tore into the hall, grabbed her school bag and shot out of the front door, and shook his head in bewilderment.

The dear child really was full of surprises. It must be with her being a girl.

8.30 a.m.
Class 9C, West Green Upper School

Jade Williams dumped her kitbag on the classroom floor and sat down. She was glad no one else had arrived yet. Getting to school early was the one way of getting time out for herself. Being alone was a total impossibility at home.

Not that she could get into the way of thinking of her aunt's house as home. Home had been the little Regency house in Brighton, so close to the sea that you could hear the waves breaking on the shingle. Home had been her attic bedroom with the sloping ceiling and wonky floorboards. At home no one teased her about being thirteen and still having fluffy pandas and rabbits and a giant kangaroo at the foot of her bed. Home had been friendly and comfortable. Home had been Mum and Dad.

Jade felt the inevitable tears pricking at the back of her eyes again and gave herself a shake. There was no Mum and Dad any more. There hadn't been since that awful Tuesday evening back in May when they had driven off in their clapped-out old Escort, waving and laughing, to celebrate their wedding anniversary with dinner at *Mon Plaisir* in Worthing.

'Now don't go spending all evening on the phone and do your homework and don't leave lights on all over the place,' her mother had said. 'Oh dear, I do wish we'd asked Karen to come over and sit with you – I hate leaving you here on your own.'

'Oh, Mum, for heaven's sake,' Jade had snapped. 'I'm not some stupid kid. I don't need looking after.'

'Oh, and Jade,' her mother had added, as her husband elbowed her towards the door, 'you could try and tidy your room. It is a tip.'

'Nag, nag, nag,' said Jade, pulling a face. She wished she hadn't. Her dad had given her a hug.

'See you later, Sunshine,' he had grinned, giving her a friendly punch on the shoulder.

But she hadn't seen them later. She had never seen them again. On the way back from the restaurant, a joyrider driving a stolen BMW had crossed the central reservation on the new bypass and crashed into her parents' car. The policewoman told her that her mum had died instantly. Her father died in the ambulance on the way to hospital.

Jade blocked out the rest the way she always did. She refused to think about the funeral, about the family discussions on 'what to do with Jade'. She wouldn't let herself think about the 'For Sale' board being hammered into the pocket-sized lawn or her mum's clothes being bundled up in plastic bags by her gran and taken to a charity shop.

She missed her parents so much. And she missed Tanya, who had been her best friend since primary school. On the day that her mum's sister, Paula, had driven down with her husband, David, to fetch her and bring her to Dunchester, Tanya had come to say goodbye. Jade had cried and cried. She had hugged Tanya and they had promised one another that they would write and phone and visit, but next to hearing the news about Mum and Dad, driving away and leaving Tanya waving frantically was the worst feeling in the whole world. Paula and David had kids of their own and Jade felt as if there was no one left who was just for her.

'Don't worry, cherub,' Paula had said comfortingly. 'You'll make lots of friends at your new school. And just think, you've got Allegra for a buddy now.'

Jade started unpacking her school bag and sighed as she thought about her three cousins. She could just about handle Joshua, who was sixteen and a total dweeb who kept out of her way most of the time, and Nell, who was seven and quite cute when she wasn't picking her nose and sticking snot on the skirting boards, but Allegra was something else. She was fourteen and a half – a year older than Jade – and went to a stage school on the other side of town. She was stunningly beautiful – and didn't she know it! Her dressing table was covered with lotions and creams and almost every shade of eye colour ever manufactured and her wardrobe was full of the funkiest gear you could imagine. She had stacks of CDs which she played all the time, refusing to let Jade play any of her own, which she said were totally sad.

The worst thing of all was that in front of her parents, Allegra was all sweetness and light, saying how lovely it was to have Jade around, and of course she would be nice to her, poor little thing, and would she like to borrow her chenille sweater. But as soon as they were on their own, she turned really bitchy and catty, saying that Jade's clothes were more suited to an unimaginative nine-year-old than a teenager and rummaging through her make-up basket saying things like, 'Oh, puhleese!' and 'That colour went out three seasons ago.'

Ever since Jade first moved in, she and Allegra had had to share a bedroom which was something Jade just couldn't get used to.

'It will do you good to have someone with you to take

your mind off things, cherub,' Paula had explained, as if talking about blusher and boys would make Jade forget her mum and dad. In fact, Paula didn't seem to want Jade to talk about the past at all. If she found Jade crying, she would jolly her along and offer her a game of Outburst! or a trip to the cinema. She even suggested that Jade should put away her collection of family photographs because they might be upsetting her – but Jade flatly refused. She loved to look at them; to see bits of her mum and dad in herself. She had her mum's mass of honey-coloured hair which tumbled untidily over her head, and her father's piercing green eyes. The last thing she did at night and the very first thing she did in the morning was talk to the photos of Mum and Dad. Silently, inside her head, so that Allegra wouldn't tease her.

Assorted kids were beginning to drift in to the classroom. Some of them smiled briefly at Jade and said a quick, 'Hi!' but most of them ignored her. It was pretty hard starting a new school mid-year and, besides, it seemed that once the other kids knew that her parents had been killed, they got embarrassed and didn't know what to say. Jade knew they weren't being mean – it was more that they were scared about saying the wrong thing; she just wished they'd say something – anything to make her feel part of things again.

'What if no one likes me?' she had ventured apprehensively one evening when Paula was showing her the school prospectus.

'Of course they will like you,' she insisted. 'Just don't be – well, you know . . . don't dwell on the past.'

'And just think,' David had added, trying to lighten things, 'with looks like yours, you'll have all the boys in Year Nine falling over themselves to ask you out.'

To date, thought Jade, she hadn't exactly been trampled in the rush. Not that it mattered. She was so busy trying to keep cheerful and not burst into tears that flirting and chatting up boys would just be too much of an effort. Although, Scott Hamill was nice. After that horrendously embarrassing moment in the park the previous weekend, he'd been so – well, so ordinary about it. Most guys she had known in the past would have run a mile. But he was different. If she was going to try to get off with anyone, it would be him.

'Hi, Jade!' Holly Vine hurtled into the classroom. 'Hey, what's up – you look like you've been crying.'

Holly was always one to come straight to the point with her friends even if she rarely managed it with her parents.

'I'm fine,' muttered Jade, wishing her freckled nose didn't go red whenever she cried.

'Is it because of your parents?' asked Holly gently. 'It must be awful – I don't blame you for feeling mizz.'

Jade looked at her gratefully. Holly had been the first person to talk to her when she came to West Green Upper last term, and the only one not to pretend her mum and dad had never existed. Because of Holly, she was getting to know Tansy and Cleo as well – but like everyone else, they never mentioned Mum and Dad.

'It's four months today that it happened,' she whispered, scrabbling in her school bag and pulling out her geography folder.

Holly bit her lip. She didn't really know what to say. 'That's hard,' she murmured and then thought how inadequate that sounded. 'Well, anyway,' she said cheerfully, thinking that perhaps Jade needed to talk about something else, 'it's on. It's all systems go.'

'Pardon?' asked Jade.

'The party – I told you,' insisted Holly, incredulous that anyone could forget this forthcoming highlight of Year Nine's social calendar. 'My dad came up with the goods and said I could have it.'

'That's nice,' said Jade unenthusiastically. The last thing she felt like right now was a party with everyone being hip and happening and her feeling the pits.

'And you can sleep over,' said Holly. 'I'm getting my best mates to stay on after so we can have a post-mortem on who got off with who!'

Holly, who sounded quite scatty to people who didn't know her frightfully well but who was really pretty astute about other people's feelings, knew that the sleeping over bit could be the key to getting Jade to come.

As Holly expected, Jade perked up a bit.

'Who's going?' she asked. Holly thought she was one of her best mates. That was really nice.

'Well, Tansy and Cleo and you and me, and then I'm asking Tim and Becky and Alex Gregson and Nick – which means asking Ursula, of course, cos they're tied at the hip – and Scott . . .' she added, trying to look totally casual as she mentioned his name.

Scott, thought Jade. 'And Ella?' she asked.

Holly shook her head. 'She's away at some family bash,'

she said, trying to make the whole issue sound totally unimportant. 'So you will come, won't you? It'll be a blast.'

Jade thought. It seemed all wrong to think about parties with her mum and dad dead. Like laughing in church or playing tag round gravestones in the churchyard. And she didn't have anything to wear. But then again, she had to get to know people. And it would mean a whole night away from Allegra, which had to be a bonus. And Scott was going to be there.

'OK,' she said, 'that would be good.'

'Ace!' beamed Holly. 'I'm going to make next Saturday a day that no one will ever forget!'

12.30 p.m.
The cafeteria

Holly hurtled into the cafeteria, grabbed a table in the corner and scanned the crowded room for her friends. She had had no chance of talking to them all morning. Tansy was clever enough to be in the top sets for almost everything, and while Holly had been grappling with the complexities of the German language, Cleo and Jade had been making filo pastry in home economics and tie-dying in CDT.

'Hey, you guys – over here!' Holly spotted her friends struggling with laden trays and waved frantically.

'Guess what?' she enthused, after they had settled themselves down. 'It's on!'

'What's on?' asked Tansy, prising the lid off her

plastic lunch box and eyeing a carrot and cottage cheese sandwich suspiciously.

'My party,' said Holly.

'Really?' Tansy looked impressed. 'That's great!'

Holly nodded.

'So your mum agreed after all?' asked Cleo, spooning the school's idea of macaroni cheese into her mouth at high speed.

'No, I asked Dad instead,' admitted Holly. 'And he said yes, just like that. And he said I could invite loads of people. And you guys can sleep over!'

Cleo paused in mid-chew. The party might be fun, but a sleepover? No way. She couldn't. She'd have to come up with an excuse.

'I can't wait!' enthused Holly. 'It'll be so cool.'

'What'll be cool?' A broad American accent broke in on their conversation. 'Hey, Scotty, let's sit here, why not?'

The four girls turned and gawped. Deftly balancing a tray on one hand and nudging Scott Hamill playfully with his free arm was the most drop-dead gorgeous guy any of them had ever seen. He was wearing a black polo sweatshirt, joggers and a baseball cap. He grinned at them all.

That guy, thought Holly, taking in his slate-grey eyes and floppy blond hair, is seriously sexy.

That guy's sweatshirt, thought Tansy, who could smell money at twenty paces, is a Ralph Lauren and it's definitely not a fake. His body isn't bad either.

Isn't Scott dreamy? thought Jade.

'This is Trig Roscoe,' announced Scott, interrupting

their thoughts and giving them the info they were all dying to know. 'He's going to be here for a year because his dad's got a transfer to Dunchester. Mr Roscoe is an ex-Marine.'

This latter piece of information obviously impressed Scott as much as Trig's looks were impressing the girls.

'Oh, and he's American,' added Scott unnecessarily.

'From Westmont, Illinois,' declared Trig, opening a packet of crisps with his teeth.

Illinois, thought Tansy with a jolt. That's where my perhaps-father came from.

'Near Chicago,' Trig added.

'Deep pan pizzas,' said Cleo, for whom food was a source of the greatest joy. 'And the Bulls.'

'Wow!' breathed Trig. 'An English kid who knows about basketball. How come?'

'I've got a sister with a sports-mad boyfriend and a father who watches endless sport on Sky TV,' said Cleo ruefully.

Trig laughed and looked at her admiringly. Cleo was too busy demolishing an apple turnover to notice.

Tansy, who was fascinated by everything American, introduced everyone.

'Hi!' she said. 'I'm Tansy Meadows, and this is Holly Vine and Jade Williams and that's Cleo . . .'

Trig smiled at Cleo.

Just then Ella Hankinson simpered up and smiled coyly at Scott. Her school blouse was tucked tightly into her short skirt. When she sat down, she swung one leg gracefully over the other.

Holly bristled, conscious of Ella's perfectly symmetrical chest and sure she chose her blouses one size too small just in order to show it off.

'Hi, Scott – missed you,' Ella said. 'Hi, Trig! About this weekend, Scott . . .'

She continued but whispered in Scott's ear, so no one else could hear.

How pathetic, thought Holly. Trig, meanwhile, seemed to have problems adjusting to English life.

'Boy, this place is sure different from Westmont Junior High. Bizarre clothes, soggy French fries and no baseball on TV. Is everyone really sad or is there life in Dunchester?'

Oh please, thought Cleo. Attitude or what?

'Actually,' said Holly, 'there is. Or at least, there will be on Saturday.' She flicked a strand of hair over her left shoulder, a gesture which *Heaven Sent* said was a real turn-on for most guys. 'On Saturday I am having the party to end all parties. Come along, why don't you?'

For a second, Trig looked doubtful. 'I dunno,' he said. 'My girlfriend – well, girlfriends – they're both back in the States and I don't know anyone yet.' He looked upwards in mock horror. 'Did they freak out when they heard I was coming to England!'

Bully for them, thought Holly. I bet they had chests too.

'You can come with Scott,' she said, who on hearing his name promptly turned round.

Yes! said Jade to herself, mentally going through her wardrobe.

'Are you going to be there?' Trig asked Cleo.

'Yes,' Cleo replied shortly. Although preferably as far away from you as possible, she thought.

'OK,' said Trig. 'Cool. I'll come.' He said it as though he was granting a great favour. Tansy looked well satisfied.

'But you won't be going, will you, Scott?' purred Ella, her nose three centimetres from Scott's left eyeball. 'I'm going away, remember.'

Jade and Holly held their breath.

'I'll go anyway,' Scott replied casually. 'To keep Trig company.' It sounded a good excuse, but Cleo noticed that he was smiling directly at Jade. She threw an anxious glance in Holly's direction but her friend appeared not to have noticed. Ella, meanwhile, was looking like thunder. If looks could have killed, thought Cleo, Holly and Scott would be en route for the mortuary. Her thoughts were interrupted by the end-of-lunch bell.

'I must go,' Cleo said, dumping her dirty dishes on the trolley. 'Choir practice. You coming, Jade?'

Everyone started to disperse.

'Me too,' agreed Tansy. 'Drama club.' Tansy was very theatrically inclined, something which her mother said tended to point the finger of fatherhood at Jordan, who could make a drama out of a crisis. Tansy chose to ignore this, having decided that Pongo was a far better bet than a guy who painted pebbles.

'Hey, you guys,' protested Holly, as they walked from the cafeteria across the school forecourt together. 'I wanted you to help me with ideas for the party. Food and music and all that stuff. There's loads to do.'

'Indeed there is, Holly Vine!' Mr Grubb, known to everyone as Beetle, appeared from the doorway of the science block. 'Much to do. Like explaining the absence of your geography project.'

Holly gulped. The others drifted off. You didn't hang around when Beetle was roused. 'Ah well, sir, you see, sir, actually what happened was that – '

'Shall we discuss this well-thought-out excuse inside?' he replied. 'Then I can ignore it, you can complain that I am horribly unfair and we can agree that tomorrow you will stay late for detention and write me an additional essay. Agreed?'

Now I won't be able to go shopping for gear after school, thought Holly. My whole life put on hold because of some stupid essay. Who cares about river valleys anyway?

TUESDAY

8.00 a.m.
In the kitchen at The Cedars. In acquisitive mode

Holly's Birthday List	Stuff For Holly's Party
Red hipsters	Loads of cola, lemonade, etc., etc.
Lemongrass shower gel	Crisps and nuts
Mud face-pack	Mini hot dogs
Watch	Pizzas – masses
Boots size 4	That gooey chocolate cake you make
Compilation CDs	
Personal CD player	
Money – lots of it	

'Mum, I've made these lists . . .' Holly dashed into the kitchen to find her mother talking in a most agitated manner on the telephone and her father spreading lime marmalade thickly on to his wholemeal toast.

'Richard, darling, NO! Oh surely not? She did? You were? He has?' Her voice rose to a crescendo in competition with the earthmovers outside. 'But, Richard dear, of course you must – no trouble, no trouble at all. All right, talk to you later. Love you lots. Bye for now.'

She banged the receiver back on to the rest and turned to her husband. Holly opened her mouth to speak and shut it again when it became clear that neither parent was going to take the slightest notice.

'Rupert, would you believe it? Serena has walked out.

38

Just like that. Upped and offed. Poor Richard, he's in pieces, bless him.'

Richard was Holly's twenty-five-year-old married brother. He was brilliant at being an accountant and terrible at changing nappies, which was a bit of a drawback since he had an eighteen-month-old son called William who was totally circular and utterly adorable, particularly when asleep.

'Rupert!' repeated Holly's mum. 'Serena's left Richard.'

'Has she?' said Holly's father, biting into his toast and marmalade and showing about as much surprise as if he had been informed that the sun had risen that morning. 'She'll go back. She always does.'

Richard and Serena had a relationship that at best was lively and at worst explosive. Holly was very fond of her brother but felt that there were rather more pressing matters to be attended to.

'Mum . . .' She tried again, one eye on the clock.

'I must go over there,' interrupted her mother. 'She's left William with him and he's teething.'

'William or Richard?' enquired Holly's father a mite sarcastically, getting up from the table.

Her mother glared at him.

'Well,' he said, 'I must be off – I've to be in Oxford by ten and the traffic is bound to be frightful. And don't forget I'm staying over tonight – decent dinner in Hall with the Master. Serves a damn fine port, if I recall.'

'But Rupert, what about Richard?' insisted his wife.

'He doesn't like port as far as I know,' he replied, deliberately misunderstanding.

'Rupert!'

'Angela,' said Rupert firmly. 'What do you expect me to do? Richard is twenty-five, a married man and a father. He has to sort out his own problems. You fuss and worry over him as if he were Holly's age.'

You don't fuss or worry over me at all, thought Holly irritably. After her father had gone she had another go.

'Mum, about Saturday – I've done lists. Dad said –'

'Lists?' Her mother looked surprised and took the sheets of paper from Holly's outstretched hand. She had just put on her reading glasses when the phone shrilled urgently once more.

'Richard? Oh he hasn't? All right. Don't worry – I'm on my way.' She turned to Holly. 'Must dash, darling – William's stuffed Rice Krispies in his ear.'

'But, Mum, aren't you going to look at my lists?' protested Holly.

Her mother picked up the sheets of paper. 'I'll take them with me,' she said. 'I must say, it's nice that you're taking an interest. Now – want a lift as far as the roundabout?'

As Holly clambered into her mother's metallic-blue Metro she wondered why anyone wouldn't take an interest in their own birthday. Except of course that her mother wasn't a party person. And she was very middle-aged. And not at all socially switched on.

'I'll be a bit late home tonight,' said Holly as her mother pulled up at the kerbside. 'Netball practice.'

It didn't seem sensible to raise the matter of the detention. Her mother had a tendency to go ballistic over unfinished work and to do ridiculous things like

4 0

grounding you or stopping your allowance. She didn't want to mention anything that would put this party at risk. Not with her dad being so co-operative and everything finally sorted.

She gave herself a little hug. By Saturday night she would have Scott back. She just knew she would.

10.45 a.m.
In biology

Dear Tansy,

I'm writing this in biology and I'm bored! Who cares about cellular respiration? What are you going to wear to Holly's party? What are you getting her?

I reckon Jade is after Scott which is awful because Holly's desperate to get him back and Jade's supposed to be a friend. Should we warn Holly, do you think?

What did you think of Trig? Pretty full of himself, I reckon.

Love, Cleo

Cleo folded the note ready to slip it to Tansy when the bell rang. She was getting a bit worried about Holly's party. For one thing she didn't have any decent gear to wear, and for another she was quite sure that while Holly would be flirting like crazy with Scott, and Tansy would have dozens of boys round her because Tansy always did, no one would chat her up. And she knew it was all because she was fat.

Boys were perfectly friendly to her but they never got any further, not even when she took notice of all the tips given to her by her sister, Portia, who knew all there was to know about the art of seduction on account of her ongoing romance with Gareth Ferryman in Year Eleven.

'You're too uptight; you have to chill,' Portia instructed her. 'And don't look as if you care about anything – look unavailable. Boys always want what they think they can't have.'

Maybe, thought Cleo, shoving her biology folder into her bag as the bell rang, she should impart this information to Holly. Cleo was absolutely certain that Jade was after Scott and she knew full well that Holly wanted him back more than anything else in the world. The two of them had been friends ever since playgroup. Holly had always stuck up for her when people called her Fatty. Cleo really wanted Holly to be happy and if keeping Jade away from Scott would do the trick, then that's what she would have to spend the party doing. There was unlikely to be much else on offer.

11.30 a.m.
In physics

Dear Cleo,
Thanks for the note. I haven't got a single garment worth wearing, but I'm working on Mum. I fancy

a suede miniskirt – what do you think?

I don't know that you are right about Jade – I reckon that because of her mum and dad she's not likely to be in the mood for pulling. And even if she did fancy him, she's too timid to try it on. Why don't we club together and get Holly some smellies?

Love, Tansy.

PS Trig's OK-ish, I suppose.

Actually, thought Tansy, doodling a clown face at the end of her note, Trig is a lot more than OK. Trig is utterly swoon-inducing and to die for. It wasn't just his glorious eyes and that sensational smile, it was the whole confidence bit, the way he was totally at ease, completely sure of himself. OK, so he poked fun, but even that was a turn-on. Ever since yesterday at lunch, she had been unable to stop thinking about him, which was an unusual experience for her because although heaps of guys chatted her up, she frankly found most of them boring, immature and ordinary. And Tansy had no place for ordinary in her life.

There was, of course, the added bonus that Trig was American. And from Illinois. For all she knew, he might live in the same town as her unknown father. Half of her knew that this was about a zillion-to-one chance, but the other half was quite enjoying fantasising about Trig falling madly in love with her, and inviting her to America when he went home, and them meeting Tansy's dad who would recognise her instantly and rush over with tears in his eyes and –

'Tansy Meadows!' Mrs Bainbridge interrupted her reverie. 'For the third time, could you possibly rouse yourself enough to give us the answer to question nine?'

'Er . . .' murmured Tansy, trying to find her place.

'Or perhaps you would like to share with the rest of us whatever fascinating thought was occupying your mind when you should have been considering terminal velocity?' added Mrs Bainbridge sarcastically.

No, thought Tansy. I don't think so. I think that just for now, I shall play it really cool. If Cleo is right and Jade and Holly are both after Scott, and Cleo doesn't even like Trig, then it's up to me to make him feel at home.

Thinking about just how she might do that kept her occupied for the rest of the day.

3.30 p.m.
During study period – not studying

Dear Tanya,

Thanks for your letter and the photograph. Your new hairstyle is brill – you look heaps older!

I need your advice. There's this guy in my year and he's really cute. I think he might like me but he's going out with this girl, Ella, who's got an amazing figure and is really flash. Anyway, Holly – that's the girl I told you about last term – is having a party on Saturday and Scott's going WITHOUT ELLA! What shall I wear? How do I play it? And do you think I'm awful to be thinking about boys after all that has happened?

It would be nice to have someone just for me.

Tons of love,

Jade XXXXX

Jade licked the envelope and stuffed the letter in her bag to post on the way home. She could have phoned Tanya but if she did that, Allegra would hover in the hallway, eavesdropping on every word and mimicking her every expression, and no way was Jade going to admit to her cousin that she fancied a boy. She felt guilty enough about even thinking of having a good time with Mum and Dad dead, and besides, if she didn't admit her feelings to anyone she wouldn't feel a complete nerd if Scott totally ignored her.

As soon as the bell rang, she piled her books in her bag and ran downstairs to the girls' cloakroom. As she turned the corner to her locker, she bumped into Holly.

'Hi!' she said. 'Walk to the bus stop? I could do with some advice on what to wear for your party.'

Holly shook her head. 'Detention,' she said, pulling a face. 'But say, why don't you come on over tonight? You can help me try this new super-seductive makeover that's in *Heaven Sent* magazine and we can sort out the music and stuff.'

'Great!' enthused Jade. 'But won't your mum mind me just turning up?'

'Course not,' said Holly emphatically. 'Chances are she'll be out at some committee meeting or other.'

5.15 p.m.
After detention

'All right, hand in your work and you may all go.' Miss Partridge (who was taking detention) put the top on her pen and picked up her bag.

Holly slouched up to her desk and handed in the essay that Beetle had set her.

'Oh, Holly dear,' said Miss Partridge, who had a very soft spot for Holly because she was as brilliant at English as she was dire at geography, 'will you thank your father so much for his note?'

'Miss?'

'About the battle re-enactment on Saturday,' she said. 'I shall be there – dressed up and ready to go as Worried Bystander.' She gave a peal of laughter. 'I'm so thrilled your father got me involved in the Sealed Knot – isn't it exciting?'

It was, thought Holly, amazing how some people got their thrills.

'Oh very,' she said. 'Can I go now?' She grabbed her rucksack and charged downstairs. If she was lucky, she might meet up with Scott who had athletics practice on Tuesdays. She dashed through the double doors into the main corridor. Straight into Trig Roscoe. He was wearing a black tracksuit and trainers but still managed to look like a pin-up in *Cool Girl*.

'Hey, where's the fire?' he said.

'Oh, hi!' Holly gulped. 'Sorry.'

He grinned and Holly felt her cheeks burn. 'That's

46

OK – can't wait to get out of the place, eh? Me neither.'

'Were you in detention too?' asked Holly, thinking it was unusual for a new guy to get punished that early no matter what they'd done.

Trig shook his head. 'Extra history – we don't do English history in the States.'

'Lucky you!' said Holly.

'I kind of like it,' said Trig. 'All your kings and barons and stuff – it's great. I'm really into all that.'

'My dad's an historian,' commented Holly. 'That, and sadly deranged on the side.'

'Really? You mean, he earns his living through history? Wow! I'd sure like to meet him.'

No way, thought Holly. He's best kept behind closed doors.

Trig glanced at his watch, which had as many dials on it as the flight deck of Concorde.

'Come on – I said I'd meet Scott at the bus stop.'

Scott. Holly's heart gave a little flutter.

Trig opened the outside door and stood back for her to go through. He grinned. Holly's heart decided to go into overdrive.

'So what gives on your party?' he said as they crossed the yard to the bus stop.

'How do you mean?' Holly asked, thinking what gorgeous eyes he had.

'Well – you know – what's the scene? Is it a cookout or a rave? It's not a pool party, is it?' He looked slightly anxious.

Holly laughed. 'No,' she said. 'We don't have

swimming pools left, right and centre like you do in the States.'

Trig looked relieved. 'We have some great parties back in Illinois,' he said. 'My cousin had a swell Rock and Rodeo party last fall. But then I suppose you uptight Brits never get to hang loose like that,' he teased.

Holly swallowed. She had been so ecstatic at getting her dad to agree to the party that she hadn't thought further than buying some cola and crisps and borrowing as many of her mates' CDs as she could.

She was about to say that it was just an ordinary, run-of-the-mill, dark room, loud-music, parent-free-zone party when she stopped. For some reason she didn't want Trig to think she was in any way ordinary. Not that she fancied him or anything. Well, not much. But she wanted him to think her hip and happening and really at the cutting edge. (She wasn't sure what the cutting edge meant but she'd read somewhere that it was where you were meant to be.)

'Oh,' she said airily, in what she hoped was a husky and seductive voice, 'now that would be telling.'

'Go on, tell me,' he urged. 'Does Scott know?'

'Do I know what?' Scott loped up to the bus stop, still dressed in his white running shorts and singlet. I do love him, thought Holly, and I will get him back. I will, I will, I will. And of course, if for any reason I don't, there is always Trig.

'Do you know the theme of Holly's party?' Trig repeated.

'She's not letting on.'

'Theme?' asked Scott in a bewildered voice. Most parties were just opportunities for dancing, chatting and, if you got lucky, a bit of serious kissing. 'Isn't it just an ordinary party?'

Holly shook her head. 'There will,' she asserted, 'be nothing ordinary about it.'

6.00 p.m.
Intent on sorting her mother

When Holly arrived home her mother was on the phone. She covered the mouthpiece with one hand, mouthed, 'It's Dad,' and carried on talking.

Holly went upstairs, tore off her uniform, put on her favourite jeans and her 'I'm So Cool' T-shirt and picked up a pad and pen. She hoped Jade wouldn't be long – and that she was hot on ideas. Now that she had hinted to Trig and Scott that this party was going to be something special she had to come up with something truly amazing.

She kicked off her shoes and lay on the bed. Trig was gorgeous. She wondered what it would be like to be kissed by him. She closed her eyes and did a little puckering of the lips. Then again, she really loved Scott big time. She imagined him running his hands down her back. She was just getting to the shivery tingly bit when she remembered that she hadn't got her mum sorted yet.

As she ran downstairs, she heard her mother raise her voice.

'I said, I really ought to get something good to wear for Saturday – can't let the side down! Well, of course it's important. Well, it is to me anyway.'

Oh no, thought Holly. She doesn't actually think she is going to *appear* at my party, does she? Everyone knows parents go out or at the very least sit upstairs in their bedroom with the TV and sandwiches. They certainly do not hang around in their idea of high fashion making spectacles of themselves. She walked into the kitchen just as her mother hung up.

'Er, Mum,' said Holly, 'you're not going to actually be *at* my party on Saturday, are you? I mean, while it's actually going on?'

Her mother walked purposefully to the fridge and took out a packet of sausages. She was not a mother who worried about low-fat diets.

'No, Holly dear, I am not,' she said, peeling off the cling film.

Thank heavens for that, thought Holly.

'Because I'm afraid you've got a little carried away with all this,' she continued, piercing the sausages with a skewer. 'There is absolutely no way you can have a party on Saturday night.'

Holly's stomach suddenly felt as if it had been filled with lead. No party? There had to be a party. She had told everyone there was going to be a party. Even Dad had agreed that there was going to be a party. What was her mother going on about?

'But, Mum, Saturday's my birthday,' she protested.

'Oh, I know that, darling, of course I do,' chirruped

her mother (who in truth had got confused and only remembered when she perused Holly's list in a boring bit of the committee meeting that morning). 'And of course you'll have your presents and I thought maybe a nice cake and then on Sunday you, me and Dad could go to Bella Italia for lunch . . .'

That did it. No way, thought Holly, am I settling for a slice of chocolate sponge and a dollop of tagliatelle for my fourteenth birthday.

'Mum! I'm not a kid any more – I don't want to celebrate my birthday with my *parents*, for heaven's sake! Get real!'

Her mother raised an eyebrow, which should have been a warning to Holly. She, however, was too irate to notice.

'And anyway, you can't do this to me because Dad said I could have a party!' she shouted. 'What's more, he said I could invite loads of friends – he PROMISED!'

Her mother raised the other eyebrow. 'Oh, he did, did he?' she said.

'Yes he did,' said Holly. 'He said it was a big day and he was looking forward to it.'

Her mother sighed. 'Well, you know your father; he lives in a world of his own. I think you will find you were talking at cross-purposes. Saturday is Dunchester Battle Day. Dad seems to think you are bringing a crowd of mates along to that.'

Dunchester had been the scene of a minor skirmish during the Civil War, when a crowd of hot-headed peasants had taken a stand against a section of

Cromwell's army and lost in a rather messy manner involving bodies in the blood-drenched river and limbs lying around in fields. Not content with erecting a plaque in the local church and a statue of a rather distressed-looking farmhand on the river bank, the town had in recent years turned the whole fiasco into a money-making event, with re-enactments of the battle (orchestrated, needless to say, by Holly's father), side shows and a raft race on the River Cress.

Holly's heart sank. Her father surely couldn't have been so thick as to imagine she'd want to take her friends to that naff do.

'So what's that got to do with anything?' demanded Holly, deciding that her mother was just fishing for an excuse not to have to fork out for the food and drink. 'Just because Dad's going to spend the day playing soldiers doesn't mean I can't have a party.'

Her mother sighed. 'Holly, don't you ever take an interest in anything that goes on? I do so try to make you aware of social issues.'

And I do try to make you aware of the mess that is my life, thought Holly. Not that I get very far.

Her mother sat down on the kitchen stool. 'I told you ages ago about the protest,' she said. 'There are plans to build the new hypermarket on Swan's Meadow and if that goes ahead, they will demolish all the old warehouse buildings.'

'So?'

'So that means losing the Lowdown Centre and the crèche and everything.'

'Oh dear, oh dear, what a disaster!' said Holly sarcastically.

'Yes, it would be,' said her mother fiercely. 'For scores of young mums and their children, it would be. Not everyone lives in a large house with heating and a garden, you know, and that centre is a lifeline to single mums.'

Holly looked suitably chastened.

'And so on Saturday we're not only going to run our usual crèche, we are going to have a rally. Lots of us – mums, the committee, teachers, all sorts,' her mother finished. 'And I've thought up a slogan: "Dunchester Battle was lost in 1642 – to win the playcentre battle, we need YOU!" Good, isn't it?'

'Mind-boggling,' muttered Holly, thinking, not for the first time, that having an elderly mother carried untold risks.

'We have to fight,' said her mother. 'These youngsters must be given a future.'

What about my future? thought Holly. 'But,' she said hastily, 'my party will be in the evening. After you've done all that campaigning and stuff. And I'll do all the food. And vacuum,' she added, knowing how hot her mother was on blemish-free carpets. 'So you won't have to do a thing.' Except keep well out of the way, she added silently.

Her mother shook her head. 'No, because after I've spoken at the rally – '

'You're speaking?' For a moment the shock of having a second parent threatening to do something embarrassing in public in one afternoon diverted Holly's attention from the matter in hand.

Her mother nodded eagerly. 'Yes, and we've got TV coming,' she beamed.

Heaven save us, thought Holly.

'And then, in the evening, it's the Battle Ball and guess what?'

Holly sighed. 'What?' she said. 'You are going to tap-dance on the table between courses?'

Her mother ignored her sarcasm. 'Tim Renfrew's going – you know, our MP – and I've been seated next to him.'

Holly had had enough. 'Oh, great. I get it. A poxy rally, and dinner with some stuffy MP means more than your own daughter's birthday. Oh well, great.' A tear trickled down her cheek. 'I bet you never did this to the boys. I bet they had parties and things. But of course, I'm not important.'

Her mother put an arm on her shoulder. 'Oh, sweetheart, it's not that, of course you're important. But it's not like fourteen is a special birthday like going into double figures or being eighteen or anything.'

Holly grunted. 'It's special to me,' she said.

'Look, love, if we can just get the local MP on our side, we could swing this thing,' her mother continued.

'Big deal.' Holly shrugged her mother off and turned away.

'I'll tell you what,' said her mum, remembering a lecture she had heard on 'Communicating With Your Teenager', 'why don't you have Cleo and Tansy and that nice new girl, what's her name – Jane?'

'Jade,' mumbled Holly.

'Oh yes, Jade – have them round for a film. I'll get pizzas delivered for you. That would be nice, wouldn't it?' she added in a soothing tone of voice.

Holly swung round, crying hard now. 'Oh big deal, Mum, we had film and pizza parties when we were seven. And you can't have films because the boys don't like the weepy ones and – '

'Boys!' Her mother's pupils dilated in a most alarming manner. 'You are not having boys round when your father and I are out.'

'Come off it, Mum! Some of my best mates are boys.'

Her mother held up a hand. 'I'm sorry, Holly, that is my final word – you are too young to be left alone with boys. Especially some of the ones you seem to find attractive.'

'Oh, that's it, slag off my friends, why don't you!' shouted Holly. 'And what do you think is going to happen? We're not stupid, you know. Just because your generation messed up.'

'It is not up for debate,' said her mother, waving her hand dismissively. 'Just you four girls or nothing.'

'I shall look like the biggest dweeb in the whole school,' Holly wailed. 'God, Mum, you are so unbelievably selfish! Why are you being so mean? Don't you trust me?'

Her mother bit her lip. Holly saw the moment of weakness and went in for the kill.

'Or is it just that you're bored of having me around? You never really wanted me to be born, did you?'

Her mother looked pink. It was working.

'You care more about the kids at the crèche than you

do about me,' she went on. 'You tell everyone that I was an afterthought – I'm just a nuisance in your life.'

Two tears rolled satisfactorily down her nose. Her mother pressed her lips together and looked distressed, as Holly had hoped she would.

'Of course you're not, darling. Well, I suppose, maybe – if it was just – '

Holly held her breath. At that moment the front door bell rang. Her mother went through to the hall.

'Oh, hello, Jade dear – come along in,' Holly heard her say, in the tone of voice mothers use when they don't want anyone to suss that ten seconds before they were screeching like a crazed parrot.

'Thanks, Mrs Vine,' said Jade, following Angela through to the kitchen. 'Hi, Holly – how was detention?'

Holly frantically signalled to her but it was too late.

'Detention?' Her mother swung round to face her. 'You told me you had netball practice. And two minutes ago you were asking me if I trusted you. That's it then – forget the party. It's a DVD or nothing. And you're lucky to get that.'

Jade gulped and threw an apologetic glance to Holly. Holly was past caring. Her credibility was wrecked, her chances of ever getting a life as good as over.

'I just don't believe you can do this to me!' she hissed at her mother. 'I hate you – I really, really hate you!'

Angela Vine did not look particularly distressed by this outpouring of venom, but simply smiled, picked up her car keys and hurried out.

'Well, thanks a million, Jade,' snarled Holly. 'You have just ruined my birthday. I hope you're satisfied.'

WEDNESDAY

In that dark hour before the dawn

Worries . . .

Holly didn't have a very good night. When she was awake, she was worrying about what everyone would say when she told them the party was off. But when she was asleep she dreamed that Scott told her she was a total rat and went to Norwich with Ella while Trig, who refused to speak to her ever again, went off to play basketball with Cleo. She hoped that by the morning her mother would be suffering from pangs of terminal guilt and change her mind. She didn't think it was very likely.

Guilt pangs . . .

Jade's night was not exactly restful, either. She felt awful for having dropped Holly in it with her mum. Not only was she worried that Holly wouldn't want her as a friend any more, but she realised with a sickening thud that now there was no chance of getting Scott on his own. If only she could turn the clock back. But she couldn't. Not about anything. Holly said she was never going to speak to her mother again. But she would. Jade would never speak to hers again. She couldn't. She rolled over and buried her face in the pillow and cried.

Fantasies . . .

Tansy, meanwhile, was dreaming that she and Trig were driving along a freeway in a white Cadillac, driven by her father, who turned out to be a millionaire businessman who had always wanted a daughter. Tansy was dressed in a long scarlet evening dress with her hair, now perfectly manageable, piled on top of her head. It was just as Trig was pulling her towards him in a passionate embrace that the alarm clock woke her with a jolt. She smiled like a satisfied kitten. It didn't matter. She could find out what happened next when she got to Holly's party.

And more worries . . .

Cleo was lying on her back, staring at the ceiling and worrying. Her mum said that if they had worrying as an event in the Olympic Games, Cleo would come away with the gold medal.

This time she was worrying about Holly's party. Well, not the party itself, actually – the sleepover bit. What if she had one of her bad dreams and shouted or screamed out? She would never live it down; just thinking about it made her shake. She was always nervous about staying over in other people's houses because she felt embarrassed if she had to go to the loo in the night and couldn't find the light switch and she sometimes slipped her thumb into her mouth when she was falling asleep and then she got teased. She would have to think of an excuse to go home after the party. Maybe she could say her dad was coming up the next morning. That would be a good one. Everyone knows that when you only get to see your dad once a month, every second counts.

Now that she had found an escape route she felt

better. Of course, she didn't have anything halfway decent to wear. If only she hadn't been what her mum called pleasantly rounded, she could have borrowed some of Portia's clothes. Portia was tall, slim and very clever. She was also the sort of person who could wear a bin liner and look a million dollars.

Cleo sighed. She wondered how old you had to be to have liposuction.

9.00 a.m.
In a foul mood

'I'm really sorry about dumping you in it last night,' said Jade to Holly as they went to registration.

'So am I,' said Holly curtly.

'So the party really is off?' ventured Jade, hoping that something might have changed.

'Thanks to you, yes,' she snapped a trifle unfairly. 'Look, you got me into this mess so now you can just shut up, OK? Don't you dare say a single word to anyone about the party being cancelled.'

Jade's eyes widened. She had never seen Holly so angry. 'OK,' she said shortly, 'but you're going to have to tell them sometime.'

'Oh get lost!' said Holly.

And hated herself for being so horrid.

11.30 a.m.
In an even more foul mood

'Hey, Holly, come shopping with me tomorrow after school? Mum's given me some cash for a new skirt!' Tansy hopped excitedly from one foot to the other.

Holly swallowed. 'Can't,' she said. 'Dentist.'

2.15 p.m.
Approaching panic stations

'Great about the party, Holl!' called Ursula Newley from across the classroom. 'Me and Nick are really looking forward to it! What time?'

Holly squirmed. 'I'll let you know,' she muttered. 'Must dash.'

3.15 p.m.
At the end of her tether

'Er, Holly,' said Cleo nervously after biology. 'About Saturday – I don't think I can sleep over – my dad's coming the next day and – '

'That's OK,' said Holly. 'It doesn't matter.'

Oh, thought Cleo. And rather wished it did.

7.15 p.m.
Doing the grovel – big time

'Look, Mum, I'm sorry about not telling you about detention, and I'm sorry I was horrid, and I didn't mean it. But please, please, can I have a party? Just a small one? Without food? Ending at eleven? OK, ten-thirty. Pleeeeeese. No? What do you mean, no? I said I was sorry, didn't I? I hate you.'

10.00 p.m.
In despair

I'll have to tell them. All of them. That the party's off. And they will ask why, and I will have to say that it's because my mother cares more about a handful of snotty-nosed infants and my father's dressing up in black knickerbockers and running amok with a pikestaff. I can't tell them. I have to. I will never be happy again.

THURSDAY

After lunch
Sitting by the tennis courts

'And she just wouldn't listen to reason!' Holly concluded after she had plucked up the courage to tell her mates the disastrous news.

'Look, if you want the party to happen,' said Tansy determinedly, 'you have to make it happen. You can't just sit back and say, "Oh well, that's it then."'

Not when Trig was going, you couldn't, she thought. At last she thought she was really falling in love.

'If you've got a mother like mine you can,' retaliated Holly. 'Honestly, sometimes parents are more trouble than they are worth.'

Cleo pulled a face at her, and Holly remembered Jade. Seeing her downcast expression, she felt a pang of guilt, even though she was still mad at her for wrecking everything.

Jade, in fact, was at that point not thinking about her mum but about the fact that without Holly's party as an excuse she wouldn't get to see Scott on his own. That shouldn't matter but it did. A lot. Ever since he had thrown that frisbee for his dog, Fitz, and it had landed on Jade as she sat behind a laurel bush thinking about Mum, she had thought about him all the time. He'd been so nice – he hadn't asked her what was wrong; he hadn't teased her. Just asked if she was hurt and then talked about how daft Fitz was and how he couldn't catch a frisbee to save his life. And Jade found herself telling him about the accident – and she hadn't even asked him not to tell anyone she had been crying. She just knew he wouldn't.

'Maybe your mum will change her mind,' Cleo suggested. She didn't really mind one way or the other but she hated to see people unhappy.

'Maybe pink pigs will fly past the art block,' mumbled Holly.

'Tell me again,' said Jade slowly. 'Just why won't she let you?'

'Because,' said Holly with mock patience, 'my sad father is fighting mock battles while my oh-so-noble mother waves placards and tries to save a playground. And then they are going to put on evening dress and pretend to be normal people again and go to some boring ball and suck up to politicians.'

'There has to be something we can do,' said Tansy.

'There is,' said Jade.

Everyone looked at her in surprise. Jade was usually so quiet.

'What if we all offered to help out on Saturday?' suggested Jade. 'I mean, you said she was doing a crèche and stuff – we could look after the kids, or wave a banner or something.'

'Oh, big deal,' said Holly, still miffed at Jade for messing things up in the first place. 'And that's supposed to make up for not having a party, is it? You have a weird idea of fun.'

'I get it,' said Tansy, eyes brightening. 'We trade our

help for your mum's permission to have a party. Jade, that's brilliant.'

Jade looked chuffed.

'It might work,' said Holly doubtfully. 'But my mum is so hung up on boys being in the house, I can't see she'll change – and there's no point in a party without guys.'

There is when they never take any notice of you anyway, thought Cleo.

'It's worth a try,' said Tansy, clutching at straws. 'We've nothing to lose.'

6.30 p.m.

Holly did her homework in record time. She emptied the garbage, fed Naseby, and made her mother, who was trying to write her speech, a large pot of tea and a toasted teacake.

'What's all this in aid of?' asked her mother with a smile. 'Or can I guess?'

Holly took a deep breath and recited word for word what Jade had told her to say.

'I know I should have told you about the detention and I'm sorry; I was just ashamed of myself and didn't want to upset you. And I'm sorry I yelled at you. And I do understand about your evening being important. So could we compromise?'

Her mother looked impressed. Jade had said that parents warmed to the word compromise. 'What are you suggesting?'

'What if Jade and me and Cleo and Tansy all come along on Saturday to help?' Holly sat back and waited for an outpouring of maternal gratitude.

Her mother laid down her pen and eyed her quizzically. 'Well,' she said, 'that would be very nice.'

'And then, if we did, could I have a party afterwards?'

Her mother sighed. 'Oh, Holly, it's not that I want to be a killjoy,' she said, 'but I can't let you have a party when there is no one responsible in the house to keep an eye on you. The other mothers would go spare.'

'No, no they wouldn't, honestly,' insisted Holly. 'They realise that at our age we need to extend our social horizons.' Holly remembered the phrase from a PSHE worksheet and rather liked the way it rolled off the tongue.

Her mother roared with laughter, which was not the idea. 'Good try, darling, but no,' she said, without a glimmer of remorse. 'Look, why not wait until half-term and have a party then? That would be nice, wouldn't it?'

Half-term is no good, thought Holly. Ella will be around at half-term. I need the party now.

'Think about it, sweetheart,' cooed her mother. 'Settle for a girlie night in. Remember, life is what you make it.'

Not when you're a teenager, it's not, thought Holly angrily. It's what your stuffy parents choose to make it.

FRIDAY

8.50 a.m.
Talking boys

Dear Jade,

It was great to get your letter. This guy sounds cool – and after all, your mum and dad wouldn't want you to live like a nun for ever, would they?

And remember, if other girls want this guy, that's up to them. Go for it, kiddo – and be sure to let me know how you get on.

Miss you heaps.

Oodles of love,

Tanya

'Jade?' Cleo hurled her books into her locker and turned to her friend.

'Yes?'

'Do you fancy Scott Hamill?'

'Me?' squeaked Jade. Was it that obvious? She didn't want anyone to know. 'No, why?'

'Just that you look at him a lot – and he seems quite keen on you too.'

Jade took a deep breath. Keen? Whoopee!

'Wouldn't be any point, would there?' she said, trying to sound unconcerned. 'He's going out with Ella.'

'Oh, I know he is,' agreed Cleo, 'but that's not the point. Holly used to go out with him.'

Jade didn't know that. That did it: if Scott could dump someone as stunning as Holly there was no way he'd take a second look at Jade. He was obviously just being kind to her.

'And she wants to get him back,' said Cleo. 'I mean, like desperately.'

'Fine,' said Jade, trying to sound disinterested. 'I'm not into boys anyway.'

'That's OK, then,' said Cleo.

No it's not, thought Jade. She could, of course, be really nice and tell Scott that Holly still fancied him. But she didn't want to. Not at all. She wanted someone in her life who was for her and her alone. She would do what Tanya said. She would go for it.

A little tingle of excitement ran down her spine. It was a new feeling.

Lunchtime
First advances

'Hi, Jade!' Scott Hamill sauntered into the library where Jade was on returns duty.

He perched on the desk. 'How are you doing?' he asked.

'Fine,' she said, conscious that Cleo was watching her from behind the 'Geography – Europe' section.

'How's Fitz?' she asked, knowing how much Scott loved his mongrel. 'Learned to catch frisbees yet?'

Scott laughed. 'That dog will never learn anything – thick as two short planks,' he said affectionately.

There was another awkward silence.

'You going to Holly's party?' he asked.

Jade nodded, trying to look casual.

'Great,' said Scott. 'I'm glad. See you around.' And he scuttled out of the room.

He's glad, thought Jade. That must mean something. She felt a surge of happiness for the first time in months. If Holly wanted Scott, she'd have to fight her for him first.

2.15 p.m.
More advances

'So did you get your mum to change her mind?' Tansy asked Holly as the bell rang for afternoon lessons.

Holly shook her head and sighed.

'So no party?' Jade asked. Typical. Just when she had got her act together.

Holly shrugged. 'Just us four – big deal,' she said with a sigh. 'I suppose I'll have to tell the others.'

Cleo tried to cheer her up. 'We can still have a laugh,' she said. 'And at least the oldies won't be there to tell us to keep the noise down.'

'That's it! Cleo, you're brilliant!' Holly suddenly grinned.

'What?' chorused Tansy and Jade.

'If Mum and Dad aren't there, they won't know what goes on, will they?' exclaimed Holly triumphantly. 'So we make like it's just a sleepover and then, when they've

6 8

left for the dance, we get the other guys round.'

Cleo chewed her lip. 'But what if they come back early and we get found out?' she ventured. *And how do I get out of this sleepover idea?*

'So – I get grounded,' admitted Holly. 'But at least we'll have had our fun and they can't take that away from us.'

Tansy nodded. 'And if we still do this oh-so-helpful bit on Saturday, and you do get found out, you just throw your mum the "after all I did for you" line that they keep hurling at us.'

Holly grinned and nodded. 'Ace!' she said. 'Spread the word with the others to come round at eight o'clock – and tell them to keep *shtum* about it. That way, nothing can go wrong, can it?'

2.25 p.m.
Lurking behind a locker

'Holly Vine!' Mrs Harvey, who was head of PE and whose legs would have done very well as replacements for a Chippendale chair, laid a hand on Holly's shoulder, remembered Guidelines to Teachers and took it off again. 'Why are you not getting changed for swimming?'

'I can't, please, Mrs Harvey,' lied Holly. 'Time of the month.'

'Holly, you have used that excuse for the past three Fridays. Maybe I should write to your mother suggesting a trip to the doctor.'

Holly tried again. 'Verruca,' she said, cursing the dead governor whose bounty enabled West Green Upper to be the only school in town with an indoor pool.

'Swim,' said Mrs Harvey.

Half a minute later . . .
. . . in the boys' changing rooms

'Trig Roscoe! You should be changed and in the pool by now.'

Trig smiled what he hoped was a winning smile at Mr Wynne. 'We don't swim during fall semester in the States, sir,' he said.

Mr Wynne, a man who was absent when God handed out humour, glowered. 'It may have escaped your notice, Roscoe, that you are not in America now, and here we do swim – all year round. Change. Now.'

Trig tried again. 'No kit, sir,' he said.

Mr Wynne was not impressed. He couldn't make the boy swim with no gear, and he did so hate to lose.

'Next week, you come fully equipped. Or take a detention.'

'Yes, sir,' replied Trig meekly, knowing full well he would opt for detention any day. Anything was better than having to endure a swimming lesson.

'Hey, Holly, what are you doing?' Holly jumped out of her skin. She was in her swimming gear, with her tracksuit top buttoned to the neck, hiding behind the benches at the end of the pool and hoping Mrs Harvey's eagle eye wouldn't spot her. The last person she expected to see was Trig.

'Ssh,' she whispered urgently. 'Don't drop me in it – I'm bunking swimming.' She looked at him. 'Why aren't you in the pool? Can't you swim?'

'Of course I can swim – pretty well, actually,' he said shortly. 'I forgot the gear. What about you? You're changed.'

Holly thought fast. 'I hate it,' she said. 'Dumb sport – and when I don't want to do something, I don't do it.' She hoped that she sounded really chilled and in control.

'Holly Vine! Into the pool. Now. Four lengths backstroke and no arguing.'

Holly's heart stopped. She couldn't. Bad enough at any time. But now, standing right next to Trig, whom she fancied more and more each day, she couldn't. She stared at Mrs Harvey.

'I could, of course, write to your mother!' boomed Mrs Harvey, striding towards her down the poolside, her trainers making squishing noises as she approached.

No way, thought Holly. 'Coming,' she shouted, turning her back on Trig, ripping off her tracksuit top and jumping into the water. It was so cold she caught her breath. Now all she had to do was make sure she kept well under the water and was the last out of the pool. Then maybe no one would notice how deformed she was.

3.45 p.m.
Civil war

'Holly! Hang on a minute!' She turned to find Trig sprinting across the school yard towards the gate.

'Hey, Holly, can I ask you a favour?' His eyes crinkled at the edges as he gave her a lopsided grin. Holly's kneecaps began dissolving. She wished she didn't smell of chlorine.

'Of course,' she said, only it came out all squeaky and not at all deep and sophisticated as she had intended.

'Mr Eastwood has given me this history project to do: *"My favourite period in English history"*.'

'Poor you,' said Holly, who had had enough history rammed down her throat at home to last her a lifetime.

'I was wondering . . .' Trig paused and kicked an empty cola can with the toe of his shoe.

'Yes?' said Holly, trying to keep her heartbeat to some sort of regulation norm.

'Well, could I come round to your house and maybe ask if your dad had some info and books and stuff – I've chosen the Civil War.'

Holly gaped at him. 'You've chosen the Civil War?' she repeated incredulously.

Trig nodded. 'Sure have. So, will your dad mind?'

'Mind?' said Holly. 'He will probably go into paroxysms of joy. I think he feels cheated because none of his own kids actually like dead people.'

'So when can I come?' he said.

Holly was never one to waste an opportunity. 'Now?' she said.

72

4.05 p.m.
Heading for high drama

'Neat house!' said Trig admiringly as he and Holly scrunched up the gravel drive. 'Is that the date it was built?' He pointed to the ivy-clad wall above the bedroom windows where a diamond-shaped stone bore the figures 1884.

Holly nodded.

'I love old things,' said Trig.

'You'd better come and meet my father then!' replied Holly dryly.

When Holly pushed open the kitchen door, she stopped dead in astonishment. And horror. And then sent up a very rapid, silent prayer that the ground would open, right there, and swallow her up.

Standing in the middle of the kitchen, beaming from ear to ear, was her mother. Dressed as a white rabbit. With large floppy ears. And as if that wasn't enough, her father, wearing a tin helmet and leather jerkin, was charging the vegetable basket with a battered pikestaff.

I think, thought Holly, I am part of a very dysfunctional family.

'Darling,' said her mother, 'wonderful timing – you can tell me how I look. Oh, I'm sorry, I didn't see you had a friend. And this is . . .?'

'Trig,' said Holly, wondering if anyone else's mother was in need of certification. 'He's from America and he wants Dad to help him with some Civil War thing he's got to write.'

Rupert Vine stopped in mid-charge, adjusted his helmet and beamed with delight.

'If you don't mind, sir,' said Trig politely.

'Mind? I'd be delighted. Just let me get this manoeuvre right – one must sidestep as one thrusts, you know.'

My father should be put away somewhere very quiet, thought Holly. Her mother flicked a rabbit ear out of her face, and smiled at Trig.

'Nice to meet you, Trig,' said Mrs Vine, holding out a pink padded paw. 'Isn't this fun?' She gave a little grin and wiggled her white cotton-wool tail. Holly decided it was time to die.

'It's for Saturday,' said her mother. 'We're dressing up,' she added for Trig's benefit.

'I get it,' said Trig. 'You're having a fancy-dress do for your par – '

'Have a biscuit,' said Holly hastily, grabbing the tin off the counter top and thrusting it under Trig's nose. She knew that if Trig said the word 'party' her mother would go into overdrive.

'Your mum's a rabbit and your dad's a – '

'Roundhead, young man,' Rupert said robustly. 'It's all because of Dunchester Dozen Day. Though, of course, you don't know about that, do you? Well, you see, in sixteen forty-two at the very outset of the Civil War, twelve peasants . . .'

Holly sighed. Once her father got started, they could be here all night.

'Look, come upstairs and I'll get you some books,' said her father, leading Trig to the door.

After they had gone, Holly looked at her mother. 'I know Dad dresses up for kicks, but surely you're not going to make a speech looking like something out of *The Flopsy Bunnies*?' she asked wearily.

'Oh, darling, of course not,' said her mother. 'We're doing the crèche in fancy dress and then marching to the other end of Swan's Meadow for the rally.'

'Dressed like *that*?' gasped Holly.

'Yes, darling, we hope it will attract people's attention,' said her mother.

'You can bet on it,' observed Holly. 'I imagine the men in white coats will be hauling you away.'

Her mother pulled a face. 'Then I shall slip out of the costume and address the meeting,' said her mum. 'I am a bit nervous about it but it has to be done. These children are – '

'Our future. Yes, I know,' said Holly, sighing.

Holly's mother pulled off her rabbit ears and was unzipping her costume when Rupert burst into the kitchen, followed by an eager-looking Trig.

'Angela dear, where is the costume box? You know, the one with all the spare bits and pieces?'

Mrs Vine looked at him in surprise. 'In the cupboard under the stairs – why?'

'Need to kit out young Trig here,' said Rupert.

'Your dad says I can be a peasant boy,' affirmed Trig, with as much excitement as if he had just been given permission to help himself to the gold reserves at Fort Knox. 'I'm going to take part in this battle thing. On Saturday.'

'You are *what*?' Holly looked aghast.

'That young Jeffreys lad has dropped out,' said her father. 'French exchange or some such – so we are short of a bystander.'

'Dad, Trig doesn't want to get involved in – '

'Sure I do,' said Trig. 'I told you, I love this stuff.'

'Well now, I think this will do – slip your shirt off, Trig, and we'll see if it fits.' Rupert held up a peasant smock of uncertain age and somewhat strange odour.

'Er . . . no, no . . . I'll take it home and try it on there,' said Trig hastily. 'No problem.'

'As you like,' said Holly's dad, handing him some brown leggings. 'But what if it's the wrong size?'

'It will be fine,' said Trig, snatching it out of Mr Vine's hand. 'Truly.'

'So we'll see you about lunch-time,' said Mr Vine. 'Then I can show you the ropes.'

SATURDAY

Noon
On Swan's Meadow

The four girls were out of breath by the time they reached Swan's Meadow, where Dunchester Battle Day was in full swing. Holly was wearing the new red hipsters and trouser boots that her parents had given her and was smelling rather strongly of the exotic perfume that Tansy and Cleo had chosen. She hoped that the combination would have the desired effect on either Scott or Trig. The girls pushed through the crowds and found the marquee that housed the crèche.

'Over here, dears!' Holly's mother waved frantically from inside a bright yellow playpen, her rabbit ears flopping.

The things I do to get a social life, thought Holly.

For the next two hours they made Lego houses and pushed toddlers round on bikes and read stories and played with finger-paints. Holly was just doing battle with a three-year-old who was attempting to kill her with a plastic sword, when her mother rushed up.

'I've got to get ready for the march,' she said breathlessly. 'Can you girls take this banner over to where Dad's lot are going to do the battle scene? Tie it to a tree or something.'

Great, thought Holly. I can find Trig.

Neat, thought Tansy. I can start working on Trig.

I wonder, thought Jade, if Scott will turn up.

'Supposing we can't find a tree?' asked Cleo.

1.15 p.m.

'Isn't that your dad?' Tansy pointed to where a tall figure was instructing a group of guys on how to dismember a pretend Cavalier.

'Sadly, yes,' muttered Holly. 'And there's Trig – over there, talking to Scott.'

They knotted their banner to the fence and ran over to where the two boys were trying to persuade Scott's dog, Fitz, to give up his attempt to catch his own tail. Trig was doing his best to look like an old English peasant, although his smock looked a lot cleaner compared to when Holly last saw it.

'Happy birthday!' Scott said, grinning at Holly and yanking at Fitz's lead.

'Yeah – happy birthday,' echoed Trig.

Holly's neck tingled and her knees almost gave way. There was something very exciting about being keen on two guys at the same time.

'How do I look?' asked Trig. 'Historical, eh?'

'Great!' said Holly.

Dangerously kissable, thought Tansy. This is very definitely IT.

Holly's father strode over to them. 'Come along, Trig,' he said excitedly. 'We're about to get underway. This is no time to be chatting up the girls.'

Holly cringed. Her father was so utterly uncool and totally without shame.

'You're mad, Trig,' said Scott, as Trig followed Rupert into the arena. 'But go for it!'

They settled down on the grass to watch the proceedings. The sun was shining and it was very warm for September. Holly, who had been to loads of these things before, yawned in a bored fashion and lay back on the grass, ignoring the spectacle of her eccentric father. For some reason, her friends seemed to think the whole thing was pretty cool. The Roundheads and Cavaliers did a lot of shouting and bashing about with pikestaffs, whilst a crowd of pretend peasants with hoes and shovels marched purposefully up the hill. Then a bunch of women waved their fists and sobbed into shawls.

'Isn't that Miss Partridge?' said Tansy, pointing to a woman dressed in a black shawl and long brown skirt who was walking unsteadily with four or five other women.

'You're right,' said Holly. 'She doesn't look as if she is totally with it. Not that there's anything unusual about that.'

Suddenly, a group of Roundheads, led by Holly's dad waving a pikestaff, charged down the slope towards the peasants. Mr Vine, getting into the mood of the occasion, yelled a few expletives in the local mediaeval dialect and plunged the tip of his staff towards a burly farmer. Unfortunately, the tip of the pikestaff stuck in the ground and Holly's father, still shouting, shot inelegantly into the air, over the top of his weapon and straight into Miss Partridge who collapsed to the ground in an untidy heap. Her groans were frightfully authentic – but then with all fourteen stone of Holly's father on top of her, they were unlikely to be anything else.

Cameras clicked as the photographer from the

Evening Telegraph captured the moment.

'I don't think,' said Holly, 'that was meant to happen.'

Her father rolled over and lay on the ground, motionless. A lot of Roundheads suddenly stopped being Roundheads and started having a little panic.

Miss Partridge sat up and stared at Holly's dad. 'Oh dear,' she said. And fainted.

The photographer was having a field day.

It was when Mr Vine tried to stand up, blood pouring from his nose, and fell instantly back to the ground that Holly realised this was serious.

'Dad's hurt!' cried Holly. 'Scott, go and get Mum! She's waiting for the march to start. Down by the river.'

'OK,' said Scott, jumping up, snatching Fitz's lead and heading off down the hill. Jade hesitated for one moment and then sped after him, much to Cleo's annoyance.

'We need to stop the bleeding,' shouted someone. 'And his ankle looks as if it might be broken. Get the St John's Ambulance up here now!'

A young reporter, notebook in hand, sped over to the scene, scribbling as he ran. Holly's heart raced. She ran over to her father, her two friends close on her heels. Trig was hovering some distance away, chewing his lip.

'You, lad!' shouted someone. 'Give us your shirt.'

Trig froze.

'Come on, boy, for heaven's sake – quickly.'

Trig stood motionless, his gaze averted from where Holly's dad lay on the ground.

'Trig!' Cleo snapped. 'Get on with it!'

Trig glanced at her, pulled off his shirt, threw it at the man and ran off.

Holly and Tansy looked at him in amazement. 'What's up with Trig?' asked Tansy.

Before Holly could reply, two bustling St John's Ambulance men arrived and set about examining Rupert's still bleeding nose. Then they strapped up his foot and lifted him into the vehicle, followed by a slowly reviving Miss Partridge, who kept saying 'Oh dear,' somewhat ineffectually.

'Dad – Scott's gone to get Mum!' said Holly, leaning over her father.

'No need, no need,' he said bravely. 'She's got her march – I'm fine. Just a bit of a knock. Tell her I'll see her in casualty when she's done her speech. And wish her luck.'

'I'll come with you,' said Holly.

Her father shook his head. 'Enjoy the day,' he said. 'It is your birthday after all. And say sorry to Trig for spoiling his fun, won't you?'

Holly nodded and turned to find him. But Trig had gone.

2.55 p.m.
Trying to be cool

'Excuse me, but did I hear you say that guy was your father?' The young reporter, pen poised, grinned at Holly. 'Don't look so worried, he'll be fine.'

'He wasn't rambling or incoherent or anything,' said

Tansy comfortingly. 'Which means his mind is OK.'

'Makes a change,' said Holly with a watery smile.

'I'm Leo Bellinger, from the *Evening Telegraph*,' said the reporter. 'Now, could you give me a few details . . .'

'Sorry,' said Holly, 'can't stop. I have to find my mother – she's speaking at the rally in a minute.'

'Really?' The reporter pocketed his notebook. 'I'll try and catch that – two people in the same family making the headlines – great!' He beckoned to the photographer and the two of them dashed off.

Holly scanned the crowds. 'Where is Scott? He should have found Mum by now.'

'And where's Trig?' questioned Tansy.

'I think he was embarrassed,' said Cleo. 'I saw he had this huge birthmark all over his chest.'

'Oh . . . how unsexy,' commented Holly. Maybe I'll go for Scott instead, she thought.

Cleo stared at her. 'Looks aren't everything,' she said, surprising herself. Not that she liked Trig that much or anything, but she couldn't help thinking about how miserable he looked. And she hated to see anyone unhappy. And when he wasn't posing he looked – well, more lovable.

'Look,' said Tansy, pointing across the field. 'There's your mum.'

Holly stopped dead in her tracks. 'Oh no, please, please no,' she breathed.

Standing behind a table on a wooden platform with a microphone in one paw was a large white rabbit. And everyone in the crowd was laughing. A cameraman from

TV East was focusing his lens on her white bobtail.

'She's supposed to have changed into a dress or something,' wailed Holly. 'I can't bear it!'

They stood on a bench to get a better view. Everyone was still laughing and Holly spotted Leo the reporter, leaning against a nearby tree and scribbling frantically.

Holly's mum held up a paw. 'Go on, please, do laugh,' she said fiercely to the crowd. 'It is, I agree, amusing that the zip has broken and I am stuck in this costume for the foreseeable future.'

The crowd chuckled, but it was a kinder chuckle this time.

'Your laughter can't hurt me,' declared Mrs Vine. 'But let the developers knock down the day centre and you can hurt a lot of young people who need our support – young people who have very little to laugh about.'

'She's good,' whispered Tansy.

'She's amazing,' agreed Cleo.

'This is one heck of a story,' said the reporter, flipping over a page.

Holly opened one eye. She had to admit that her mum sounded pretty in command.

'Would you sleep easy in your bed at night knowing that you had done nothing to save a day centre that gives support to the disadvantaged, just so that you could have yet another hypermarket?'

A murmur went through the crowd. The cameraman moved closer and beckoned to a girl in a green jacket carrying a furry mike. Holly opened the other eye.

'Fight the closure,' stormed Mrs Vine, waving a white

furry arm in the air. 'Because if you don't you are condemning a lot of young people to a life on the streets.' Applause echoed round the crowd.

'Get a picture of that woman, Jack.' Leo obviously couldn't believe his luck. Holly felt quite proud, and began to edge forward so that she could let her mum know about the accident.

Mrs Vine turned to the table, and took a sip from a glass of water, which was difficult through several centimetres of fur and wire whiskers.

Just then, a tall man with a big moustache, wearing a waxed jacket and green moleskin trousers, pushed to the front of the crowd and jumped on to the platform. 'Good riddance to the layabouts, that's what I say! Glue-sniffing, no-good wasters, that's all they are!'

Mrs Vine wheeled round to face the heckler, her rabbit ears bouncing up and down. 'What did you say?'

The man repeated it louder and more aggressively.

Mrs Vine drew herself to her full height, took three steps forward and threw the glass of water in his face. And then the entire contents of the jug. The man gasped, staggered around the platform and almost caught hold of Mrs Vine's flapping rabbit ears.

'No!' cried Holly involuntarily. *Stop it, Mum. Please.*

It would have been all right if her mum had been wearing shoes. But little pink padded paws are very slippery and as she stepped backwards to avoid the angry heckler, she slid on the spilled water and shot over the edge of the platform, landing on top of the young policeman who had spent all morning feeling bored.

The audience gasped. The photographer, unable to believe his luck, took picture after picture. Holly considered putting herself up for adoption.

The constable, who was supposed to be on crowd control but was hoping for a real crime, decided that, in the absence of bank robbers on the run or a defecting spy, he supposed a deranged woman would have to suffice.

'Come along now, madam, I think it's time we finished up, don't you?' he said, picking himself up and trying to look dignified, despite being covered in bits of grass and the odd lump of nylon rabbit fur.

'Don't you patronise me!' shouted Holly's mum.

The TV crew moved in closer.

Holly shut both eyes again. The shame of it all. She heard her friends gasp. She opened her eyes. The policeman's helmet was on the grass and Mrs Vine was being marched ceremoniously towards a white van with POLICE in large letters on the side, followed by the camera crew and the reporter.

It's OK, thought Holly. In a moment I'll wake up. It's all a nightmare. She ran up to the van, closely followed by Cleo and Tansy.

'Mum!' she cried.

Mrs Vine turned round and waved. 'Not to worry, sausage!' she called. 'No problem.'

Oh great, thought Holly. You call me sausage in public, get arrested and then say there's no problem.

'Just tell your father what's happened, there's a love.'

'But, Mum – '

The van door shut.

Holly suddenly felt very small and burst into tears. She hadn't managed to tell her mum about her dad and her dad wouldn't know her mum was in custody and she didn't know what to do.

'Don't cry, love,' said the reporter. 'They'll let her out after they've given her a caution. It's only a formality.'

Formality or not, Holly felt miserable. Trig was nowhere to be seen and Scott had disappeared too. Her birthday wasn't turning out at all the way she imagined.

3.20 p.m.

Holly, Cleo and Tansy were just wondering what to do next when Jade came rushing up to them, out of breath and flushed in the face.

'Have you seen Fitz?' she gasped, brushing a strand of honey-coloured hair out of her eyes.

'Who's Fitz?' asked Tansy, wondering if this was yet another dishy guy she had hitherto overlooked.

'Scott's dog,' explained Jade. 'He broke loose from his lead when Scott was looking for Holly's mum – did you find her, by the way?'

'Not exactly,' said Holly and told Jade the whole story.

'That's awful,' said Jade. 'Are you going to the police station to find your mum? Because if you are, I'll come too and report Fitz lost.'

'That's a great idea,' agreed Holly. 'Where is Scott? He ought to come too.'

'He's down by the river asking people if they've seen

anything,' said Jade. She paused. 'Poor thing, he's in pieces about it. I'd love to be able to find Fitz for him.'

Holly stared at her. And it hit her like a stone. Jade fancied Scott too. Well, tough. Jade had already blown the chance of a proper party, so she certainly wasn't going to get Scott. Holly was going to make quite sure of that.

3.40 p.m.
Just when you thought it couldn't get any worse

'What's your relationship to the dog's owner, dear?' The policewoman looked up from filling in the lost-property form. 'Girlfriend, are you?'

'No she's not, she's just his friend,' interrupted Holly instantly. 'We are all friends of his.'

DUNCHESTER POLICE – LOST-PROPERTY REPORT

Item lost	One mongrel – male, brown and white short-haired, scruffy. Answers to the name of Fitz. Last seen Swan's Meadow 20 September
Owner	Scott Hamill, 2 Dulverton Road, Oak Hill, Dunchester
Person reporting loss	Miss Jade Williams, 53 Lime Avenue, Oak Hill, Dunchester

At that moment a side door opened and Holly's mother emerged, looking extremely cheerful for someone who had been on the wrong side of the law. Holly rushed up to her and gave her a big hug, for once not minding what her friends thought.

'Holly, darling! What are you doing here? And your friends! What a day – people did notice me, didn't they?'

'Notice you? Mum, the whole thing was filmed by TV East.'

Her mother clapped her hands in delight. 'Brilliant!' she cried. 'Couldn't be better!' She caught the eye of the police officer on the desk. 'Only of course I didn't mean it to end like that – very silly of me,' she said, sounding as if she didn't mean a word of it. 'Dad outside with the car, is he?'

'No, he's in hospital because . . .'

'Hospital!' Her mother grabbed the edge of the desk and turned pale. 'What – ?'

'Don't worry, Mrs Vine, it's not serious,' said Cleo. at once.

'He pole-vaulted over his pikestaff and hurt his ankle,' said Tansy.

'And his nose bled like anything – Miss Partridge fainted and Trig . . .' Holly gabbled.

'I must get to the hospital at once,' said Mrs Vine.

'I'll come with you,' offered Holly.

'No, dear, you go home,' said her mother. 'And can you phone Mrs Heatherington-Smythe?'

'Why?'

'Well, if your father is hurt, we won't be going to the ball tonight, will we? And she'll need to make a few changes of plan on the top table.'

The girls looked at one another, all thinking the same thing.

If Holly's parents didn't go to the ball, it wasn't just Mrs Heatherington-Smythe who would be changing her plans.

4.15 p.m.
The seed of an idea

'What are we going to do?' asked Holly as they walked home along Riverbank Road. 'Scott and Trig and the others will be turning up at eight o'clock and if my parents haven't gone out, all hell will break loose.'

Tansy frowned. 'But if they are at home, they won't mind you having boys round,' she reasoned.

'The fact that I had arranged it all without telling them will cause my mother to do a major flip,' said Holly. 'And believe me, that is not a pretty sight.'

Jade paused before crossing the road. 'If Scott hasn't found Fitz, there is no way he will come to the party anyway,' she said. 'He'll just spend all evening hunting for him. And if he does that, Trig is bound to stay and help him.' And so will I, she added silently.

'But it's my birthday!' Holly stressed, her heart sinking. Scott had to come. And Trig. She was pretty sure it was Scott she wanted, especially now she knew Jade was after him – but then again, if that didn't work out, there was always Trig to fall back on.

'And Fitz is Scott's dog!' retorted Jade. 'He could be

hurt or locked in somewhere or anything. An animal's life matters more than your stupid party.'

Holly glared at her. She didn't want anything diverting Scott's mind from falling in love with her. An idea slowly formed in her mind. An idea that would make it certain that Scott came along.

It might just work. Of course, it wasn't exactly honest – but then again, all was fair in the cause of love. Wasn't it?

'I wonder what happened to Trig,' Tansy said casually after she and Holly had waved goodbye to Cleo and Jade.

She hadn't been able to get him out of her mind all afternoon. When he had pulled off his shirt and run away, she had realised just what it was that made him so attractive. It wasn't just the blond wavy hair and those incredible liquid eyes. It wasn't even his bouncy confidence. It was the fact that she was quite certain that Trig had something secret in his life, something that all his bravado and teasing was a cover-up for. He was actually quite vulnerable and sensitive.

'He probably joined up with Scott after the accident,' said Holly. 'Guys always stick together. He'll turn up.'

6.00 p.m.
Drastic events call for drastic actions

'Is that the *Evening Telegraph*? Oh good. This is Holly Vine speaking. Can I speak to Leo Bellinger, please? Yes, yes, I'll hold.'

Holly closed her eyes and sent a prayer heavenwards.

'Oh, hi, it's Holly Vine – you took pictures of my mum and dad . . . yes, that's right, the Roundhead and the Rabbit. That's going to be the headline? On the front page?'

The shame of it all.

'Well, anyway, I thought you'd like to know that my mum is going to be at the Battle Ball tonight trying to persuade our MP to join her campaign. Well, no, she doesn't always throw jugs of water around, but she is quite . . . volatile.' Holly's love of English meant that when pressed she could always find the right word for the moment. 'Oh yes, I think there might be a great story there . . . You were thinking of going? Oh do . . . Yes, she has a few tricks up her sleeve . . . All right then . . . Oh, you're welcome.'

She hung up. Stage one completed with success.

6.27 p.m.
The scheming continues

She had just changed into her navy suede miniskirt and was trying without great success to put her hair up when she heard a car scrunching to a halt on the gravel drive. She ran downstairs to see her mother climbing out of a taxi.

'Hi, Mum! How's Dad?' she called.

'Not so bad, not so bad,' said her mother, handing a five-pound note to the driver and picking up her bag. 'But they are keeping him in overnight, just to be on the safe side.'

Yes! said Holly to herself. One parent dealt with, one to go.

'Come on in, Mum, and I'll make you a cup of tea,' offered Holly in her most soothing tone. She eyed the kitchen clock. Six-thirty. Cleo, Tansy and Jade would be arriving at seven, and she had a lot to get sorted before then. She had to word this next bit very carefully. 'And when you've had your tea, I'll run you a bath,' she said.

Her mother shook her head. 'No, darling, I'm just going to sink into a chair and do nothing for a couple of hours.' She yawned expansively.

Oh no you are not, Mother dear, thought Holly.

'Why don't we cut your birthday cake?' her mum suggested. 'It's in the larder – I did the chocolate layer one you like so much.'

'You did? That's so nice of you!' exclaimed Holly, genuinely chuffed that her mum had remembered. 'But, Mum,' she added hastily, in wide-eyed innocence, 'what about the ball? And Tim Whatever – you know, the MP? I mean, after your triumph today you can't pass up the opportunity of meeting him.'

Her mother shrugged. 'It's a shame, I'll admit it,' she agreed, 'but Mrs Heatherington-Smythe will have found someone to take my . . . you did remember to phone her, didn't you?'

Holly clamped her hand to her mouth in mock horror. 'Oh, Mum, I forgot – I'm so sorry. You see, what with worrying about Dad, and talking to the reporter . . .'

'Reporter? What reporter?'

Holly regaled her mother with the story of meeting

9 2

Leo at the showground and how he thought that Dad's chivalry and Mrs Vine's social awareness would make a wonderful story.

'And he phoned to say he's going to be at the ball tonight to hear that MP man speak,' said Holly. 'And he wants to do a big piece on your campaign.'

Well, twisting the truth just a little didn't matter when it was in a good cause. And there was no better cause than her party.

'Well, I don't know,' began her mother, but Holly noticed that she was drinking her tea rather rapidly and eyeing the clock. 'I suppose I could go – but without Dad . . .'

'He would hate to think you had passed up an opportunity like this, just because he was in hospital,' said Holly emphatically. 'And you did say that saving the centre was very important. But it's up to you.'

It was with great satisfaction that Holly watched her mother scoot upstairs to the bathroom.

7.25 p.m.
We can't – can we?

'And she's really gone?' Tansy's eyes lit up as she flung her sleeping bag on to the floor of Holly's bedroom.

Holly nodded.

'Brilliant!' said Tansy. 'What's happened to Jade and Cleo?'

'They should be here soon,' said Holly. 'Which is why we need to get a move on. I need your help.'

'Do you want me to put out crisps and stuff?'

Holly shook her head. 'No, it's much more important than that. Jade says that if Scott doesn't find Fitz, he won't come to the party. So this is what I thought . . .' And she told Tansy her plan.

Tansy's eyes widened. 'But that would be a total lie!' she gasped.

Holly stared at her. 'You were the one who said that if you wanted something enough you had to make it happen,' she insisted.

Tansy nodded slowly. 'And I suppose it wouldn't really do any harm, would it?' she said.

'So?'

Tansy thought. Where Scott went, Trig was bound to follow. And no one was interested in Trig except Tansy. 'Yes – let's go for it!' she said.

7.40 p.m.
Lying through her teeth

'Hi, may I speak to Scott, please? Holly. Holly Vine.'

She covered the mouthpiece and gave the thumbs-up sign to Tansy.

'Scott, it's me – Holly. Have you found Fitz? No? Well, listen. I don't know whether this is any help but Tansy and me both think we've seen him. Running through my back garden.'

She held her breath.

'Pardon . . .? Well, sort of white with browny-black

bits . . . It is? Yes, come straight away. Must go, some of the others are arriving.' She replaced the receiver and grinned at Tansy.

'Is Trig coming with him?' asked Tansy anxiously.

'Don't know,' Holly said, shrugging. 'But Scott is and that will do for starters.'

8.10 p.m.
Hanging in there

Within half an hour, the sitting room was full of people. Nick and Ursula were entwined round one another in one corner, apparently competing for the longest kiss in the universe competition, and Alex Gregson was rifling through Holly's collection of CDs and tapes. Cleo was sitting on the arm of a chair watching him and wishing she could think of something mind-blowingly witty to say. Jade kept going to the back door and peering into the garden, because Holly had told her that Scott's dog had been spotted in the shrubbery and she rather thought she wanted to be the one to find him.

The doorbell rang.

'Hi, Holly, have you found him?' Scott, breathless and red in the face, scanned the front garden hopefully. Trig hovered behind him, staring at the gravel with deep concentration.

'Well, no – but I'm sure he's around here somewhere,' she said. 'Why don't we go into the garden and have a good look?' Amongst other things, she added silently in her head.

'I'll help,' said Trig, still not looking anyone in the eye.

'Oh, no,' interrupted Tansy. 'I don't think too many people should go searching. It might frighten him off,' she improvised quickly.

She grinned at Trig. 'Come through and I'll get you a drink,' she said, praying that the fifty minutes she had spent getting the Smouldering Chestnut eyeshadow and Purple Passion lip-liner just right would pay off.

Trig followed Tansy, rather more reluctantly than she would have liked, and Holly took Scott into the back garden. She was just about to start the first chat-up line from *Cool Girl*'s 'Get Your Guy' supplement when Jade appeared at her elbow.

'Any luck?' she said brightly.

If you'd disappear, I might have, thought Holly. She sighed as Jade and Scott began peering behind bushes and prodding undergrowth.

'He might be on the building site,' suggested Jade. 'He could be stuck somewhere.'

And with that, she headed through the gap in the fence, closely followed by Scott. Holly had an overwhelming desire to throttle her. If she went too, she would ruin her new shoes. If she didn't, Jade might get her mitts on Scott. On balance, the shoes would have to suffer.

8.20 p.m.

Tansy had never seen Trig so subdued before. She had tried all the best flirting techniques she knew, but all he did was sip his cola and answer in monosyllables. There was nothing for it: she would have to come straight to the point.

'What's wrong?' she asked, looking him straight in the eye. 'Is it something to do with this afternoon?'

Trig coloured and turned to look out of the window. 'I'd better get out there and help Scott,' he muttered, heading for the door. 'I wasn't going to bother coming to a dumb party anyway.'

'Wait!' said Tansy, grabbing his arm. She was desperate to make the most of this moment alone.

Trig shrugged her off. 'I guess I'll go home soon,' he said. 'There's baseball on Sky Sports.'

'You can't do that,' gasped Tansy. 'We've only just started.' Or in our case, not started, she thought. 'Anyway, you want to get to know everyone, don't you?'

Trig shrugged. 'I guess they won't want to get to know me – not after, well, you know, running off like that. And anyway,' he added, looking straight at her, 'what's the point of a party when there's no chance with the girl you really like?'

Tansy's heart did a double flip. 'But there is a chance, you know,' she said softly. 'A very good chance indeed.'

Trig stared at her. 'There is? Do you really mean that? Even though . . . well, despite everything?'

Tansy nodded, imagining the long, slow, lingering kiss that, if she played it right, would follow in about twenty seconds.

'Oh yes,' she breathed, hoping she sounded huskily sexy. 'Very definitely.'

This was it. She was falling in love. It was happening.

'So should I tell her how much I fancy her? Right now?'

Tansy's eyes widened. 'Tell – who?' she quavered.

'Cleo – should I tell her I think she's incredible?'

'Tell her what you like,' snapped Tansy, and went to the loo. Loos are pretty good places for people whose hearts are breaking.

8.40 p.m.

'Hi,' said Trig, sidling up to Cleo who was sitting on the bottom of the stairs feeling fat and wishing it was time to go home. 'I brought you some crisps.'

Cleo looked up in surprise. 'Thanks,' she said. There was no doubt about it – Trig might be a world-class bragger but he did have the most beautiful eyes.

'Has Scott found the dog?' asked Cleo, shouting over the persistent beat of jungle music.

'They're still out in the garden looking,' replied Trig. 'I want to ask you something,' he added in a rush.

Cleo looked at him questioningly.

'Will you go out with me?'

Cleo gasped. 'Pardon?' she said.

'OK, OK, I get it! It was dumb of me to ask anyway!' Trig stood up and headed down the hall.

'Hang on,' Cleo called after him. 'Give me a chance.'

Trig paused.

'I thought . . . I mean, what about these girls in the States? You said . . .'

'OK, so I lied,' he said. 'There are no girls. There never were any girls. I guess there never will be.'

Cleo stared at him. And realised that Trig was really upset. 'Tell me,' she said gently.

'Where do I begin?' asked Trig.

'Try the beginning,' said Cleo.

8.50 p.m.
Last-ditch attempt

'It's getting dark,' said Holly. 'Let's go in.' And then I get you to myself, she thought, eyeing Scott with longing.

'You go,' muttered Scott. 'I'll just go and check round once more.'

'Oh, come on,' said Holly, who was feeling desperate. 'Don't be such a party-pooper!'

Scott turned on her. 'My dog matters far more than your stupid party,' he said, his voice wobbling. 'Just go, why don't you? You'll stay, won't you, Jade?'

'Course I will,' agreed Jade.

Holly got the distinct feeling that she had made a bad move.

8.55 p.m.
So this is love . . .

'I'm sorry, really I am.' Scott was sitting on an upturned wheelbarrow close to tears. 'I suppose you think I'm pretty wet, getting upset over a missing dog, especially when . . . well, compared with what you lost and all that,' he added, not certain quite how to put it.

Jade shook her head and smiled. 'Of course I don't,' she declared. 'Love is love – what or who you love doesn't come into it. You're worried sick about Fitz and I'm missing Mum and Dad – it's still pain.'

'Do you know something?' said Scott softly, leaning towards her.

'What?' asked Jade.

'You are lovely,' said Scott. And gently kissed her forehead. It was very nice.

'Would you . . . I mean, suppose we went out together sometime? If you don't mind, that is.'

'I don't mind,' said Jade. 'I don't mind one little bit.'

At which point Scott kissed her again. This time on the lips. For quite a long time. So this, thought Jade, as little electric shocks galloped up and down her spine, was what falling in love was all about.

9.00 p.m.
Gee!

'I've never talked to a girl like this before,' said Trig, looking embarrassed. 'In fact, I've never talked to anyone like this before.'

He had told Cleo how he had been born with a huge strawberry-coloured birthmark which spread all over his chest and back, across his shoulders and down the tops of his arms. Even though he was having treatment, it would never disappear completely, which was why he wore polo-neck sweaters and long sleeves all the time.

She discovered that he had an elder brother who had won a sports scholarship to an American university and a sister who was brilliant at athletics.

'My dad thinks they are the greatest,' he had said ruefully. 'He keeps on at me to get involved in sport and says I'm a weed and a wimp. He says he doesn't know how an ex-marine like him could produce a runt like me. But because I hate the idea of people staring at me, I've never got involved in sports.'

'I understand,' said Cleo. 'Surely your dad does too?'

'He says I have to learn to be a real man. He skis, and shoots, and does white-water rafting – the whole bit.'

'So?' said Cleo. 'That doesn't mean you have to like that stuff.'

'But real cool guys are into that kinda thing,' said Trig. 'And what with having a hideous body – '

Cleo had had enough. 'Your body is not hideous!' she exclaimed. 'Trig, you've got a birthmark. A mark, that's all it is. I'm really sorry but it's no big deal. It's just skin, not the real you. You're a nice guy – a really nice guy,' she added, suddenly realising that she meant every word of it. 'Especially when you stop pretending,' she added.

Trig gave a half smile. 'Oh yeah,' he drawled. 'But no girls ever fancy me when they see . . . well, you know . . .'

'What you mean,' said Cleo, 'is that you imagine that just because you've got a birthmark, no one will fancy you. That's crazy. Holly fancies you,' she added hastily, worrying that she was coming on too strong.

'It's not Holly I'm interested in,' he said. 'It's you I asked to go out with me. But you don't want to.'

'Who says I don't?' demanded Cleo, her conscience clear now she had got the Holly thing out of the way. 'In fact, I can't think of anything nicer.'

Trig grinned. And this time it was a real grin. 'Gee,' he said.

Gee indeed, thought Cleo.

9.10 p.m.
Found out

'Did you find him, Scott?' Ursula unwrapped herself from round Nick long enough to shout the question above the music as Scott and Jade came into the room, adding to the lumps of mud which Holly had trodden all over the carpet.

Scott shook his head and looked miserable. Tansy, who had got bored with sitting in the loo, turned to Alex Gregson, who was demolishing a dish of peanuts at record speed.

'Hardly surprising,' she muttered. 'Holly made the whole thing up just to get Scott over here.'

It was unfortunate that this remark was made at precisely the moment when the music stopped.

'You did what?' Scott wheeled round to face Holly.

'So you never really saw Fitz at all?' Jade looked incredulous.

'And I've been wasting all this time here when I could have been looking all over for him,' shouted Scott. 'Well, thanks a bunch, Holly! I'm leaving.'

Holly felt sick. She knew she'd been a total idiot, and mean, and selfish – but she couldn't bear being made to look a dweeb in front of all her friends. 'Hey, don't go!' she said. 'The party's about to hot up.'

'You are unbelievable!' shouted Scott, wrenching open the door into the hall.

Holly followed him out of the room. 'Scott, don't! I didn't . . .'

She paused as she heard a car pull up outside. Mum! She was back. She couldn't be.

Scott grabbed his denim jacket off the coat hook and pulled open the front door.

'Get lost!' he yelled at Holly, and careered out of the door, straight into Mrs Vine who was standing on the step in her peacock-blue cocktail dress, grappling with her door key.

She did not look happy. As Scott mumbled an apology and ran down the drive, she stepped into the hall, her eyes widening at the persistent beat of music echoing around the house.

'Holly,' she said, in those ominous measured tones that mothers use just before they explode in fury, 'what is going on?'

Holly's heart sank to below floorboard level. What possessed her mum to come home so early?

'I, er . . . we . . . well, you see . . .' began Holly, praying that her mother would hold back on the exploding

103

front until they were on their own.

She didn't. 'You were told specifically that you could have the girls over for the evening,' she said, marching over to the stereo and switching it off. A deathly hush fell over the room and people stopped dancing in mid-jig. 'You were also told that boys were not allowed.'

Ursula tittered. Alex spluttered into his hand. Holly hoped that death would be rapid.

'Mrs Vine?' Cleo stood up. 'Actually, it wasn't really Holly's fault.'

Mrs Vine's eyebrows elevated.

'You see, Scott has lost his dog and Holly thought she had seen it in your garden so he came over with Trig and the others – ' at this point she gave them all a 'stick to this story or else' stare '– to help hunt for him. Only we didn't find him, and most of us have to phone for lifts from our parents to get home so we decided to play music till they came.'

Holly, Tansy and Jade stared at her. Cleo, quiet, anxious, correct Cleo, had told a lie to save her friend. Cleo was equally stunned at her actions. She would never have believed she could speak out like that.

Trig looked at her in admiration. He took a deep breath. 'No, ma'am, it's my fault, really. When Scott said Holly had seen Fitz, I rounded up the guys to help us search – I guess we never thought about asking if it was OK.'

Cleo squeezed his hand.

Mrs Vine eyed them all intently.

'I see,' she said, mellowing slightly. 'Well, I suggest

you all have a slice of Holly's birthday cake and then I will drive you all home.'

'Mum!' cried Holly. 'We told their parents to come at ten-thirty and . . .' She stopped. She knew she'd blown it.

'You did? So you knew in advance about this search party for this missing dog, did you?' her mother said through gritted teeth. She turned to the gang. 'Coats. On. Now.'

No one argued.

10.00 p.m.
A life in ruins

Holly stood in the kitchen in floods of tears. Tansy put an arm round her shoulder.

'I'm really sorry,' she said. 'I didn't mean anyone to hear what I was saying. I was just in a bad mood.'

Holly sniffed. 'It's not that,' she said. 'It's just that I wanted this to be the best party ever. I wanted Scott and Trig and everyone to think I was really cool and it's all gone wrong. Scott hates me. Jade's gone home in a huff and Trig completely ignored me.'

'And me,' Tansy said with a sigh.

Holly stared at her. 'Do you fancy Trig?'

Tansy nodded. 'Much good it did me,' she said. 'He's besotted with Cleo. And now Scott's gone off with Jade – you wanted him back, didn't you?'

Holly nodded. 'Or Trig . . . or, I suppose, anyone,' she said, suddenly realising that it was not the guys she wanted for their own sake, but just so that she could say she had a boyfriend. And Trig and Cleo had stood up for her, even though she'd been pathetic. They were real friends, regardless of who they fancied. She saw that now.

'I just don't know how my mum could be so embarrassing, treating me like that in front of everyone.' Holly sighed. 'If only she hadn't decided to come home early. I just don't know what I'm going to do.'

'You can start, my girl, by washing the mud off the sitting-room carpet.' Her mother appeared at the kitchen door. 'Tansy, dear, how nice that you're staying. You could have asked Cleo,' she added, turning to Holly.

'Her dad's coming up early tomorrow so she had to go home,' said Holly.

Her mother nodded. 'Well,' she said, 'I shan't say any more about this incident, Holly, except to remind you that there are rules in life which have to be followed. And if you don't learn them at home, how are you ever going to be a reliable member of the community?'

'That's rich,' said Holly, 'coming from a woman who got arrested while dressed as an overgrown rabbit.'

Her mother tried not to laugh. She opened her arms.

'I'm sorry, Mum,' said Holly, giving her a hug. 'Really.'

'Me too,' said Tansy. 'Sorry, Mrs Vine.'

'Let's have some birthday cake,' said Holly's mum. 'And tomorrow we can celebrate with a slap-up meal and have a really relaxing day. Now, isn't that a nice idea?'

SUNDAY

9.00 a.m.
More shared secrets

Holly and Tansy didn't wake up till nine o'clock because they had talked for hours before going to sleep. Tansy had told Holly how she wanted to be rich and famous and find her father, and Holly had told Tansy how she wanted to be shorter.

'On balance,' Tansy had said, 'I think I stand a better chance of getting my wish. You try being tiny like me – it's a total pain. I had to get my skirt in the kids' department of a clothes shop – but don't you dare tell anyone!'

'My boobs aren't doing what they should,' Holly had confessed. 'One's bigger than the other.'

'Really? No one would ever notice. Anyway, I saw this programme in biology and it said that lots of girls have lopsided boobs in their teens. At least you've got a chest, which is more than I have.'

Holly felt better. 'But it would be nice to be utterly gorgeous – like Ella – wouldn't it?' she said.

'Well,' Tansy had murmured, just before falling asleep, 'she may have legs up to her armpits but she hasn't got a guy any more, has she? Which just goes to show that there's hope for you and me yet.'

9.45 a.m.

On Sunday morning, Mrs Vine left Holly and Tansy eating their breakfast and went to the hospital to fetch her husband.

'Just don't do anything catastrophic while I'm gone,' she admonished them.

'As if,' said Holly. Her mother had only been gone about five minutes when the doorbell rang.

Standing on the front step, with William on one hip and a towelling holdall in his hand, was her brother Richard.

'Mum in?' he asked, pushing past Holly into the hall.

'Hi, Holly. Did you have a good birthday, Holly? So sorry I forgot to send you a present, Holly. Here's a tenner to make up for it, Holly,' chanted his sister.

'Birthday? Oh cripes, yes. Sorry, Holly – sort it with you later. Look, where's Mum?'

'Gone to the hospital to fetch Dad,' she said. 'She won't be long.'

Richard tutted. 'That's too bad. Nothing serious, I hope,' he said. 'Look, you'll have to take William – I've got to go to Leicester.'

'What on earth for?' asked Holly, as Richard thrust William into her arms.

'Serena's there – at her mum's – and she wants to come home,' he said triumphantly. 'Look, I've put toys and biscuits and stuff in the bag. I'll . . . we'll get back as quickly as we can. Must dash.'

'You'll have to pay me!' said Holly. 'And I don't come cheap!'

'Fine,' said her brother. And with that he hurtled through the front door and into his dilapidated Renault 5.

'Bye bye,' said William, waving his chubby hand at the closed door. 'Bikky?' he added hopefully.

'He's so cute,' said Tansy. 'Can I stay for a bit and play with him?'

'Whatever turns you on,' said Holly.

10.15 a.m.
Child-minding crisis

Half an hour later, the bell rang. Holly went to the door with William padding after her.

'Remember me?' Leo, the reporter from the *Evening Telegraph*, stood grinning on the doorstep. 'Wondered if I could come in and have a word with your parents? Get a bit of background colour for this piece I'm doing.'

'Doddy,' said William, leaning out of the doorway excitedly.

'Be quiet, William,' hissed Holly. 'They're not here,' she said to Leo. 'Mum's fetching Dad from the hospital. But you can come in if you like – they'll be back soon.'

She was about to shut the front door when a sleek racing-green Jaguar pulled up the drive. An overweight man in a pinstriped suit stepped out. 'Good morning, good morning,' he boomed, holding out a hand. 'Tim Renfrew, MP for Dunchester West. Is Angela Vine about?'

'Doddy, doddy,' said William, jumping up and down and banging Holly on the knee.

Holly ignored him and repeated the story. 'But do please come through,' she said politely. 'This is Leo Bellinger from the *Evening Telegraph*. He's a reporter.'

Tim Renfrew looked as though he had just been introduced to a small and rather muddy earthworm.

'Oh, I know Mr Bellinger,' he growled, his already red face diffusing with even more colour. 'Our paths have regrettably crossed before. This whippersnapper besmirched my good name.'

Leo tried a friendly smile. 'Oh, come, Mr Renfrew,' he said, 'I was only doing my job. I only gave the people the facts.'

The MP snorted and sank into an armchair. Leo placed himself as far away as he could. Tansy, who never missed an opportunity to ingratiate herself with anyone with even a modicum of fame, had come smartly into the room as soon as she overheard the words 'MP'.

'Can we get you both some coffee?' she asked.

'How very kind,' said Tim Renfrew. 'Black, two sugars, please.'

Tansy and Holly went through to the kitchen.

'I hope Mum hurries up,' said Holly. 'I'm not into all this polite conversation stuff.' She poured boiling water on to the coffee and carried the tray through to the lounge. 'My mum won't be long,' she said again.

She had better not be. She felt very awkward standing here.

'Want some juice, William?' she asked, turning round.

There was no sign of William. 'William? Tansy, where's William?'

10.30 a.m.
With her heart in her mouth

Holly felt sick. Her heart was pounding in her chest and her legs had turned to water. The front door had been left open. William was nowhere to be seen.

Holly rushed down the front drive, calling his name at the top of her voice. The gate was open and she looked frantically up and down the road, but there was no sign of the little boy. She flew back through the side gate and into the back garden, closely followed by Tansy.

'He can't have gone far,' Tansy said encouragingly. 'He's only little.'

'I know,' sobbed Holly. 'And if anything has happened to him it will all be my fault.'

They looked all round the back garden and then Tansy spotted the gap in the fence. The same thought crossed their minds – building sites were no place for a toddler.

Holly pushed through the gap in the fence, closely followed by Tansy. 'Look!' said Holly urgently.

Outside one of the half-built houses, a large lady in a pair of black leggings and a red sweater was squatting down on her haunches, talking to William and holding his hand. Then she picked him up in her arms and turned towards the road.

'Stop it! Stop!' Holly rushed across the broken bricks and building debris littering what had once been their vegetable garden. 'Put him down!'

The woman turned.

'That's my nephew!' said Holly, remembering all the

stories of attempted kidnap that she had ever read. 'Give him to me.'

The woman handed him over, smiling broadly.

'Doddy,' said William.

'Oh my dear, I meant him no harm,' said the woman. 'I was just afraid he would get hurt – there's broken glass and all sorts of stuff round here. You really should keep a better eye on him, you know.'

Holly glared at her. She felt guilty enough without this woman reading the riot act.

'Doddy,' said William.

'What's he saying?' asked the woman, attempting to break the icy atmosphere.

'Nothing,' said Holly. 'Good morning.'

10.45 a.m.
Thank heavens for little boys

'The parents – they're back!' said Holly, as they led a giggling William back into the house. 'If they see William covered in mud, I'll really be for it. You take him upstairs and clean him up, Tansy, and I'll do the charming daughter bit.'

When she went into the sitting room, she found her father sitting in an armchair, his bandaged foot resting on a footstool, trying not to look bored as Tim Renfrew talked politics. Mrs Vine was pouring sherry from a cut-glass decanter and looking rather pink and Leo was sitting on the windowsill looking mildly amused.

'How's the foot, Dad? Anything I can do to help, Mum?'

The bell rang yet again. This place, thought Holly, is getting more like a railway station every day. Serena and Richard were standing on the doorstep, holding hands and looking all dewy-eyed and soppy.

'We've come for William,' said Serena. 'Where is my little precious lambkin?'

On cue, Tansy came down the stairs, holding a sparklingly clean little lambkin by the hand.

'Who's Mummy's darling boy, then?' cooed Serena.

'Tarky doddy, Mamma,' said William.

'Did William see a doggy then?' murmured Serena, who apparently had a degree in baby talk.

Holly looked at Tansy. Tansy looked at Holly.

'Come in and have a sherry, darlings,' called Mrs Vine, anxious to portray herself as the together mother-in-law.

'It might not be that doddy – I mean, dog,' said Tansy to Holly.

'And we can't make the same mistake twice,' said Holly.

'But then again . . .'

They sped upstairs.

10.55 a.m.

'Hi, Scott. Holly here. We really do think your dog is round here somewhere . . . No, no, I'm not, honestly. William says he saw a dog . . . William? My brother's kid . . .

113

No, no, it's not a wind-up – really I – He's hung up,' said Holly.

'It probably wasn't his dog, anyway,' said Tansy. 'I mean, babies yabber on about anything, don't they?'

Holly marched into the sitting room and squatted down beside William who was systematically eating the *Radio Times*.

'Where's the doggy?' she demanded, oblivious to the astonished gaze of her parents and their guests.

'Doddy,' said William, smiling beatifically.

'Where?' repeated Holly. 'In the garden? In your book?'

'Doddy sleeping,' said William. 'Dirty doddy.'

'Good boy!' yelled Holly. 'Come on, Tansy.'

They rushed from the room. Mrs Vine smiled nervously at her MP. 'The young,' she cooed. 'So vibrant, so full of life. Have another sherry.'

11.00 a.m.

The girls pushed their way back through the fence.

'He must have seen the dog and followed it,' reasoned Tansy. 'So it has to be here somewhere.'

They peered into the first of the half-built houses.

'We ought to go in and look,' suggested Holly.

They were just climbing through the unfinished doorway when they heard a whimper.

'Listen!' said Tansy.

They heard it again. In the hole that would one day be a stylish fireplace lay Fitz. He was damp, very muddy

114

and one paw was crusted with blood. He raised his head and stared dolefully at the two girls.

'It's him!' breathed Holly. 'We've found him. Give me a blanket.'

Tansy pulled a face. 'Oh yes, building sites are awash with freshly laundered bedding,' she said. 'Here, take this.'

She slipped her arms out of her denim jacket and handed it to Holly who tenderly picked up the whimpering dog in her arms.

'You can see,' she said, looking at its liquid-brown eyes, 'why Scott loves him so much.'

Tansy smiled. 'Now all we have to do is tell him how you risked life and limb to rescue him, and maybe he'll love you too,' she said.

I wish, thought Holly.

11.10 a.m.

When Holly, closely followed by Tansy, carried Fitz into the sitting room, she found her mother and father and Tim Renfrew sitting coyly on the sofa, while Leo aimed a camera at them.

'Just one more!' he said, squatting on his haunches. 'Terrific, absolutely terrific.'

Holly's mother turned her gaze on her daughter, and her mouth fell open. 'Holly dear, what on earth is that?' she said.

Holly went through the whole saga again and Leo clapped his hands in delight.

'Amazing!' he said. 'The theme continues, "The Vine Family: Champions of the Underdog". I love it! What a headline!'

It is, thought Holly, an improvement on 'The Roundhead and the Rabbit'.

'Get into the picture, Holly – with the little dog.'

Holly shook her head. 'I've got to get him back to Scott,' she began. 'He won't believe me if I phone.'

'Why not?'

'It's too complicated to explain,' said Holly hastily.

'OK, do the pic and I'll phone him,' he said. 'People believe reporters.'

'Not all of them,' commented the MP dryly.

Noon
Things get better

Scott was down on his knees hugging Fitz and trying to hide the tears in his eyes.

'Thanks, Holly,' he said, his voice muffled as he pressed his face into Fitz's grubby coat. 'Sorry I didn't believe you.'

'It's OK,' said Holly. 'I don't blame you. Don't you think you should take him to the vet?'

Scott nodded.

'My dad's outside with the car – I'll take him now. Can you let Jade know we've found Fitz? She's been brilliant.'

Holly sighed. 'Yes,' she said. 'Of course I will.'

'Thanks again,' said Scott with a grin, and Holly's battered heart did another lurch.

'Don't worry,' whispered Tansy as Scott drove off with his dad. 'There are plenty more guys where he came from.'

Maybe, thought Holly. But they don't seem to be falling over themselves to get to me.

'Right, Angela, so that's all agreed, is it?' said Tim Renfrew, downing the last of his sherry and standing up. 'You'll get me all the details and I'll take this matter up in the House. It's too important to sweep under the carpet.'

'Of course, Tim, and thank you,' Mrs Vine purred.

'Oh no, thank you,' said the MP. He turned to Holly. 'You must be very proud of your mother – one day I hope we'll see her on the benches. This country needs more people like her. People who really care.'

Yes, thought Holly, she does care, doesn't she? And not just about other people. She really does care about me. She'll probably know what to do about the boobs.

1.00 p.m.

Mrs Vine was in the kitchen singing. It was not something she was good at, but Holly was so relieved to have her mother in a good mood that she put up with her unique rendition of 'Don't Cry For Me Argentina'.

'Are you staying for lunch, Tansy dear?' she asked, chopping carrots with ferocious determination.

Tansy shook her head. 'I'd love to,' she said, 'but Mum said I had to go home. She's got that awful

Laurence coming for lunch – he's enough to put anyone off their food.'

Mrs Vine laughed. 'I'm sure he can't be that bad, Tansy,' she said. 'Not if your mum likes him.'

'She is,' commented Tansy dryly, 'very easily pleased.' She picked up her jacket and rucksack and beamed at Mrs Vine. 'Thank you very much for having me. Bye, Holly!'

A thought crossed Holly's mind. 'Hang on,' she said. 'I'll walk to the end of the road with you.'

'Hey,' said Tansy. 'You're going the wrong way.'

'I'm not really going to walk with you, stupid,' said Holly.

'Charming,' said Tansy mildly. 'Where are you going then?'

Holly took a deep breath. 'I was completely out of order last night,' she admitted. 'I'm going to set things straight with Scott. No, it's OK,' she added as Tansy opened her mouth. 'I know Jade and him are an item; I just want to say I'm sorry.'

'Good on you,' said Tansy.

1.20 p.m.
Taking a very deep breath

The door of Scott's house was opened by a large lady with jet-black hair and an unrestrained bosom. From inside came the sound of noisy laughter and glasses clinking.

'Is Scott in?' Holly asked nervously.

'But of course,' the woman beamed. 'Scott! Scott!'

Scott appeared from the kitchen. 'Thanks, Gran,' he said. 'Hi, Holly. Excuse the noise – it's my uncle's birthday. They're drinking Chianti and being utterly stupid.'

Holly breathed a sigh of relief. Scott sounded quite normal with her.

'Look,' she began hastily, 'I am really sorry about lying to you yesterday. Can we still be friends?'

'Of course,' said Scott. 'I like you a lot. You're a good mate, really you are.'

That, thought Holly, is enough for me. For now at any rate.

3.00 p.m.
A newcomer with possibilities

Halfway through Sunday lunch, the doorbell shrilled.

'Oh no,' said Mrs Vine with a sigh. 'What now?'

'I'll get it,' said her husband. 'I've got to get used to these crutches.' He hobbled to the door and returned with the woman Holly had shouted at on the building site.

'Hello again,' she chirruped, smiling at Holly. 'So sorry to intrude but I found this after you had gone.' She held up an exceedingly mangy blue toy elephant. 'I think the little lad – '

'Thank you so much,' gasped Holly, snatching the toy. 'Isn't it odd what strange things dogs play with?'

Please don't mention William, she prayed. I can't stand getting into any more trouble.

'Let me introduce myself,' the woman continued to Holly's relief. 'I'm Deannie Bennett, and I'm going to be your new neighbour. Over the back – the house on the left.'

'How charming!' said Mr Vine politely, hoping she would go so that he could get on with his roast pork.

'It's perfect for my tribe,' she said. 'Our bungalow in Ridgeway is far too small for three teenagers.'

'You have children then,' said Mr Vine, praying they would be of the quiet variety.

'Kirsty's thirteen, and the twins are fifteen,' she said. 'Honestly, who'd have teenage boys?'

'Me,' said Holly without thinking. And everyone laughed.

9.00 p.m.
Making up

By nine o'clock Mr Vine had retired to bed to rest his aching foot and Holly and her mum were sitting in the kitchen drinking hot chocolate and stuffing themselves with coconut cookies.

'Mum,' Holly began, suddenly feeling very shy and little. 'Can I ask you something?'

'Of course you can, sweetheart,' her mother assured her. 'What is it?'

Holly took a deep breath. 'The thing is, what I'm

trying to say is . . . one of my boobs is bigger than the other.' She chewed her lip.

'Oh, darling, isn't it irritating when that happens!' cried her mother, as if commenting on a cake that had failed to rise. 'Mine were totally out of kilter when I was your age. It's no big deal – but if it bothers you, we'll see the doctor, just to put your mind at rest.'

She paused. 'I'm sorry, Holly, really I am,' she said.

'What for?' asked Holly in surprise.

Her mother sighed. 'Well, I've been so keen on giving you personal space and privacy – and maybe I overdid it. I don't know – after the boys, I was so thrilled to have a daughter that I was determined not to blow it by becoming an over-protective mum.'

'Were you?' interrupted Holly. 'Were you really thrilled to have me?'

'Darling, of course I was. I just wish I had known that you were worrying – then we could have sorted it all out sooner.'

Holly hugged her mother. 'That's OK,' she said. 'Everything's sorted now.'

WHAT A WEEK TO MAKE IT BIG

*For Ellen, Ursula, the two Claires, Alex, Matthew,
Nick, and the two Sarahs – a constant source of inspiration!*

MONDAY

7.00 a.m.
3 Plough Cottages, Cattle Hill

A Problem Shared – *Heaven Sent*'s Dee Davies talks it over . . .

Dear Dee,

My father is ruining my life. He criticises my clothes, moans that I wear too much make-up and won't let me stay out late like all my friends. He is really off with my mates too. My mum travels away on business a lot and when I tell her what he's like she just says that I'm lucky he cares. Please tell me how to make him see I have to get a life.

Sarah Lovell (age 14)

Tansy Meadows sighed, tossed her magazine on to the floor and kicked off her duvet. That kid didn't know she was born – at least she had a father to argue with. Tansy wouldn't have minded dragging a dad into the twentieth century had she been lucky enough to have one. All her friends had fathers somewhere or other – even Jade Williams had a dead one – but Tansy's problem wasn't how her paternal parent behaved. Her dilemma was that she hadn't a clue who he was.

Her mother, Clarity, who had once been a New Age traveller and was very good at yoga and caring for small forests and not much good at noting the parentage of her child, assured Tansy that the choice was limited to two: Jordan, who had spent a whole summer painting pebbles in a dilapidated bus parked outside Glastonbury, or Pongo, an American university student from Illinois, who was a great source of comfort to the grief-stricken Clarity when Jordan decided to abandon the pebbles and set off for the Faeroe Islands with a flaxen-haired girl called October.

Tansy hoped it was Pongo – after all, with a university degree, he could by now be rich and famous, with a home in Florida and holidays in the Bahamas. You don't, she thought, get wealthy drawing on stones. Money meant a great deal to Tansy, largely because to date she had not seen as much of it as she would have liked. Her mother, who earned a sort of living from gardening, said that job satisfaction and communing with nature meant more than large pay cheques. Personally, Tansy couldn't understand how anyone would prefer talking to a cauliflower when they could be engaged in some serious shopping.

The older she got, the more Tansy daydreamed about finding her father. Back in primary school, when she had had to write stories about 'Me and My Family', she would invent a father who had fair hair just like her and who gave her piggybacks and took her to the zoo. As she got older, she gave this father a job on an oil rig, to account for his non-appearance at school sports day or Christmas concerts. Of course, in the end she had to give up pretending and just told people that her dad had left when she was a baby. But that didn't stop her imagining that one day she would find him.

Tansy knew that this was pretty unlikely. Jordan must have got tired of the Faeroe Islands and could be anywhere in the world, and all she knew about Pongo was that he had been a student in 1984, sang country and western songs and liked English fish and chips. She didn't even know the name of the town he came from. Her mother said he was fun and spunky and that they had met on the top of Glastonbury Tor while he was on a walking tour of Somerset, trying to find his ancestral home. Tansy had pestered her mother continuously to tell her more, but Clarity said there was no more to tell. Pongo had spent a couple of months with the travellers, during which time Clarity, still seething with anger at the departed Jordan, had fallen for him in a fairly major kind of way. And then, one morning, he was gone.

'But he must have left an address or something,' Tansy would insist. 'You don't have a passionate fling with someone and just leave it at that.'

'Well, we did!' her mother would reply shortly. 'Now just forget it, please.'

But Tansy never did forget it. She wanted a father – and one with an ancestral home sounded hugely promising. Because the other thing that Tansy was adamant about was that she was going to be Somebody. Anybody. As long as it meant she could live in a house with her own TV and DVD player and fitted carpets and a Jacuzzi and never have to hear the phrase 'We can't afford it' again. She wanted to be recognised when she walked down the street and to hear people whisper, 'That's Tansy Meadows – you know, she's the famous . . .'

Only at this point Tansy got a bit stuck. Some days it was 'famous film star', on others it was 'chat-show host' and once in a while, when she had been chosen for the debating team, it turned into 'the well-known politician'. Whatever it turned out to be, Tansy had made one vow. She would never, ever be ordinary.

In view of this ambition, it was, she thought ruefully as she pulled her school sweater over her head and brushed her sandy-coloured flyaway hair, pretty unfair that she was hampered by an excessively ordinary body. She had eyes the colour of snail shells, tiny features and a skinny frame which made her very fast over hurdles and, in her opinion, utterly unacceptable in clingy Lycra. Her mother, who was well built with a mass of auburn hair and the sort of placid disposition that simply couldn't get agitated about things like zits and broken fingernails, told her that she was worrying unnecessarily. But then, thought Tansy, what would you expect of a woman whose idea of make-up was to slap some moisturiser on her cheeks before facing the elements and who on special occasions wore bright-blue eyeshadow which appeared to have been layered on with one of her gardening trowels. Clarity wore floaty Indian cotton dresses when she was at home and cord dungarees while she was working and said things like, 'Your body is simply a dwelling place for your soul.' To which Tansy was prone to reply that her soul would feel a lot happier if its dwelling place could be clothed in a Kookaï cardigan and a charcoal suede miniskirt.

'Tansy! It's getting late – breakfast's on the table!'

Her mother's voice carried up the stairs.

'Just a minute!' Tansy puckered her lips and applied a generous amount of Peach Passion lip-gloss. Miss Partridge would probably tell her to wipe it off, but hopefully not until she had thrown a few alluring smiles in the direction of the gorgeous Todd Butler.

She cluttered down the uncarpeted staircase and went through to the kitchen. As she opened the door, an overpowering smell of spices assailed her nostrils.

'Yuk!' she gasped. 'What on earth . . .?'

'Now, darling, don't do your usual thing,' pleaded her mother, poking at the frying pan determinedly. 'Just try these before you say anything.'

She put a plate of what appeared to be burned potato cakes in front of Tansy, who prodded them suspiciously with a fork. Despite having given up the travelling lifestyle when Tansy was a baby, her mother was still in what could only be called the experimental stage of home cooking.

'They're awfully good, darling,' enthused her mother, brushing a strand of damp hair from her face. 'Spiced lentil cakes.'

Tansy put down her fork and turned to face her mother. 'Mum,' she said, in the gentle tone one employs when addressing those of limited brain power, 'most people have things like cereal and toast for breakfast. Some even go as far as doing something interesting with a sausage. No one in their right mind eats lentils, spiced or otherwise.'

Her mother sighed. 'Oh, darling, you really are so

limited in your view of food. Did you know that in countries where they eat a lot of pulses, they have far fewer cases of heart disease?'

'And a lot more cases of stomach cramp, I shouldn't wonder,' said Tansy. 'Thanks but no thanks.'

Clarity sighed again. 'Laurence says that today's teenagers eat far too much junk food and it is up to parents to re-educate their palates,' she said.

That, thought Tansy with a sinking heart, explained it. Laurence was the latest in a collection of boyfriends that her mother had acquired over the years and simply served as further proof that, when it came to men, her mother shouldn't be allowed out on her own. Some of the others had been pretty dire but Laurence was something else. He had the haircut from hell, the kind of smarmy smile that made you want to throw up and an irritating habit of being jolly all the time. He was a librarian with the Schools Library Service and thought that made him a world authority on everything. What was majorly embarrassing was the way he kept turning up at school with boxes of books and insisting on chatting to Tansy whenever he saw her – which meant she had to acknowledge that she knew him. Worst of all, he kept telling Tansy how he wanted them to be 'best buddies'. Having a mother with rotten taste in men was bad enough, but how she had the nerve to fall for someone who talked like a character in a bad movie was beyond belief.

Despite all Laurence's shortcomings, Tansy hadn't been too worried at first. Clarity normally kept her relationships on a pretty low-key footing and waved a firm goodbye if things got too involved, but time was marching on in Laurence's case. Clarity had gone all dewy-eyed and glowy and had started wearing tangerine lipstick, which made her look like a rather surprised hen. Tansy really felt that the time was coming when she would have to intervene.

'That guy is so weird,' muttered Tansy, pushing her plate away and going to the fridge. 'Surely you can do better than him?'

Her mother turned pink and dropped her eyes. 'He's a dear man with very sound values,' she insisted. 'And he's extremely knowledgeable.'

'He's a patronising git!' muttered Tansy, ripping the top off a hazelnut yogurt. 'He talks to you as if you've got half a brain.'

Clarity pulled back her shoulders and bristled. 'He's broadening my horizons,' she said. 'And he likes to take care of me which makes a nice change. Anyway, I'd like you to try to get to know him better.'

She fiddled with a strand of curly hair like a teenager on a first date. 'I mean, I get the feeling that Larry might be around for a long time.'

Tansy was so gobsmacked that she dropped her carton of yogurt on to the floor. 'You're not . . . I mean, you don't intend to . . .'

Clarity held up her hand. 'I'm not saying anything, it's far too soon,' she said. 'We shall have to wait and see. He wants to take me skiing for New Year. He's very special. She took a sip of dandelion coffee.

'Special! Mum, he is awful!' gasped Tansy, picking

bits of hazelnut off the tiled floor and trying to picture her chunky mother hurtling down a mountainside in a snowsuit. 'You can't be serious. And no way can you go on holiday with him.'

'Why on earth not?' demanded her mother.

'You hardly know the guy,' remonstrated Tansy. You would have thought that by now her mother would have some grasp on morality.

Her mother looked pained. 'So can't I have a life?' she asked. 'Anyway, I think it's written in my path of destiny. Madame Zarborski saw a man with a pile of books in her crystal ball.'

Tansy raised her eyes heavenwards. 'Oh, for heaven's sake, Mum!' she snapped. 'You are so gullible. You've probably told her a zillion times that you're going out with a librarian. Anyway, I thought you said you weren't going to any more clairvoyants after she told you that she saw large sums of money the night before you beat me at Monopoly.'

Clarity said nothing, so Tansy tried again. 'You can do much better than Laurence, Mum,' she said persuasively. 'What do you see in him?'

Clarity screwed up her eyes and smiled dreamily. 'He makes me feel wanted and cherished. And he's sensible and sorts me out. Besides, you've always said you wanted a father, haven't you, darling?'

This, thought Tansy, is seriously dangerous. 'Not just any old father!' she snapped. 'My own father, yes!'

'Oh, darling, let it rest — that's all in the past now.'

'It isn't in the past, it is my past!' retorted Tansy, her

throat tightening in the way it always did when her mum got all dismissive. How dare she expect to fob her off with a nerd in cord flares who had all the charisma of a dying pot plant?

'You just don't care how I feel, do you?' she snapped accusingly.

Clarity shrugged. 'I do care – but after all, what is the point of tormenting yourself over a father you will never meet – someone who doesn't even know you exist? Forget it, darling. What's done is done.'

Tears pricked at the back of Tansy's eyes and she swallowed hard. 'Oh, and that's it, is it? Oh great. Terrific. This is my life we're talking about. But you couldn't care less about who my real dad is, do you? You didn't care who you hung out with then and you don't care now!'

Tansy stopped. She couldn't believe she said that.

Her mum stared at her, open-mouthed. 'That's not true,' she said softly and Tansy saw that her eyes were damp. 'But whatever mistakes I made, I can't change the past. The future is what matters now.'

Tansy was about to reply when there was a repeated knocking on the back door. Clarity, relieved to have a diversion, peered through the window.

'Oh, it's Andy, darling!' she chirped. 'How nice!'

Tansy cringed. How come Andy Richards, who had sticking-out ears and crooked front teeth, followed her around like a forlorn puppy, while Todd Butler, who was funny, drop-dead gorgeous and had money to burn, ignored her very existence? Life was excessively unfair.

'Tell him I've left already,' she hissed, jumping up from the table and sidling through to the sitting room.

'But Tansy . . .' began her mother, her hand on the back-door handle.

'Mum!' There was no mistaking Tansy's warning tone. 'Do it!'

Her mother sighed, opened the door, and did as she was told.

Tansy flopped into an armchair and reflected on her life. She knew at thirteen and three-quarters she should really be in love. Or at least very much in like. But the only guy who made her stomach flip and her heart race, like all the magazines said they should, was Todd, who didn't even notice when Tansy deliberately bumped into him. She had got pretty near to it last term with Trig Roscoe, who was American and had the most amazing eyes. But when her best friend, Holly Vine, had had her somewhat disastrous birthday party, Trig had been all over Cleo Greenway and now they were a total item. She tried not to be jealous, because Cleo was a mate, but she did wonder how it was that her timid, anxious and overweight friend could get the only fit guy in Year Nine without even trying.

Her mother finally returned from what appeared to be an unnecessarily long conversation on the doorstep. 'Sweetheart,' she said encouragingly, 'Andy does seem such a nice boy.'

With a track record like yours, thought Tansy, I would do well to avoid any guy you deem suitable. Besides, I want passion and Andy just isn't passion material. Whereas Todd . . .

'So why don't you like him?' her mother persisted. 'I mean, he's – '

'Mum! It's my life, OK. And I hardly think you are qualified to comment on boys.'

Clarity pursed her lips and turned away.

'It's late,' Tansy mumbled. 'I'll see you tonight.' She stood up and picked up her school bag.

'Anything exciting happening this week?' Clarity asked, in an attempt to put the conversation on a less risky footing.

Tansy shook her head. 'Exciting?' she snapped. 'At West Green Upper? In your dreams.'

8.30 a.m.
Top-secret news

As Tansy turned into Weston Way she saw Holly and Cleo walking ahead of her, deep in conversation. Usually Tansy was pleased to see her friends and to catch up on the news from the weekend, but this morning she had a lump in her throat and didn't feel like talking. She slackened her pace and hoped they wouldn't turn round and spot her.

Perhaps her mum was right, she thought. Perhaps she should just put all ideas about her somewhere-father out of her mind and accept that she would never know who he was. After all, she had managed for nearly fourteen years without knowing. But for some reason which she didn't really understand, not knowing about one half of herself was getting harder, not easier.

She did feel rather guilty for having yelled at her mum. She guessed she must get lonely at times, although in Tansy's opinion solitary confinement would be preferable to an evening with the dreadful Laurence. But sometimes she wondered whether her mum really understood what it was like to be fatherless. Even though Tansy's granddad had died suddenly three years earlier from a heart attack, he had always been there while Clarity was growing up so she had loads of memories about her own father. She knew that her auburn hair came from his side of the family and that he loved dark chocolate and Westerns and was brilliant at drawing and terrible at remembering where he put things. And most importantly of all, she knew that he loved her.

Clarity had told her often enough how it was Granddad who had stood up for her when she returned home at eighteen, broke and four months pregnant with Tansy. He had understood when she refused to have an abortion and had taken her side when she had told them that she wanted to keep the baby. And he had smoothed everything over when Gran had totally flipped and refused to talk to Clarity for days.

It wasn't even as if Tansy could pump Gran for information, because she had re-married and now lived in Scotland. She sent Tansy presents on her birthday and at Christmas, and they talked on the telephone. But whenever Tansy brought up the subject of fathers, Gran would simply say, 'Best let sleeping dogs lie,' and start telling her all the wonderful things that darling Beth was doing.

Beth! Tansy's mind started racing. Her mother's sister was twenty-two – ten years younger than Clarity – and a real high-flyer. She lived in London, in a tiny flat right on the King's Road, and worked as a feature writer for *Savoir Faire* which was the sort of magazine people put on coffee tables because it showed their friends that they had good taste. Beth had a wicked sense of humour and changed her boyfriends as often as Tansy's mum, but at least Beth chose presentable ones with decent cars and the ability to match the right socks to their trousers.

Tansy had never talked to Beth about Pongo or Jordan – after all, Beth had only been eight when Tansy was born and no one would have told her anything, but she might have some ideas on how Tansy could get more information. She might even be able to persuade Mum to open up or get Gran to tell her something. It wasn't very likely, but the way Tansy was feeling right now, anything was worth a try. She was tired of being fobbed off with feeble excuses. It was time everyone started treating her like an adult. And Beth was more likely to do that than anyone.

Once she had made that decision she felt better and by the time she caught up with her friends at the bus stop, she was smiling broadly and looking her normal, cheerful self.

'Hi, Tansy – guess what?' Holly Vine was hopping up and down on one leg in excitement, her nutmeg-brown hair flopping over her face.

'You're in love again?' suggested Tansy. She knew that Holly's main aim in life was to get a guy and, generally speaking, when her friend was in high spirits a boy was involved somewhere.

'No, silly – although one of the boys who are going to be moving into the new house behind us is to die for.'

Cleo and Tansy exchanged 'here we go again' glances and grinned.

'No,' continued Holly excitedly, 'it's even better than that! You know *Go For It!* – that TV game show on Saturday mornings?'

Tansy nodded. *GFI!* was one of the coolest shows for teens on cable – everyone watched it, partly because of Ben Bolter, the dishy presenter, and partly because it was so wickedly off the wall and different from any other show on TV.

'Go on,' urged Cleo. 'Tell her.'

'Well,' began Holly, savouring her role as bringer of great tidings. 'They're coming to Dunchester. For Saturday's show! And West Green Upper's going to be one of the schools taking part!'

Tansy's eyes widened in disbelief. 'You're kidding!' she breathed. 'How do you know? No one ever knows.'

What made *GFI!* so different from anything else on TV was its unpredictability. Schools wrote in for a chance to send a team of kids, but it wasn't until the week of the live show that they got to know whether they had been picked.

Go For It! was all about ambition and making dreams

come true. It had Go for Cash, Go for Glory and Go for the Top rounds, and if your team got through to the final round, you each got to Go for IT – your own personal dream. The prizes were ace, and the whole thing was brilliant viewing. To take part, thought Tansy, would be the funkiest thing ever.

'Isn't it great?' said Cleo, hitching her rucksack over her shoulder as the school bus came round the corner. 'Who do you reckon will get on the team?'

Me, if I have anything to do with it, thought Tansy, her brain whirring as she imagined being spotted by a talent scout and whisked off to a life of indulgence on a film set in Beverly Hills. This could be my passport to fame.

'But how do you know they're really coming?' she asked Holly again, as the bus pulled up. She couldn't afford to get excited and then discover that Holly had got the wrong end of the stick.

'Miss Partridge let it slip to my dad at one of their stupid dressing-up sessions,' Holly explained.

Holly's father was an historian who wrote intelligent books all week and then behaved in a most unintelligent manner at weekends, dressing up as a Roundhead and fighting mock battles at carnivals and county shows. Elinor Partridge, who for obvious reasons was nicknamed Birdie, taught English to Year Nine and had such a sad life that her idea of excitement was to take part in these re-enactments as a bystander or mother of just-killed son (she was very good at weeping to order).

'She wasn't meant to say anything,' said Holly, 'but

you know how dippy she is and, apparently, it sort of came out because she has to take the team to *GFI!* on Saturday and can't be "A Fallen Woman at the Siege of Camber Hill".'

'And your dad actually told you?' queried Tansy as they piled on to the bus. 'It's meant to be top secret until the last minute.'

'My father,' Holly said with a sigh, 'is not of the real world. He hadn't even heard of *GFI!* – can you believe it?'

She glanced quickly round the assortment of kids jostling and chattering around them. 'So don't say a word to anyone else,' she urged, dropping her voice to a whisper. 'Birdie would have a fit if she knew Dad had told me.'

'But we can tell Jade, can't we?' asked Cleo anxiously. 'I mean, if we three know, it's not fair to leave her out, is it?' Cleo was a firm believer in fair play and keeping everyone happy all the time.

'I don't know,' said Holly hesitantly.

'She won't tell anyone,' urged Cleo, grabbing the handrail as the bus lurched round a corner. 'It might help cheer her up.'

Jade Williams had joined their set last term when she had come to Dunchester to live with her aunt, who already had three kids of their own. Jade's mum and dad had been killed in a car accident and even though she was trying hard to get over it, she had spells when she was really down in the dumps. Cleo thought it must be the most awful thing in the world to suddenly find yourself an orphan. She missed her dad like crazy now he lived with his new girlfriend, Fleur, but at least she got to see him from time to time, and she still had her mum. And, of course, her two sisters, although whether Portia and Lettie qualified as things to be thankful for was somewhat debatable. Even with all the rows between her mum and stepdad, Roy, and her mum and Portia, and Lettie and Portia, and practically every other combination you could think of, Cleo reckoned she was a lot luckier than Jade, who must feel really alone.

Holly chewed her lip and looked thoughtful.

'Come on,' urged Cleo. 'You're not still miffed with her, are you?'

Actually, yes, thought Holly. After all, it was me that stood by Jade when she first came to West Green Upper, and then she actually chose my birthday party to snog the guy I fancy. Scott Hamill could still make Holly's toes curl with desire, and the fact that he and Jade had been a major item since the party didn't help Holly to feel kindly disposed towards her.

But she was basically a pretty fair person and knew deep down that it wasn't actually Jade's fault that Scott fancied her more than Holly. Rotten, tragic, heartbreaking and very short-sighted on Scott's part – but not Jade's fault.

'OK,' she said at last, 'but absolutely and positively no one else. Cross your heart?'

'And hope to die,' asserted Cleo.

'Promise,' echoed Tansy, whose mind was working overtime. She had to get on this show. She simply had to. 'How do you think they choose people?' she asked

Holly, trying to sound as if it didn't matter to her in the slightest.

'I'm not sure,' admitted Holly. 'But I reckon this is a good week to suck up to the teachers.'

'I read in a magazine that they send people from the show into schools,' said Cleo. 'Only you don't know they are from *GFI!* – they pretend to be someone else.'

'So really,' said Tansy, thinking fast, 'we have to be especially nice to the teachers and chat up every stranger we see in school.'

Holly nodded. 'And remember,' she urged, 'they are bound to ask you what your ambition is – that's the whole point of the programme. So we need to think up some pretty mind-blowing ideas that they've never done before.'

'What if you don't have an ambition?' asked Cleo, who currently found that getting through each day with a family like hers was enough to be coping with, never mind thinking years ahead.

'Then you wouldn't get on, would you?' said Tansy in exasperation. 'The idea is that you don't get days and days to think up something wacky, just to get on TV – it has to be what you really want and know something about.'

Holly grinned. 'Of course, we've got a head start. We know they're coming. I'd die to get on that show.'

Cleo pulled a face. 'I don't somehow think pulling a dozen guys in five days is allowed as an ambition,' she teased. 'Anyway, none of us know what we want to do for sure.'

Speak for yourself, thought Tansy. She had so many ambitions, the problem would be choosing one. Not that even *GFI!* could grant her dearest wish. Finding fathers wasn't part of the programme's schedule. But getting on TV would mean being noticed and she was determined that somehow she was going to get picked. No matter what it took.

9.00 a.m.
During registration

Holly, Cleo and Tansy looked for Jade, eager to tell her the secret. She was nowhere to be seen.

'Maybe she's missed the bus,' said Cleo.

'Or perhaps she's ill,' suggested Tansy. 'We could phone in the lunch hour and find out.'

'And tell her about *Go For –* ' began Cleo and stopped when the toe of Holly's trouser boot addressed her left ankle.

'I told you not to say a word,' said Holly. 'Your voice can be heard right across the room.'

Cleo looked suitably apologetic. As the school's star soprano, she was used to being told to project her voice, which was useful in school plays and when subduing her little sister, Lettie, but not a great advantage in the keeping of secrets.

'Do you want to get chosen for you-know-what?' Tansy asked Cleo. She had been pondering on just how awful it would be if one of them got chosen and not the others. Particularly if she was one of the others.

Cleo shook her head. 'All those people watching me

make an idiot of myself? No, thank you. What about you, Holly?'

Holly nodded eagerly. 'You bet,' she said. 'Just think of all the guys you'd get to meet from the other teams.'

'Is every decision you make governed by boys?' Cleo said in mock desperation, sighing.

'Yes,' said Holly happily, and began daydreaming about the sexy brothers who would soon be her over-the-fence neighbours.

11.15 a.m.
Cleo makes plans

It was boys – or rather one particular boy – that occupied Cleo's own thoughts in geography. Thinking about Trig Roscoe was a lot more gripping than considering oxbow lakes. Cleo had never expected to get a boyfriend; she had always thought that because she was fat, useless at sport and blushed easily, she would always be the one without a guy. But at Holly's fourteenth birthday party, Trig Roscoe, who was American and had hair the colour of a crème brûlée, had actually asked her out. Her! Not Tansy, who was small and lively and always remembered the punchlines to jokes; not Holly, who was tall and willowy and never worried; but her. Dumpy, boring Cleo. Even more surprisingly, Cleo had said yes. Since she had spent the previous week thinking that Trig was an arrogant poser with attitude, this was quite a turnaround. But she had discovered that all Trig's apparent confidence and boasting about girlfriends back in Illinois was just a ploy to hide his worries about his body. He had a huge scarlet birthmark which ran from his neck to his waist and even though he was easily the best-looking guy in Year Nine, he seemed to think that no girl would give him a second look once they knew.

In the few weeks since they had got together, Cleo had discovered that Trig's life was pretty tough even though all the kids at school reckoned that dashing off round the world for a year at a time was the height of glam living. Trig's dad was an ex-Marine who worked in IT and earned wads of money. He was in England for a year setting up a complicated computer system for an American bank and they lived in a big rented house in Dulverton Road. Trig's elder brother, Pierce, was on a sports scholarship at an American university and Jodie, his seventeen-year-old sister, had decided to stay in Chicago because she was representing Illinois in the Junior Sportathon.

'I'm hoping my dad will get to like me better, now there's only me at home,' Trig had told Cleo the previous Monday as they dawdled home from school.

'What do you mean?' Cleo had asked in surprise. 'Of course he likes you.'

'Not really,' Trig had muttered. 'Not as much as Pierce and Jodie anyway. They are really into athletics and sport and all that stuff – Pierce is six-foot-four and he plays American football and baseball and runs for his uni. I'm useless at all that stuff – my dad says I'm a total waste of space.'

Cleo had gasped. That was awful – the sort of thing you expect bullies in the playground to yell at you, not your own father.

'I expect he was just joking,' Cleo had assured him, secretly thinking that it was a pretty poor kind of joke.

Trig shrugged. 'Maybe,' he had said. 'But like I told you at Holly's party, Dad's really into body-building and action stuff. He keeps on at me to get a life and stop being a nerd.'

'You're not a nerd! You're clever and funny and you like a laugh. And you know so much about history.'

Trig had sighed. 'Oh yeah – great, isn't it? I mean, "I like history" doesn't sound quite as cool as "I scored a home run" or "I'm captain of the hockey squad", does it?' He had pulled off his Chicago B's baseball cap and twiddled it round in his fingers. 'Dad says real guys don't bury themselves in the past but go out and create the future. That's his favourite line.'

Cleo liked Mr Roscoe less the more she heard about him.

Trig had shrugged. 'I guess that until I do something earth-shatteringly wonderful, Dad will still just keep on at me. He's a great one for fame and recognition. And there's not much chance of me getting either of those in Dunchester, is there?'

When he had said that, Cleo had felt quite sorry for him. But now, sitting in Beetle's boring geography lesson, the seed of an idea crept into her mind.

If Trig could get on to *GFI!*, he could show his dad that he was up there with the cool guys. And if he did well, his dad would be really proud of him which would do Trig's confidence the power of good. And of course, if Trig took part in *GFI!*, Cleo could go along to cheer from the audience. And give him a congratulatory kiss at the end. Which wouldn't exactly be bad for Cleo either.

The whole thing was luck, of course. But if only she could find out who was doing the choosing, it might be a way to give luck a bit of a helping hand.

11.45 a.m.
'Bonjour, mes enfants!'

Tansy chewed the end of her rollerball and reread her first paragraph with some satisfaction:

> Monday – in French
> Hi, Beth!
> I am writing to you because I need your help to sort out something really important and I reckon you are the only person around who is going to take me seriously and not treat me like some dippy kid.

Beth was bound to sit up and take notice after an opening like that.

'Tansy Meadows! What are you doing?' Mrs Chapman barked across the classroom.

Tansy slipped the letter underneath *Allez en France, mes enfants!* and smiled winningly.

'Nothing, Mrs Chapman,' she lied.

'Well, instead of concentrating all your undoubted talents on nothing, perhaps you could address yourself to writing three paragraphs on the subject of *Ma Famille en Vacances* which means . . .?'

Mrs Chapman waited with that air of hopeful expectation that teachers adopt when school inspectors are due any day.

'My family on holiday,' said Tansy with a sigh.

Momentarily satisfied, Mrs Chapman turned her attention to Ursula Newley's inability to grasp the past tense of *avoir*. Tansy slipped her letter from underneath the book and thought hard. The next bit had to be just right.

Lately I can't stop thinking about my dad – whoever he might be. Mum gets all upset when I mention the subject and you know how Gran just won't talk about it at all. So I was wondering whether you knew anything. I know you were only little when it all happened but if you knew how I could find out a bit more about him – then it would be wonderful. Mum says it was either a guy called Jordan Walters who went off to the Faeroe Islands or else a student called Pongo from America. I suppose I should have asked Granddad while he was still alive, but when I was younger it didn't seem so important. Now it does. Please tell me anything you know, however small. And please reply really, really soon.

Love, Tansy XXXXX

That sounded about right, thought Tansy with satisfaction. She stuffed the letter into an envelope and rammed it into her rucksack. She could post it on the way home. She felt a little shiver of excitement ripple through her body. Within a few days, she could be on the way to finding a father, and even, if luck was on her side, being discovered by a TV producer as the next big thing.

I do believe, she thought as the bell rang for lunch break, that my life might actually start to get exciting.

12.45 p.m.
Making enquiries

At lunchtime the three girls clustered around the payphone in the locker room and dialled Jade's number.

'Hi, is that Paula? I mean, Mrs . . .' Holly paused. She knew Paula didn't have the same surname as Jade, but she couldn't remember what it was. 'Oh, sorry, Mrs Webb. Yes, well, this is Holly Vine. I was just wondering if Jade is OK?'

The others could hear a gabbling voice at the other end and saw Holly frown.

'Jade – is she OK? I mean, when we realised she wasn't at school, we just wondered whether she . . . oh, I see.' She clamped her hand over the mouthpiece.

'Paula says of course she's at school,' she hissed to her friends. 'You don't think she's bumming off, do you? What shall I say?'

Holly jigged up and down looking worried and Tansy

151

snatched the phone from her hand.

'Hi, Mrs Webb, this is Tansy Meadows,' she chirped. 'Don't worry, it's my fault. One of the guys said Jade was off sick, and I thought he meant your Jade, but he meant Jade Connolley. Jade's probably tied up. . . doing library duty or something. Bye!' She slammed the receiver on to the cradle and turned to Holly and Cleo. 'Did that sound even vaguely like a true story?' she asked.

She noted their expressions. 'No, I didn't think it did.'

'Do you think we've landed her in it with Paula?' asked Cleo anxiously as they headed towards the cafeteria. 'And if she's not at home, where is she? Shouldn't we tell someone?'

'We can't really,' said Tansy with a frown. 'If we do, she'll be in trouble big time and there's probably a perfectly simple explanation.'

'We could ask Scott,' suggested Cleo who was always the one with the sensible ideas. 'He's bound to know – they're hardly ever apart these days.'

Holly felt a stab of jealousy hit her in the chest. She had tried and tried to forget Scott Hamill but she still thought that he was the cutest guy in their year and having one of her closest friends hanging out with him didn't help the forgetting process one bit.

'He's over there,' said Cleo, pointing across the crowded cafeteria to a table in the far corner. 'Let's sound him out.'

They pushed through a crowd of Year Sevens who were being even more infantile than usual and moved towards Scott's table. As they passed the drinks machine, Andy Richards appeared from nowhere and nudged Tansy's arm.

'Hi, Tansy,' he said, his cheeks turning bright pink. 'Are you coming to computer club?'

Tansy glared at him. 'Are you?' she asked.

Andy nodded eagerly. 'Then no,' she said, turning away.

'That,' said Cleo, 'was not very nice.'

Tansy shrugged. 'He'll never get the message unless I spell it out,' she said. 'Why can't he find someone else to drool over?'

'Because he fancies you, of course,' grinned Cleo. 'He's as crazy about you as Scott is about Jade. I think he's kind of cute. Don't you like being adored?'

Not, thought Tansy, unless it's Todd doing the adoring. And right now there seems little chance of that.

When they reached Scott's table, they saw that Ursula and Nick were with him, and the three were deep in conversation.

'Hi, Scott!' interrupted Tansy, who was never one to observe the niceties of social etiquette. 'Do you know where Jade is?'

Scott looked up. 'No,' he said shortly.

'She's not in school,' added Cleo.

'So?' said Scott, dipping a chip into some tomato sauce. 'Maybe she's ill.'

It occurred to Holly that he didn't seem particularly concerned. Maybe he was falling out of love with Jade already. She knew that shouldn't please her, but it did. A lot.

'She's not ill,' continued Cleo. 'We phoned her house, and her aunt thinks she's in school but she's not.'

For a moment Scott looked concerned.

'And we thought, what with you two being such lovebirds – ' began Tansy.

'Get lost!' snapped Scott.

'Pardon?' said Tansy. She had just spotted Todd Butler moving towards them and was trying to look as if she didn't know he was there, while still making sure he noticed her.

'Just leave it out, will you?' Scott interjected. 'You can't fool me – Jade's put you up to this. Well, I'm not that dumb. If she wants to talk to me, she can come and do it face to face. Not,' he added, stabbing a fish finger with unnecessary force, 'that I care one way or the other.'

Cleo and Holly stared at him, for once in their lives lost for words. Tansy was too busy smiling extravagantly at the approaching Todd to notice just how angry Scott was looking.

Cleo was the first to recover. 'Hey, hang on a minute!' she retorted. 'I haven't a clue what's going on with you two but this isn't some stupid game. It's the truth. We don't know where Jade is.'

Scott said nothing but lowered his eyes. Tansy was busy pursing her lips in what she hoped was a provocative manner and willing Todd to stop at their table.

'Does it occur to you that Jade could be in some kind of trouble? Anything might have happened to her,' said Cleo sternly. 'That's why I can't help thinking we should tell someone.'

'She's probably just skiving off school,' suggested Ursula. 'It's no big deal.'

'It is with Jade,' asserted Holly. 'She's not the skiving off sort.'

'Yes, well I thought I knew Jade and, boy, was I wrong!' snapped Scott, and Cleo noticed that he was clenching his fists.

Tansy sighed. Todd had walked straight past her. He hadn't even noticed her existence. She turned reluctantly back to the conversation. 'Have you two had a row?' she asked.

'We've split up,' said Scott.

Oh goody, thought Holly. And then felt very guilty for being so delighted.

'That's awful,' said Cleo, thinking that the last thing Jade needed right now was a broken relationship on top of everything else.

'What happened?' asked Tansy. 'You two were such an item.'

'Well, we're not now,' said Scott. 'Just forget it, will you? It's no big deal.'

And with that he pushed back his chair and stomped off towards the door. The girls looked at one another.

'What was all that about?' Cleo asked Ursula.

'Scott says that Jade's being really off with him,' replied Ursula, stuffing chips into her mouth. 'He says she's stuck up – apparently she won't go round to his house because she doesn't think his family is good enough.'

Scott came from a big and boisterous family and

Holly remembered that there always seemed to be one or more of his mum's Italian relatives staying over. When she was going out with Scott, she never managed to sort out all the different cousins and uncles that kept appearing for tea and talking nineteen to the dozen, switching from fluent Italian to accented English and back again at the speed of light.

'That's ridiculous!' Tansy burst out. 'Jade's nothing like that — he must be crazy!'

Ursula shrugged. 'I'm only saying what he told us,' she said. 'Maybe you should ask her what's going on.'

'We will,' agreed Holly.

'When we find her,' added Cleo.

3.00 p.m.
In Beckets Park

Jade sat huddled on a bench in Beckets Park. She couldn't believe she was doing this. She had skived off school for a whole day. She had never, ever done that before and she didn't even care. Or at least, she was trying to convince herself that she didn't care. She knew that if she got found out, she'd be in big trouble but that was tough. Nothing mattered any more. Nothing at all.

She stood up, shoved her hands in her pockets and began wandering down the path towards the kids' playground. Mums were pulling children off the slide and bundling them into pushchairs, ready to fetch their older children from school. Further along, a dad was playing frisbee with a small boy, while an elderly lady nursed a squealing baby. Everywhere she looked, the world was full of families. Proper families. Like she would never have again.

Just for a bit over the past month, she had begun to think that maybe life would get back to normal one day. She would never forget her parents, never stop missing them for one single second, but when she and Scott had started going out, she had begun to feel that maybe there was someone in the world to whom she would be special. It wasn't that Paula, her mum's sister, or David, Paula's husband, were horrid or anything; they did all they could to make her happy. But they had kids of their own and a whole life before Jade came to live with them, and she felt like an intruder, a sort of spectator watching other people's lives but never being part of them. She knew Allegra, her fourteen-year-old cousin, who went to stage school and had a whole host of really trendy friends, resented Jade's presence. Josh, who was sixteen, simply ignored her. Only Nell, who was seven and pretty timid, seemed to be pleased to have her around. Jade spent a lot of time reading to Nell and playing with her, which caused Allegra to say that she was at last finding someone of her own emotional level. Allegra could win the Olympic gold for cattiness.

Jade kicked at a patch of gravel and sighed. When she and Scott had got together, it had been such a relief to have someone to talk to about anything, someone who didn't seem to mind her chatting about the past. Paula hated it when Jade mentioned her parents but Scott asked her questions and laughed at her stories and made her feel that things might just be getting better.

And then it had all gone horribly wrong. She wished she could turn the clock back, have Saturday all over again. Then she would never have said yes when he asked her back to his house for tea, never have faced that enormous family, never have made such a mess of everything.

She stopped and brushed the tears away from her eyes. She wouldn't think about it. It was over. Scott hated her. He had every right to hate her. She was horrible. No one would ever love her again. She knew that now.

She began wondering how she could avoid school tomorrow.

4.00 p.m.
Muddy and miffed

Clarity Meadows loaded her garden tools into the back of the van and brushed the mud off her dungarees. Usually she found her job as a gardener a real delight, but today, while she was raking up leaves and pruning roses, she had been worrying about Tansy. And wondering whether the past would ever lie down and go to sleep.

She knew it was hard on her daughter, not knowing who her father was. Maybe, she thought as she climbed into the driving seat and slammed the door shut, I did it all wrong. Maybe I should have told her everything when she was small. But how could I? I only did what I thought was right and now she thinks I don't care.

If she had married when Tansy was little, her daughter might not have this desperate need to find her real father. But the right guy never came along. I haven't had a lot of luck with men, she thought as she adjusted the driving mirror and turned the ignition key. Until now. Until Laurence. I think this time things might just work out.

Clarity knew Tansy wasn't very keen on Laurence. But he was kind and generous and, most important of all, he took charge of her. It had been great to be wild and independent when she was younger but now she was in her thirties the novelty was wearing off, and having someone to remind her about things like tax returns and taking cod liver oil for her knees was very comforting. It was a shame that Laurence worked so hard as it meant she didn't see him much during the week – and she was beginning to think it would be rather nice if he was around a lot more. It was a long time since Clarity had had someone there for her. And she rather liked it. But she wanted Tansy to be happy too.

It wasn't even as if she could talk it over with any of the other mums. To do so would mean admitting what a mess she had made of things. Angela Vine, Holly's mum, was really nice but Clarity was sure that people like her, who did good works and sat on committees, would think she was a total failure. So would Cleo's mum, who was an actress and who had been in TV adverts and even had a small part in a film with Scarlett

Johannson. She couldn't talk to her mother, because she was of the mind that Clarity had made her own bed and should learn to lie in it, which was probably true but not enormously helpful, and Dad, who had understood, was dead. And Beth – well, she still thought of Beth as her baby sister, despite her high-powered job and frenetic social whirl.

Clarity felt very alone. Being a single mum had been hard enough when Tansy was a baby; but that was a doddle compared to knowing what to do now.

Anyway, she told herself firmly, it's probably just a phase Tansy is going through. After all, she thought, teenagers do go through phases, don't they? I did – I was headstrong and ran away and did all sorts of crazy things and I'm perfectly normal now, whatever my daughter says. That's what it will be – just a passing phase.

She kept telling herself that all the way home. But when she pulled up outside the cottage, she still hadn't managed to convince herself.

4.15 p.m.
Anxious auntie

Paula Webb had been thinking about that phone call all afternoon. There was something odd about it. First Holly asking how Jade was and then Tansy coming on the line and saying that it was all a mistake and it was another Jade who was ill. It couldn't be that Jade really hadn't turned up at school, could it? Well, of course it couldn't. Jade was such a quiet little mouse, not like her mum Liz, Paula's sister. Paula remembered when she was twelve and Liz was ten, they had gone . . . Stop it. Don't remember. Lizzie's gone. Oh, Lizzie.

Paula shook herself and switched on the kettle. She did so want to get things right with Jade. Of course she worried about her own three, but Jade was Lizzie's daughter and it seemed even more important that she should do everything perfectly for her.

She had thought of telephoning the school, just to check that Jade was there, but then decided against it. After all, the girls must have found Jade or they would have phoned again. And she didn't want to be seen as a worrier.

She looked at the kitchen clock. Normally she would have been at work all day but Nell had tonsillitis and she had brought some work home so that she could be with her. 4.35 p.m. Jade would be in soon and she'd ask her outright. Jade would always tell the truth. She was that sort of child.

4.25 p.m.
Thoughts horticultural

Holly's mother stood at the kitchen sink, staring out at the mess that was their back garden. Once it had been beautiful with a long sweeping lawn, lots of fruit trees and a big vegetable garden. But because her husband refused to leave their rambling old house, despite its rattling windows and clanking radiators, and because the bank were not exactly delighted at the size of the Vines' overdraft, they had been forced to sell most of the garden to a builder. He had built two new houses whose curtainless windows glared unsympathetically at Mrs Vine as she washed dishes.

'What we really need, Naseby,' she informed the cat who was sitting on the draining board licking a used teabag, 'is a gardener. But gardeners cost money and we don't have any to spare.'

Unless, she thought, I ask Tansy's mum. She might not charge as much as these big landscaping firms. And she's young enough to cope with digging which is more than I am.

Mrs Vine was beginning to feel every one of her fifty-four years. She adored Holly but having a child years after you thought your family was complete had come as a bit of a shock and sometimes she thought that she'd made a mess of motherhood third time round. Clarity Meadows was only in her early thirties and, if that delightful Tansy was anything to go by, the perfect parent, despite doing it all single-handed.

There would be no harm in just asking her what it would cost to make a patio and a lawn and maybe a little rockery. With a small fountain, perhaps. They could have a coffee and a chat. She might pick up a few tips on motherhood as well as climbing roses.

Angela began hunting for the telephone directory.

8.00 p.m.
On line for a good idea

Tansy had sat for what seemed like an eternity at the supper table, enduring not only her mother's unique version of fish pie but Laurence's patronising lecture about how she really should read something more illuminating than *Heaven Sent* magazine.

'I am what I am today because of reading,' he told her.

'Now there's a good reason never to pick up a book again,' remarked Tansy through gritted teeth. She was spared her mother's irritated riposte by the ringing of the telephone.

'I'll get it,' she cried and fled. 'Dunchester five-seven-seven-zero-seven-eight,' she began.

'Hi, Tansy? It's me, Holly. Listen, I've been thinking about this *Go For It!* thing. You do want to get on it, don't you?'

'Of course I do,' said Tansy shutting the door in an attempt to blot out Laurence's droning voice. 'Trouble is they could pick anyone.'

'I know,' agreed Holly. 'But at least we know they're coming. What we need are some really unusual ideas to have as our *Go For It!* dream. That's why I'm phoning – what if I say I want to be the nation's youngest newsreader?'

'Do you?' asked Tansy.

'Not especially,' admitted Holly. 'But no one's done that before. What about you?'

'I haven't thought yet,' said Tansy. But the seed of an idea suddenly began sprouting in her mind. I wonder, she thought. I just wonder.

8.30 p.m.
Lies down the line

Jade rushed to the telephone and grabbed it on the second ring. After ten minutes of being questioned she had managed to get Paula to believe that she had been at school all day, and one wrong word from any of her friends would really blow it.

'Dunchester eight-double-one-one-two-three,' she gabbled. 'Oh, hi, Cleo – how's it going?'

'Are you OK? Where were you? We rang and Paula said – '

'Did you really?' Jade tried desperately to make it sound as if she was having a perfectly normal conversation. 'And what did he say?'

Cleo paused. 'Someone's listening?'

'Sure,' said Jade, as Paula brushed past her on the way to the kitchen.

'You did bunk off, didn't you?' she said. 'Jade, why? What's happening? And what's with you and Scott?'

Jade's heart sank. He'd told them. She hadn't thought he would do that. Not yet. What had he said? 'What do you mean?' she said, playing for time.

'He said you'd split up,' said Cleo gently.

Jade's eyes filled with tears. So he really had meant it.

And he was telling everyone. She had hoped that he might just change his mind. It was all her fault.

'Jade? Are you still there? Are you OK?'

Jade swallowed and took a deep breath. 'Yes, fine.'

Cleo realised that Jade was far from fine and decided that this was not the time to tell her just what Scott had said about her. Not over the phone.

'Anyway,' she said, adopting a bright and cheerful tone of voice. 'Brilliant news.' And she launched into the story of *GFI!*.

Jade listened as Cleo told her about the researchers coming, and made her promise not to say a word. She said yes and no in all the right places and agreed half-heartedly that it would be great if one of their friends were chosen.

'Isn't it exciting?' enthused Cleo.

'Yes,' said Jade flatly. How could she get excited about some stupid TV show when her whole life was in pieces?

'So who do you reckon is likely to get picked?' Cleo babbled on, realising that her attempts to cheer Jade up were failing miserably. 'Do you reckon Tansy is in with a chance?'

'How the hell should I know!' shouted Jade. 'What does it matter anyway?'

'Sorry,' muttered Cleo.

Why did I say that? thought Jade. What's wrong with me? Why am I becoming so horrid?

'Jade, I'm sorry about you and Scott, honestly I am.' Cleo sounded really concerned and for one instant Jade wanted to pour out everything.

'Poor you,' added Cleo.

Suddenly Jade had had enough. Poor Jade, whose parents got killed. Poor Jade, who had to leave her home and all her friends in Sussex. Poor Jade, who can't even hang on to a guy. She was fed up of pity. She wanted to be like everyone else.

'It's no big deal,' she said. 'Who cares about some naff guy who flips over the slightest thing?' Even as she said it, she knew she didn't mean it. She just couldn't help it.

There was a long pause at the other end of the phone.

'Well,' Cleo said eventually, 'I've got to go. Trig's coming round later – and Mum will go ballistic if I haven't done my homework first. See you tomorrow.'

When Cleo had hung up, Jade stood for a long time staring into space. Tomorrow. She knew what it would be like. Everyone would be quizzing her about what had happened between her and Scott. Her friends would try to be nice and that would make her want to cry. On the other hand, if Scott really had told them everything, they would be thinking she was really horrid. Cleo probably thought she was the pits. She hadn't meant to snap. It was just that she felt so miserable and fed up and alone.

She dragged herself upstairs to finish her homework. Some stupid English essay entitled 'If only . . .' that she was meant to finish a week ago. If only I hadn't said those things; if only Mum and Dad were here; if only I didn't have to go to school tomorrow.

8.55 p.m.
Ambitious and able

'Tansy Meadows, superstar!' Tansy answered the phone, sure that it was Holly phoning back. 'Oh, sorry, Mrs Vine – I thought it was Holly . . . Yes, fine thanks – I'll get her for you.'

She crashed into the sitting room where her mother and Laurence were watching *The Bridges of Madison County*. Clarity was sprawled across Laurence's lap in a manner which Tansy considered deeply unsuitable for someone of her age.

'Holly's mum's on the phone for you,' she said curtly, noting with disgust the way Laurence was playing with her mother's hair and kissing the top of her head. 'So if you could put each other down for a minute . . .'

Clarity grinned, totally unmoved by her daughter's disapproval, and pressed the pause button. Meryl Streep and Clint Eastwood froze in an embrace on the screen. Everyone, thought Tansy, is at it. Except me.

'So, how's school?' asked Laurence when Clarity had gone to take the call.

'That,' declared Tansy, wondering how anyone could possibly go out in a blue cord shirt and brown trousers and not be arrested, 'is the most naff question anyone can ask. But since you ask, it's as good as it gets.'

Laurence pursed his lips and clasped his hands together as if in prayer. 'And what do you want to do when you leave the place?'

Tansy stared at him. How weird that he should ask

that question just now, when she had spent all day thinking of little else. Not that it was any of his business – but still, she could sound him out. It would be good practice.

'I want to be an archivist,' she said, and took great satisfaction in watching Laurence's amazed expression.

He cleared his throat. 'And do you know what an archivist is?' he asked.

Tansy raised her eyebrows. 'Oh no, that's why I want to be one,' she snapped. 'They find out about the past, trace family histories, all that sort of stuff.'

'That's right,' said Laurence. 'That's a very unusual ambition.'

Oh whoopee, thought Tansy. Perhaps he's not as pompous as I thought.

'Of course, I know a great deal about all that sort of thing,' he assured her.

Yes he is, she observed.

He took a notebook and pencil from his trouser pocket and began scribbling. 'I'll get you some books from the library – you can read up on it. Now what you probably don't know is this – '

Tansy was about to make her escape when Clarity burst into the room. 'Guess what?' she said with a grin.

'We've won the lottery?' asked Tansy hopefully.

'No, silly – Holly's mum wants me to quote for redesigning their garden. I'm going for coffee tomorrow.'

It is, thought Tansy, utterly amazing what excites some people.

TUESDAY

8.10 a.m.
Guess who's here again?

'Oh, Tansy,' said her mother, peering out of the sitting-room window. 'Look who's here!'

She made it sound as if Brad Pitt had put in an appearance outside their door. Sadly, as Tansy followed her mother's gaze, she saw it was only Andy Richards, duffel bag in one hand and trainer laces flapping, who was crossing the road to their front door.

'Get rid of him, Mum!' hissed Tansy urgently. 'Tell him I've left.'

'Don't be silly, darling,' said her mother. 'I did that yesterday. It's very rude.'

'Mum! Just get rid of him!'

It was too late. Clarity had opened the front door and was standing on the step with the sort of smile normally reserved for visiting royalty.

'Morning!' she said brightly. 'Have you come for Tansy? Do come in.'

Tansy cringed.

Andy stepped into the room looking a little sheepish. 'Hi,' he said. 'I thought we could walk to school.'

Clarity looked unaccountably pleased. 'Brilliant idea!' she cried as if Andy had just mapped out plans for the next moon landing. 'Off you go, sweetheart – have fun!' She planted a kiss on Tansy's forehead.

I think, thought Tansy, I might quite like to die now.

* * *

'Your mum's really nice,' said Andy as Tansy stomped along beside him in stony silence. 'What does she do?'

'Gardening,' said Tansy curtly. And makes a profession out of embarrassing me, she thought grimly.

'And what about your dad?' persisted Andy, flicking a wayward strand of brown hair out of his eyes.

Oh no, thought Tansy. You're not getting me on to that subject.

'What is it with you?' she snapped. 'You want a rundown of all my relatives?'

Andy looked mortified. 'Sorry. I just wondered.'

'He left when I was a baby, OK?' she said abruptly.

Andy frowned and shoved his hands deeper into his pockets. 'That's tough,' he said, in the sort of voice that suggested he wasn't in the least shocked. 'Still, at least you don't remember him. That makes it easier.'

Tansy turned on him.

'Easier!' she expostulated. 'Easier than what? And anyway what would you know about anything?'

Andy chewed his bottom lip and pushed his glasses up the bridge of his nose. 'My mum left. Last year. I haven't seen her since and I don't know where she is. She just went.'

Tansy felt the pits. She couldn't imagine what that must be like. At least she'd never known her father but her mum was everything. Without her – it didn't bear thinking about.

'I'm sorry,' she said. 'Really.'

Andy looked at her and nodded slowly. 'It's OK,' he said. 'She'll be back one day. I'm sure she will.'

It occurred to Tansy that he didn't seem too sure at all.

9.00 a.m.
In registration

'Hi, Jade, are you OK?' Tansy touched her friend on the shoulder.

'Yes, why shouldn't I be?' replied Jade shortly. When people were nice to her, she wanted to cry.

'What happened yesterday?' persisted Tansy, noticing how pale and drawn Jade was looking.

Jade shrugged. 'You mean apart from you lot almost landing me in it with Paula?' she said. 'She said you phoned to find out where I was.'

Tansy nodded. 'But once we realised that she thought you were at school, we wriggled out of it,' she pointed out. 'We were worried, though.'

Jade gave a half smile. Maybe Scott hadn't said too much after all. 'Well, don't be. I just took a day off to chill, OK? I'm fine now.'

It occurred to Tansy that she had never seen Jade looking less fine. She would have asked more but the bell rang for first period.

9.45 a.m.
On the trail

Holly was sitting in maths, wondering why on earth it was necessary to know the percentage profit some mythical greengrocer made on his tomatoes, when Mr Boardman, the head teacher, came striding into the classroom, followed by a tall, lean woman with a pointed chin, enormous scarlet-rimmed spectacles and a pair of bright-yellow fish earrings.

Amid much scraping of chairs and dropping of pencils, 9C stood up. Mr Boardman was very hot on what he called the finer points of old-fashioned etiquette.

'Good morning, 9C,' he boomed, beaming at them with the caring expression reserved for use in front of parents, governors and visitors. 'Excuse me for interrupting your class, Mrs Bainbridge, but I would like to introduce Frau Dimmerstucker from Hamburg. She is here to observe English teaching methods as part of a report she is writing for the European Parliament.'

A stranger! Holly's brain went on red alert.

Mrs Bainbridge beamed at the visitor and held out her hand. 'How nice to meet you!' she simpered.

'I very much would like to watch you in zis class,' said the visitor. 'It is for me very good zat I see ze way of teaching is zis countreee.'

Oh puh-leese, thought Holly, that accent! Naff, or what? You're no German – you're a spy for *GFI!*

Her heart raced with excitement. She had to let the others know that she had it sussed already. And she had to make sure that Frau so-called Dimmerstucker noticed her.

'Miss Dimmerstucker will be sitting in on a number of lessons over the next couple of days,' announced Mr Boardman, turning to face the class. 'And I trust you will give her all the help she needs.'

You bet, thought Holly. I shall be charm itself. Because I know who she really is. She doesn't fool me one little bit.

Tansy hugged herself in excitement. Only Tuesday, and already she knew exactly who the guy from *GFI!* was! Just wait till she told the others. Of course Mr Boardman had passed him off as a photo-journalist taking pictures for a book called *The Teenager Observed*, but Tansy wasn't stupid enough to be taken in by that garbage. It was obvious; all the observing that Phil Douglas was doing was not for a non-existent book, but to spot some kids for the show. And now that Tansy knew that, she was going to make sure that his lens focused on her as much as possible.

And she would make sure she got to chat to this guy. Soon. And let slip about her ambition. Or at least just enough to get her on the show. The rest could wait. For now.

Cleo was feeling all tingly. She was only in the same set as Trig for two subjects – English and history – and he sat just in front of her, which meant she could gaze at the way his hair curled into the nape of his neck, but did little for her ability to concentrate on the War Poets.

At the end of English, he turned to her with a somewhat desperate look on his face. 'I need your help,' he confessed.

Cleo, who liked nothing better than feeling needed, felt a warm glow.

'It's my English homework,' Trig continued. 'It was

173

supposed to be in last week and now Birdie says if I don't hand it in tomorrow, I'll get detention. I haven't a clue what to write. It's a dumb subject anyway.' Trig always got sullen when he was worried.

'Is it that "Twenty Years On" thing she gave us last week?' asked Cleo.

Trig nodded.

'I'm useless at that sort of stuff,' admitted Cleo. 'I did a thing about what Dunchester might be like in twenty years' time. You know, monorails and shopping by TV, that sort of thing. But I guess you're more interested in the past than in the future!'

Trig nodded. 'The further back the better,' he said.

'Do you really want to be an archaeologist?' she asked.

'You know I do – why?'

Cleo couldn't tell him about *GFI!* but she needed to know more. 'I just wondered what the fascination with digging up bits of pottery could possibly be,' she said teasingly.

'Oh, so you think I'm a weirdo too, do you?' Trig snapped. 'Why don't you just come right out and say so?'

Cleo gulped. Trig always got defensive if he thought someone was sending him up. 'I don't – I just wanted . . . I mean, I just like to know what makes you tick.'

'What – so you can snigger about me to all your mates?' Trig slammed his textbook into his bag.

'Hey, hang on!' Cleo was beginning to get cross. 'What is it with you? No one thinks being an archaeologist is naff — half of them don't know what one does anyway. Can't I show an interest without getting my head bitten off?'

Trig looked contrite. 'Sorry,' he mumbled. He picked up his bag and turned to face Cleo. 'It's like putting a jigsaw together – finding out all the bits of the past that have got lost and buried, and making it all into some kind of sense. And then there's always the chance . . .' He stopped.

'Go on,' urged Cleo.

'Well,' Trig said in a rush, 'I might just discover something really big, like the guy that found Tutankhamun's treasures, and then I'd be really famous.' He grinned, his bad mood evaporating. 'I might even get to make one of those documentaries – *Lost Civilisations* or something,' he said. 'I can see myself in the white jacket and Ray-bans, telling the world about my latest discoveries! You never know – in twenty years' time you might be watching me on TV!'

Hopefully it won't take twenty years, thought Cleo, itching to tell Trig about *GFI!*. 'There you are then,' she said instead.

'What?' Trig frowned.

'Twenty years on – write about what you will be doing twenty years from now! That way you get to write about archaeology which you find easy anyway, and . . .' She stopped. An amazing thought had just hit her.

'That's a brill idea!' exclaimed Trig, grabbing his books. 'See you later.'

'Mmm,' murmured Cleo.

It couldn't be, could it? Perhaps she should tell the others. But then again she often got things wrong and she didn't want to look an idiot. And besides, if she was right, it was too late for anyone to do anything about it.

12.30 p.m.
Lingering over lunch

'Where's Jade?' Holly dumped her plate of burger and beans on the table and glanced round the cafeteria. She wanted to be sure that all three other friends heard her news.

'Getting some food – I wish she'd hurry up,' said Tansy, wriggling on her seat with excitement at her discovery.

'Did you find out what happened yesterday?' asked Cleo anxiously. 'She was pretty vague on the phone.'

Tansy shook her head. 'I tried talking to her in registration,' she said. 'But she was pretty short with me. Sssh – she's coming.'

They're talking about me, I know they are, thought Jade miserably, balancing a bowl of soup and a roll on her tray. They're probably saying that I'm the pits and they don't want anything more to do with me.

'Hi, Jade,' said Holly brightly. 'You OK?'

'Why shouldn't I be?' said Jade and then wished she hadn't. She stared gloomily at her vegetable soup.

'No reason,' said Holly placidly. 'Anyway, you lot, just listen to this.'

'Hang on,' said Tansy. 'What I've got to tell you is really important.'

'Not compared with this,' interrupted Holly. 'Guess who I've seen?'

'Who?' asked Cleo through a mouthful of macaroni cheese.

'The researcher from you know what,' stressed Holly.

Tansy felt decidedly irritated. She thought she was the only one to have it sussed.

'She's posing as some German woman,' said Holly. 'But that is obviously just a front. She even calls herself Frau Dimmerstucker!'

'Unreal!' said Tansy. 'Well, they must have sent two people down because I have definitely sussed out someone.'

Cleo and Holly stared at her. Jade went on stirring her soup absent-mindedly. 'He's called Phil Douglas and he's supposedly taking pictures for some book about teenagers,' she said, unwrapping a cheese slice. 'But it's pretty obvious that's just a cover to allow him to walk round school with a camera.'

'Brilliant!' exclaimed Holly, spilling baked beans down her shirt in her excitement. 'Now we know who they are, we need to make absolutely sure they notice us.'

Cleo looked thoughtful. 'I was just wondering,' she ventured, 'whether you are both wasting your time. You see, I – '

Tansy looked irritated. 'Of course we're not,' she said. 'You always look for the problems, Cleo. You may not want to get on the show but Holly and I do. Just because you're not interested – '

Cleo gulped. 'I am, I am,' she insisted. And kept quiet. After all, she was probably wrong.

WEDNESDAY

7.30 a.m.
Relative surprises

Tansy was clattering downstairs for breakfast when the telephone rang. Her mother picked up the receiver just as Tansy opened the kitchen door. 'Dunchester five-seven-seven-zero-seven-eight . . . Beth! What a surprise!'

Tansy stopped. Beth must have got the letter. Brilliant! Only not so brilliant if she let on about it to Mum. She realised with a jolt that she hadn't told Beth to keep it a secret.

'Can I talk to her?' she said quickly, hand out-stretched. Her mother shook her head impatiently and turned her back.

Tansy prayed hard. 'What's that, Beth . . . Really? What, in Dunchester? Terrific!'

Tansy held her breath.

'Today! Better still! Of course, love to see you. I get back from work about five . . . I'll leave a key in the plant pot by the front door . . . Wonderful. Ciao!'

Clarity put the phone down and turned to Tansy with a broad grin on her face. 'Beth's coming up for a couple of days!' she exclaimed. 'New boyfriend's up here working for a bit, she's got some holiday owing and felt like seeing us both. Isn't that great?'

Tansy nodded eagerly. Beth must, absolutely must, know something. People don't bomb up motorways for no reason and the story about boyfriends and holidays was

178

just a ruse. She was so excited that she could hear her heart beating in her ears. Things were starting to happen.

She was just about to leave for school when Laurence loped through the back door with a broad grin on his face.

'Oh, you're still here, Tansy,' he said.

'That is stating the obvious,' commented Tansy dryly.

'Tansy!' Her mother did not see the funny side. 'Hi, Larry.'

She gave him an unnecessarily lengthy kiss and Laurence ruffled her hair as if she was a small child and wiggled her nose with his finger.

Why is it, thought Tansy, that when my mother talks to any man she goes all pink and pathetic?

'Coffee? Tea? Can I cook you some breakfast?' asked Clarity.

Heaven preserve us, thought Tansy. She'll be lying down and inviting him to walk all over her next.

'No thanks,' said Laurence, flicking his unspeakable fringe out of his eyes and beaming at Tansy. 'I just brought these round for Tansy. Those books I was talking about.' He handed her a couple of paperbacks.

'Thanks,' said Tansy. Much as it annoyed her to admit it, these might be pretty helpful when it came to impressing the *GFI!* people.

'Oh, and there's this one,' he said, passing her a crumpled carrier bag. 'You might have fun with this.' He handed her a big hardback book, with a card sticking out of the top, covered in spidery handwriting.

Tansy,
I thought you might like to browse through this. I gather it's a cult thing with your age. The quizzes at the back are fun – if you get stuck, ask me. I'm pretty hot on general knowledge.
Enjoy!
Laurence

Conceited git, thought Tansy, reading the note. And then looked at the cover of the book. The heart-stopping features of Ben Bolter gazed up at her. It was the all-new *Go For It! Annual*. It had to be an omen. It just had to be.

Phil Douglas certainly got round the school with his camera. Tansy beamed at him in the science lab while he snapped away at kids with Bunsen burners and angled her computer screen to show her best profile during computer studies.

Unfortunately, he wasn't around during hockey practice, which was a bit of a downer since she scored two goals, but her moment came during the last period of the afternoon when she spotted him sitting on a bench outside the gym.

'Hi, Mr Douglas,' she said. 'Are you getting loads of good pictures?'

'Pretty good, I guess,' said Phil, unscrewing one lens and fitting another. 'The worst part about it is having so short a time to work in. The head teacher is only letting me stay for a couple of days.'

That fits, thought Tansy. 'Do you think I am photogenic?' she asked, inclining her head to one side and hoping that she looked sophisticated.

Phil grinned and ran his fingers through his curly black hair. 'That's what all you girls want to know,' he said. 'I bet you want to be a supermodel!'

Bad move, thought Tansy. That's been done to death.

'Oh no,' she said hastily. 'My ambitions are far bigger than that. I want to be an archivist, a family historian, a genealogist . . .' She quoted all the words she could remember from the books that Laurence had given her, and which she had been reading during study period when she should have been learning French verbs.

'Now that really is interesting!' said Phil, impressed. 'Why would you want to do that?'

This is it, thought Tansy. I've got to get this right. And couldn't think of a thing to say that wouldn't give the game away.

'I just think it really matters that you know where you came from,' she said lamely. 'And not everyone does. I'd like to run a company that found people – I mean, found out about people.'

That came out all wrong, she thought miserably.

'That,' said Phil, 'is one hell of a bright idea. Good on you. I hope it works out for you.'

'So you like the idea?' Tansy pressed, hope rising.

Phil looked surprised. 'Yes . . . not that it is anything to do with me,' he said.

'Of course not,' said Tansy knowingly. 'Of course not.'

Cleo was getting more and more certain that her idea was the right one. Frau Dimmerstucker had hardly shown a glimmer of interest when Cleo told her that there was this Year Nine guy who wanted to be an archaeologist, and her ring binder was full of pretty official-looking papers with rubber stamp marks all over them.

And when Phil Douglas interrupted their CDT lesson to take pictures, she dropped big hints about ambitions and careers, but he just told her she had a fascinating bone structure and took her picture while she made papier-mâché.

There was no doubt in Cleo's mind that the test had already been set. And none of them had known about it.

2.00 p.m.
Feeling miserable

Jade sat on a bench in the shopping arcade, picking half-heartedly at a packet of cheese-and-onion crisps. She had tried so hard. She had managed to get through maths because she wasn't in the same set as Scott or any of her closest friends. She'd missed French by saying that she felt sick and had spent break sitting in the loo. But on her way to the art block she had bumped into Scott in the corridor and, with her heart thumping in her chest, she had tried to make amends.

'Scott,' she had begun, 'about Saturday. I am really sorry.'

'I'm not,' he had retorted.

'You're not?' The relief had been enormous.

'No,' he retorted. 'At least now I know what you are really like. So I'm not good enough for you? Fine. You're not good enough for me either.' And with that he had stomped off down the corridor.

When Jade had reached the art block she had walked straight on past the door, and then out of the school gates. She knew she was being stupid, but that didn't stop her. Half of her wanted to cry and the other half wanted to smash something into a zillion pieces. Right now she was angry with everyone. Angry with Mum and Dad for dying; angry with Paula for never talking about them; angry with Scott for thinking all those things about her which just weren't true. And most of all, angry with herself for being like this.

She didn't know why she was being so horrid to everyone. Especially now, when she wanted them all to like her and be kind to her. For ages, her parents' death had seemed like a bad dream, something that she would wake up from and suddenly everything would be all right. But it was getting worse, not better. She missed them more every day. She wanted her mum right now, here, telling her that it would be OK, that she loved her, that she would take care of her. How could she just go and die?

Mum would hardly be chuffed if she skived off school. In fact, Mum would go ballistic. But Mum wasn't here. No one really cared what happened and neither did she. She threw the wrapper into the bin and began walking again.

* * *

She was ambling down the hill, hoping that no one would notice her red eyes, when a silver-grey Granada pulled up beside her and a young woman with long dark hair wound down the passenger window.

'Excuse me,' she began. Jade pretended not to hear and quickened her pace.

'Excuse me, but can you tell me where West Green Upper School is?' the woman called again.

Just as Jade was taking a deep breath and attempting to look composed, a large woman with a poodle on a lead came the other way.

'Young of today – no manners at all,' she muttered, glaring in Jade's direction before turning to address the woman in the car. 'Can I help you at all, my dear?'

Jade sighed with relief and hurried to the other side of the road. The afternoon stretched ahead of her. She didn't know what to do but one thing was certain – she wasn't going back to school.

She didn't notice Miss Partridge until it was too late. 'Jade? What on earth are you doing out of school?'

She looked up and there was her English teacher, dressed in a long, flowery skirt and pink angora sweater and looking like a small marshmallow.

Jade took a deep breath. 'Dentist,' she said.

Miss Partridge nodded slowly. 'And you've handed in a note?' she asked.

'Yes, Miss,' Jade lied.

'Well,' said Miss Partridge decisively, 'I'm walking back to school. I'll keep you company.'

Oh terrific, thought Jade. Here comes the lecture.

But Miss Partridge merely chatted amiably about school and holidays and how her flat was being redecorated, and what fun it was to have a place of her own. She told her that she had just been out to book a skiing holiday with her boyfriend and how she did hope she would be able to stay upright because he had told her he was an expert skier.

Jade was just thinking that she had got away with it, when the teacher suddenly changed the subject.

'I suppose it feels to you as if nothing will ever be fun again,' she said conversationally, slowing her pace to allow for the steepness of the hill. 'No wonder you feel like getting away from it all, escaping.'

Jade stared at her.

'OK, OK,' said Miss Partridge. 'We'll stick with the dentist story for now if it helps.' She smiled gently at Jade who relaxed just a little. 'My dad died when I was eleven, you know,' Miss Partridge added. 'It was awful.'

'I'm sorry,' whispered Jade. Her throat tightened as it always did when anyone mentioned death.

'I was so upset and I missed him,' said Miss Partridge. 'And I was so very, very angry with him.'

Jade's eyes widened and she blinked back a tear. 'You felt angry too?' she asked. 'Really?'

'Furious,' asserted her teacher. 'I couldn't believe he'd just died and deserted me and my mother. Of course, I felt guilty for being cross and that just made it worse.' She paused while they crossed the road towards the school gates.

'My father used to encourage me so much – and I felt angry that he wasn't there to see me win a prize or get the lead in a school play. And I always told him I wanted to be a teacher – and do you know, even on the day of my first job, I was cross that he wasn't there to see me.'

Jade nodded slowly. 'My dad used to say that he'd be ill deliberately so I could nurse him,' she said with a faint smile. 'And Mum used to keep on about how I might be the first Williams to go to uni.' She paused. 'You see, I've always wanted to be a doctor.'

Miss Partridge nodded. 'You mentioned that in your essay,' she said. 'I love the idea you had about injections being a thing of the past in twenty years' time. Cowards like me would much prefer your melting patches idea!'

Jade grinned. 'I'm probably too thick to be a doctor,' she said, 'but I will be a nurse. In Africa. Don't laugh,' she added hurriedly.

'Jade,' said Miss Partridge, 'why would I laugh? I think that's wonderful.' She paused and leaned against the wall. 'And, Jade, you are not thick. You are very bright and capable. Saying you are thick is just another way of being angry with yourself. Anger has its place, Jade; grief, and loneliness and feeling scared – they are all OK. Running away isn't.' She turned to her. 'All those feelings are inside you – when you run, they just come with you.'

That makes sense, thought Jade. I don't feel any better for having skived off. In fact, I feel worse.

'End of lecture,' said Miss Partridge briskly. 'It will get better, you know.'

Jade sighed. 'I wish it wasn't taking so long,' she said.

2.15 p.m.
Late back

When Jade got back to school, chemistry had already started.

'Oh, you've deigned to join us, Jade,' said Mr Cole sarcastically. 'And what pressing engagement causes you to be late for my class?'

'Sorry, sir,' said Jade meekly. 'I was talking to Miss Partridge.'

Mr Cole looked peeved. 'Oh,' he said, obviously irritated at being given a good excuse. 'Well, go over to the far table and join Scott. We're carrying out the experiment on page seventy-six of your textbook.'

Jade took a deep breath. She was aware of at least six pairs of eyes watching her, Holly and Cleo's among them. She had no choice. She had to face him.

For a while she and Scott didn't say a word but merely set up their equipment and listened to Mr Cole droning on about heat conductors. They didn't look at each other.

This, thought Jade, is ridiculous.

'Look,' she said, taking a deep breath and feeling slightly sick, 'can we talk about things? I don't like – '

'Jade Williams!' Mr Cole snapped. 'Not only do you do me the discourtesy of turning up late, but now you see fit to talk instead of work! Go to that spare table and work on your own, where you cannot distract those who do come to school to learn!'

Jade heard a few muffled titters behind her. Why was everything in her whole life going wrong?

3.15 p.m.
Holly makes progress

Holly was certain her moment had come. She was clearing away her books after English, when Frau Dimmerstucker, who had been 'observing' the lesson from a seat at the back of the classroom, tapped her on the shoulder.

'I zort zat your reading of ze part of Viola was very, very gut,' she said. 'You have a most musical speaking voice.'

Holly beamed and felt her cheeks glow. This was it. This was *it*!

'Thank you, Frau Dimmerstucker,' she said in her most polite voice. 'I hope you are right – you see, I want to be a newsreader.'

The German woman's chin thrust itself forward in excitement. '*Sehr gut!*' she cried. 'A child with ambition. I like zat!'

Holly was so thrilled that she didn't even mind being called a child. She had done it – she could feel it in her bones. It was only a matter of time before everyone would know that Holly Vine was going to be big on TV. At home time, Holly couldn't contain her excitement. She knew she shouldn't say a word until it was absolutely definite, but it was so obvious that Frau Dimmerstucker had singled her out that when she spotted Cleo in the locker room she just had to tell her.

'So, you see,' she babbled after she had given her the news, 'I'm sure I'll be chosen. I can't wait.'

Cleo looked at her anxiously. 'Don't get your hopes

up too much,' she began. 'I mean, Frau Dimmerstucker might not be . . . well, she might not have meant . . .'

'Oh, for heaven's sake, Cleo!' retorted Holly. 'Can't you just be glad for me? Do you always have to be such a wet blanket?'

Cleo gulped. 'Of course I'm glad,' she said hastily. 'That's terrific.'

I hope, she thought.

'What were you and Scott talking about when old Cole blew up?' asked Cleo as she walked home with Jade.

Jade bit her lip. '*We* weren't talking about anything,' she said miserably. 'He doesn't want to know me any more.'

Cleo looked sympathetic. 'Poor you,' she said. 'Look, why don't you write him a note? You know — making up. I mean, he might walk off if you try talking to him, but he's bound to read a letter.'

Jade thought. It might work. But she didn't want to look as if she was grovelling.

'Oh . . . who cares?' she said, shrugging her shoulders and trying to look laid back.

'You do,' said Cleo. 'You don't fool me for one minute.'

4.00 p.m.
Beth makes an entrance

Tansy sped down Weston Way and into Cattle Hill. Great! Her mother's disreputable van wasn't parked outside their cottage, which meant she was still at work.

She let herself in the front door and immediately knew that Beth had arrived. The smell of Eternity perfume pervaded the air and a number of expensive-looking carrier bags were dumped at the bottom of the stairs.

Tansy galloped up the stairs and knocked on the guest-room door. 'Hi, Tansy, how are *you*?' Beth opened her arms and gave her niece a bear-like hug. She was wearing a snappy little navy suit and slingbacks and looked a million dollars.

'Fine – it's so good to see you!' exclaimed Tansy, wishing she was tall and stylish. 'So you got my letter?'

'Letter?' Beth frowned and ran her fingers through her immaculately bobbed hair. 'No – mind you, I've been away for two days. Round at PJ's.'

'PJ?'

'The new guy in my life,' explained Beth. 'He is so cute – you'll die when you meet him. Hang on a minute – I went back and grabbed my post before we drove up.' She rifled through her bag and pulled out a handful of mail. 'Bill, bill, junk, bill,' she muttered, flicking through the pile.

'That's the one,' said Tansy, pointing to a lime-green envelope. 'It's about my dad.'

Beth looked up. 'Your dad?' she said in surprise. 'Oh what, that Pongo person?'

Tansy's mouth dropped open and her mouth went dry. 'You mean, you know which one – ' She stopped as a car door slammed outside. 'That's Mum,' she said hastily.

'She doesn't know I've written – she gets upset . . .'

Beth gave her a quick hug. 'That's OK,' she said. 'I won't breathe a word. I'll read your letter and then we can talk later.'

'Promise?' Tansy had never been this close to knowing something about her dad before.

'Promise,' Beth assured her.

The front door slammed and Beth stuffed the letter into her handbag. 'Beth? Tansy? Are you there? I'm back!' Clarity's voice floated up the stairs.

'Coming!' Beth sped down the stairs. Tansy followed more slowly.

Pongo. She had been right all along. So why had her mum said she didn't know who her father was?

4.30 p.m.
Gossing

'So what's new, Tansy?' Beth asked.

They had spent the previous half-hour sitting round the kitchen table, eating huge wedges of carrot cake that Beth had brought up from Harrods food hall and opening the presents she had bought. She had given Clarity loads of expensive bath and body oils in big bottles and Tansy a silver make-up bag packed with lip-gloss, eyeliner and some wicked purple mascara, as well as a big and very expensive-looking bottle of Desire perfume.

'You shouldn't spend all this!' Clarity had exclaimed,

uncomfortable that her little sister could produce gifts that would take her a month to save up for.

'I didn't,' Beth reassured her. 'They are all freebies sent to the magazine – I'm drowning in smellies and potions, so you might as well have them.' She nudged Tansy who was staring into space. 'Hey, you – you're miles away. So let's have all the goss – what's going on in your life?'

Tansy blinked. She had been thinking about fathers. And mothers who didn't tell you the truth. 'Not much,' she said. 'Oh, except that guess what? *GFI!* are coming to our school to choose kids.'

'What's *GF* . . . whatever you said?' asked her mum.

'*Go For It!*,' interrupted Beth, who was far more into the current scene than Clarity. 'It's a big hit on cable – audience expanding every week.'

'Is that the programme with that guy you drool over?' asked her mother.

Tansy pulled a face. 'Ben Bolter, yes it is!' she said. 'But I shouldn't have said anything because no one is supposed to know they are coming until they turn up. Except that they have turned up and I know who they are.'

Beth raised an eyebrow. 'And no doubt you want to get on the show?' she said with a smile.

Tansy nodded. 'I think one of the research guys was dead impressed with my ideas,' she said confidently. 'What I came up with was this – ' She was about to tell Beth all about her idea when the doorbell rang.

'That'll be PJ,' cried Beth, leaping to her feet in excitement. 'Clarity, just wait till you see him. You will positively die!'

She ran to the front door and Tansy heard that sort of slurping sound that people make when they kiss so passionately that they appear to be eating one another.

'Come through and meet my sister and Tansy,' said Beth.

She appeared in the doorway, a little pink and dishevelled, holding the hand of a twenty-something guy with a huge grin and a mop of unruly black hair.

'This,' she announced proudly, 'is PJ.'

Tansy turned round. And caught her breath.

'Well, hi there,' said PJ, holding out a hand. 'We meet again.'

Tansy's heart soared. PJ was Phil Douglas, the TV guy. He was Beth's new man and he was here. In her house.

'Hi!' she said, giving him what she hoped was a winning smile. 'Great to see you again!'

If I play this one right, thought Tansy, I can't lose. *GFI!* here I come!

5.00 p.m
Preparing for stardom

Tansy stood in front of her dressing-table mirror, casting a critical eye over her appearance. She thought that maybe she had gone just a little over the top with the styling wax, but when your hair was totally undisciplined at the best of times, it seemed sensible to make spikiness into a feature. She had gone to town with aubergine eyeliner and the new purple mascara and thought she looked quite sultry. She just hoped PJ would recognise latent talent when he saw it.

She was about to gallop down the stairs when she remembered that she was trying to look sophisticated. Pulling herself up to her full five-foot-one, she endeavoured to glide into the sitting room.

Beth was sitting in an armchair, with PJ on the floor beside her.

'So you've already met PJ, I hear,' she said, passing Tansy a glass of fruit juice. 'Has he captured you on film?'

PJ nodded. 'I have indeed,' he said. 'Although according to the head teacher, I'm not supposed to tell kids they've been snapped – he says it raises their hopes of fame!'

I knew it, thought Tansy. I absolutely knew it.

'Who else did you take pictures of?' she asked. It would help to know the competition.

'Oh, loads of kids,' PJ said airily. 'The thing is, at this stage, one needs – '

'Oh, come on,' urged Beth, scrambling to her feet. 'Enough work talk – what about this Chinese you said you owed me?'

PJ laughed. 'OK, OK,' he said. 'Bye, Tansy – nice to have met you. See more of you soon, no doubt.'

'You bet,' said Tansy. And began planning what to wear on *GFI!*.

7.00 p.m.
Boy talk

'Hi, Tansy – it's me, Holly.'

Picking up the phone, Tansy was just about to tell Holly the amazing news when she thought better of it. It would only upset her friend and, anyway, she would know soon enough.

'Listen,' Holly was gabbling on the other end of the phone. 'You know that family I told you about – the ones moving in to the new house at the end of our garden? Well, they have.'

'Have what?' asked Tansy.

'Moved in, silly,' said Holly. 'And these two guys are to die for. Honestly, Tansy, they are totally gorgeous. They're twins only they don't look much alike. Apart from their legs. They have the most amazing legs.'

Tansy giggled. 'So are you about to vault over the fence and make advances on them?' she teased.

'Better than that,' said Holly excitedly. 'The boys go to Bishop Agnew College.' She named the posh private school in Dunchester.

'So?' said Tansy.

'And Bishop Agnew are sending a team to *GFI!* as well — so the boys will be in the audience, and I can get to chat them up.'

'Cool,' said Tansy. I wonder, she thought, whether these twins are as dishy as Todd. One thing was certain: they couldn't miss her. She was going to be the star of the show.

10.00 p.m.
Past imperfect

'Tansy! Tansy, are you still awake?' There was a knock on the bedroom door.

Tansy, interrupted from her daydream of winning *GFI!*, jumped up and opened the door. Beth, wearing a divine cream Joseph jacket and a jersey dress the colour of cappuccino coffee, gave her a conspiratorial wink and slipped into the room.

'PJ's gone back to the hotel – and Clarity's still out with the lurid Laurence,' she announced. 'My sister has a strange choice in men, doesn't she?'

Tansy sighed. 'Tell me about it,' she said. 'Why can't she choose someone like PJ? At least he's got a life.'

Beth flopped down on the bed and took off her jacket. 'Speaking of men, I read your letter,' she said. 'And this seemed like a good opportunity to talk. I don't know how much I can help. But I'll do what I can. Everyone has a right to know where they came from.'

Tansy looked at her gratefully. 'I know you were only little when Mum got pregnant,' she said. 'And I know you won't have been told anything but – '

'Hang on,' said Beth. 'I had to listen to heaps and heaps.'

'What?' Tansy gasped.

Beth clasped her hands behind her head and closed her eyes. 'I was only seven when Clarity left home,' she said. 'And when she came back, she had to share my bedroom for a while because Mum had turned her old

196

room into a study. So she would lie in bed and talk to me. Well, more to herself really – I guess she thought an eight-year-old wouldn't take much notice. But I did. I hung on her every word.'

Tansy's heart quickened. 'And?'

Beth screwed up her face in thought. 'She went on a lot about a guy called Jordan who was really arty and who painted flowers and birds on pebbles and sold them in the local craft shops,' she recalled. 'She said she was in love with him, but he went off with someone else and she was devastated.'

Beth paused and looked at Tansy. 'I remember thinking how sad and how romantic it was – you know, like you do when you're a kid.'

Tansy nodded.

'Clarity was really miserable. She was homesick but didn't want to admit that she had been silly to leave home. I remember she told me the story, over and over, how one day she was walking on the hills and couldn't stop crying. And that's where Pongo found her.'

'And they . . . well, you know . . .' said Tansy.

Beth nodded. 'They became an item. As a kid, I thought it so romantic but I reckon it must have been awful.'

'How come?' asked Tansy.

'A couple of weeks later, Pongo told her that he was engaged to a girl back in Illinois.'

Tansy involuntarily clamped her hand to her mouth.

'He said his time with Clarity was just a bit of fun, no big deal, and that he was going back to the States the following day,' continued Beth, kicking off her shoes and tucking her feet under Tansy's duvet. 'He left – and a few weeks later your mum discovered she was pregnant.'

Tansy cupped her chin in her hands and stared at Beth. 'So she really doesn't know which one my dad is?' she said with a sigh. 'But when I mentioned my father to you, you immediately said Pongo.'

Beth nodded. 'It was the photograph, I suppose,' she said. 'She had these pictures and as soon as you were born it was pretty obvious that you were Pongo's daughter. You are the image of him – same shaped face, same colouring, everything.'

Tansy caught her breath. 'Photograph?' she gasped, her mind racing. 'I've never seen a photograph.'

Beth shook her head. 'I don't suppose you would have done,' she said. 'Clarity knew that by the time you were born, Pongo would be married to this American girl. She didn't have an address for him, and for some reason she didn't want to let on that she was having his baby. She couldn't tell you that Jordan was your dad, when she knew it wasn't true, so she decided to say she didn't know.'

Tansy couldn't understand quite why, but she wanted to cry. Not that she ever cried in front of anyone, least of all Beth who was so together and sophisticated. So why were tears trickling down her cheeks? And why couldn't she stop?

Beth wrapped her arms around her and gave her a hug. 'It's hard, isn't it?' she said, offering Tansy a tissue.

Tansy nodded, sniffed and blew her nose. 'Am I stupid to want to meet my dad so much?' she sobbed, her shoulders shaking. 'To know what he's like and how he talks and everything? Do you think that's crazy?'

'Of course not,' said Beth. 'It's perfectly natural – he's part of you, after all.'

Tansy wiped her eyes. 'He might have kids – I might have half-brothers and half-sisters, and I'll never know.'

Beth sighed. 'Maybe it's best that way,' she said.

Tansy sniffed. She wasn't sure that she agreed. 'I wish I had a photograph – that would be better than nothing,' she said.

Beth bit her lip. 'I remember that your mum had this tapestry bag. She kept secret stuff in it. I know that because she yelled at me once when I touched it. The pictures were in that.' Beth paused and looked hard at Tansy. 'I probably shouldn't say this,' she said, 'but I know my sister. There is no way she would ever throw those pictures away. No way at all.'

Tansy stared at her. 'One thing is certain,' concluded Beth. 'Those photographs must be somewhere in this house. All you have to do is find them.'

The one advantage of having an aunt who was only eight years older than you, thought Tansy, was that she's still young enough to think up scams. They had got it all sorted. Beth was going to meet Clarity from work the following day and take her shopping.

'Knowing your mum it will probably be wind chimes and organic carrots,' laughed Beth. 'But I'll do my best to keep her out of the way while you have a root around for the pictures.'

After Beth had gone to bed, Tansy lay awake wondering where the photos could be. The cottage was tiny and Clarity was always complaining that there was nowhere to put anything. She kept on saying that when she got a really big garden design commission, they would have the loft converted and then they could . . . the loft! That's where she'd look. They must be in the loft.

Suddenly Tansy needed to see that picture more than anything else on earth. Even getting on to *GFI!* seemed unimportant by comparison. Although . . .

Tansy sat bolt upright in bed. She couldn't! Could she? It might just work. If she had a photograph of her father and the whole world was watching *GFI!*. Yes! That was it. If only she could manage to see it through.

THURSDAY

9.00 a.m.
Assembly

'It has to be today!' whispered Tansy to Holly as they filed into the school hall for assembly. 'The show's on Saturday so they can't leave it any longer to make the announcement.'

Holly nodded in agreement. She just hoped that Tansy wouldn't be too jealous when she got picked for the show.

Cleo, who was just behind them talking to Jade, glanced at the platform. Mr Boardman was ushering a young woman and a tall thin man to chairs beside him.

'Who are they?' she hissed to Jade.

Jade looked across the room and frowned. There was something familiar about the woman. She had seen her somewhere before, quite recently. But she couldn't think where.

'Good morning, everybody!' boomed Mr Boardman.

'Good morning, sir,' they chanted respectfully.

'Now, before we begin I want to give you all an exciting piece of news. West Green has been chosen to appear on *Go For It!* this very Saturday.'

The whole hall erupted into a babble of sound and he held up his hand for silence.

Tansy nudged Holly. 'Where are the so-called Frau and PJ?' she whispered.

Holly shrugged.

'You will recall that we set you some essays last week,' Mr Boardman continued. 'Some of you were given the title "If Only", and others "Twenty Years On".'

I was right, thought Cleo. I knew I was right.

'Well, with me today I have two researchers from *GFI!* – and they've read all your work and chosen West Green's team!'

Tansy gasped. What about PJ? He'd said he was . . . no, he hadn't. He hadn't actually said anything about television. Surely he wasn't really doing all that snapping for a book after all?

Holly's heart was sinking. If Frau Dimmerstucker really was a German, all that effort had gone to waste.

Jade suddenly realised where she had seen the woman – in the car asking the way to school. If only she had guessed, she could have warned the others.

'And now,' said Mr Boardman, holding up his hand for silence, and picking up a red folder, 'for the big moment. Just who has been picked to appear on *Go For It!*?'

Tansy held her breath and crossed her fingers.

Holly told God that if he let her get on the show she would never, ever do anything horrid ever again.

Cleo willed them to read out Trig's name.

Jade was trying to work out what to say in her letter to Scott, the last ten attempts at which she had torn up in disgust.

'Over to the *GFI!* team,' said Mr Boardman.

Oh, get on with it, thought Tansy.

The girl with the ponytail stood up.

'Hi,' she said brightly. 'I'm Val Porter, and I'm a researcher for *GFI!*.'

Get on, urged Tansy silently.

'We've picked six people,' she said. 'Four from Year Nine and two from Year Ten.'

The hall fell silent.

'Andy Richards, who wants to be an investigative journalist,' she began. A cheer went up from Andy's mates. Tansy couldn't believe it. She had no idea Andy was ambitious. She liked ambition in a guy.

'Abigail Reilly – marine biologist; Matthew Santer – jockey; Trig Roscoe – archaeologist . . .'

'Yessssss!' said Cleo. And turned scarlet as everyone around her burst out laughing.

Please, please, God, prayed Holly.

'Ursula Newley – she wants to dance with the National Ballet.'

Holly felt sick. Only one more name to go. Tansy wanted to cry. If only she had known that the essay was for the show, she would have worked a zillion times harder.

'And finally . . .'

You could have heard a pin drop.

'Tansy Meadows! A lovely essay about helping people to find their roots. She'd like to be a genealogist.'

Holly swallowed, closed her eyes, opened them again, and put a smile firmly on her lips. 'Well done!' she said, trying desperately not to feel insanely jealous.

Tansy's eyes were unusually bright. 'Thanks,' she whispered.

She'd done it! She had really done it! Now all she had to do was get to the final and her whole life could be transformed. She was so excited that she began to feel sick.

'And lastly,' said the researcher, holding up her hand to silence the chattering pupils. 'We have two names as reserves – just in case any of the team fall ill. And these are . . .'

Me, me, me, Holly pleaded silently.

'Jade Williams and Scott Hamill. Jade hopes to nurse in Africa, and Scott wants to be a sports commentator.'

Jade's mouth dropped open in amazement. Cleo hugged her. Tansy grinned.

Holly turned away. Not only had Jade got the guy Holly fancied but now she had all the limelight as well. Life was distinctly unfair.

Jade, meanwhile, was in a daze. She would get a whole day with Scott. A whole day in which he would ignore her existence. She couldn't bear it. She would have to write him that letter. And soon.

While Tansy was relishing the thought of forthcoming fame, her mother was sitting at the Vines' kitchen table silently doing sums. She mustn't undercharge, or Mrs Vine would think she didn't know what she was doing, but then if she overcharged she wouldn't get the job.

'I think,' she said tentatively, 'that I could do what you want for nine hundred and eighty pounds.' That sounded so much less than a thousand, she thought.

'Oh, wonderful!' Holly's mother clapped her hands in glee. 'When can you start?'

'The week after next?' suggested Clarity, and then hesitated. 'Oh – that's half term. I don't really like leaving Tansy every day . . .' She paused.

'No problem,' said Angela, waving a hand in the air. 'She can come and spend time with Holly. Such a lovely girl, your daughter. You must be very proud of her.'

'Yes,' said Clarity. 'Yes I am.'

The problem is, she thought, that right now I don't think Tansy is very proud of me.

'It can't be easy bringing a child up on your own,' commented Angela, pouring more coffee from the cafetière.

'It's not,' admitted Clarity.

'It's none of my business,' said Angela, who made a profession out of sorting other people's lives, 'but when did you and her father split up?'

Clarity swallowed. She could tell the old story of him disappearing when she was a baby. She could say he died. But she was tired of stories.

'We were never together,' she said in a quiet, slightly shaky voice. She raised her eyes.

Angela Vine was watching her closely.

'Tansy believes that I don't know who her father is,' Clarity said.

'But you do.' Angela Vine's remark was a statement, not a question.

She nodded. 'Yes,' she said. 'I do. And I have a feeling Tansy won't rest until she finds out.'

'Have another slice of ginger cake,' said Mrs Vine and settled down to listen.

2.05 p.m.
Team spirit

'It's brilliant, you and me being on the team together, isn't it?' Andy beamed at Tansy as they gathered with the rest of the team to have their photographs taken for identity badges.

Tansy was so over the moon at being chosen that she felt kindly disposed to the entire universe. 'Great,' she said, smiling, as Val the producer handed out bright-green T-shirts with *GFI!* printed across the back in gold.

'I wish my mum could see me,' he said wistfully. 'Still, she might be watching somewhere, you never know.'

So might my dad, thought Tansy. Or at least someone who knows him. And if my plan works, we could be reunited really soon.

Val clapped her hands to attract everyone's attention. 'Your parents all signed consent forms when the school applied to take part,' said Val. 'And, of course, mums and dads can come along and watch the show.'

Mine can't, thought Jade, and for a moment the excitement faded. She knew Paula and David would come but it wasn't the same.

'Don't forget that for the first round, "Go For Points", you are competing for your school and not yourselves,' explained Val. 'You play in pairs – we've put Tansy Meadows and Andy Richards together, Trig Roscoe and Abigail Reilly, and Matthew Santer with Ursula Newley.'

Andy tapped Tansy on the shoulder.

'I'm really glad it's you,' he said. 'Because I'm absolutely determined to win.'

Tansy looked at him in surprise. He sounded as if he really meant it. Perhaps he wasn't so drippy after all.

Except that he'd have to realise that he wasn't going to win the individual prize. She was.

2.55 p.m.

'Well, Jade, I expect you are secretly hoping someone falls by the wayside so that you can take part?' suggested Miss Partridge that afternoon, when Jade apologised for missing English.

'No way,' said Jade, shaking her head vigorously. 'I'd die of fright. I can't think why I was chosen in the first place – I mean, it's not as if I'm clever or anything.'

'Jade Williams!' exclaimed Miss Partridge in mock desperation. 'Will you stop running yourself down? Someone who wants to be a nurse in Africa needs faith in themselves. Oh, and by the way, I thought you might like to read this.' She handed Jade a glossy hardback book called *Fever, Famine and Flame Trees*. 'I'd like it back when you've finished with it,' she said. 'It's about a mission hospital – I think you'll enjoy it and I'm sure it will give you something to think about.'

3.05 p.m.

Holly was trying very hard to feel happy for Tansy and Jade. But it wasn't easy. Now she and Cleo would be in the audience while the other two were stealing all the limelight. And even Cleo would have Trig to cheer for. Holly felt like a reject. Probably nothing exciting would ever happen in her whole life.

Never mind ambitions. She might as well become a nun.

4.15 p.m.

The moment Tansy got home, she flew upstairs, tore off her school uniform and pulled on her stonewashed jeans, an old sweatshirt and trainers. She reckoned she had about an hour to find the photographs and she wasn't going to waste a minute. It was even more vital than before that she found the picture of Pongo.

She grabbed a torch from her bedside drawer and went on to the landing. Pulling down the loft ladder, she clambered up the metal steps. The attic was so dark that she had to spend several minutes scrabbling around and waiting for her eyes to become accustomed to the dim light.

She hadn't realised that there was so much junk up here. There were boxes of books, and dozens of *Gardening Today* magazines. Her old rocking horse leaned lopsidedly against an artificial Christmas tree and a rusting doll's pram was propped beside some deckchairs.

'Think!' she told herself firmly. 'Where would she put them?'

Stacked against the wall were three battered suitcases. Tansy wrenched open one of them. It was full of baby clothes. Was I ever that small? thought Tansy in surprise.

The second was packed with blankets and old pillows but when she opened the third suitcase, she gave a sharp intake of breath. Underneath a pile of somewhat weird and wacky clothes was a small tapestry bag.

As Tansy lifted it out, she realised that her hands were shaking.

She found it tucked at the bottom of the bag. It was bent at the edges, and there was a small tear on one side. Written on the back in fading blue ink were the words:

Pongo – at Tansy Fields, Somerset

The picture blurred as her eyes filled with tears. Her mother had known all along. She must have been named after the place and her mother hadn't even told her that. How could she? How could she?

For a long time after she had come down from the loft, Tansy sat on her bed, stroking the photograph with one finger. Beth had been right: the guy in the photograph was just like her. The same floppy hair, the same heart-shaped face. This was her father. Her dad. And no one had ever told her. And he was out there, somewhere in the world, not knowing she existed.

She had thought that when she found the photograph she would feel overjoyed, but instead she felt so angry it was like a physical pain in her chest. She would confront her mother the moment she got home. She would make her tell her the whole story, from start to finish.

And on Saturday . . . She stopped. If she said too much to her mother right now, she could very well blow her big idea for the TV show. Maybe she should keep quiet for a bit longer. There was too much at stake to mess up now.

Tansy heard her mum slam the front door. 'Tansy, sweetheart? We're back!'

Tansy slipped the photograph into the pocket of her jeans and ran her fingers through her hair. For just a little while longer, she would act as if nothing had happened. She wiped her eyes on her sleeve, took a deep breath and went downstairs.

'Guess what!' she said, bursting into the kitchen and hoping she looked normal. 'I've been chosen for *Go For It!* on Saturday.'

'Wow!' breathed Beth. 'Clever you!'

'That's terrific!' exclaimed Clarity, giving her a hug. 'Oh, darling, I'm so thrilled for you! Can I come and watch?'

Tansy nodded. And then wondered whether after all that was such a good idea. Not that she could do anything. 'Yes, of course,' she said.

'Great.' Her mum beamed. 'I'll bring Laurence.'

'Oh,' said Tansy, thinking that there were limits beyond which no teenager should be asked to go. 'Must you?'

'Yes,' said her mother. 'He'll love it.'

'Did you find it?' Beth whispered to Tansy while Clarity

was in the kitchen preparing pasta for supper.

Tansy nodded. 'But don't tell Mum,' she pleaded. 'Please.'

Beth held up her hands in mock surrender. 'I won't say a word,' she said. 'Anyway, I'm off tomorrow morning early. PJ's going to be taking photographs at a rock concert and we've got free tickets.'

'Well, thanks for listening to me,' said Tansy. 'It's more than Mum ever does.'

Beth took her hand. 'Don't be too hard on her,' she said. 'Being a mum isn't easy.'

'Being a daughter isn't exactly a blast either,' said Tansy, sighing.

9.30 p.m.
A romantic read

Jade was sitting up in bed, reading avidly. But it wasn't the book that Miss Partridge had lent her that was gripping her attention, but what she had found tucked inside one of the pages. It was a letter – or at least the second page of a letter. And it was very obviously a love letter.

2

which was wonderful.

You must never think I don't love you – how could I look at anyone else when I have you? Of course I wish I could see you every night – but you know I have to work late at least twice a week and after all, it is our future I am working for – the wonderful future we shall have together. You must realise how important my job is – frankly, the whole place would crumble without me.

You matter to me so much, my darling – I love everything about you. There has never been anyone like you before and never will be again.

By the way, don't keep telephoning me at work – it really is frowned upon and I have told you before how distracting it can be.

Just think – in a few months we shall be far away from here, just you and I together.

Take care, my sweetest Cuddles, and I will see you again very soon.

Your ever-loving,

Pootle

Jade giggled. Pootle! And Cuddles! Wait till she told the others – they would die. The thought of Birdie in a passionate clinch was just bizarre!

She hugged herself and imagined her friends' faces when she told them. She'd have to work out what to do about the letter – should she tell Miss Partridge that she had found it and risk embarrassing her? Or just leave it in the book and pretend she hadn't seen it?

She'd ask the others. They'd know what to do. Right now, she had more important things to do. She was going to write to Scott and try to explain her side of the story. Then maybe, just maybe, by Saturday he would at least be speaking to her again.

FRIDAY

8.20 a.m.
Birdie's boyfriend

Tansy arrived at school much earlier than usual, because Beth and PJ had given her a lift in PJ's cool convertible. Tansy decided that the day started off far better when you didn't arrive at school in the company of three bags of compost and a dozen small conifers.

She found Jade already sitting in their classroom, reading a book. She looked up as Tansy walked to her table and grinned. 'Hey, Tansy, I have to tell you – Birdie's in love!'

Tansy grinned back, pleased to see Jade looking happier. 'Birdie? How do you know?'

Jade beckoned her over. 'Look,' she said, handing Tansy the letter.

Tansy scanned the page. 'Pootle!' she exclaimed. 'Oh yuk! Pompous, more like – he talks to her like she was a kid.' Suddenly Tansy's voice faded and a puzzled expression came over her face.

Jade laughed. 'Maybe she likes being bossed around – makes a change from doing it to us all day,' she said. 'What should I do though – should I give her the letter back or what?'

Tansy was staring hard at the page.

'Tansy? Tansy, are you listening?'

'Oh – sorry. What did you say?'

'I said, should I tell Miss Partridge about finding

213

the letter?' repeated Jade.

Tansy frowned. 'I don't know,' she said distractedly. 'That writing – I've seen it somewhere before. You don't think it's one of the other teachers, do you?'

Jade peered over her shoulder. 'I don't recognise it,' she said. 'We could ask Cleo and Holly later.'

Tansy nodded. 'Best not say anything to Miss Partridge – well, not till *GFI!* is over, anyway. She will only get in a state.'

'OK,' said Jade, glad to have the decision taken out of her hands. 'Whatever.'

'Can you actually imagine Birdie in the throes of passion?' Holly giggled when Jade showed her the love letter during morning break.

'But it is romantic, isn't it?' Jade said with a sigh. 'I mean, having someone think you are that wonderful?'

'Don't you think we should hand the letter back?' asked Cleo anxiously.

'Tansy said we shouldn't do anything until *GFI!* is over,' commented Jade. 'Because of getting Birdie all embarrassed.'

Cleo, who liked everyone to be happy all the time, nodded in agreement. 'OK,' she said. 'After all, it's no big deal.'

3.15 p.m.

By the end of Friday afternoon, everyone was in a state of high excitement. All of Years Nine and Ten were going to be in the audience for the show, and there was a great deal of discussion among the girls about what they should wear just in case the amazing Ben Bolter actually spoke to them.

'Should I put my hair up, do you think?' Holly asked Cleo as they left the cafeteria after lunch. 'In case I have my photograph taken?' And in case the amazing Bennett twins really do show, she thought.

'You won't,' said Cleo. 'You're not taking part.'

'She might,' Tansy said. 'You all might. They put pictures of all the school audiences in the annual each year. I'll show you.'

She scrabbled in her school bag and pulled out the *GFI!* annual that Laurence had given her. As she opened it, his card fell to the floor and she bent down to pick it up. And froze.

As she stared at the handwriting, she knew at once where she had seen it before. It was identical to the writing on the letter which Jade had found in her book.

Laurence Murrin was Pootle. Laurence Murrin was Birdie's boyfriend. And what was worst of all, Laurence Murrin was two-timing Tansy's mum.

3.50 p.m.
In contemplative mode

Tansy walked home deep in thought. In one blazer pocket was the card from Laurence and in the other, Miss Partridge's letter, which Tansy had slipped out of

Jade's bag when her friend went to the loo.

How could her mum be so stupid? How come she hadn't sussed that Laurence had something to hide when he told her he could only see her two nights a week? What was it with her and men?

She took the letter out of her pocket and read it yet again. Quite what she was going to do with it she wasn't sure. She could tell her mum the whole story at once and get it over and done with. But even though her mother needed some firm talking to, she knew this was going to make her really miserable – and that would spoil the weekend and *GFI!*.

Perhaps she should confront Laurence and get him to back off. Or she could just pretend she had never seen the letter and let things be. But she knew she wouldn't do that. Her mum had a right to know before she made a fool of herself yet again. She was so useless at managing her love life that she needed Tansy to sort her out. And once the show was over that was precisely what she would do.

4.15 p.m.
Panic stations

Clarity was still at work when Tansy arrived home. She ran upstairs and rummaged through the debris on her bedroom floor to find her jeans.

Her jeans weren't there. She pulled open every drawer and scrabbled through the hangers in her wardrobe.

Where were they? And much more importantly, where was the photograph of Pongo? The photo she simply had to have with her for tomorrow.

She flew into the bathroom and pulled the lid off the wicker laundry basket. Her mum had probably had a clean-up and chucked her jeans in, ready for washing on Monday. The basket was empty. Tansy suddenly felt incredibly sick.

4.20 p.m.
In the kitchen

Tansy pulled open the door of the washing machine and pulled the jumble of damp clothes on to the floor. Tangled among the blouses and nightshirts were her jeans. She grabbed them and stuffed her hand into the pocket. As she touched a wad of soggy paper, her worst fears were confirmed.

Lying in her hand were the remains of the photograph of Pongo Price. The ink from the back had run, streaking what was left of the picture with blue smudges. As she tried desperately to smooth it out, it disintegrated into even more pieces.

The only thing she had to show her what her father was like had gone for good. And without it, all her plans for tomorrow's show were shattered.

Tansy sat down on the kitchen floor, put her head on her knees and cried.

4.30 p.m.
Totally tense

She was still sitting there, wearing her school clothes and holding the few remaining segments of Pongo's picture in her hand when her mum came home.

'Tansy! What on earth are you doing? And the washing – it's all over the floor. For heaven's sake, is this what I have to come home to after a tiring day!'

Suddenly Tansy had had enough. She jumped to her feet and shoved the damp paper into her pocket 'You washed my jeans!' she shouted. 'You actually went into my room and took my clothes and washed them without asking! You had no right!'

Her mum raised an eyebrow and dumped her groceries on the table. 'If you fling clothes on the floor, you can't blame me for thinking they need washing,' she said. 'Your bedroom should carry a government health warning.'

'Oh, that's right, make like it's my fault!' snarled Tansy, clenching her fists. 'You have no respect for my privacy.'

Clarity eyed her daughter suspiciously. 'You've been crying,' she said gently. 'Surely not over a pair of jeans?'

Tansy swallowed hard. She couldn't tell her mum about the photograph because then she would know Tansy had been searching through her stuff and go totally ballistic.

'Not just the jeans!' retorted Tansy. 'Everything. The way you treat me like some kid; the way you don't tell me about my father; the way you make a total idiot of yourself with a man who doesn't give a fig for you!'

Clarity sighed. 'Oh please, don't start on that all over again,' she pleaded. 'I can have a life too, you know. Laurence and I love one another and that's something you are simply going to have to accept.'

'Oh no, I'm not!' shouted Tansy, who was feeling such a mix of anger and misery that she didn't care what she said. 'Because Laurence doesn't love you at all. Not one little bit.'

Clarity's expression hardened. 'Tansy! That is enough!' she exploded. 'Since you are so keen that I should show you respect, maybe you would care to afford me the same privilege. You know nothing about Laurence or his feelings for me.'

Tansy glared at her. 'Well, that's where you are wrong!' she stormed. 'Look at that!' And she pulled the love letter from her pocket and stuffed it under her mother's nose.

Clarity leaned against the fridge, her eyes scanning the scrawly handwriting. As she reached the end, the colour drained from her face and she bit her bottom lip. 'And where did you find this?' she asked Tansy in a whisper.

Tansy thought fast. If she told her mother the whole truth, Clarity would probably have a blazing row with Miss Partridge at the show, which would be too embarrassing to contemplate.

'Jade found it,' she said. At least that wasn't a lie.

Clarity pulled back her shoulders. 'Then it obviously is nothing to do with Laurence,' she said with obvious relief. 'It's just someone with similar handwriting. It's as simple as that.' She didn't sound convinced.

'It's you that's simple!' yelled Tansy. 'Mum, can't you

see? You're just doing it again – hurtling blindly into some stupid relationship before you know anything about the guy! What are you going to do? Carry on till you get pregnant and then tell some other kid that you haven't got a clue who her dad is! Won't you ever learn?'

Tansy had shouted so loudly that she began coughing. Clarity gripped the back of the kitchen chair and closed her eyes. 'That isn't fair,' she began.

'Oh, we're on to what's fair now, are we?' yelled Tansy. 'That's rich, coming from you. Do you think it has been fair of you to pretend you hadn't a clue who my dad was when you knew it was Pongo all along?' She stopped, heart thundering in her ears. She hadn't meant to say that – it had just come out.

Her mother stared at her but didn't say a word. Tansy noticed that she was clenching and unclenching her fists and breathing rapidly.

Now Tansy had started, she couldn't stop. 'Oh yes,' she cried. 'I found out about the photograph.'

Her mother gasped and Tansy began sobbing again.

'Mum, why? Why didn't you tell me? Why?'

Clarity took a deep breath and locked her hands together. 'I want you to tell me how you got hold of the photograph,' she said evenly. 'And then I want you to give it back to me.'

Tansy felt awful. What could she do? She'd let it slip and now she would have to confess to her mother about what had happened.

'Beth said you had one and I found it in the attic,' she said.

'I see,' said her mother. 'So you have been rifling through my things. And you talk about privacy.'

'It's my father, for heaven's sake!' yelled Tansy. 'I have a right to know.'

Clarity nodded slowly. 'OK,' she said at last. 'Give me the photograph and I'll try to explain.'

Tansy lowered her gaze. 'I haven't got it,' she said.

Her mother stared. 'Where is it?' she asked with icy calm. 'Answer me. Now.'

Tansy slipped her hand into her pocket and pulled out the fragments of damp paper. Opening her fist, she showed them to her mother.

For a moment, neither of them spoke. Tansy watched as her mother's eyes filled, and one solitary tear trickled slowly down her cheek.

Tansy felt awful. Mixed in with the anger towards her mum was a lump of guilt for having gone behind her back and made her cry, and misery at losing the only picture of her father she was ever likely to have. But it wasn't all her fault, was it?

'If you hadn't taken my jeans, the photograph would still be in one piece,' she muttered.

Suddenly her mother's composure snapped. 'Well, I hope you're satisfied!' Clarity shouted. 'You try to turn me against Laurence, you rummage through my things and you ruin my best photograph of the man I once loved. You had no right! No right at all!'

That did it. 'I have every right!' screeched Tansy. 'Everyone has the right to know where they came from. If you had been honest from the start, this need never have happened. It's all your fault for keeping secrets!'

'Oh, that's right, blame me!' Clarity shouted. 'Blame me for doing my best for fourteen years, blame me for trying to think of other people, blame me for wanting to protect you – blame me, in fact, for everything, why don't you!' And with that she stormed out of the kitchen and ran up the stairs.

Tansy didn't move. She wished she could have the last ten minutes over again. She knew she'd handled it all wrong.

As she went slowly upstairs to change, she noticed the letter lying on the stairs where her mother had dropped it, and she picked it up. She thought she might need it. From behind her mother's closed bedroom door she heard the sound of sobbing. Tansy touched the doorknob, half wanting to go in and say she was sorry. But why should she? Wasn't it up to her mum to apologise first?

It wasn't until she was lying on her stomach on the bed that a thought struck her. Her mother had yelled at her for ruining her best photograph of Pongo. But if that had been the best, it meant there must be another one. But it was too late to find it now.

7.00 p.m.
Calming down

Tansy was staring out of the window, feeling miserable, when there was a knock on her door.

'Tansy, can I come in?' her mum called.

Tansy opened the door. Despite having red-rimmed eyes and tousled hair, Clarity gave her a watery smile. 'Come down and have some supper,' she said, trying to sound cheery and upbeat. 'It's spaghetti bolognese, your favourite.'

Tansy wanted to make her mother feel really guilty by saying that she was too upset to contemplate even a mouthful of food, but giving up spaghetti on a matter of principle was too much to ask even of her.

'Are you looking forward to tomorrow?' her mother asked brightly as they sat over their supper. Tansy shrugged. 'I suppose,' she said. In fact, she was excited but didn't think that someone who had been so badly treated by a parent should let anything but abject misery show on their face.

Her mother laid down her fork and began fiddling with her serviette. 'Look,' she said in a rush, 'Laurence is coming to *GFI!* tomorrow and I don't want you to say anything to him.'

Tansy stared at her mother, a strand of half-sucked spaghetti hanging from her mouth. Laurence was going to have the audacity to go to the show, knowing Miss Partridge would be there! How could he? What kind of guy was this? He might think that neither of his two women knew about the other but he couldn't possibly imagine he was going to pull it off.

And her mother was still determined to believe nothing was going on. I've got to do something, thought Tansy. Mum may be totally insane but I don't want her hurt.

'Mum! You're crazy! You should be telling him where to go, not hanging out with him in public. You're . . .' She stopped. Her mother's eyes were filled with tears and her lips were pressed firmly together.

'I'll handle it, Tansy,' she said softly but firmly. 'My way.'

She knows, thought Tansy. She knows that letter was from him. So why doesn't she phone and tell him where to go?

The workings of the parental mind were sometimes quite beyond her.

SATURDAY

Noon
Practice makes perfect?

Dunchester Leisure Centre was buzzing with noise as the teams broke for lunch. The whole morning had been spent rehearsing the games and being told what to do if you got knocked out of a round. Three other schools were taking part including Bishop Agnew College, the posh private school whose playing fields backed on to West Green's.

'Whatever happens,' said Tansy, as she and the others filed up to collect sandwiches and drinks, 'we have to slaughter them.'

'I'm determined to get to the final,' said Andy. 'I hope our team wins the school prize, but I really want the individual one. But then I guess we all do.'

'Not me,' said Jade. 'I just hope you all stay upright so I don't have to take part.'

'Me too,' said Scott spontaneously and then turned away, obviously annoyed that he had spoken to Jade. She took an envelope from her pocket and passed it to him, and before he could speak, moved off to chat to Cleo.

'What is the prize anyway?' asked Trig who, being newly arrived from America, had never seen the show.

'You get a whole day doing a job connected with your ambition,' said Andy. 'Last week a kid who wanted to be an airline pilot got to sit in the cockpit of a jet all the way to Malta and back.'

Trig looked impressed.

'You could get to go on a dig,' said Cleo, who had come across to wish them all good luck. 'And you'd get to work on a real newspaper, wouldn't you, Andy?'

Andy bit into his cheese roll. 'Actually, I don't want to be a journalist,' he admitted. 'I really want to be a merchant banker.'

'So why didn't you write about banking?' said Tansy, who was eavesdropping on the conversation.

'I just chose journalism because if I win, I want to spend a day on a national newspaper,' Andy explained.

'So you knew what the essays were for!' exclaimed Tansy, impressed. Andy was a lot more perceptive than she had realised.

'It was obvious,' said Andy. He dropped his voice so that Trig and Cleo couldn't hear. 'I want,' he said, 'to find my mum. And if I write a big feature in a paper and put her picture in, she just might know I love her and come home.'

Tansy noticed that he was close to tears. She didn't really know what to do. But it did make her think. She wasn't the only one with a missing parent. And she was not the only one determined to do something about it. In lots of ways Andy was worse off than she was.

Not that she wanted him to win. No way. She was definitely going for it!

1.00 p.m.
Tansy's big moment

After lunch, Tansy went to look for her mum and make sure she knew that she was not to cheer or call out or get herself noticed in any way at all.

She spotted her mum almost at once, which wasn't surprising since she was wearing a bright-orange beaded jacket, yellow palazzo pants and a black velvet hat that looked as if someone had sat on it for an extended period of time. Whenever Clarity was uptight, she reverted to the Seventies. It was not a part of her nature that Tansy found endearing.

As she hurried over to join her, she saw to her horror that she was talking to Miss Partridge. And in between them, beaming like a Cheshire cat, was Laurence Murrin.

How could he do that? thought Tansy. How come he has the nerve to sit there with the two women in his life, and expect to get away with it? Well, if she had anything to do with it, he wouldn't.

'Oh, Laurence, you are so funny!' she heard Miss Partridge gush in her breathy voice as she drew nearer. I'll give him funny, thought Tansy angrily.

Clarity didn't look amused either. In fact, Clarity looked as if she was about to commit a punishable offence.

Tansy was about to interrupt and sort them out, when Val the producer stepped into the centre of the hall and held up her hand for quiet.

'In just a moment, Ben Bolter will be joining us for the final run-through,' she said. 'Before we start recording the show Ben will ask each contestant about their ambition. It's just to get a sound check and make sure all of you know what to say. Right, let's get going.'

The teams nodded. Tansy's stomach began fluttering as she took her place with the others.

A make-up girl dusted their faces with powder, a weedy guy with a voice like an angry budgie did important-looking things with a tape measure and a piece of chalk, and the sound technician, whose dress sense was only marginally better than Laurence's, began checking dials.

Tansy listened as a girl from Bishop Agnew told how she wanted to be a deep-sea diver and a boy from Cedarwood School went on at some length about driving a team of huskies.

'Tansy Meadows from West Green Upper, please!' Val beckoned her to step in front of the camera.

'Go for it, Tansy!' A booming voice echoed round the hall and Tansy closed her eyes in horror as she realised that Laurence was punching the air and grinning at her.

One of the Bishop Agnew girls tittered behind her and she could see Trig and Andy exchanging smirks. She thought she might as well die now and not bother with the show. Not that it mattered what Andy thought.

She was prevented from dying by Ben Bolter, who beamed at her and turned a page on his clipboard.

'And this is Tansy Meadows, whose ambition is to be a family historian – a genealogist, in fact. That's someone who traces people's family trees, for those of you not into long words.' He gave a stagey sort of laugh. 'That's an unusual ambition, Tansy. Tell us why.'

Tansy took a deep breath. She didn't have the photo of Pongo any more. She didn't have a mum who would be any help at all. And the way she was feeling right now she didn't have anything to lose.

'I think it would be a fascinating career,' she said in her clearest voice. 'But I do have a very personal reason.'

'Yes?' encouraged Ben Bolter, casting a hasty eye over his crib sheet. Tansy took a deep breath and remembered everything that she had learned about the Dramatic Pause. This was the moment when she would have raised the photograph to the camera and looked deeply moved.

'I want,' she said, looking straight into the camera, 'to help people trace their ancestry. But first, more than anything, I want to find my father.' She was aware of a gasp from some of the kids in the audience and then a muffled murmur.

'And where is your father?' asked Ben, conscious that no one had told him that this was going to happen, but aware that it might make a good publicity story for the show.

'I don't know, Ben,' she said, hoping she looked pitiful but pretty. 'I don't even know who my father is.'

1.20 p.m.
Trouble in store

After that, things happened rather fast. Val the producer ordered an immediate break and went into a huddle with Ben Bolter and the film crew. The man with the tape measure and chalk flounced across the studio looking ruined and muttering about schedules and his migraine coming on. Andy, Jade and the others rushed up to Tansy and were about to start pumping her for information when Laurence and her mother appeared, with Miss Partridge close on their heels, wearing her 'I am most displeased' expression. Her friends melted away, sensing that what was to come was not going to be a bundle of laughs.

'Tansy,' said her mother with a catch in her voice. 'How could you? Our private business – here? In front of all these people?'

Tansy looked at the floor and then at her mother's stricken face. What had seemed a great idea a moment before suddenly seemed something of a mistake.

Miss Partridge looked pink and agitated. 'You were supposed to talk about investigating family trees,' she gabbled. 'Just as you did in your winning essay. This . . . this . . .' She waved a hand in the air. 'Well, it was very thoughtless.'

Tansy kept staring at the floor.

'How could you do that to your mother?' demanded Laurence. 'Going behind her back like that – it's despicable!'

That did it. 'You're a fine one to talk after what

230

you've been doing!' she exploded with tears in her eyes. 'Carrying on with another woman and pretending to my mum that she's special!'

Clarity gasped. Laurence gulped. Miss Partridge stepped forward.

'Tansy, please, not here, not now . . .'

Tansy stepped back. 'Oh no, you wouldn't want me to make a fuss now, would you? Not since you are the other woman!'

Elinor Partridge's mouth dropped open in horror and she turned pale. Clarity looked close to tears.

Laurence looked from Clarity to Miss Partridge and back at Tansy, who was staring at him defiantly. 'I think,' he said, 'it is time you did some explaining, young lady.'

Before Tansy had a chance to open her mouth, Val the producer strode over to them, clipboard under her arm. 'We simply have to start recording the show in twenty minutes,' she said briskly. 'And our schedule is so tight that we can't possibly run the risk of any more disruptions. I think we had better substitute Jade Williams in your place, Tansy.'

Tansy looked at her in disbelief. 'But you can't . . . I mean, that's not fair!' she cried. 'I haven't done anything wrong. And Jade doesn't even want to do it!' she added for good measure.

Val fixed her with a steely stare. 'I'll give you ten minutes,' she said. 'If you cannot give me a guarantee that, in the event of getting to the final, you don't mention missing fathers, then I'm afraid your place in the team is forfeit. Understand?'

Tansy nodded dumbly. So much for her brilliant scheme. Even if her father was out there next Saturday morning, watching the show, he would never know who she was. Not now. Not ever.

1.30 p.m.
Examining the evidence

'So,' said Laurence firmly, after they had all gone out into the foyer to talk, 'what is all this ridiculous nonsense about me carrying on with Miss Partridge? As if!'

Elinor Partridge glared at him. 'Not, of course,' he added hastily, 'that it wouldn't be delightful to . . .'

Clarity glared at him.

'Though, of course, I wouldn't . . . that is, couldn't. . .'

'Oh, shut up!' Tansy shouted. 'You may fool my mum but you don't fool me! You see, I've got this!' She pulled the letter from her pocket and shoved it under Laurence's nose.

'What's this?' he said.

For the first time, Tansy's mother spoke. 'I think,' she said, 'that is what we both want to know.'

1.35 p.m.
Sorting things out

Tansy felt a bit stupid. Clarity looked overjoyed. Miss Partridge clucked around them and bought polystyrene cups of tea which in her excitement she spilled all over the table.

'So you see,' said Laurence, 'I must have put the first page in the envelope and mailed it to you and left the second page in the book. I gave the book to Miss Partridge on Thursday because she said she had a pupil interested in Africa.'

Tansy had one last go. 'But Mum hasn't had a letter from you,' she protested.

Clarity smiled the blissful grin of a woman reprieved. 'The post hadn't come when we left,' she said. 'It'll be waiting when we get home. Everything's just fine.'

For you, maybe, thought Tansy. It seems that not only am I destined never to find my dad but I may well get permanently lumbered with Laurence. There is no justice.

1.45 p.m.
The show begins

'Are you OK?' asked Andy as Tansy took her place with the team, having promised Val the producer that she would behave like a perfect angel.

Tansy nodded.

'Don't worry,' said Andy, 'you can still find your dad. There are lots of ways of hunting people down. I'll help if you like,' he added, squeezing her hand unexpectedly.

What happened next was equally unexpected. Tansy's mouth went dry. Her heart did a sort of back flip with double pike and the skin at the back of her neck tingled. She looked at Andy. He looked at her. And grinned.

He is, thought Tansy, very caring. And if you ignore the ears, rather cute.

Not, of course, that I fancy him. Not at all.

2.00 p.m.
Half-time

The show was going brilliantly. By the end of the Go for Cash rounds West Green were in the lead, but the team games were still to come. Andy and Tansy had to run back to back down the room which for some reason made Tansy's knees turn to water, but West Green fell behind. Bishop Agnew were now four points ahead.

Then just before the next round, Matthew Santer announced in a weak voice that he felt slightly ill – and proceeded to faint in a rather ungainly heap in front of the floor manager.

'Take a break!' called the guy with the tape measure, as he swallowed two painkillers and muttered about youth programmes being awfully dire for his blood pressure. 'West Green reserve, please!'

Jade turned to Scott, who was sitting behind her. 'That's you!' she said. 'Boys replace boys, girls replace girls. Good luck!'

Scott froze.

'Go on, Scott!' several of his friends urged. 'Good luck, mate!'

Scott didn't move.

Jade noticed that he was looking very pale. Maybe there was a bug going round. Perhaps that was what Matthew was suffering from.

'Are you OK?' she asked gently.

Scott glanced at her. 'I can't do it,' he whispered. 'I can't.'

'Yes you can,' urged Jade. 'Once you are up there, you'll be fine. I promise.'

The floor manager, whose face was turning a livid shade of puce, flicked his hair with the back of his hand and tutted. 'We don't actually have all day, you know!' he simpered. 'It's too, too trying!'

'Scott,' whispered Jade. 'Go for it. You can do it. I know you can.'

He gave her a long steady look and Jade noticed that her letter was sticking out of his jeans pocket, and it was open. He nodded slowly. 'OK,' he said. 'I'll try. Thanks.'

Jade took a deep breath and started praying.

West Green pulled back to level pegging after the brain-teaser round and everything depended on the Go For the Finish obstacle race.

Ursula put the team into an early lead, and Andy and Tansy kept up the pace. Poor Abigail got caught in the crawling net, which put them back in third place, but Trig kept up a cracking pace and by the time Scott was due to go, they were neck and neck with Bishop Agnew.

'Come on, Scott!' Jade yelled so loudly that her voice carried above everyone else. 'You can do it!'

Tansy didn't dare look. They had to win. They *had* to.

Scott belted round the course and reached the finish two seconds ahead of Bishop Agnew.

They'd done it. West Green had won.

Everyone cheered, Jade loudest of all. Scott looked across into the audience and caught her eye. And grinned from ear to ear. Jade was so happy she wanted to cry. And very nearly did.

'And on the individual points, we have a tie,' announced Ben Bolter, grinning at the camera. 'Tansy Meadows and Andy Richards – a tie-breaker to decide.'

Tansy's heart was racing. If she got this question right before Andy did, she would win the major prize. She could ask for someone to start tracing her dad.

As Ben Bolter was explaining the rules to Camera Three, Tansy glanced at Andy. He was pale with concentration and she noticed he was digging his fingers into the palms of his hand. He looked as if his whole life depended on getting this right. He looked so nervous. He looked so cute.

She thought about Clarity. How infuriating she was, how embarrassing, how irresponsible. And how much she loved her. If her mum went missing, Tansy knew she would never be happy again.

'And the question is – fingers on buzzers, please – Who built St Paul's Cathedral?'

That's easy, thought Tansy. Go on, Andy. Go on.

Andy pressed the buzzer. 'Sir Christopher Wren,' he said triumphantly. A cheer went round the hall. Andy had won. And to her great surprise, Tansy didn't mind at all.

* * *

'You were brilliant!' said Jade. 'We'd never have won if it hadn't been for you.'

'It was luck,' said Scott modestly. 'The others had done all the difficult bits – I'd have been useless if I'd had to talk.' He looked at the floor and scuffed the toe of his shoe. 'Actually,' he said, 'we ought to talk.'

Jade nodded. 'Yes, we should,' she said.

'And until I read your letter, I thought you hated my family,' he said. 'I never thought about it making you miss your folks.'

Jade nodded. 'It was just that round at your house, with your parents and brothers and sisters, and that aunt from Italy – well, it all came back. How we used to have tea on Saturdays while Dad watched the rugby and how Mum and I used to tease him when his team lost — and then how Gran would come round and play cards and cheat like crazy to win. And I was jealous. Horribly, madly jealous.'

Scott stared at her. 'Jealous?' he asked.

Jade nodded. 'Don't you see?' she said. 'I wanted what you had. A family, noise, teasing — all that stuff. I was cross that your mum and dad were alive and nagging you about homework and mine were dead and . . .' Her voice caught and she stopped. 'I just wanted to run away from it all,' she said. 'But not because they weren't good enough. Because it was so good. And I missed it all so much.'

Scott sighed. 'I've been a jerk, haven't I?' he said. 'Can we start over?'

Jade's eyes widened. 'You mean . . .?'

'Can we go out again?' asked Scott. 'Only if you want to.'

'Oh yes,' said Jade. 'I want to.'

'Oh good,' said Scott. And he kissed her. In front of everyone. Even Miss Partridge. And Jade didn't mind one bit.

5.00 p.m.
Celebration time

After the show, everyone crowded round Andy to hear about his prize. Not only did he get a whole day in London with the features editor of the *Daily Mail* but he was going to be on Mega TV's *Kids Speak Out!* show. For a moment, Tansy couldn't help feeling jealous – after all, she could have been the winner. But then Andy grinned that lopsided grin and she knew she'd done the right thing. She just hoped that she wasn't going to get too much of a blasting from her mum when they got home.

Certainly Clarity didn't look too miffed right now. She and Laurence were holding hands, which was fairly obscene given that half of Year Nine could see them. If this relationship was going to continue, Tansy would have to give her mother a few firm guidelines about her behaviour.

She was about to suggest that they went home, away from public view, when Andy came over, followed by a tall, thickset man with greying hair and red cheeks.

'My dad's taking me and my brother out for a pizza to celebrate,' he said. He pulled his ear lobe and looked around the car park as if it were the most fascinating place on earth.

'Do you want to come – you don't have to,' he said in a rush.

Tansy grinned. Andy looked really endearing when he was embarrassed. If she went to supper with him, not only could she get to know him better – which she quite liked the idea of – but she'd be out of the way of any punishment her mother had planned.

'I'd love to,' she said. 'Mum!' She beckoned her mother who thankfully released Laurence's hand and came over.

'Andy's asked me out for a pizza – is that OK?'

Clarity looked as excited as if Tansy had announced her forthcoming attendance at a Buckingham Palace garden party. 'Wonderful, darling!' she enthused. She beamed at Andy. 'And are you two an item?' she asked.

'Mum!' hissed Tansy.

There were times when she thought her mother should carry a government health warning.

'Sorry,' she muttered to Andy as they climbed into his father's car which, Tansy noted with some satisfaction, was a Series 5 BMW.

'That's OK,' said Andy, dropping his voice so that his small and rather muddy brother wouldn't hear. 'Can we?'

'Can we what?' asked Tansy.

'Be an item?' said Andy.

Tansy hesitated. Andy certainly wasn't a dish like Todd. But then Andy was understanding about missing parents and took time to listen. And Andy was here and Todd was nowhere.

She grinned at Andy. 'Why not?' she said.

When Tansy got home, full of pepperoni pizza and double-chocolate fudge sundae, she found her mum sitting on the settee, idly channel-hopping on the TV. Now I shall be for it, thought Tansy, hanging up her jacket and praying that her mother would not go totally ballistic.

'Have a good evening?' asked Clarity.

Tansy nodded. 'Where's Laurence?' she asked, playing for time.

'I told him I wanted to be alone with you,' replied her mum. 'I think it's time you and I had a talk.'

She is going to kill me, thought Tansy. Maybe it would be best if I got in first.

'Look, Mum,' she began, 'I'm really sorry about this afternoon. I didn't think about all the other parents and how you would feel about them knowing.'

Clarity inclined her head. 'No, you didn't,' she agreed, 'but then I didn't think years ago about how you would feel not knowing who your father was, did I?' She took Tansy's hand. 'Darling, I thought I was doing what was best. But perhaps I was wrong all along. You see, I haven't been totally honest.'

Tansy stared at her.

'When I knew I was going to have a baby, I really wasn't sure whether Jordan or Pongo was the father. I know, I know,' she said as Tansy tried to interrupt, 'it was irresponsible and dangerous – I've regretted it all my life. But that is how it was.'

Tansy nodded slowly.

'As soon as you were born, it was obvious. Those wonderful eyes, the heart-shaped face, everything was just like Pongo. I knew Pongo had gone back to America to get married but I was clutching at straws, and I wrote to him.'

Tansy gasped. 'You said you didn't have an address,' she accused.

'I lied,' her mother admitted. 'I was trying to protect you – I didn't want you to know that he never wrote back.'

'Never?' whispered Tansy.

Clarity shook her head. 'I wrote five times in all, and I even sent a photograph. He never replied. Not once.'

Tansy's shoulders sagged. Somewhere in the world she had a father. The father she had dreamed about, the one who would take her out and make a fuss of her and be over the moon to have found her. Now she knew that dream would never come true.

My own father doesn't care, she thought. I don't matter at all.

'Why didn't you tell me all this ages ago?' she asked, trying not to cry.

Clarity sighed. 'I always thought it would hurt you too much – knowing that your father just didn't want to know. And as time went on, I figured that he would have a family of his own and that even if I did find him it would just mess up a whole lot of lives. I guess it seemed easier to let you blame me, because I was around for you and could prove I loved you. I'm sorry. Really I am.'

Tansy chewed her knuckle. 'You could have flown out to Illinois and confronted him,' she suggested.

Clarity laughed. 'A single mum with a tiny baby – hardly feasible, sweetheart!' she said. 'Besides, I got to thinking that if he didn't even care enough to reply to my letters, then he wasn't good enough for my daughter. I decided to try to be a mum and a dad rolled into one. I'm sorry I didn't make a very good job of it.'

Tansy leaned over and gave her mother a bear-like hug. 'You did! You did!' she cried. 'You're the best mum in the world!'

Clarity slipped her hand in her pocket. 'This,' she said, 'is for you.'

She handed Tansy a picture. It was of Pongo. Not as clear or as large as the one that got washed, but Pongo nevertheless.

'Keep it,' said Clarity as Tansy tried to hand it back. 'Whatever he did and wherever he is now, he is your father after all. And I did love him.'

Tansy nodded. 'Thanks, Mum,' she said. 'But you keep it. I don't need it now. After all, I've got you.'

SUNDAY

10.00 a.m.
Tansy's kitchen

Tansy and her mum were enjoying a Sunday morning slop around in their dressing gowns, when the front door opened and Laurence walked in. This, thought Tansy, was getting seriously worrying. Giving the guy his own key was only one step short of him moving in. He might not be quite as bad as she had thought but she certainly wasn't having him living here.

'Morning!' he said brightly, hugging Tansy's mum and planting a kiss on her forehead. 'Did you get the letter?'

Clarity nodded happily and pulled a sheet of notepaper from her handbag. 'Page one of two,' she laughed. 'So it was all a big misunderstanding. I'll go and make us all some coffee.'

After she had gone through to the kitchen, Laurence looked at Tansy. Here comes the lecture, she thought. Let's get it over with. 'Has your mum told you?' he asked.

Oh great, thought Tansy. She's even discussed my parentage with him. 'Yes, as it happens,' she said curtly.

'Great!' said Laurence. 'So which have you chosen?'

Tansy frowned. What was the guy on about?

'The skiing holiday, silly,' said Laurence. 'Do you fancy France or Switzerland?'

Tansy's mouth dropped open in amazement. 'Me? Are you going to take me too?'

Clarity, coming back with a tray of coffee and biscuits, laughed. 'Of course,' she said. 'You don't think we'd leave you behind, do you?'

Laurence nudged Tansy's mum playfully, almost making her spill the coffee. 'Of course, she probably couldn't bear my company for a week,' he said.

True, thought Tansy. And then thought about mountains and skiing. And après-ski. And dishy bronzed instructors. 'Oh, I don't know,' she said hastily. 'I think I could hack it.'

2.30 p.m.
News from Holly

Tansy was supposedly doing her biology homework, but actually drawing red biro hearts and writing 'Andy' all over them, and wondering how it was he kept creeping into her mind, when the door bell rang.

'Get that, sweetheart,' called her mother, who for reasons best known to herself was lying on the bedroom floor, listening to a *Sounds of the Ocean* tape with a mud pack on her cheeks and two cucumber slices over her eyes.

Holly was on the doorstep, with her baby nephew William in a pushchair. She was wearing new black hipsters, a floral cardigan and pink vest top and looked stunning.

'Don't ask,' she said hastily. 'It was taking William out or doing mum's ironing.'

'No contest,' agreed Tansy. 'But what's with the glamour bit?'

Holly grinned. 'That's what I have to tell you – it's unbelievable!' She jigged up and down and little William shook in his pushchair.

'What's happened?' asked Tansy.

'It's this guy,' began Holly.

'Oh,' said Tansy with a grin. 'I should have guessed.'

2.45 p.m.

'You have to push William,' ordered Holly, thrusting the pushchair at Tansy and flicking her hair over her shoulder, as they walked down the road.

'Why me?'

'Because,' said Holly, 'he might see me and I want to look cool.'

'Who might see you?' asked Tansy patiently.

Holly sighed ecstatically. 'This guy Paul – from the new house. He was at *GFI!* yesterday and he is so gorgeous!'

For the next five minutes, Holly talked non-stop – about Paul's eyes, Paul's deep voice, Paul's muscles and the combined effect of these attributes on Holly's heart. 'I have to see him again,' she said.

'He lives right behind your house, silly – of course you'll see him,' said Tansy reasonably.

'I have to see him *alone*,' persisted Holly. 'So this is what you have to do.'

'Hang on,' said Tansy. 'What I have to do?'

Holly nodded. 'He told me he plays tennis every Sunday afternoon in Beckets Park,' she said.

'That's where we're going.'

'I rather thought it might be,' said Tansy. 'But where do I come in?'

'You,' said Holly, 'are going to faint.'

Tansy couldn't stop laughing. Holly was crazy. When Tansy said that no way would Paul rush to the aid of a fainting West Green kid, Holly suggested Tansy should scream and pretend to have been bitten by a snake.

When Tansy pointed out that Beckets Park was not known for its adders, Holly thought that maybe they should let William loose on the tennis court and then retrieve him.

'He'd notice me then,' she said.

Tansy shook her head. 'Holly,' she said patiently, 'just shut up.'

Holly looked mortified.

'I think,' said Tansy, 'you had better leave it to me.'

The two girls walked over to the courts.

'That's him!' hissed Holly. 'Over there! Don't look!'

Tansy sighed. 'If I don't look, I can't see him, can I?' She followed Holly's gaze to where a tall, athletically built guy was standing at the kiosk buying a drink.

'Stay there,' she said, and pushing William she marched over to Paul.

'Are you Paul?' said Tansy firmly. The guy looked up in surprise and nodded.

'Oh good,' said Tansy, 'because my friend Holly met you yesterday at *GFI!* and she's dying to talk to you and if you don't get over there, I shall have to endure another ten minutes of hearing how great you are!'

3.15 p.m.

'I am definitely in love!' declared Holly. 'I mean, really, properly, this time. I think Scott was just a childish infatuation.'

Tansy said nothing.

'Did you hear him say he'll phone me?'

Tansy nodded.

'Do you think he will?'

Tansy nodded again.

'When? What should I say? Should I be really cool or what? Do you think he'll ask me to go out?'

Tansy shook her head. 'I doubt it,' she said.

Holly looked horror-struck. 'Why not?' she asked.

'Because he's unlikely to get a word in edgeways,' Tansy said, grinning.

Holly pulled a face. 'You just don't understand what it's like to be truly, madly, deeply in love,' she said.

'Yes I do,' said Tansy.

'You do? Who?' Holly gabbled.

Tansy paused. 'Andy,' she said.

Holly looked gobsmacked. 'But he's not your type at all!' she protested. 'You said your dream guy had to be tall and clever and rich and – '

'I know,' said Tansy. 'But on second thoughts, dreams can be disappointing. Andy's really cute. And understanding. And what's more he's here. Now. And that's what counts.'

WHAT A WEEK TO BREAK FREE

For Kate, who invented Shiny Vinyl,
and for all the pupils of the Royal High School, Edinburgh

MONDAY

7.00 a.m.
53 Lime Avenue, Oak Hill. Facing reality

Jade Williams rolled over in bed and opened one eye. And just for a moment, she thought she was back in her attic bedroom in Brighton and that the last six months had been one very long bad dream. For an instant she imagined she could hear her father's cheerful, if somewhat tuneless, singing as he beat Jade into the bathroom, and half expected the door to open and her mum to appear with a mug of tea, teasing her about being the sleepiest teenager in town.

But then her eyes fell on the prone form in the bed next to hers, and she remembered that these days she had to share a room with Allegra, the cousin from hell. She picked up the silver photograph frame on her bedside table and stared at it.

'Oh, why did you have to die?' she said out loud to her smiling parents. 'Why did you have to go and leave me?'

They smiled wordlessly back.

'Oh, please! It's bad enough having pictures of dead people all round the room, without you holding conversations with them!'

Jade turned round. Allegra was propped up in the adjoining bed, leaning on one arm and giving Jade the sort of look normally reserved for lower forms of reptilian life.

'Oh, shut up!' spat Jade, trying hard not to cry, mortified that she had been overheard. 'It's all right for

253

you, your parents are still alive. Mine are – '

'Dead. I know. You keep telling me,' said Allegra, yawning and running her fingers through her mahogany-brown hair. 'Isn't it time you stopped wallowing in self-pity and got on with life?'

She clamped her hand to her mouth in mock dismay. 'Oh, sorry, Jade, I forgot. You haven't got a life, have you?' she sneered, swinging her long tanned legs out of bed and standing up. 'You just loll around looking pathetic and driving us all demented. My mother says it's time you pulled yourself together.'

'Oh, does she?' yelled Jade, grabbing her bathrobe and heading for the door. 'Well, I don't care what she says. It's not up to her. She's not my mother.'

'A fact,' snarled Allegra, picking up her hairbrush and following her, 'for which I imagine she is truly thankful. My parents didn't have to take you in, you know. They only did it because there wasn't anyone else. I heard them say so.'

Jade caught her breath. She knew it. They were all sick of having her around. Joshua, who was sixteen and a total dweeb, had ignored her from the start, but then Joshua ignored most people unless they happened to be fascinated by his collection of stick insects and spiders and other revolting creatures which he kept in glass tanks in his bedroom. Nell, who was seven years old, small, chubby and apparently terrified of practically everything in the universe, had been delighted to have a cousin who would read *The BFG* over and over again. But recently she had refused to speak to her and pushed her away when Jade tried to hug her. David, Paula's husband, would smile at Jade in a vague sort of way, as if trying to recall who she was. And even Paula, who had been nice in the beginning, had changed lately. She used to cook all her favourite dishes, and make sure that no one watched the regional news on television in case they reported a car crash and made Jade cry, but lately she had been snappy and impatient whenever Jade mentioned her parents or the past. Jade was pretty certain that the whole family would like her to disappear.

'At least we have next weekend to look forward to,' said Allegra as if to reinforce her thoughts. 'You don't know how good it's going to be not having you dripping around the place all the time.'

Jade whirled round to face her, her hand on the door handle. 'Not half as good as being miles away from you!' she shouted. 'I wish the school trip was for a month, not just three days. In fact, I wish I could just go to Dorset and never come back!'

'You and me both!' retorted Allegra. 'Now, if you don't mind, I want a shower.' She pushed Jade to one side and opened the door.

'It's my turn to go first!' shouted Jade.

'Tough!' replied Allegra.

Jade glowered at her. 'That's not fair!' she shouted. 'Why should you always have things your way?'

Allegra turned and gave her a condescending smirk. 'Because,' she said snappily, 'I was here first. Remember?' And with that, she disappeared into the bathroom and slammed the door.

Jade sank down on to her bed and gazed miserably at the photographs. Her mother and father were frozen in time, beaming at her from behind the glass, as if they didn't have a care in the world. Dad wouldn't sing songs in the shower ever again and Mum wouldn't nag her to get a move on. They were dead, killed by a teenage joyrider in a stolen car. And because of that, Jade was living a hundred and twenty miles away from her gran and all her old friends, feeling as if she would never properly belong anywhere again.

She knew she should be feeling a rush of love, or a sharp stab of sadness, but instead she was overcome by a violent, gut-wrenching anger. Anger with them for dying, for abandoning her to this ready-made family, who were already tired of being kind and were starting to make it quite clear that they wished she wasn't around. And no one was better at doing that than Allegra. Allegra hated her.

'Of course she doesn't hate you, darling!' her aunt, Paula, had exclaimed the previous Saturday when Jade complained that no matter how hard she tried, her fifteen-year-old cousin was determined to make her life a misery. 'She loves having you here, we all do. Although – '

'Although what?' Jade had retorted. 'Although you wish Mum and Dad hadn't made you guardians in their will? Although you wish there was someone else to palm me off on?'

'JADE! For heaven's sake!' Paula had burst out, slamming the bread knife down on the kitchen counter top and clenching her fists. She had closed her eyes, taken a deep breath and turned to face her niece. 'I'm sorry, sweetheart,' she had said, steadying her voice and giving Jade a hug. 'All I meant was that . . . well, you should try not to dwell on things so much. It's been six months now and it's time you were putting it all behind you. It does make it hard for Allegra, for all of us to – '

'Hard for you?' Jade had stormed, shrugging her away and choking back tears. 'Oh, and I suppose you think that it has been a real doddle for me, is that it? You think I should just forget about my parents, like you have. Well, you may not care that Dad and Mum are dead, but I do!'

She had seen the shadow pass across her aunt's face and had waited for Paula to protest that of course she cared, that she missed her sister and brother-in-law just as much as Jade. But she hadn't. She had merely taken a deep breath and carried on chopping vegetables.

'It doesn't do you any good to brood, Jade,' she had said. 'There's nothing to be gained from looking back.'

But Jade couldn't help looking back. The awful thing was that already there were odd moments when she would shut her eyes and be unable to picture her father's face. Or to hear the sound of her mother's voice inside her head. She was terrified that one day she might forget completely. Just as Paula appeared to have done.

Jade could remember her mother, Lizzie, saying that she and Paula had been really close as children so it seemed odd that her aunt never wanted to chat about things now. She could have talked to Gran, but Gran had gone to America to stay with her sister after Dad died and although Jade had received postcards, she hadn't a clue when she would be home.

A tear trickled down her cheek.

'Oh, puh-leese, you're not going all pathetic again, are you?' Allegra, a towel wrapped turban-style round her head, crashed back into the bedroom. 'By the way, there's no hot water left.'

'What?' gasped Jade. 'There has to be – I've got to wash my hair before school. It looks a real mess.'

Allegra gave a sarcastic laugh. 'What's unusual about that?' she jibed. 'You've had that same hairstyle – well, no, sorry, I can't even call it a style – since you were about eight. Even Nell wouldn't be seen dead in baby curls. I think it's going to take a little more than a hair wash to make you look halfway decent.'

'I hate you!' spat Jade.

'The feeling,' replied Allegra, 'is entirely mutual.'

7.30 a.m.
Behind closed doors

After a ten-minute battle with her hair, in which the score was Hair – 5, Jade – nil, she stomped downstairs to breakfast. The sooner she had something to eat, the sooner she could leave for school. While most of her friends hated Monday mornings, Jade was actually relieved to get out of the house. When she was with Holly, Tansy and Cleo, she could forget her problems and even go for a whole day without thinking of her parents. Best of all, she would be with Scott. She had never had a proper boyfriend before and just thinking about him made her toes curl and little shivers dance up and down her spine. This weekend had been worse than most, because Scott had gone to a family wedding in London and it had been sixty-one hours and thirty minutes since she had seen him. But next weekend, she thought with a grin, she would have him for three whole days. Year Nine's trip to the Hoppinghill Activity Centre in Dorset was the highlight of the term and although Mr Boardman, the headmaster, told them that it was intended to build their characters and improve their communication skills, everyone else (especially Holly) saw it as a brilliant opportunity to get in some serious chatting up behind the rocks they were supposed to be climbing.

All these thoughts of Scott and passion cheered her up enormously and she ran along the hall towards the kitchen, eager to swallow a bowl of cereal and get to school early enough to spend time with him before first period. And what's more, she'd ask Paula for some money to get her hair cut. She knew her aunt was dead against it because she'd tried it on once before.

'Darling, your hair is lovely as it is,' she had protested when Jade had mentioned a new style. 'You look so sweet.'

'I don't want to look sweet!' Jade had shouted. 'I want to look grown up. Of course, if it's left to you I won't ever grow up at all!'

'We'll discuss it later,' Paula had said lamely. But she never had. Today, though, she would. Jade would make sure of that.

It was as she passed her uncle's study that she heard raised voices.

'I've really had just about enough of her,' she heard her aunt complain. 'It's all right for you – you don't have to deal with her whining day after day.'

Jade froze. 'Oh, I expect she'll get over it,' she heard David's calm voice reply. 'Although I must admit, she is very babyish. Perhaps we've all been too soft on her.'

Jade heard her aunt sigh.

'She's so different from Allegra,' she said. 'And I'm not getting any younger. If I'd known that it was going to be this hard, I honestly don't think I would have had her.'

Jade clamped her hand to her mouth to stop herself crying. They really didn't want her. It wasn't just her imagination. They thought she was a baby just because she got tearful sometimes. They wished she was like Allegra.

Then her misery gave way to anger. It wasn't her fault she was here. She hadn't asked for her parents to die. She grabbed her jacket off the hook in the hall. If they wanted her out of their way, she'd keep out of their way.

She snatched up her school bag and opened the front door. Breakfast could wait. She wasn't going to watch them pretending to care, when all the time they couldn't wait for her to go.

She'd show them. She didn't need any of them. Friday couldn't come quickly enough.

8.00 a.m.
6 Kestrel Close, West Green. Worrying

While Jade was storming through her front door, Cleo Greenway was pushing a piece of toast disconsolately around her plate and hoping for a miracle before Friday. Maybe, she thought, I will come out in spots, or break my ankle, or start throwing up all over the place. It might even be worth eating rancid prawns if it got me out of going to Dorset.

All her friends were ecstatic at the thought of three days of rock climbing and canoeing and abseiling. Cleo would have preferred to spend the weekend in the dentist's chair having root-canal work than face looking a total nerd in front of the whole of Year Nine.

'I don't know what you're worried about,' her elder sister Portia had said the night before, when Cleo had asked her to breathe all over her in the hopes of passing on her sore throat. 'I had a brill time when I went.'

It was, thought Cleo, easy to have a brill time when you were five-foot-ten, slim as a reed and thought hurling yourself off a viaduct on the end of a piece of rope was a great way to spend a Saturday. It wasn't quite so simple when you were five-foot-four, fat, and totally uncoordinated.

'You're not fat,' Holly would protest whenever Cleo bemoaned her flabby thighs. 'You're just well built.'

Cleo didn't want to be well built. She wanted to be slim with legs up to her armpits and to have the ability to do the hundred-metre hurdles without the need of a life-support system at the finishing line. She was sure that if she went on this wretched activity weekend, she would be the one who capsized her canoe or got stuck halfway up a rock face.

But even more worrying than what would happen during the day was what might occur at night. What if she had one of her bad dreams? And shouted out? Everyone would hear her. She couldn't go. She would simply have to think of something. Maybe she should start praying now.

'Darling, there you are!' Her mother, Diana, burst into the kitchen, dressed in a crimson kaftan and matching embroidered Chinese slippers, and waving a letter above her head. 'Sweetheart, the most divine news! You'll never guess!'

Cleo grinned despite herself. Her mother was an actress and even when she was out of work, which was rather too much of the time, she managed to make the most mundane event sound as dramatic as the first moon landing.

'Darling, it's just too exciting!' enthused Diana, waving the letter under her nose. 'I've got a screen test!'

Cleo's eyes widened. Now that was news. When she was younger, her mother had done two seasons with the Royal Shakespeare Company, but the arrival of three daughters in quick succession had put a stop to that. Then Mum and Dad had split up and Mum had married Roy and by the time she returned to acting, it seemed everyone had forgotten her. She did get a few small parts; Cleo's friends had been fairly excited a few months before when her mother appeared, sipping a tomato juice, in the Rovers Return on *Coronation Street*, and there had been a high spot when she was in a film with Nicole Kidman for a whole thirteen seconds, playing 'woman at bus stop'. But the big time had passed her by, a fact which Cleo knew upset her mother enormously. A screen test, however, sounded hugely promising.

'That's brilliant, Mum!' she exclaimed, shrugging her arms into her school blazer and glancing at the clock. 'What's it for?'

'Fittinix,' said her mother, dropping her eyes slightly and sipping her coffee.

'Pardon?' asked Cleo.

'You know, angel,' said her mother, 'those new knickers – the ones that flatten your tummy and make your bottom invisible. They want a more mature woman for the TV advertising campaign.'

Cleo's jaw dropped and she stared at her mother. 'You are not telling me,' she said in disbelief, 'that you intend to appear on national television in your underwear?'

Diana nodded enthusiastically. 'It's rather flattering, don't you think, to be chosen for one's bottom at the age of forty-four? You know, if the campaign took off, I could end up as Rear of the Year. What fun!'

Cleo cringed. The idea of her mother's bottom being displayed on TV at peak-viewing time was bad enough. That it should feature on the pages of every tabloid newspaper and be giggled over by every kid at West Green Upper was simply too much to contemplate.

'Mum, you can't! What will Roy think? Does he

know?' Cleo could hardly imagine that her chauvinistic stepfather would warm to the idea of his wife making an exhibition of herself in public.

'No, he doesn't know yet – he's left for work,' Diana snapped. 'Anyway, what he thinks is irrelevant. I am my own woman. No man tells me how to live my life.'

Cleo sighed. That's what her mum had said when she and Dad had all those rows before they split up three years ago. And lately, her mother and Roy had been arguing a lot. It worried Cleo a great deal, especially since whenever they had a row, Lettie threw up and Portia stormed out of the house, because she said the tension was bad for her karma. While her sisters were throwing wobblies, her mother would get one of her heads and her stepfather would lock himself in the garden shed, muttering, 'If I had known it would be like this, I would never have taken them on.' It was left to Cleo to calm everyone down.

'You're so sensible, darling,' her mother would croon afterwards. Sometimes Cleo wished she was the one being pacified with chocolate buttons instead of Lettie. Everyone spoiled Lettie. Still, she thought, if Mum gets work, Roy will be pleased and maybe the rows will stop. I would just rather she found something that involved remaining fully clothed.

'The trouble is,' continued Diana, interrupting Cleo's thoughts, 'the screen test is on Saturday – Roy will be at that golf tournament at The Belfry, Portia's going to Stratford with the sixth form and you'll be away in Dorset. I just don't know what I can do with Lettie. I have to leave for London at six in the morning.'

If I offer to look after Lettie, I won't have to go to Dorset, thought Cleo gleefully. I won't have to worry about dangerous sports or nightmares.

'I won't go to Dorset,' she said eagerly. 'I don't much want to, anyway.'

'Of course you want to go, darling!' exclaimed her mother.

'No, truly, I – '

'Sweetheart, it's divinely dear of you but I wouldn't dream of stopping you. All your friends will be there – and that nice new boyfriend – Trig, isn't it?'

Cleo nodded. There was that, of course. Three days with Trig would be good. She had to admit she was surprised that Trig wasn't as determined as she was to find a way out. After all, he hated sport and was desperately self-conscious about the huge strawberry birthmark which covered his body from his shoulders to his waist. But when she had suggested that they work out a ruse together to get out of going, he had refused.

'My dad's really chuffed that I'm going,' he said. 'You know what a disappointment I am to him. And there must be something there that I'll be good at.'

Mr Roscoe was the sort of father who thought sons should spend their time kicking balls and leaping over hurdles. Trig was trying hard to please him and failing miserably.

'That reminds me, angel,' said Cleo's mother, 'I must get you a new sleeping bag.'

'Mum, honestly, don't . . .' Cleo began. And stopped.

A particularly detailed image of her mother in cling-fit knickers swam before her eyes. If it was a choice between risking life and limb in a sailing dinghy or making it even easier for her mother to make a spectacle of herself, it would be better to risk drowning.

8.45 a.m.
A crisis of confidence

By the time Jade reached the school gates, she was convinced that Allegra was right. She looked a nerd. It wasn't easy to look hip and cool in West Green Upper's dire chocolate-brown and gold uniform but the rest of them seemed to manage it. And it wasn't just rebels like Ella Hankinson, with her designer shoes and drastically shortened skirts, who managed to be trendy. Ursula Newley had put blond streaks in her hair, which made her look about three years older, and Emily Wilkes had got a babe bob and wore lime-green sunspecs on top of her head, even when it rained.

And I look just the same as always, thought Jade in irritation. Wet, wimpish and boring. Something would have to be done. Fast.

Jade had had long curly hair ever since she was little and suddenly she hated it with a passion. She wished she could take some scissors and chop the lot off right now.

'Hey, Jade! Over here!' She turned to see Holly Vine, waving frantically from the other side of the forecourt. Holly was one of her best friends, which was pretty amazing considering that she had really fancied Scott Hamill and even thrown a party in the hope that he would fall madly in love with her. Only it had been Jade he had kissed and Jade he had asked out. Luckily, Holly was the sort of person who fell in love with the utmost ease and only last week she had announced that Scott had been a mere adolescent fantasy and that she was about to embark on a Real Relationship with Paul Bennett who went to Bishop Agnew College, the posh independent school in Oak Hill. Whether or not Paul knew about this impending love affair, Jade was not certain, but as he had just moved into the house behind Holly's, there was no way he was going to be able to shake her off.

'Guess what?' began Holly excitedly as soon as Jade got within earshot. 'Shiny Vinyl are coming to The Danger Zone! On Wednesday! Can you believe it?' She waved a fluorescent-pink flyer in Jade's face. A somewhat smudged photograph of four faces in mid-shriek stared out from the page.

'Don't you think they are just amazing?' urged Holly, flicking her sleek, nutmeg-brown hair over her shoulders. '*Heaven Sent* magazine says they are going to be really big one day. I would kill to see them play.'

I, thought Jade, would kill to know who on earth they are. Not only do I look a dweeb but I can't even sound hip.

'What's that?' Tansy Meadows panted up to them, her school bag bouncing on her skinny hips. Tansy was Jade's second-best friend, and not someone who liked to be left out of the action.

Jade handed her the flyer, hoping fervently that Tansy wouldn't have a clue as to who they were either.

'Wow!' she exclaimed. 'Wicked! What do you reckon, Jade?'

Jade fixed a bright smile on her face. 'They're great,' she said, hoping she sounded convincing. To her relief, at that moment the bell rang for registration. 'Did you understand that French homework?' she asked Holly, hoping desperately to change the subject before she got caught out.

'No,' said Holly, as they pushed their way through the double doors into the school building. 'But then languages and me never did get on.' She sighed. 'I'd give anything to go,' she said.

'To France?' asked Jade, frowning.

'No, stupid, to see Shiny Vinyl,' retorted Holly.

'Me too,' said Tansy.

'So why don't you?' asked Jade as they reached their classroom.

'Because of that,' said Holly, stabbing a finger at the small print on the bottom of the leaflet.

Jade and Tansy peered over her shoulder.

'*Tickets, currently on sale at Discdate music stores, will not be sold to anyone under the age of sixteen,*' read Tansy. 'Typical! Honestly, how is anyone supposed to get a life around here?'

'Well, at least there's the weekend to look forward to,' said Jade, dumping her bag on the table and unloading her books. 'That will be cool – with the disco on Saturday and everything. I can't wait, can you?'

Holly stared at her. 'Oh, please,' she said. 'You can hardly compare a school trip with a chance to see Shiny Vinyl. I know which I would rather do.'

'Oh, me too,' said Jade hastily. Now Holly thought she was a nerd as well.

'I suppose,' said Holly thoughtfully, perching on the edge of the table, 'we could get someone older to buy our tickets and then hope that we could sort of slide in unnoticed.'

Tansy perked up. 'That,' she said eagerly, 'is a brilliant idea. Who? What about your brother, Holly?'

Holly raised her eyes heavenwards. 'No way,' she said. 'Ever since he got married and had a kid of his own, he's gone all moral and stuffy and keeps saying things like, "Shouldn't you be studying, Holly?" and 'What *are* you wearing?". He'd never agree.' She paused. 'I know,' she said triumphantly. 'Jade, you can ask Allegra. I mean, I know she's not sixteen but she looks it, and, anyway, she's got attitude.'

'Tell me about it,' muttered Jade, miffed at yet another reminder of her cousin's attributes. 'Anyway, I'm not asking her any favours – she hates me and, besides, she'd just go and tell Paula and then I'd be for it.'

Holly tossed her head. 'For all you know, she might want to come along – then she'd keep quiet! But I suppose if you're too chicken even to try it, we might as well forget the whole thing!'

Jade took a deep breath and put a bright smile on her face. 'No need,' she said as coolly as she could. 'I'll get the tickets.'

'YOU?' gasped Tansy and Holly. 'Don't be silly!'

'Girls!' Mr Grubb roared, slamming his books on his desk. 'Is it within the realms of possibility that you could silence your overactive tongues for more than ten seconds at a time?'

'Sorry, sir,' they chanted.

'You'll never get away with it!' hissed Holly from behind her hand.

'Watch me,' said Jade, and noted with great satisfaction the expressions of sheer amazement on the faces of her two friends.

10.15 a.m.
In geography, deeply regretful

How could I have been so dumb? thought Jade, making a half-hearted attempt to draw a diagram of a glacial valley. They're right; I'll never convince anyone that I'm sixteen. I won't mention it again and they'll just forget about it. That's cool.

11.00 a.m.
At break. A quick rethink

'Hi, Jade! Is it true?' Scott flopped down on the bench beside her and grinned. Jade's knees turned to jelly.

'Is what true?' she asked. That I love and adore you? she thought. Yes.

'That you're going to be able to get tickets for Shiny Vinyl?'

Jade took a deep breath. 'Ah, well,' she began. 'I'm not – '

Scott beamed at her. 'I'd never have guessed you'd be up for it! That's so cool. Do you reckon you can get one for me?'

He thought she was cool. He hadn't said she had no chance. She loved him so much.

She looked at him from underneath her eyelashes, the way she had seen Allegra flirt with her snooty boyfriend, Hugo.

'No problem,' she said. 'Consider it done.'

12.30 p.m.
In the cafeteria, assessing the odds

'Jade reckons she'll be able to get tickets for Shiny Vinyl, no trouble,' Holly was telling Cleo enthusiastically as Jade came up to the table with her lunch tray. 'That's right, isn't it, Jade?'

Jade bit her lip and nodded half-heartedly.

'You're crazy!' gasped Cleo, attacking her tuna and vegetable bake with enthusiasm. 'You'd never get away with it. You don't even look fourteen, never mind sixteen.'

'Oh, thanks,' muttered Jade. She didn't need Cleo to tell her what she already knew.

'No offence, but she's right,' agreed Tansy, peering

with some distaste at the contents of her onion bagel. Her mother was very into natural foods, which meant Tansy kept finding obscure bits of plant life in her lunch box. 'You're the least likely of any of us to pull it off.'

That does it, thought Jade, pulling the ring pull on her can of lemonade. I'm fed up with the way that everyone sees me as a kid and I'm fed up with people telling me what I can't do. I'll get those tickets if it's the last thing I do.

'I can look any age I like if I put my mind to it,' she said airily.

Cleo frowned and shook her head. 'Even if Jade got the tickets, which is unlikely . . .'

Jade glowered at her.

'. . . you'd never get past the bouncers on the door. It wouldn't work.'

'It might,' said Tansy thoughtfully, 'if we all wear a lot of make-up and dress really cool.'

'What,' insisted Cleo, 'if we get caught?'

Jade shrugged. 'All they can do is chuck us out,' she said. 'It's no big deal.'

Cleo looked at her in stunned silence. She had always thought of Jade as being the one person in their set who was most like her – anxious to do the right thing and keep out of trouble.

'It's worth a try,' said Tansy, warming to the idea. 'Go for it, Jade – you get the tickets and we'll make sure we get in. After all, we've nothing to lose.'

'There is just one small problem,' remarked Holly, tipping the remnants of her crisp bag into her hand and licking them up with her tongue. 'Sorting the parents.'

'Oh, sugar,' said Tansy. 'If my mum hears it's over-sixteens only, she's bound to say no.'

Tansy's mum had been a New Age traveller when she was young and it seemed very unfair to Tansy that she should have decided to start worrying about convention and common sense and early nights just as Tansy got old enough to do without any of them.

'Mine too,' agreed Holly. 'Why is it parents always imagine that you're going to drink or get in with a bad crowd? As if we'd be that stupid.'

Tansy grinned. 'Best keep their blood pressure down and just say we're going to the cinema together, right? After all, The Danger Zone and the Multiscreen are both in the Rainbow Centre. As long as we stick to the same story, we'll be fine. OK, Cleo?'

Cleo swallowed. She had no intention of going. She didn't like crowded places and she wasn't that keen on indie bands either. But there was no way Jade would get the tickets so it would never happen.

'Fine,' she said. 'Just fine.'

Tansy ditched the onion bagel and peeled a satsuma. 'So are us lot going to share a room at the weekend, then?' she enquired, biting into a segment and squirting juice all down her blouse. 'Beetle said we had to sign the list today.'

Mr Grubb was known as Beetle behind his back, on account of his name and shiny black hair.

'I suppose so,' said Holly unenthusiastically. 'Not that I can bear to contemplate three days away,' she added tragically. 'I shall have to leave Paul behind.'

Jade frowned. 'Paul?' she asked.

'This guy Holly's besotted with,' Tansy said, grinning.

Jade turned to Holly. 'Are you two an item, then?' she asked.

'Well, not exactly,' admitted Holly. 'But he does fancy me, I know he does. He said hello this morning and he had this look in his eye. He'll realise how he feels any day now and if I'm not here . . .' Her voice trailed off as the horrific enormity of the situation hit her.

'You could always ask him to the Shiny Vinyl gig,' suggested Jade. 'Shall I get an extra ticket?'

Holly's face lit up. 'Would you? Could I? What will I say? Do you think he'd say yes?'

Jade grinned. 'I'm not too sure,' she said, laughing.

'Why not?' gasped Holly.

'Because,' said Jade, 'it would mean you being quiet for more than two seconds.'

3.30 p.m.
In the locker room, getting cold feet

'Tansy?'

'Mmmm?'

'Will you come with me to get these tickets? I mean, just for the company. I'll do the talking.' Jade crossed her fingers behind her back and sent up a silent prayer.

Tansy shook her head. 'Sorry. Drama club. Must dash.'

3.35 p.m.
Feet getting colder

'Hey, Holly, wait for me!' Jade ran to catch up with her friend.

'Do you fancy coming into town – to get the tickets?' she asked.

Holly quickened her pace. 'I'm in a tearing hurry – I'm planning to accidentally-on-purpose bump into Paul when he gets off the Bishop Agnew bus. Must run.'

3.40 p.m.
Feet nearly numb

'But, Cleo, honestly, it would only take half an hour. Please come.'

Cleo grabbed a sheet of music from her locker. 'I can't – I've got choir practice. Why don't you just forget it? It won't work anyway.'

Oh, thanks, thought Jade. Thanks a bundle.

4.05 p.m.

**Shiny Vinyl
AT THE DANGER ZONE
WEDNESDAY 8.00 P.M.
GET YOUR TICKETS HERE FOR THE ULTIMATE GIG!**

Jade took a deep breath and surveyed her reflection in the music-store window. She had tied her hair back in a ponytail and piled on loads of Raspberry Shocker lipgloss which she had bought at the chemist next door.

'Remember,' she told herself severely, pushing open the shop door, 'it's attitude that counts.' She strode purposefully up to the counter where a young guy with greasy hair and a blank expression was chewing gum and gyrating half-heartedly to a rock track.

'Six tickets for Shiny Vinyl, please!' demanded Jade, tossing her head and hoping that she looked really cool.

'Sorry, love,' said the assistant, hardly pausing in mid-chew. 'Sixteen and over only.'

'I am sixteen,' said Jade, pulling herself to her full height, and giving him what she hoped was a sultry smile. 'How much are they?'

'Fifteen pounds each. And I'm the prime minister of England,' drawled the guy. 'Nice try.'

4.15 p.m.
Simmering with rage

Of course, I don't have to tell them that the guy thought I was a dweeby kid, thought Jade, stomping up Abbey Street – Dunchester's main shopping area. I'll just say that I didn't have enough cash on me.

But then, she thought, staring in the window of Gear Change and wondering whether a black lace slip dress would make a difference, if I do that, they'll just give me the money and expect me to go back tomorrow. And I'm not going to look any different tomorrow than I do today. Unless I get the new haircut by then.

That was it! That's what she had to do. That way, she'd get the tickets, and everyone would shut up about how babyish she was and start giving her a bit of respect.

There was just the small problem of how much it would cost. Perhaps she could persuade Paula to cough up her allowance earlier, if she really grovelled. She didn't feel like being nice but if it meant getting a new look, she'd just have to grit her teeth and do it.

4.30 p.m.

Holly stood in the telephone booth, wrinkling her nose. It smelled foul, and she was bored with reading and re-reading the instructions on how to make a call. She wished Paul's bus would hurry up. She had it all worked out. When she saw him getting off the bus, she would run out and bump into him. That way he would have to talk to her.

She knew he fancied her. Or at least, she thought he did. Ever since that Sunday afternoon when Tansy had let on to Paul that Holly liked him, he had eyed her with interest. They hadn't actually had much of a conversation yet, but then, as everyone knew, when guys really had the hots for someone, they found speech difficult. It was up to Holly to make it easy for him.

To her relief, the Bishop Agnew school bus lurched

into view. Holly's heart beat faster. She peered through the glass and saw Paul, long legged and lean, jump from the step. This is it, she thought to herself. Remember what *Heaven Sent* magazine said. Be cool.

She was about to rush out when she noticed that Paul wasn't alone. He was with another Bishop Agnew guy and they were deep in conversation. Holly's heart sank. He'd never chat her up now – not with his mate listening in. But she'd give it her best shot anyway.

She shoved the door open and burst out, bumping straight into Paul who fell onto his mate, pushing him against the wall.

'Sorry!' she gasped, widening her eyes and trying to look alluring. 'Oh, Paul – I didn't realise it was you! I wasn't looking where I was going.'

Paul grinned. 'Clearly,' he said. 'You OK, Steve?'

The other guy rubbed his elbow and nodded. 'Just about,' he said. 'You're the kid that lives at The Cedars, aren't you?'

Holly bristled. Kid, indeed.

'The one that is mad as a hatter, right?'

Who did this guy think he was? This was not the image she was trying to convey.

'Do I know you?' she asked in what she hoped was an ice-cool voice.

Paul laughed. 'This is my twin brother, Stephen,' he said.

Holly was surprised. He didn't look a bit like Paul who was tall and fair with the most remarkable legs. Stephen was shorter, plumper and had a shock of reddish-brown hair that flopped over his face.

'Take no notice of him, he's a nutter,' added Paul.

'*I'm* a nutter?' Stephen exclaimed. 'If anyone's nuts round here, it's . . . oh, sorry, what's your name?'

'This is Holly,' said Paul.

Holly's spirits rose. He remembered her name. He'd probably been saying it over and over to himself, plucking up courage to talk to her.

'Well,' said Stephen, 'it's Holly that's nuts. She must be, to fancy you!' He gave his brother a friendly punch. Paul laughed.

Holly thought she might as well lie down in the gutter and quietly die.

'Take no notice of him,' said Paul hurriedly. 'I told him how your friend set you up and pretended that you liked me.'

Holly was relieved that he didn't realise it was she who had made Tansy go with her to drool over Paul a couple of weeks before when he was playing tennis in the park.

'I know it was all a joke,' Paul added. 'Just a laugh.'

Holly swallowed. Now what did she do? They didn't tell you about this bit in *Heaven Sent* magazine. 'Sure!' she said with a bright smile. 'Tansy's always doing that kind of thing for a laugh.'

Paul's expression faltered for just a moment.

'So,' Stephen said as they walked towards Holly's house, 'what do you do when you're not swooning over my brother?'

'Give it a rest, Steve!' snapped Paul.

Go for it, Holly told herself.

'Oh, this and that,' she said airily. 'I'm going to the Shiny Vinyl gig on Wednesday, and then we've got this activity weekend and – '

'Shiny Vinyl?' gasped Steve. 'Wicked!'

'Activity weekend?' said Paul at precisely the same moment. 'Where?'

'Dorset,' said Holly, stopping outside her front gate.

'Oh . . . that's nice,' said Paul. 'We're going on one this weekend from school as well. Down in Sussex – sailing and orienteering and canoeing and stuff.'

'He's boat mad,' interjected Steve. 'Now, about this Shiny Vinyl gig . . .'

'I don't suppose by any chance you sail?' Paul continued.

'Off and on,' said Holly casually. Her experience amounted to being sick in her uncle's Laser off the Isle of Wight one windy day last summer but he wasn't to know that.

'Great!' exclaimed Paul. 'Maybe – '

'Never mind sailing,' said Steve. 'How come you can get tickets for this gig? I thought it was sixteen-plus only.'

Holly glared at him in irritation. How dare he interrupt? 'I have connections,' she said.

'Can you get some for us?' asked Steve eagerly.

Us? thought Holly joyfully 'Yes, I should think so,' she said. Jade had better come up with the goods. This was going to be it.

'Count me out,' said Paul.

Holly's face fell.

Steve laughed. 'You should know that my brother is the least hip person I know,' he grinned. 'He'd rather be getting soaked to the skin in a force-five wind than going to a gig. Bad luck, kiddo!'

I think, thought Holly, that I might very much like to kill you.

'It doesn't bother me,' she said. 'And actually, my contact has run out of tickets.'

Steve's face fell.

'So I can't help you,' said Holly. 'Bad luck, kiddo!'

4.45 p.m.

Jade stood at the reception desk of Talking Heads feeling very self-conscious. She wasn't used to hairdressing salons – her mum had always trimmed the split ends for her and the only time she had ever been to a hairdresser was when she was a bridesmaid four years ago.

'Can I help you?' The assistant looked up and smiled.

'I'd like an appointment for tomorrow, please,' said Jade.

'Certainly – what would you like done?'

Jade took a deep breath. 'I want it all cut off. Very short.'

The receptionist tapped a few keys on her computer keyboard and yawned. 'Melanie could do it for you at half-past four,' she said.

Brilliant, thought Jade.

'Er, how much will it cost?' she asked.

'Twenty-five pounds,' said the receptionist.

'*What?* I mean, that's fine. Thanks. See you tomorrow.'

She'd need all her ingenuity to get that much cash out of Paula. But she'd have to do it. Her street cred depended on it.

5.30 p.m.
Plan of action

As Jade turned the corner into Lime Avenue, she saw Paula standing at the front door, casting anxious glances up and down the street.

'Jade! Where on earth have you been – I've been worried sick!'

'Sorry,' said Jade in what she hoped was a suitably meek voice. 'Netball practice – I forgot to tell you.'

Paula sighed. 'I've had Nell's teacher on the phone demanding to see me because Nell's falling behind with her reading, and Joshua got bitten by one of his spiders and had to go to Casualty, and I can do without worrying myself silly over you!'

Jade was about to interrupt this outpouring with a stern reminder that she was practically fourteen and quite capable of looking after herself when she remembered that she had planned to be charming.

'I'm really sorry,' she said. 'You have had a bad day. Shall I make you a cup of tea?'

6.00 p.m.

Jade was standing at the kitchen sink, putting part two of her campaign into action by helping Paula to peel potatoes for supper, when Joshua ambled in with his hand in a bandage, and clutching something black and creepy in a jam jar. He leaned over his mother's left shoulder and dangled it in her face.

'Aaah! Oh, Josh, take it away, whatever it is. It's revolting. Put it in one of your tanks.'

Josh eyed his new beetle with affection. 'I can't,' he said. 'It would eat the others.' He put an arm on his mother's shoulder.

'Could you sub me for a new tank? Please?'

Paula sighed. 'And if I do, that wretched creature will be locked up for eternity?'

Josh grinned and nodded.

'OK. How much?'

6.10 p.m.

Part three of the campaign involved laying the table. Jade had just got to the napkin-folding bit when Allegra crashed in.

'Mum, can I have ten pounds? Please. It's vitally urgent.'

Paula heaved a sigh. 'Allegra, you are always asking for money. What is it this time?'

'*The Deep Blue Sea*'s on at the Rep – Terence Rattigan,' she added.

'I do,' said Paula, 'know who wrote it.'

'Yes, well, a group of us are going on Wednesday – it's very educational.'

Paula sighed again. 'OK – get my purse.'

6.15 p.m.

'Can I have some money like Legs and Josh?'

Nell stood in the doorway, chubby and scowling.

'Don't be silly, Nell – what do you need money for?'

'Things,' said Nell.

Paula laughed. 'Well, things will have to wait,' she said. 'Now wash your hands for supper.'

Nell hiccuped and burst into tears. 'It's not fair,' she said. 'You're horrible.' Slamming the kitchen door, she stomped upstairs.

'Silly child,' muttered Paula.

Jade took a deep breath. 'By the way, Paula,' she said as casually as she could manage, 'could you let me have some money to get my hair cut?'

Paula opened the oven door and prodded the cottage pie. 'I'll trim it for you, sweetheart,' she said. 'Much less expensive.'

'No, I mean a proper cut,' said Jade. 'Short.'

The oven door slammed shut and the saucepans on the hob leaped alarmingly. 'Jade, I've told you,' asserted Paula. 'Short hair wouldn't suit you. Believe me.'

'Oh, great,' said Jade. 'You've decided, have you? Never mind what I want to do with my hair.'

Paula threw her a warning glance.

Jade tried again. 'I only need to borrow a bit,' she said.

'No, Jade,' returned Paula. 'If you want a haircut you will have to wait until you can afford it yourself.'

'Oh, I get it!' yelled Jade. 'It's OK for Josh and Allegra to get handouts whenever they want, but I don't count, do I?'

Paula opened her mouth to speak but Jade was in full flood. 'Well, that's fine by me,' she shouted, 'because I'm going to get my hair cut and there's nothing you can do to stop me!'

6.30 p.m.
Little worries

Jade was in the bedroom, seething with fury. It wasn't fair; her mum would never have made such a fuss over something simple like a haircut. Mum used to say that part of growing up was learning to express yourself. Well, Paula could carry on all she liked. Jade wasn't going to be told what to do any longer.

The trouble is, she thought, making bold statements is one thing, but finding the money was quite another. She had eleven pounds left in her bedroom drawer, which wasn't nearly enough for the sassy new hairstyle she wanted.

She was just debating whether to ask Talking Heads what they could do for eleven pounds when she heard sobbing from the next room. She dropped the magazine she was looking at and went on to the landing.

'Nell!' she said, pushing open her door and finding the little girl curled up on the bed with tears streaming down her face. 'What's the matter?' She crouched down beside the bed and took Nell's hand.

Her cousin snatched it away and sat up. 'Nothing,' she said, sniffing. 'I'm not telling. Nothing.' She sniffed and rubbed her fists across her eyes.

Jade's heart went out to her. She knew what it was like to sit alone in your room feeling miserable. And she was thirteen, not seven. 'You can tell me, Nell. Maybe I can make it better.'

Nell stared at her solemnly, her big brown eyes filling once more with tears. Jade remembered what Paula had said earlier. 'Is it school?' she asked.

'No, I didn't say that, I didn't!' shouted Nell. 'It's not!'

'OK, OK,' said Jade soothingly. 'I just thought maybe you were worried about your reading.'

Nell screwed her face up. 'Reading's stupid!' she shouted. 'School's stupid! You're stupid! Go away!'

Jade sighed and got to her feet. 'I'll get your mum,' she said. She'd know what to do.

'No!' gasped Nell. 'Please, Jade, don't tell my mum. Look, I'm happy now. See?' She smiled a watery smile.

Jade grinned back. 'OK, I'll believe you,' she said. 'But tell me if I can help, won't you?'

Nell gulped and nodded her head slowly.

Jade closed the door and went thoughtfully back to her bedroom. She wasn't convinced. She knew that sometimes explaining to people what was really wrong was so hard that it was easier to pretend everything was fine.

6.45 p.m.
Cousinly confrontation

'Hey – that's my magazine!' Allegra leaned over Jade's shoulder and snatched it from her hand. 'How dare you touch my stuff!'

'Pardon me for breathing!' retorted Jade. 'I was only looking.'

'Well, don't!' snapped Allegra. 'Buy your own if you want one!'

Jade counted to ten, and then to twenty. She still wanted to kill her cousin.

'Now would you please mind getting lost?' asked Allegra. 'I need peace and quiet to learn my part.'

'What part?' asked Jade.

'Saint Joan,' said Allegra proudly. 'I've got the lead in the school play.'

'Saint Joan?' queried Jade. 'Isn't she the one who got burned at the stake?'

Allegra nodded.

'That's nice,' said Jade. 'What a pity your school won't be using real flames.'

7.15 p.m.
On the line

They were halfway through supper when the telephone rang.

'I'll get it!' cried Allegra. 'It's bound to be for me.' She grabbed the receiver. 'Dunchester eight-double-one-one-two-three. Oh. Yes, she is. Hang on.' She turned to Jade. 'It's for you,' she said sullenly. 'Holly someone.'

Jade jumped up.

'Jade, did you get them?' Holly shouted so loudly down the phone that Jade was sure that everyone would hear.

'No,' she said.

'I knew you wouldn't! You should have asked Allegra!'

'Ssshh!' hissed Jade, looking hastily over her shoulder. 'Anyway, I can get . . . do it, but you have to give me the money.'

'Oh . . . sorry,' said Holly. 'How much?'

Jade was conscious that both Allegra and Nell were staring at her. 'Fifteen pounds.'

'*What?*' Holly gasped.

'Look, we're eating. I'll call you back.' She went back to the table and smiled.

'Was you being horrible to her?' demanded Nell, pushing a chip round and round on her plate.

'Not was you, were you,' corrected Paula instinctively. 'Of course she wasn't. Don't be so silly, Nell. Eat your supper.'

Allegra was eyeing Jade with suspicion. 'What do you want fifteen pounds for?' she demanded.

Jade thought fast. 'Cinema,' she said. 'We're going on Wednesday. I'm in charge of getting the tickets.'

Paula put her knife and fork down with a clatter. 'Oh no,' she said firmly. 'Not on a school night. No way.'

Jade glared at her. 'That's not fair!' she said. 'All my friends are allowed to.'

'Well, I'm not responsible for your friends, but I am in charge of you and the answer is no!'

Jade thumped her fist on the table, sending peas spinning over the tablecloth. 'I don't believe you! You said Allegra could go out this Wednesday – I heard you!'

'Allegra is a year older than you and, besides, she's going to the theatre. It's different.'

Jade pushed back her chair and leaped to her feet. 'Oh, well, it would be, wouldn't it?' she stormed. 'You make quite sure everything's different for your kids. I'm just the hanger-on, aren't I? You don't – '

'*Jade!* David, say something.'

David glaced up from the evening paper he had been reading. 'Apologise to your aunt, Jade,' he said mildly and returned to the financial pages.

'What for? Wanting a life? I'd have thought you'd be pleased I was going out. After all, you don't like me being here, do you?'

Paula was opening her mouth to reply when the front door bell rang. 'I'll get it – then you can all sit and talk about me behind my back!'

Jade stormed out of the kitchen, slamming the door behind her. I mustn't cry, she told herself firmly. I won't give them the satisfaction.

She opened the front door to find a large woman in a waxed jacket holding an even larger dog on a lead. 'Oh, jolly good show! You're in,' she said. 'Is there a Miss Williams at this house?'

Jade nodded in surprise. 'Me,' she said.

'Oh, spot on,' she boomed. 'This letter was popped through my door today – it's addressed to thirty-five, you see, not fifty-three.'

She handed Jade a blue and red airmail envelope. 'It's from Gran!' said Jade, without thinking. 'She's always getting things wrong! Oh, sorry – thank you. Thank you ever so much.'

'No probs,' said the woman enthusiastically. 'Get vague myself sometimes. *Anno domini*, you know. Come along, Lucretia, walkies!' And with that she bounded off down the path, turning to give Jade a cheery wave.

Jade sat on the bottom of the stairs and ripped open the letter. A twenty-pound note fell out. She picked it up and hugged it to her chest.

Brilliant! she thought. It's an omen. I'm meant to have my hair cut. Now there is nothing Paula can do to stop me. The thought of getting one up on her aunt was as rewarding as the idea of a new look.

She sat at the bottom of the stairs and attempted to decipher her grandmother's flamboyant handwriting.

113 Heath Place, Westmont, Illinois, USA

Darling Jade,
By the time you get this letter I shall be home! I've had a marvellous time here with Alice but I must

admit I'm ready to get back to normal and more than ready to see my darling granddaughter again. I'm sure you are terribly grown up by now. We've so much to talk about – so when shall it be?

'Jade! Come and finish your supper.' Paula, looking flushed, stuck her head round the kitchen door. 'And who was at the door?'

Jade ambled back along the hall, still reading her letter. 'A woman from number thirty-five,' she said. 'She delivered this. It's from Gran.'

Paula began scraping leftovers into the bin and gestured to Jade to finish her cottage pie. Jade went on reading.

You can help me sort through some of your parents' pictures – I am sure there are things you would like to have.

I'll be back in Brighton on Friday next – give me a ring, darling. I can't wait to hear your voice.

Loads of love

Gran

'She says she's got stuff of Mum and Dad's that I can have. Can I go soon? How about the weekend after next?' Jade begged.

Paula hurled dinner plates into the sink and turned on the tap. 'I can't just drop everything and go tearing down to Sussex,' she said shortly. 'Besides, Allegra has rehearsals on Saturdays.'

Jade glared at her. 'So? You don't have to take me. I can catch a train, you know. I'm not totally incapable.'

'No?' muttered Allegra. 'You had me fooled.'

David threw her a warning glance.

Jade ignored her. 'So can I? Saturday week?'

'No!'

Paula wheeled round to face her. David redirected his warning glance at his wife.

'What do you mean, no?' exploded Jade. 'It's my life, I'll do what I like!'

'I don't mean that you can't go at all, but not yet!' shouted Paula. 'It's too soon. It's – '

'Too soon!' yelled Jade. 'I haven't seen her for six months. I need to see her.'

Paula took a deep breath. 'So, we'll invite her up here,' she said, trying to keep her voice level. 'For a weekend. That would be nice, wouldn't it?'

Jade shook her head vigorously. 'No, it wouldn't! I want to go to Brighton. I want to see Tanya and all my other friends, and my old house and . . . I just want to go back home!'

A shadow passed over Paula's face. 'This is your home,' she said.

'No, it isn't!' Jade cried, choking back tears. 'This is where I live. But it isn't home. And it never will be! Brighton is home and I want to go back there!'

And with that she rushed out of the kitchen, up the stairs and into her room. Flinging herself on the bed, she grabbed the photograph of her parents.

'I want to go back!' she shouted at them. 'I hate it here! It's all your fault – why did you have to die? Why? Why? WHY?'

And hurling the picture to the floor, she buried her face in the pillow and began to cry as if she would never stop.

7.30 p.m.

'Hi, Cleo? Holly. I've spoken to Jade. She didn't get the tickets.'

Thank heavens for that, thought Cleo.

'But don't worry, it's only because we didn't give her any money. She needs fifteen pounds from each of us. I've told Tansy.'

Cleo swallowed. She didn't want to part with that much money for something she wasn't even keen to go to. But if she said that, she'd sound wet.

'OK,' she said. 'I'll bring it to school tomorrow.'

It would be all right. Jade would never manage to get the tickets. She'd get her money back. No problem.

TUESDAY

8.00 a.m.
3 Plough Cottages, Cattle Hill. Red-letter day

'Tansy! Andy's here!'

Tansy was peering in the dressing-table mirror, wishing she had hair that would lie down and behave itself, when her mother called up the stairs. She grabbed her school bag and opened her door.

'She'll be thrilled that you've called for her,' she heard her mother say as she pounded downstairs.

Tansy cringed. Didn't her mum realise that it was totally uncool to let a guy know that you were even mildly chuffed by his presence? Not that her mother had a clue when it came to men. It had been ages before she worked out who Tansy's own father was, and all the time Tansy was growing up, she had had a series of extraordinarily unsuitable boyfriends.

'So are you two looking forward to your weekend away?' enthused Clarity, beaming at Andy who was standing in the hallway with a broad grin on his face and glasses halfway down his nose. 'Give you a chance to get to know one another better and – '

'*Mum!*' hissed Tansy. Honestly, she was such a liability. 'We're going. See you at four thirty.' She gave her mother a quick kiss, and steered Andy firmly through the front door before Clarity could utter one more embarrassing syllable.

'Guess what!' cried Andy, the instant the front door

closed behind them. 'I've had a postcard from Mum – and this time she's actually written lots.'

Tansy beamed at him. 'Brilliant!' she said. 'Where is she?'

Andy's mum had disappeared months before; just walked out one day and never come back. She sent Andy a postcard every few weeks from a different place so the police weren't worried about finding her.

'They say an adult has the right to go off if they want to,' he had told Tansy miserably one day. 'She's not a missing person because she sends us cards. But all she writes is "Love you lots, Mum".'

Tansy thought it was an odd kind of love, just leaving Andy and his little brother, Ricky, like that. Usually when Andy got a postcard he was pretty quiet for a couple of days but now he seemed really excited.

'Listen,' he said excitedly, pushing his glasses up the bridge of his nose and peering at the card.

Dear Andy,

I'm thinking of you a lot this week because I know you're going on a school trip. Have a lovely time. I do miss you, you must believe me. One day I will tell you everything and then maybe you will understand and forgive me. I am writing this sitting by the sea watching the seagulls fighting over bread.

I've sent Ricky a Thomas the Tank Engine card – look after him for me.

Much love, Mum

'Isn't that brilliant?' he urged.

Tansy swallowed. 'Well, yes,' she replied hesitantly. 'But does she give an address?'

'No, but the postmark says Brighton and Hove,' he said eagerly. 'But that's not the point. Don't you see – she said one day she'll tell me everything. That means she will be coming back.'

Tansy squeezed his hand. 'That's great, Andy.'

'And she knows about the school trip,' he gabbled excitedly. 'Which means someone is telling her all our news – and that someone knows where she is! If only I could find out who it was!'

Tansy felt so sorry for him. It had been bad enough for her to accept the fact that she would never know her real father, but she couldn't imagine what it must be like to have the person you loved most in the world walk out on you.

Andy slipped the card carefully into his jacket pocket. 'I just get the feeling she'll be home really soon.'

Tansy prayed that his hopes for his mum wouldn't be dashed like her own for her unknown dad.

8.10 a.m.
5 Kestrel Close. Calming troubled waters

While Tansy and Andy were discussing absent parents, Cleo was hovering in the hallway, fiddling with her blond hair and trying to put off going to school. Behind the closed kitchen door, her mum and stepfather were having a row. Another row. And there was no way Cleo was going to leave her mum while Roy was in one of his angry moods.

'I do think I'm in with a good chance for this knicker advert work,' Mrs Greenway was saying with a pleading tone in her voice. 'And it would pay quite well, you know.'

'Quite well!' thundered Roy. 'It had better pay damn well, the way you spend money! If I had known how you and your confounded kids were going to drain me of cash, I would never have – '

'Never have married me, is that it?' shouted Diana with a catch in her voice. 'I didn't plan to be out of work! You know how many auditions I've been to.'

'Oh yes,' sneered Roy. 'And when you don't get a job you console yourself by going to the shops and spending more money. I can't carry this family single-handedly, and what's more I don't intend to go on doing it.'

Cleo winced. What did he mean? Was he going to walk out, just like Dad had? If Roy went too, Mum would be in pieces all over again. Roy was horrid when he was in a bad mood but he was OK the rest of the time and she couldn't bear to think of Mum being as upset as she had been after Dad had left.

'You don't have to,' said Mrs Greenway hastily. 'Max sends money for the girls each month.'

Cleo heard the sound of a fist thumping the kitchen table.

'Oh, yes – a pittance compared with what it costs to clothe them and pay for Lettie's riding lessons, and now there's this activity camp or whatever for Cleo and – '

That did it. Cleo pushed open the kitchen door.

'Don't keep shouting at Mum!' she cried. 'I won't go on the weekend. If it'll save money, I can cancel.'

Roy turned round and a guilty smile crept across his rugged features. 'I didn't know you were there,' he said. 'It's OK – you go. Saving that amount would be like trying to stop a tidal wave with a teacup. I must get going.' He paused to pick up his briefcase and newspaper. 'Someone around here has to earn some money,' he stressed, throwing a stern glance at Cleo's mother. He left without kissing either of them.

'Are you all right?' whispered Cleo to her mum. 'Let me cancel the weekend and stay home with you.'

Mrs Greenway's laugh was brittle. 'No way, angel,' she said. 'It will do you good to get away.'

No it won't, thought Cleo. 'But Mum – '

'Darling, I'm fine. Absolutely fine,' insisted her mother.

Cleo wished she believed her.

8.20 a.m.
The Cedars. Boy-watching

Holly was hanging out of her bedroom window and quietly drooling. From there, she could see into the kitchen window of the house that had been built on what was once her family's vegetable garden – Paul's house. And she could actually see Paul, leaning against the work surface, mug in hand, talking to his mum.

He was divine. He had a body to die for. And he was

298

hers. Well, not quite hers yet, but it was only a matter of time.

As she watched, Paul turned to put his mug in the sink and glanced up. His eye caught hers. Her mouth went dry and, as she lifted her arm to wave to him, he smiled. Her stomach lurched.

He fancied her. She could see it in his eyes. Please God, she prayed, could you make something happen to bring us together? Soon. Very soon. Amen.

8.35 a.m.

It was as Jade turned the corner of Lime Avenue that she saw Scott ambling ahead of her along Dulverton Road. She frowned. He usually waited for her outside his house so that they could walk together.

She broke into a run. 'Scott!' she called. 'Wait for me!'

He paused and turned.

'Hi!' she said breathlessly as she drew alongside him and linked her arm through his.

'Hello,' he said somewhat flatly and gently shifted his arm out of her way. 'Did you get the tickets?'

Jade frowned. 'No, I need the cash,' she said. 'Fifteen pounds.'

Scott's eyes widened. 'Oh well, count me out, then,' he said reluctantly. 'There's no way I can spend that amount. I'm skint!'

'But you have to come!' exclaimed Jade. 'Fifteen pounds isn't that much.'

'Well, it is to me!' snapped Scott. 'Fitz is ill again.'

Jade bit her lip. Fitz was Scott's dog and he adored him with a passion.

'He's never been right since he got stuck on that building site,' Scott said. 'He's losing weight and he's not nearly as bouncy as he used to be. I'm taking him to the vet but my mum says I have to help pay.'

Jade said nothing. If Scott didn't come to the concert, there wasn't much point in going.

'So,' said Scott, changing the subject as the bus pulled up, 'how's things with you?'

'Dire,' she said. 'My gran's back from America and wants me to go and visit.'

'What's dire about that?' he asked.

'Paula won't let me,' she said. 'Can you believe that? She's so selfish – she doesn't want me to see my old friends or anything.'

'Why?' asked Scott, puzzled.

'How should I know?' said Jade. 'Probably because she hates me!'

Scott sighed. 'Don't start all that again,' he said wearily. 'It's pretty obvious she doesn't hate you. You don't ask people to live with you if you hate them.'

'She didn't have any choice!' retorted Jade. 'It was in Mum and Dad's will.'

Scott kicked at a stray pebble on the pavement. 'She could still have said no,' he remarked.

'Whose side are you on anyway?' asked Jade snappily.

'No one's!' returned Scott. 'I'm just getting a bit tired of you going on and on about how hard done by you are.

It's getting very boring.'

Jade's heart missed a beat. 'Don't you like me any more?' she whispered.

Scott paused. Rather too long for Jade's liking. 'Yes, of course I do,' he said. 'I'm sorry. I'd just like it if you were a bit more . . . well, cheerful.'

Jade took a deep breath. Scott wanted her cheerful. OK, OK. 'So what about this weekend, then?' she said brightly. 'Three whole days together. It'll be great, won't it?'

Scott sighed. 'Mmm,' he said.

Jade felt he could have sounded a little more enthusiastic. He was supposed to be in love with her. It must be the worry about Fitz. She'd just have to find ways to take his mind off his dog.

9.00 a.m.
West Green Upper School. Change of plan

'What's with this special assembly?' muttered Tansy to Cleo as they filed into the hall.

Cleo shrugged. 'Probably one of Mr Boardman's little pep talks about SATs and keeping noses to the grindstone and making something of ourselves,' she said, grinning. 'He has to have his little fix of being head teacherly now and again.'

Mr Boardman was waiting for them on the platform. 'I have,' he said, 'some unfortunate news.'

A governor's died, thought Holly, eyeing her

fingernails and thinking that she really should paint them ready for when she caressed Paul's hair.

Someone's daubed graffiti on the games pavilion, thought Tansy, staring at the way Andy's hair curled into the nape of his neck.

You have unfortunate news, thought Jade sullenly. My whole life's unfortunate right now.

'There has been a serious fire at the Hoppinghill Centre. As a result, I am afraid that the Year Nine activity weekend cannot be held there.'

A gasp went up from the assembled pupils, followed by an outbreak of anguished chattering.

'Oh no!' chorused Tansy, Jade and Holly.

Oh whoopee! thought Cleo, and tried to look sorrowful in front of her friends.

'However,' continued Mr Boardman, holding up a hand for silence, 'all is not lost.'

An expectant hush fell across the room.

'Bishop Agnew College have arranged a similar weekend for their Year Ten pupils at another centre. Luckily for us, their group is quite small and there is space available.'

A murmur rippled between the pupils.

'Provided I get your parents' consent, we shall be joining Bishop Agnew at the Downsview Centre in Sussex!'

'Bishop Agnew!' gasped Holly. 'That's Paul's school! I'm going away with Paul!' Thank you, God, thank you, she added silently in her head.

'Isn't Brighton in Sussex?' Andy whispered to Tansy.

Mr Boardman held up his hand again. 'There will be

a wide range of activities on offer and I am sure you will all have a marvellous time. Any questions?'

Jade put up her hand. 'Whereabouts in Sussex is it, sir?' she asked.

'How silly of me not to mention it,' he said. 'The centre is at Poynfield. Just outside Brighton, right by the sea.'

He was gratified to see how delighted at least three of his pupils appeared to be.

11.30 a.m.
In the lab but not in the interests of science

Jade wasn't concentrating on the properties of hydrochloric acid. All she could think about was that by Friday night she would be just a few miles from her old home. She would have the chance to phone Gran and tell her how hateful Paula was being. Gran would get it all sorted. She was so excited she could burst.

'Jade!' Tansy called to her as she walked from the art block to lunch. 'Here's my money for the Shiny Vinyl ticket. Andy's not coming – he has to look after Ricky while his dad works late – and I've told Mum we're going to the cinema so don't let on, will you?'

Jade's excitement evaporated a little. She still had to get these tickets or look a nerd in front of everyone. It seemed daft to be going to all this trouble for a concert she wasn't interested in, but she couldn't get out of it now.

'You will get them, won't you?' queried Tansy.

'Of course,' she said casually. 'Leave it to me.'

4.00 p.m.
Preparing to be beautiful

Jade hadn't expected it to be this nerve-racking. Looking at her reflection in the salon mirror, she wondered whether she dared to go ahead with it. She fingered her long curly hair. When she was little, her dad used to call her Goldilocks and tell her that he never wanted her to cut it off.

But Dad wasn't here and she had to make a fresh start. Wasn't that what everyone was telling her?

'Hi, I'm Melanie,' said a young assistant, holding out a black gown. 'What can I do for you?'

'I want it all cut off,' said Jade in a rush. 'Like this.' She thrust the picture she had surreptitiously torn from Allegra's magazine at the girl.

'Wow! What a change!' said Melanie, running her fingers through Jade's hair. 'You are quite sure?'

'Yes,' said Jade emphatically. 'Absolutely certain.'

'You don't want the colour change, do you?' asked Melanie, eyeing the picture.

Jade hesitated. 'I suppose you are a bit young . . .' murmured the hairdresser.

'I'll have it,' said Jade.

5.30 p.m.

Don't cry, Jade told herself firmly. Seeing the heap of caramel-blond curls lying on the floor, and observing this copper-headed stranger with a shaggy five-centimetre crop staring at her from the mirror, she wondered whether she had made the most awful mistake. It didn't look nearly as good on her as it did on the model in the photograph. And she didn't feel full of confidence, as she had thought she would. She felt exposed and vulnerable as if she wasn't quite sure who she was. It was so . . . different.

'Stunning!' drooled Melanie, holding up a mirror to show Jade the back.

'It's a bit . . . spiky,' said Jade.

Melanie looked affronted. 'That's the essence of the look,' she retorted. 'Get some giant earrings on and a bit of make-up and your friends won't know you!'

I suppose it does look quite cool, thought Jade uncertainly. But still . . .

'How old does it make me look?' she asked shyly.

'Oh, sixteen at the very least,' said Melanie, unplugging the hot brush.

Maybe, thought Jade, it's not so bad. In fact, I might quite get to like it. Mightn't I?

5.45 p.m.
Success at last

Discdate music store was packed with people by the time Jade got there. She had gone heavy on the lip-gloss and eyeliner, and just hoped that the school uniform wouldn't detract from her new-found sophistication.

She took a deep breath and strode up to the counter. 'Four tickets for Shiny Vinyl tomorrow, please,' she said, pulling the money from her purse.

'Sure,' said the guy. 'Sixty pounds, please. Doors open at seven-thirty p.m. No refunds.' He handed her the tickets. 'Enjoy!' he said.

I did it, thought Jade in amazement. I really did it. I'm not a kid any more. I've got attitude. It was worth the haircut.

She ran her hand over the short layers. It would grow, of course. And the colour wasn't permanent. It was no big deal.

It was while she was on the bus travelling home that it occurred to her that she still had to face the one person who would undoubtedly think it was a very big deal.

6.00 p.m.
Hair-raising reactions

When Jade arrived home, Paula was out. She sped upstairs and crashed into the bedroom, anxious to have another look at her hair before facing the inevitable argument. To her dismay, Allegra was sitting on the end of the bed, varnishing her toenails.

'Don't come near me,' she began, turning to face Jade. 'You'll only smudge my . . . Jade! Your hair!'

Jade grinned.

'What have you done to it? It's . . . it's . . . so short!'

Allegra gasped. 'And the colour – it's red!'

'Burnished bronze, actually,' retorted Jade.

Allegra stared at Jade for a long moment without speaking. 'My mother will kill you,' she said eventually.

Jade shrugged. 'Tough,' she said. 'It's done now.'

'It doesn't suit you,' said Allegra snidely. 'And it's badly cut at the back.'

'Oh, and what would you know?' retorted Jade. 'That's the essence of the look. It's done for impact.'

Downstairs a door slammed.

'Mum's back!' smirked Allegra. 'Now you'll find out all about impact. Come on – this I have to see!'

Paula was in the kitchen, unloading supermarket bags.

'Hi, Mum!' Allegra bounced across and gave her mother a hug. 'Jade's back!'

'Oh, good,' said Paula, turning round. 'How was school? Oh my . . . Jade! Oh!' She clamped her hand to her mouth and grabbed the back of a kitchen chair for support. 'What have you done?' she wailed. 'Your lovely hair? Jade, how could you!'

Jade took a deep breath. 'It's my hair and I can do what I like with it.'

Paula was close to tears. 'It's awful! And that hideous colour – it's so brash, so tacky.' Paula slumped into the chair. 'How could you be so thoughtless, so stupid? How do you think your mother would feel?'

Allegra gasped. Jade gulped. She felt really guilty. Her mum would have hated it. She knew that. But then she knew she couldn't stay looking the same for ever either.

'Mum, that's not fair.' Jade looked in astonishment as Allegra spoke. 'Jade can't go through life doing what you assume Auntie Lizzie would have wanted. Auntie Lizzie's dead. Jade's alive.' She paused, obviously stunned at her outpouring. 'Not that I'm saying that's a good thing,' she added hastily, reverting to her normal sarcasm. 'But it's not the end of the world. The hair will grow and that awful red will wash out. It's no big deal.'

Paula sniffed and wiped her eyes on a tea towel. Jade was speechless. If anyone had told her that Allegra would ever stand up for her, she would have told them they were mad.

But there was something else. Paula had mentioned Mum. And that hadn't happened in weeks. Maybe it was only by making her aunt cross that she was ever going to get her to talk. It was a thought.

'I had been considering allowing you to go to the cinema tomorrow,' said her aunt. 'But you can forget it. You're grounded.'

Jade stared at her. 'You can't!' she breathed. 'You can't do that to me!'

Paula pursed her lips. 'Oh, can't I?' she said. 'Just watch me.'

'Thanks for standing up for me,' muttered Jade to Allegra as they went upstairs.

Allegra shrugged. 'Well, at least you weren't being your normal wimp-like self,' she said. 'That was a pretty brave thing to do – even if you do look like an angry radish.'

Jade glared at her. 'I can't believe she grounded me,' she moaned. 'I simply have to go out tomorrow night. I have to.'

Allegra eyed her sharply. 'Why? What's so special about tomorrow?'

Jade paused. Could she confide in Allegra? 'Playing out with your little friends, are you?'

No, she couldn't.

'Oh, go boil your head,' Jade said.

Jade was coming out of the bathroom when she bumped into Nell on the landing.

Nell stared at her wide-eyed. 'Who did that to you?' she asked, her eyes filling with tears.

Jade looked at her in bewilderment.

'What are you on about, Nell?' she said. 'The hairdresser did it. I wanted it short. Don't you like it?'

Nell shook her head furiously and stomped downstairs.

Oh, terrific, thought Jade. So much for new looks. She began to wonder how long it would take to grow her hair back.

WEDNESDAY

8.00 a.m.
The Cedars. A question of fashion

'Mum, I need some clothes. Urgently.' Holly stood in the doorway of the kitchen, knowing that when requests for cash were forthcoming, her mother was prone to look for a speedy escape.

Mrs Vine looked up from the list of figures over which she was tutting with ever-increasing impatience.

'Oh, darling, don't be silly!' she admonished. 'You have a wardrobe full of clothes. What on earth do you need more for?'

It never ceased to amaze Holly that a woman who could organise the fund-raising for women's centres and keep the accounts for at least three charities had such a poor grasp of life's essentials.

'Because,' said Holly patiently, 'of this weekend. I need a new sweater, trainers, some hipsters, and I've seen this amazing mesh top, and – '

Angela put down her pen in exasperation and pushed back her chair. 'Holly, this is an activity weekend, not a session on the catwalks of Paris,' she said. 'You need trainers, I agree, but apart from that you can take what you've got.'

'Mum!' cried Holly. 'Get real! There's a disco on the Saturday night and, anyway, I can't wear things my friends have already seen.'

Not with Paul there, I can't, she thought. I need to

look sexy yet mysterious, trendy yet classic . . .

'OK,' compromised her mother. 'The shirt and the trainers. That is it.'

'You are,' said Holly, 'a very hard woman.'

8.10 a.m.
Perfect timing

Holly was hovering near the front door, checking her wristwatch to ensure that she left the house at precisely the right moment to bump into Paul, when the bell rang. She opened to door to find him standing on the step.

'Hi there,' he said. 'Listen, I was wondering. There's this film on tonight at MGM – *Spinnaker* – all about these guys who restore this tall ship and sail round the world and I thought, as you're keen on sailing . . .'

I am? thought Holly. Oh, yes. I am supposed to be, aren't I?

'. . . you might like to come. With me.'

Holly stood stock still, savouring the shiver that cascaded from her head to her toes. He'd done it. He'd acknowledged that he adored her. He'd asked her out.

'I'd love to,' she said.

'You would?' said Paul. 'Great. I was afraid you might still be going to that gig thing at The Danger Zone. My brother's really miffed that you couldn't get him a ticket.'

Sugar! thought Holly. I'd forgotten all about it. Suddenly the appeal of Shiny Vinyl paled into insignificance when compared to the allure of three hours with Paul. But she'd promised the others.

She opened her mouth. And closed it.

Jade wouldn't have managed to get the tickets. Not in a million years. And if she said no to Paul, only to find that Jade had messed up, she'd never forgive herself.

'No,' she said. 'It was a non-starter. What time do you want me?'

8.45 a.m.

Tansy was waiting for Holly at the school gates.

'Just wait till you see Jade!' she began the moment her friend drew within earshot. 'You won't believe it!'

Holly frowned. 'What do you mean? Is she in a miff because she couldn't get tickets?'

Tansy grinned. 'Oh, she got them all right!' She laughed. 'And how!'

Oh, thought Holly. Now what do I do?

'Come on – she's over there by the cycle park.' She set off across the playground. 'Hey, Jade!'

A girl with short hair the colour of rusty nails turned round.

Holly stopped dead in her tracks. 'Jade? Jade!' she gasped. 'Your hair – it's gone.'

'Very observant,' said Jade. 'Do you like it?'

Holly swallowed. 'It's . . . well, it's . . . very striking,' she said, not wanting to be unkind. 'But why? I'd die to have hair like yours . . . like yours was.'

Now you tell me, thought Jade.

'I was fed up with looking like a nerdy kid,' said Jade abruptly, wishing that Holly had sounded more enthusiastic. 'By the way, here's your ticket.'

Holly looked at it with some reluctance. She couldn't give up a night with Paul, and yet it was only because of her that the others were going to the gig. 'Oh, thanks,' she said.

'Is that it?' muttered Jade. 'Aren't you impressed?'

Holly nodded. 'Yes, well done,' she said.

'I think,' said Jade, 'it was the hair that clinched it.'

'I don't doubt it,' said Holly. 'Not for a moment.'

10.30 a.m.
Looking for a way out

I could always say I got a migraine at the last moment, thought Holly during chemistry. They'd never know. And it wouldn't be like letting anyone down. They'd have each other. I'll just ring Tansy at the last moment and sound ill. It won't matter.

11.15 a.m.
Should I, shouldn't I?

Grounded or not, I have to get out tonight, thought Jade. There's no way I can miss Shiny Vinyl. Not that I'm that desperate, especially as Scott's not going. But the others will think I'm chicken. Besides, they won't get in without me.

I wish I'd never opened my mouth in the first place.

12.45 p.m.
Forward planning over a pizza

'Right,' announced Tansy, as she tucked into a rapidly cooling slice of what the school called pizza. 'We need to get organised for tonight. I've told my mum we're going to the cinema and she said she'd drop me and Holly off. All we have to do is wait till she's gone and then zoom upstairs to The Danger Zone. Do you want a lift, Jade?'

Jade sighed. 'Right now, Paula is saying I can't go,' she said.

'Oh no!' gasped Tansy. 'You have to go – you're the one who's going to help bluff us all in.'

Jade fiddled with a piece of five-centimetre-long hair and thought yet again how bare she felt. 'Oh, don't worry,' she said, a lot more confidently than she felt, 'I'll sort Paula. I'll meet you all there. What about you, Cleo?'

I really don't want to do this, thought Cleo, scoffing a Danish pastry. She always ate when under stress.

'I'm not sure,' she began. 'It's not really my sort of thing.'

'Oh, don't be a weed!' said Tansy airily. 'Chill out, Cleo. It'll be a laugh.'

2.00 p.m.
Looking for guidance

Paula Webb stood beside the telephone and lifted the receiver.

Had she been too hard? She so wanted Jade to love her, but she couldn't let her get away with ruining her looks like that. David had said she had been too hard on her niece but surely the other mothers would have put their foot down too? Quite apart from the hair business, it was a school night.

'Oh, get on with it,' she told herself irritably. 'Just do it.'

She dialled the number and waited. Eventually a somewhat weary voice at the other end announced that this was Dunchester eight-six-four-five-three-five.

'Oh, Mrs Vine,' said Paula politely, 'this is Paula Webb, Jade's aunt . . . Yes, that's right.' She took a deep breath. 'Look, Jade tells me that the girls want to go to the cinema tonight and, well, I just wondered whether you really were going to let Holly go . . . You are? But I thought with homework and everything . . .'

She listened as Holly's mum held forth at some length about letting children take responsibility for their lives and the benefits of social intercourse before saying a polite goodbye and hanging up.

She tried Clarity Meadows, who said of course Tansy was going, which didn't surprise Paula because she had always had her doubts about Clarity's suitability as a parent. When Clarity suggested giving Jade a lift, Paula refused at once. No way was she letting her niece go anywhere in anyone else's car. You couldn't be too careful.

'No thanks, I can arrange something,' Paula said hastily. No way was she letting Jade go anywhere in Clarity Meadows' disreputable van.

I'll have to let her go tonight, she thought, walking to the sink and filling the kettle. I just hope she'll be all right. She's so vulnerable. Not that I'm handling any of it properly. I just look at her and I think of her mum and I want so much to say the right things and I can't. The words don't come.

I love Jade so much and sometimes I think she hates me. Oh, Lizzie, why did you have to die?

4.30 p.m.
Reprieved!

'Jade? Is that you?' Paula came out of the sitting room into the hallway as Jade opened the front door. 'Look, about tonight . . .'

Here we go, thought Jade. Another battle royal.

'. . . maybe I was a bit over the top,' continued Paula hurriedly. 'I'm disgusted about your hair – I think you were very foolish – but it's done now. You can go.'

Jade's face broke into a huge grin. 'Thanks, Paula. Thanks a lot.'

'But I'm taking you and fetching you,' she insisted firmly.

'Yes, Paula,' said Jade meekly.

She was going to Shiny Vinyl. Against all the odds, her street cred was intact for another day.

5.45 p.m.
Sick note

'Dunchester five-double-seven-zero-seven-eight. Tansy here!'

'Tansy, it's me – Holly.'

'Oh, hiya,' said Tansy. 'I'm just deciding what to wear. Do you think the purple satin skirt or those red – '

'I'm ill. I can't come,' moaned Holly, crossing her fingers firmly behind her back and hoping she sounded at the point of expiry. 'I've got a migraine.'

Tansy gasped. 'Bad luck!' she said. 'And you were so looking forward to it.'

'I know,' said Holly, sighing. 'Must go. I'll be thinking of you.'

Not, thought Holly.

7.05 p.m.
En route for disaster

'This is luxury!' said Tansy as she climbed into the Greenways' car. 'Thank goodness we didn't have to go in Mum's old van.'

'Sorry we're a bit late, Tansy!' said Cleo's mum as they drove away from her house. 'My agent phoned about the filming just as we were about to leave.'

Tansy looked impressed. 'Are you going to be in a film, Mrs Greenway?' she asked.

Diana laughed. 'I wish,' she said. 'No, I'm having a

screen test to appear in a series of adverts for those nice knickers.'

Cleo cringed. 'Knickers?' queried Tansy.

'Yes, dear, I'm going . . .' She frowned and pumped her foot up and down on the accelerator. 'What is wrong with this car? It's stopping.' She steered the car on to the hard shoulder. It stopped.

'Mum!' exclaimed Cleo in exasperation. 'You've run out of petrol.'

Mrs Greenway gazed at the petrol gauge as if it had personally insulted her. 'Well, how did that happen?' she asked.

'Probably by not filling the tank before you left,' said Cleo, checking her mobile and realising it had no credit.

'Oh, this is too irritating for words!' exclaimed her mother, opening the car door and clambering out. 'And I've left my mobile phone at home.' She stood at the edge of the roadside and began waving her arms in the air.

'Mum . . .' began Cleo.

'Don't worry, you won't miss the main film,' her mother replied. 'They always have adverts on for ages.'

Tansy and Cleo looked at one another. Never mind films. Shiny Vinyl were on in half an hour.

7.15 p.m.
Be sure your sins will find you out

'I'll meet you by the fountain at ten o'clock sharp,' said Paula. 'Be there.'

Jade ran into the cinema foyer and looked round for the others. She spotted Holly at the far side of the foyer talking to a guy Jade didn't recognise. Trust Holly to try chat-up lines at every opportunity.

'Hi, Holly! Come on, if we dash we'll just make it.' Holly spun round and stared at Jade open-mouthed. 'What are you doing here?' she said. 'You're supposed to be at the gig.'

'I thought you said it was a non-starter,' interrupted the guy. 'Hi, I'm Paul Bennett.'

Light began to dawn. Paul. The guy Holly fancied. 'Oh, great,' said Jade. 'So you're coming along too?' That would be good. He looked at least sixteen.

Paul looked bewildered. 'We're here to see *Spinnaker*.'

Holly was turning an interesting shade of puce and chewing her lip. 'Paul, can you just get me some popcorn? I'll be with you in a second.' She lowered her voice as Paul moved away.

'Holly, what's going on?' demanded Jade.

'I had to come,' Holly said with a pleading note in her voice. 'I mean, he's to die for, and if I'd said no – '

'He'd have asked you another time!' snapped Jade. 'Just let down all your friends, why don't you?'

She needed Holly there. Jade might have the new hairdo but Holly had enough attitude for all of them.

'Jade, don't be like that. This is love. I mean, the Real Thing. Like you and Scott.'

Huh! thought Jade. Scott isn't exactly pining to be with me every hour of the day.

'Look,' said Holly, as Paul reappeared with the

popcorn, 'you'd better go and find the others. See you!' And she dragged Paul off towards the entrance to Screen Two.

Jade was furious. How could Holly do this? And where were the others? She scanned the foyer but there was no sign of Cleo or Tansy.

Maybe they thought they were meeting upstairs at The Danger Zone. She'd just have to go there and hope they were waiting.

7.29 p.m.
Doing it alone

'Are you coming in or not?' The bouncer on the door was getting impatient. 'Once the band is on, we're closing the doors.'

Jade bit her lip. Maybe Cleo and Tansy were already inside. She'd murder Holly for this.

She waved her ticket in the man's face and was smugly satisfied to see that he didn't even blink an eye. She pushed through the doors and into the club. The lights were dim and the floor was a heaving mass of bodies. The warm-up band were thundering out a rock number as Jade tried desperately to spot her friends.

'Hi, sweetheart!' A tall guy with long hair and three nose studs laid a hand on her shoulder. Jade jumped, glared at him and pushed her way further through the throng. Everyone seemed much older than her, and several of them were smoking and swigging beer from cans. Jade felt very self-conscious. Everyone was pressing closer and closer to the stage. Maybe Tansy and Cleo had grabbed some good places. She edged her way nearer.

As she did so she brushed against a girl in a short black skirt and lime-green halter neck, gyrating in the arms of a broad-shouldered guy with floppy ginger hair.

It couldn't be. It was. Oh no!

She turned round to escape but someone bumped into her and she lost her footing, falling against the brown-haired girl as she did so.

'Hey, look where you're . . . Jade!'

It was too late. She'd seen her. Now she'd be for it. Most of her mates would keep their mouths shut.

But not her cousin Allegra.

7.30 p.m.
Havoc on the hard shoulder

Cleo thought she would die of embarrassment. Her mother was not fit to be allowed out on her own. She had actually stood at the side of the road, and started jumping up and down, waving her arms in the air at every passing motorist. After a few moments, a blue Granada had pulled up and Mrs Greenway had run up to the driver's door, wiggling her bottom in her white Levi's and beaming.

'I've been such a silly!' she shrilled in the sort of voice she had used when playing in Jeeves and Wooster.

'Could you possibly sort me out?'

'I'll sort her out if she carries on like that,' muttered Cleo to Tansy, as the driver wound down his window.

'Cleo! Look who it is!' Tansy burst into a fit of giggles.

Cleo peered through the windscreen. Heaving himself out of the driving seat and eyeing Diana Greenway with unnecessary interest was Mr Grubb.

'Beetle!' gasped Cleo. 'I can't bear it!'

'I think I'm out of petrol,' Diana was saying. 'Oh, Mr Grubb, dear, it's you!'

Cleo closed her eyes. What was she thinking of?

'Mrs Greenway!' Mr Grubb said, beaming. 'Girls!'

Tansy and Cleo gave him a sick sort of grin.

'Well now,' he said briskly. 'Not to worry. We'll siphon off a bit of petrol from my car.'

'You are a positive angel!' simpered Diana, flicking her hand through her hair in an actressy sort of way and smiling coyly.

'Only too pleased to help a star of stage and screen!' rejoined Mr Grubb, turning an interesting shade of ripe tomato. 'And what theatrical gem are you working on now?'

'I think,' Cleo muttered to Tansy, 'I am about to throw up.'

Mrs Greenway cocked her head to one side. 'Well,' she said, 'I hope to be doing a series of TV adverts, actually.'

'Indeed?' said Beetle, feeding the hose into the petrol inlet. 'And what delight will you be selling us?'

'Knickers,' giggled Diana.

Cleo cringed. Had her mother no shame at all? It was

bad enough to contemplate such behaviour, without telling the entire world about it.

'They say I have the right bottom for it,' Mrs Greenway added.

'Tansy,' said Cleo.

'Yes?'

'Tell me I'm dreaming. Tell me she didn't say that.'

Tansy grinned. 'I think it's wonderful,' she said.

Cleo gazed at her. 'Wonderful? You're mad.'

Tansy shook her head. 'It's a total relief to know that it isn't just my mum who is certifiable.'

7.35 p.m.
Double take

Allegra stared at Jade. Jade stared at Allegra.

'What are you doing here?' demanded Allegra. 'I thought you were supposed to be at the cinema.'

'And I thought you were supposed to be on a theatre trip,' rejoined Jade.

They stared at one another again.

'If you tell, I'll never ever speak to you again,' snapped Allegra.

'Tempting as that offer is,' said Jade, 'I am hardly likely to, am I?'

'You're not?'

Jade shook her head. 'Because if I did, she'd know I was here too, wouldn't she?'

They both smiled.

'Mum would kill me if she found out,' said Allegra. 'She used to be quite laid-back but lately she's got really uptight.'

Jade nodded. 'Tell me about it,' she said. 'She almost hyperventilated at the thought of me going to the cinema.'

Hugo shuffled at the side of her. 'Are we dancing or what?' he said.

'In a minute. Oh, this is Jade – you know, the cousin I was telling you about?'

Hugo eyed her with interest. 'Oh, hi! She doesn't look like a dweeb to me,' he added, turning to Allegra.

Allegra had the good grace to blush. 'She's not really,' she said hastily. 'She's improving.'

'Oh, thanks,' said Jade sarcastically.

The warm-up band was leaving the stage and everyone began pushing towards the front to get the best positions to hear Shiny Vinyl.

'Who are you with?' asked Allegra. 'Scott?'

Jade shook her head and told Allegra the whole story.

'So . . . you mean Mum is picking you up? Downstairs? But the gig ends at ten o'clock as well.'

'So?'

'What if she sees me? Hannah's mum is meeting us at the fountain too. Everyone meets there.' Allegra nibbled a fingernail and looked anxious.

At that moment, Shiny Vinyl came on stage. Everyone surged forward as they struck up the first number. Jade was squashed against Allegra and a huge girl with dangly earrings and BO.

For the next twenty minutes, Jade couldn't make

herself heard above the noise. It wasn't her sort of music and she was beginning to feel a bit panicky as people kept shoving and pushing against her. She turned to speak to Allegra and found that she had been pushed several metres away.

She was beginning to wish she hadn't come when a tall guy shot out his arm in time to the music and spilled beer all down her skirt.

'Oh no!' she gasped involuntarily. Now what? Paula would smell it a mile off. She just wanted to get out of there. It was smelly and hot, and she was getting a cracking headache and feeling queasy.

She glanced across to where Allegra was swaying to the beat, waving her arms in the air and clearly having a great time. If I tell her I'm going home, she'll think I'm a no-hoper, she thought. Mind you, if she starts picking on me I can always threaten to drop her in it. That gave Jade an idea. The band was coming to the end of the second number, and Jade took the chance to shove her way through to reach her cousin.

'Yuk!' said Allegra. 'You stink!'

'Precisely,' moaned Jade. 'Paula will suss immediately that I didn't get like this watching a film. And of course, if she does see you . . .'

Allegra pulled a face. 'Don't even talk about it,' she said.

'So,' said Jade, trying to sound as if she was doing Allegra a huge favour, 'I'm going home. I'll sponge my skirt down in the loo and then tell Paula I was sick or something. That way, I'm in the clear, she won't turn out to pick me up and you'll be off the hook as well.'

Allegra had watched her with ever-widening eyes as she spoke. 'That's a cool idea,' she said admiringly. 'But what about the gig? They're playing their number-one hit later on.'

Jade shrugged. 'I'm not that bothered about Shiny Vinyl,' she said. 'I only did it to prove that I'm my own person and not some nerdy kid to be bossed about. Just remember that, right?'

Allegra grinned and nodded. 'I don't reckon,' she said, 'that I'm likely to forget that in a hurry. I'll see you later. And Jade . . .'

'Yes?'

'I owe you one.'

9.00 p.m.
The best-laid plans . . .

'Paula,' she called, 'it's me – Jade.'

Paula emerged from the sitting room looking rather red-eyed and clutching a scrunched-up tissue.

'Jade?' she said with a watery smile. 'What are you doing back so soon? And your skirt . . .'

'I was sick,' said Jade.

'Oh dear . . .' began Paula, looking anxious.

'Could you pay the taxi? I didn't have enough.'

Paula opened the front door. 'How much?' she called to the driver.

'Four pounds fifty,' he shouted back.

'That seems an awful lot,' said Paula.

'Well, you see, luv, it's that new one-way system. From The Danger Zone you have to go all round the houses to get out of the town centre.'

Please don't let her have heard that, God. Please.

It seemed God was not listening. Paula virtually threw the money at the taxi driver and rounded on Jade.

'The Danger Zone!' she exploded, grabbing her elbow and propelling her back into the house. 'That sleazy down-at-heel dump in the Rainbow Centre? You went *there*?'

Jade decided to brazen it out. 'So what if I did?' she retorted. 'I'm home, aren't I? You want me to grow up. That's what I'm doing.'

Paula narrowed her eyes. 'You can grow up without going to places like that!' she stormed. 'Anything could have happened.'

'But it didn't,' said Jade.

'Well, something must have done for you to have got a cab home,' replied Paula. 'Have you been drinking? Is that it?'

'No it is not!' shouted Jade. 'Why do you always think badly of me?'

Paula put her hands to her head. 'I don't . . . it's just . . . you've changed, Jade. First this awful hair business and now going to the sort of place none of my kids would even think of frequenting . . .'

Jade wanted to tell her. To prove that she wasn't the only one fed up with being told what to do. Why should she take all the blame? But then, dropping Allegra in it wouldn't be fair and, besides, there was nothing Paula could do to her now.

'Well, you obviously need to be taught a lesson,' announced Paula. 'You are not going on this activity weekend and that is final.'

Jade stared at her. She couldn't mean it. She had to go.

'That's not fair!' she began. 'Everyone's going.'

'Everyone,' said Paula, 'except you. You have only yourself to blame. What's more, I shall go and see the head first thing tomorrow. Now go to bed.' She marched back into the sitting room and slammed the door.

'I hate you,' shouted Jade. 'I really, really hate you!' She turned and ran up the stairs, tears welling up in her eyes, and flung open her bedroom door. And stopped dead.

Standing by her bed, in a pink Winnie-the-Pooh dressing gown, was Nell. And in her hands was Jade's silver money box. And it was open.

'Don't tell, please don't tell!' the little girl whispered after Jade had removed the box and found three one-pound coins in Nell's dressing-gown pocket. 'I only borrowed it.'

Jade sat down beside her and put an arm round her shoulders.

'But why?' she asked. 'You have your own money – remember all that money you got from the grannies for your birthday?'

Nell sniffed. 'It's all gone,' she said.

Jade frowned. 'It can't have,' she protested. 'What did you buy?'

'Nuffin,' said Nell.

Jade was tired, fed up and furious with Paula for

being so mean. She didn't mean to snap but she couldn't help it. 'Oh, for heaven's sake, Nell,' she said. 'You've either spent it or you've got it. And either way you don't go round taking what doesn't belong to you. Now give it back and go to bed!' Nell rammed her thumb into her mouth and shuffled off the bed.

'And don't you ever do that again!' Jade said. 'Because next time I will tell!'

'That was pretty nice of you,' said Allegra an hour later, after she had woken Jade up by crashing into the bedroom and switching on all the lights. 'Thanks.'

Jade yawned. 'I hope it was worth it,' she said.

'Course it was – the band was just the best and Hugo kissed me. Twice. Life can't get any better than this.'

Jade sighed. 'Mine can't get any worse,' she said.

'Oh, Jade, don't start on about death again. Please.'

Jade shook her head. 'I'm not,' she said. 'It's Paula. She's grounded me for going to The Danger Zone. The taxi driver let it slip. She's even stopping me from going to Sussex.'

'Oh no!' exclaimed Allegra. 'She can't do that! It's not fair.'

Allegra cares about *me*? thought Jade in surprise.

'You *have* to go away this weekend. I've asked Hannah to sleep over. We need your bed.'

'Oh, great,' said Jade, coming back to reality. 'Thanks a million.'

THURSDAY

8.55 a.m.
Year Nine classroom. Baying for blood

'So what happened to you last night?' Jade accosted Tansy and Cleo as soon as they walked into the classroom.

Cleo looked apologetic. 'My mum's car ran out of petrol,' she said.

'Oh yes?' retorted Jade, who could only stop herself from crying by being snappy. 'That's about as feeble an excuse as Holly's migraine.'

'What do you mean?' asked Tansy, frowning.

'Holly was at the Multiscreen last night. With Paul.'

'She wasn't? Really? So you were at The Danger Zone on your own?'

Jade nodded. 'Thanks to you,' she said.

'Honestly, Jade, the car did run out of petrol,' Tansy said. 'Ask Beetle. He came to Mrs Greenway's rescue. I think he fancies her.'

'Who fancies who?' Holly appeared at Tansy's elbow.

Jade turned to face her. 'How's the migraine, Holly?' she asked.

Holly blushed. 'OK, OK, so I lied,' she said. 'But it was worth it. Paul's so gorgeous. And I shall have him for three whole days at the centre. I can't wait to get there, can you?'

'I'm not going,' said Jade, with a catch in her voice.

The three stared at her.

'What do you mean?' gasped Cleo.

'I'm grounded. And it's all your fault. I hope you're all satisfied.'

10.45 a.m.
Feelings of guilt

'Well, it's not our fault Cleo's mum ran out of petrol,' Tansy insisted. 'But you shouldn't have ditched Jade just because you had a better offer. If you'd been there, she wouldn't have gone home early and she wouldn't be grounded now.'

Holly looked abject. 'I know, I'm sorry,' she said. 'Do you really think Mrs Webb will stop Jade going to Sussex?'

Tansy shrugged. 'Sounds like it,' she said. 'Cleo saw her going into Plank's study when she was fetching some graph paper.'

Holly took a deep breath. 'Maybe we should do something.'

'*We?*' chorused Tansy and Cleo in unison.

'OK then, me,' said Holly.

10.50 a.m.
Head to head

'Mrs Webb, how nice to see you. Do please sit down.' Mr Boardman gestured to an ancient leather armchair. 'Now what can I do for you?'

Jade's aunt took a deep breath. 'It's Jade,' she said. 'I'm afraid I've said she can no longer go on the school trip.'

The head teacher clasped his hands together, inclined his head enquiringly to one side and said nothing.

'She's been very defiant lately,' Paula continued, fiddling self-consciously with an earring. 'She went against my instructions and had this terrible haircut . . .'

'Ah yes, the hair,' murmured Mr Boardman. 'I had spotted that. A little alarming, isn't it?'

Mrs Webb nodded. 'Frightful,' she said. 'And then last night she told me she was going to the cinema and ended up at The Danger Zone, which she knew I wouldn't approve of.'

'Dear me,' said Mr Boardman, as mildly as if Paula had announced that Jade had nipped into Safeway for a can of lemonade.

'So I told her straight that it wasn't good enough and the weekend trip was off,' concluded Paula.

'I see,' murmured Mr Boardman.

'I'm glad you agree,' said Paula, picking up her bag.

'Oh, but I don't,' said the head teacher.

Jade's aunt looked at him in amazement. 'You don't?'

'Oh no,' he said. 'Everything you have told me points to just one thing.'

'What?' demanded Paula.

'That Jade must most definitely come on the school trip.'

10.55 a.m.

'Will this do?' Holly shoved a piece of paper under Tansy's nose. 'I thought the hopeful anticipation bit had rather a nice ring to it,' she observed.

> Dear Mrs Webb,
> I know that Jade is in trouble for going to The Danger Zone but the only reason you found out was because I let her down, and she was fed up and decided to go home early. Please let her come on the activity weekend – she's one of my best friends and, besides, she's had a rough time lately and it will cheer her up.
>   By the way she doesn't know I am writing this so please don't think she set me up.
>   Yours very sincerely and in hopeful anticipation,
>   Holly Vine

'It's good,' conceded Tansy. 'How will you get it to her?'
'She must still be with Mr Boardman,' said Holly. 'I'll hand it to reception and they can give it to her when she hands back her security pass.'
'That's brilliant!' said Tansy.
'I know,' said Holly.

10.57 a.m.

'So you see, Mrs Webb, this sort of weekend is just what

Jade needs. She has to express her grief and her frustrations and obviously she is finding that hard to do at home.'

Paula flung him an angry stare. 'So you're saying I'm not providing her with the right environment, not being loving enough, not – '

Mr Boardman held up his hand.

'Mrs Webb, I'm saying nothing of the sort. But you must be suffering too. The loss of a sister is a terrible thing.'

To Paula's horror, she felt her eyes filling with tears. She grabbed a tissue from her handbag.

'Death affects people in so many different ways,' said Mr Boardman calmly, pretending not to notice Paula's distress. 'Some of us get angry, others try to pretend it never happened and bury it deep inside. But for everyone, it must come out some time, some way.' He paused. 'Can I get you a glass of water?'

'I'm fine,' Jade's aunt said hurriedly. 'It's not easy taking another child into the family, but I love her, and I do want the best for her.'

Mr Boardman smiled. 'Then trust me. Send her to Downsview with us. You'll be surprised at what it does for her.'

11.05 a.m.
Touch lines

Paula strode across the car park and opened the door of her Metro. Slumping down in the driver's seat, she leaned back, closed her eyes and took a deep breath.

Fancy almost making a fool of herself like that. She was over all the weeping bit. She'd put it all behind her. Hadn't she?

She tore open the letter that the receptionist had handed to her. As she scanned the contents, her eyes filled with tears again.

Jade had a friend rooting for her. A friend who was prepared to own up for her sake. Even if the head teacher hadn't persuaded her to change her mind, that letter would have done.

Turning the key in the ignition, she reversed the car out of the car park.

'Oh, Lizzie,' she said, biting her lip. 'I miss you so much.'

And this time, the tears did fall.

4.00 p.m.
The bottom line

'Do you think you have to do every activity?' Cleo asked Trig anxiously as they walked home together.

'I doubt it,' said Trig. 'I reckon if you find one you're good at, they'd let you stick at that.'

'I won't be good at any of it,' moaned Cleo. 'I'll be totally useless and everyone will laugh.'

Trig turned to face her. 'I won't laugh,' he said. 'I'm dreading it too.'

Cleo wanted to hug him. Most guys would have

pretended to be a macho man but Trig was so upfront.

'Do you want to come in for a bit?' suggested Cleo as they reached her house.

'OK,' said Trig. 'But not for long. I have to pack.'

Cleo unlocked the front door. 'Come through and get a drink,' she said. 'Then we could – '

'TA-RAR!' The lounge door flew open and Diana Greenway leaped out, arms outstretched in dancer mode. 'What do you think, darling?' She wriggled her bottom. 'How could they choose anyone else? I reckon it's a – oh. Ah. Hello, Trig.'

Cleo stood stock still. Behind her Trig swallowed and turned his eyes to examine the watercolour hanging on the wall.

Mrs Greenway was dressed in a pair of lilac knickers, adorned with small green frogs. She had on a matching bra. And nothing else.

Since she was an actress and, thought Cleo, a woman totally without shame, her mum recovered immediately.

'Fittinix – Your Firmup Friend,' she trilled, whipping a raincoat off the hall coat-stand and wrapping it over her shoulders. 'Such fun!' And with that she ran upstairs, still giggling.

'You know,' said Cleo, 'I am looking forward to this weekend after all.'

'You are?' queried Trig in surprise.

'Yes,' said Cleo. 'Anything has to be an improvement on living with a manic mother.'

4.15 p.m.
53 Lime Avenue. Saying nothing

There's Jade now, thought Paula as the front door slammed. I've got to get this right. Please let me say it right.

'Hello, darling,' she said brightly. 'Look, I went to see Mr Boardman . . .' she began.

'Oh, terrific,' muttered Jade. 'I suppose you sat there and told each other what was wrong with me.'

'No, darling, actually he . . . I . . . we decided you should go on this weekend trip,' she said.

Jade's face lit up. 'Really? Oh, thanks, Paula!'

'Wait – I haven't finished.'

I have to talk about Lizzie. I have to tell her that I'm hurting too. I can't. I'll cry. And that wouldn't help her at all, would it?

'Yes?' urged Jade.

'Nothing.'

5.00 p.m.
Saying even less

Jade was finishing her packing and wondering whether her lilac strappy slip dress would be too over the top for the disco, when she heard Nell talking to herself in the next room.

She frowned, crept on to the landing and peeped round Nell's door. Nell was sitting on her bed, with a doll in her lap. And she was shaking it furiously.

'You stupid little kid! Baby! Little wimp!'

'Nell!' Jade exclaimed. 'What are you doing?'

Nell looked up, pressed her lips together and said nothing.

And suddenly Jade knew. She was absolutely certain. She looked at the little girl's face and saw the fear in her eyes.

'Nell, someone is being horrible to you, aren't they?' she said. 'And they've told you not to tell.'

Nell's eyes widened and Jade could see the battle going on inside her head.

'Well, that's OK,' she said, 'because you haven't told me, have you? I've guessed. So when you're ready to give me some more clues, you do that.'

Nell's eyes filled with tears. She took a deep breath. Now she'll tell me, thought Jade.

'Yes,' she urged. 'Who is it? Who's being horrid?'

'No one,' said Nell.

FRIDAY

11.00 a.m.
Here we go, here we go, here we go

'Why are we waiting? Why-y are we waiting?'

The coach was stuck in a queue of traffic in Brighton and several of the boys had started chanting in impatience.

Jade had her nose glued to the window. The nearer they had got to Brighton, the more memories had come flooding back. Jack and Jill windmills where they used to go for picnics when she was small; the Brendon riding stables where she had fallen off Toffee the Shetland pony and knocked out her front tooth.

'That's where I used to live! Look, up there!'

The coach was gathering speed as they passed the bottom of Kemp Hill. Jade craned her neck to catch sight of her old house but a lorry overtaking them got in the way.

'And my gran lives round that corner!' she said, although no one was taking much notice.

The only other person who was taking any interest in what was going on out of the coach window was Andy. He didn't say a word, but Tansy, who was observing him closely, had a pretty good idea what he was thinking.

She wished she could conjure his mother up out of thin air, if only to take the sadness out of his eyes.

11.30 a.m.
Arrival at Downsview

'It's massive!' Holly breathed as the coach turned through wrought-iron gates and up the gravelled driveway of the Downsview Centre.

Ahead of them stood a rambling grey-stone house with turrets at either end and dozens of mullioned windows glinting in the sun. In front of the house was a wide expanse of lawn dotted with croquet hoops, and to the side lay tennis courts and another lawn with archery targets at the far end.

'Look at that lake!' said Scott. 'It's huge!'

'That's Pitsley Reservoir,' said Miss Partridge, 'where some of you will have the chance to try canoeing and dinghy sailing.'

A number of butterflies gathered in the pit of Cleo's stomach.

'And just beyond are Weir Rocks,' interjected Mr Grubb enthusiastically. 'That's where you shall be going for climbing and abseiling.'

The butterflies took on new recruits and assembled for action.

'Right, everyone,' said Miss Partridge, clapping her hands, 'here we are at Downsview. Bishop Agnew College have rooms in the main building and we are in the Stable Block. A quick lunch and then off to your first challenge. Dinghy sailing for Group A . . .'

Cleo's butterflies took off and flew in formation. She wished she had never come.

2.00 p.m.
I am sailing, I am . . .

'It's awfully windy, isn't it?' said Cleo nervously as they stood at the edge of the reservoir after the first hour of their basic on-shore training.

'It has to be for sailing,' said Holly, scanning the group of Bishop Agnew kids who were already on the water in dinghies. 'There's Paul – look!'

'Right,' said Graham, the senior instructor. 'These little Toppers are what everyone learns to sail in.' He gestured to what appeared to be a floating soap dish.

'What – on our own?' gasped Cleo.

Graham grinned. 'John and Tim here will be in rescue boats at your side – no harm can come to you. Now, who's going first?'

'Me!' cried Holly. She could just imagine herself whipping over the waves and coming alongside Paul, whose eyes would light up with love and passion.

She stepped into the tiny little dinghy and one of the instructors climbed into the motorised rescue boat.

'Right, three more volunteers, please – Cleo, Trig and Ursula!'

Cleo felt sick. 'I'm scared,' she said to Holly as she clambered clumsily into the boat.

'Don't be,' said Holly. 'I'll be nearby.'

This is meant to make me feel better? wondered Cleo.

One of the junior instructors pushed her off from the shingle shoreline. The wind caught the small sail and the little boat gathered speed.

Holly was trying to keep an eye on Paul's boat but the sun was in her eyes and she couldn't really see where she was going. It did feel very unstable. She tried to remember what the instructor had told her. Maybe she should lean the other way.

There again . . . perhaps not.

She looked wildly round to see where the others were. Not that she was scared or anything – just to reassure Cleo that everything was OK. Cleo was bowling along in a straight line, her face screwed up in concentration, and there was another, larger dinghy coming towards her. Very fast. How did you move these things out of the way?

Which rope was she meant to pull? This one? She tugged on the mainsheet and the little boat leaned.

The other boat got nearer. It was Paul. He'd obviously seen her. Her heart pounded. He was leaning back off the side of the boat, like the pictures she had seen in magazines, looking lean and athletic. She adopted the same pose, hoping she looked sporty and rather sultry. Out of the corner of her eye she could see the instructor waving at her from the rescue boat. She waved back.

The boat leaned. Holly tried to sit up. And slipped. The water was very cold. As she struggled to the surface, spitting a strand of green weed from her mouth, she saw two faces peering down at her.

One was the instructor, looking a little anxious. The other was Paul. And he was laughing hysterically.

3.00 p.m.

Jade and the pony eyed one another closely.

It was difficult to tell who was the more suspicious.

Scott was already sitting casually on top of a chestnut pony with milky eyes and a bored expression, and several Bishop Agnew kids were filing off across the field. She couldn't put it off any longer.

The instructor gave her a leg-up and Jade clutched the reins. It seemed an awfully long way up.

'I'll take you on the lead rein for a bit,' said the instructor. 'Just till you get the hang of it.'

The countryside was beautiful. Gradually Jade began to relax and look at the scenery around her. In the distance the sea glimmered in the late afternoon sun and she could hear the faint cry of angry seagulls cresting the air currents.

It was as they crossed the country lane outside the Centre that Jade spotted the sign – *Cycle track: Brighton four miles*.

Four miles! That was hardly any distance. She wished she had her bike with her. She hadn't ridden it much since moving to Dunchester because Paula worried about traffic and accidents, but she was pretty fit and it wouldn't have taken her any time at all to get into the town. Not that she would have been allowed out.

She sighed. She did want to see her old house. If she closed her eyes she could picture her mother standing in the tiny front garden, fussing over her hollyhocks and delphiniums, and hear her dad teasing and saying that anyone would think it was Kew Gardens, the time she spent in it. Jade's mum always said that if she couldn't have a country cottage, at least she could have a cottage garden. The very day she was killed, she had planted a new rose bush that Dad had given her for an anniversary present. Elizabeth of Glamis, it was called, but Dad had changed the label and written '*Lizzie of My Heart*', which Jade thought was so romantic for an old person.

'Right,' said the instructor, breaking into her thoughts, 'we'll try a trot.'

After that there was no time for thinking about roses or anything else.

3.30 p.m.

'I can't believe I survived that,' said Cleo to Trig as they hauled the boats ashore.

'It was cool,' agreed Trig.

'It was terrifying,' protested Cleo. 'But at least I'm in one piece, unlike poor Holly. She does look a bit bedraggled.'

'Who's the guy with her?' asked Trig.

'I think it must be Paul,' said Cleo. 'She really fancies him. I bet she's dying of shame.'

3.32 p.m.

'I thought,' Paul was saying to Holly, 'that you could sail?'

'So I lied,' muttered Holly, mortified at having made

a fool of herself in front of the one guy she needed to impress.

'You do a lot of that, don't you?' said Paul.

Holly looked abject.

'Only teasing,' he said. 'Are you OK?'

Holly nodded. 'I can't see what went wrong. You leaned back out of your boat and nothing happened.'

Paul burst out laughing. 'You really don't know a thing about sailing, do you?' he said. 'Mine was a Laser and I had a harness on. You don't do that sort of thing in a Topper.'

'I don't think,' said Holly ruefully, 'that I shall do anything in any sort of boat ever again.'

6.00 p.m.
Evening agony

'I don't think,' said Jade to Tansy as they filed into supper, 'that I shall ever sit down in comfort again.'

'Tell me about it,' grinned Tansy. 'I did rock climbing with Andy and my neck is killing me.'

'Your neck?' interjected Cleo, who was wondering whether there were any totally safe activities left to try the next day. 'You don't use your neck to hold a rope.'

Tansy grinned. 'I kept looking up at Andy's legs,' she said. 'He does have lovely thighs, you know.'

Holly sighed. 'Paul has lovely everything,' she said, 'but he will probably never speak to me again. Fate is very cruel.'

Jade and Cleo exchanged a wry smile. Holly's immersion in Pitsley Reservoir had done nothing to dampen down her sense of the dramatic.

6.05 p.m.
Failed connections

Jade fed her money into the payphone and dialled her grandmother's number.

The phone rang and rang. No reply. Maybe Gran's flight had been delayed. Or maybe the plane had crashed and Gran was . . . No, that was silly. Gran would be fine. Jade just hoped she would get the chance to try calling her again.

11.00 p.m.
Creepy conversation

The four girls lay in their sleeping bags in the darkened room.

'Do you think,' asked Holly sleepily, 'that this place is haunted?'

'Could be,' agreed Tansy. 'The house is very old.'

'But this is the stable block,' said Cleo, who didn't enjoy talk of ghosts. 'So it won't be.'

'It might,' persisted Holly. 'Maybe one of the grooms had a secret love affair with the mistress of the house and was banished for ever and now he roams what used to be the tack room in search of his forbidden love.'

'Or,' continued Tansy, taking up the theme, 'the lord of the manor is so furious that his house has been turned into an activity centre for modern kids that he paces the place every night intent on wreaking havoc.'

Cleo wriggled further down into her sleeping bag.

'Do you think dead people really do come back?' she whispered in a rather small voice.

'I wish they did,' said Jade. After that no one said any more about ghosts.

1.30 a.m.

A loud scream woke Tansy and Jade with a start. It was Cleo. 'Cleo, Cleo, wake up, you're dreaming!' Tansy shook her arm.

Cleo opened her eyes. 'Oh sorry, sorry, I . . .' Tears were pouring down her face.

'Did you have a nightmare?' asked Tansy anxiously.

'I'll put the light on,' said Jade, wriggling out of her sleeping bag. Holly snored on oblivious.

Cleo shook her head and wiped her eyes on the corner of her pyjama jacket. 'No, don't, I'm fine,' she assured her. 'Silly of me. Sorry.'

'There's nothing silly about dreams,' said Jade. 'I have them all the time.'

Tansy nodded. 'They're supposed to be very good for you.'

This kind of good I can do without, thought Cleo,

lying down and trying to blank out the terrifying images. It was as she was beginning to fall asleep that she realised that her worst fear had come true. She'd had a nightmare in front of her friends. And none of them seemed the slightest bit fazed.

SATURDAY

10.30 a.m.
Feeling terrified

Cleo was halfway up a rock and didn't dare look down
to see how far she had come, or up to see how far there
was still to go. Her arms ached and her head was
spinning. Above her Trig was laughing. Below her Tansy
was telling everyone that she was having a blast. Why am
I the only one who wishes she wasn't here? she thought,
hanging on for dear life.

11.45 a.m.
Feeling resigned

'Oh, very Maid Marion!' giggled Tansy as Cleo picked
up an arrow and aimed it at the target.

I'll be useless at this too, thought Cleo. 'You go first,'
she said to Tansy.

Tansy let fly an arrow. It veered off at an angle and
disappeared behind a laurel bush.

Oh well, thought Cleo, it won't just be me that
messes up this time. Here goes.

1.00 p.m.
Feeling smug

By lunchtime, Cleo was elated. She'd done it! She'd found something she was good at.

OK, so archery wasn't a daredevil sport and it probably wasn't very sexy. But she could do it! Miss Partridge had been very impressed when all Cleo's arrows hit the target. Tansy spent the whole hour in the bushes hunting for hers although the fact that Andy was doing the same thing probably had something to do with it. Cleo had done better than anyone. She felt she could take on the world.

1.25 p.m.
Escape route

Halfway through lunch, Mr Grubb rapped on the table and asked for silence.

'This afternoon,' he said, 'you have four hours of free time. Not for idling about, mind you. You can canoe, play croquet, take a mountain bike along the cycle tracks . . .'

Jade stopped, her forkful of apple crumble poised in mid-air. Bikes. Four hours was quite a long time.

'No one is to leave the site and I want you all back here by six o'clock sharp.'

Yes, but he'd never know if she left the site, would he? Not if she was really careful. Could she do it? If she got found out, she'd be in big trouble. But by then, she would have been able to talk to her gran and persuaded her to let her come back and live with her. And all the trouble in the world was worth that.

She'd do it. She wouldn't tell anyone, not even Scott. This was something she had to do completely on her own.

2.00 p.m.
Caught in the act

It had been surprisingly easy to slip out of the grounds. Jade had ridden a couple of times round the garden track and then dodged behind some big clumps of rhododendrons until the other bikers had headed off on one of the three tracks. Then she pushed the bike through a gap in the hedge and on to the road.

She rammed her denim jacket in the saddle bag and stopped to adjust the strap on her safety helmet.

'Where are you off to?'

The voice behind her caused her to jump out of her skin. She turned, her heart pounding. It was Andy.

'Oh, it's you!' she exclaimed in relief. 'I'm . . . er . . . I'm just looking for the cycle track.'

Andy grinned. 'And I'm looking for wild elephants,' he said. 'Where are you really going?'

Jade sighed. 'You won't let on? You have to promise.'

'On my mother's life,' said Andy.

'Don't ever, ever say that!' shouted Jade, and Andy stepped back in surprise. 'You don't know what you're saying.'

Andy's eyes dropped. 'Actually I do,' he said quietly. 'I'm sorry if I was tactless. I forgot about your parents. But my mum disappeared and I haven't seen her for a year.'

Jade gulped. 'I didn't know,' she said. 'I'm sorry.' And she told him her plan.

'I was trying to find a bus stop,' said Andy, pulling the postcard from his jeans pocket. 'Mum sent this – it's from Brighton – and then when we came here instead of Dorset it seemed like an omen and I just thought, maybe . . .' His voice trailed off. 'Go on, tell me I'm stupid.'

Jade shook her head. 'You're not – but I guess there won't be many buses on a country lane like this.' She made a quick decision. 'Get a bike and come with me. I'll wait for you round the corner.'

2.45 p.m.

The ride into Brighton had been easy. Most of it had been downhill or on the flat and once they hit the town centre, there were marked cycle paths which meant they didn't have to worry about the traffic.

'I'm going to walk along the seafront,' said Andy. 'Just in case.'

Jade nodded. 'Suppose we meet back here at half-past four. That should give us heaps of time to cycle back.'

Andy nodded and climbed back on his bike.

'I hope you find your mum,' she said.

'I don't expect I will, but I had to try,' said Andy. 'Do you know what I mean?'

Jade smiled. 'Yes,' she said, 'I know exactly what you mean.'

2.55 p.m.
Memories are made of this

Jade turned the corner into Kemp Hill and jumped off her bike, looking expectantly up at number eight. And stopped stock still in the middle of the road.

'No!' she cried out loud. 'No!'

Gone was her mother's immaculate little garden. Gone was the white-painted gate and the chain-link fence. Instead of the crowded flower bed and a pocket-sized lawn, there was a stretch of cream paving slabs and one solitary tub of flowers. A rusting bicycle leaned against the wall and a child's doll with one arm missing lay abandoned by three empty milk bottles. All that was left was the rose bush Dad had given Mum, standing bedraggled by the front gate.

She went to take a closer look. And caught her breath. Hanging from the stem, faded and torn, was a label. She fingered it. '*Lizzie of My Heart. All my love, darling, Robert.*'

Jade's heart missed a beat. Her chest ached. She couldn't even cry.

'Oh, Dad,' she whispered. 'Oh, Mum.'

She crept up to the front window and peered in. The carpet and curtains were still the same. But now there was striped wallpaper and a posh border, and the wonky bookshelves which Dad had put up two Christmases ago had been taken down and a pine bookcase stood in their place.

She was just wondering whether she dared peep through the letter box when she heard voices behind her.

'Hey, Faith, who's that?'

'Excuse me, but what do you think you are doing?' A hand landed on Jade's shoulder and, with a jolt, she spun round. A tall girl of about fifteen with auburn hair in a ponytail was regarding her severely.

'Sorry,' Jade muttered. 'I was . . . just looking.'

'Oh, and you make a habit of peering into other people's houses, do you?' retorted the girl with her.

Jade knew that voice. She turned. 'Tanya!'

The girl stared at her. 'Do I know . . . Jade! I didn't recognise you! Your hair!'

Jade shrugged. 'I know, I know, not my best decision,' she said. 'Oh, it's so good to see you! How are you?'

'Fine,' said Tanya. 'Faith, this is Jade. You know, I told you about her. She used to live in your house.'

Jade gasped. 'You live here?' she said. 'So it's your family that have absolutely ruined the garden.'

The girl nodded and gave a wry smile. 'I know, it is a shame, isn't it?' she said.

'A shame?' cried Jade. 'My mum worked flat out on that garden. She loved it. This concrete – it's horrid!'

Tanya laid a hand on her arm. 'OK, Jade, don't go on!' she said. 'It's not your house any more. They can do whatever they like with it. And they had a good reason.'

Jade glowered. 'Oh, like what?'

Faith looked her in the eye. 'Like my little sister,' she said. 'She has muscular dystrophy. She's in a wheelchair. We couldn't get the chair through the gate and there was nowhere for her to sit and watch people going by. Now there is.'

Jade felt awful. She hated it when people spoke about her family without thinking, and now she'd done the same.

'I'm sorry,' she said. 'I didn't realise. I was just cross because my mum . . . well, anyway, it was thoughtless of me.'

Faith smiled. 'It's OK,' she said. 'I suppose it's hard for you coming back and finding it all changed. Do you want to come in and look around?'

For a second, Jade was tempted to say yes. She wanted to see her old bedroom. But then she changed her mind. It would almost certainly be different and, after all, Tanya was right. It wasn't her home any more. She didn't belong.

'No thanks.' She turned to Tanya. 'Shall we go for a coffee and catch up on the news?'

Her friend shook her head. 'Sorry – can't. Me and Faith are going to this brill new disco that's opened on the pier and I have absolutely zilch to wear. I have to do some serious shopping. Good to see you, Jade.'

Jade felt hollow. She'd always been Tanya's best friend. Now it seemed she had someone new.

'Write, won't you?' Jade called after her. 'And come up to stay?'

But Tanya was already too far down the hill to hear.

3.30 p.m.

'Anyone seen Jade?' Scott wielded his croquet mallet and whacked a ball through one of the hoops.

Tansy shook her head.

'I think she took a bike out,' she said. 'She'll be somewhere on one of the cycle tracks.'

'Cool,' said Scott. 'When I've thrashed you at this, I'll get one and catch her up. I need to talk to her.'

Tansy raised an eyebrow. 'Chat-up time again, is it?' she said teasingly.

'Get lost,' muttered Scott.

3.40 p.m.
Warm welcome

As Jade cycled round the corner into Buckingham Street, she realised that before she got to her grandmother's house she needed a plan. For one thing, she had to hide the bike. Her gran, Charlotte, was great fun but she was a stickler for doing the right thing, and if she found out that Jade had bunked off from a school trip, she would go ballistic. She'd have to tell her that she had come down from Dunchester by train to surprise her. That would explain why she couldn't stay long.

She leaned the bicycle against the side of a bus shelter, smoothed her spiky hair and rang her grandmother's door bell.

'Jade! My darling! Oh . . . oh, what a wonderful surprise!'

Jade was enveloped in a bear-like hug and squeezed until she could hardly breathe.

'Oh, Gran, it's so good to see you! I've missed you so much.'

Her grandmother held her at arm's length. 'Look at you!' she said. 'So grown up. Like the haircut.'

Jade blinked. 'You do?' she said.

'Not really,' her grandmother said, grinning, 'but one doesn't like to seem elderly. One has to be – what do you call it? – trendy.'

Jade grinned. 'You are,' she said. Jade's grandmother had once been something rather big in the City and still dressed in elegant suits and heeled shoes and went to cocktail parties where, if Dad was to be believed, she got exceedingly talkative on Pimm's.

'Now, where are David and Paula? Parking the car?' She ushered Jade into the narrow hallway.

'They didn't come,' said Jade. 'I came alone.'

Her grandmother looked concerned.

'On the train? On your own? Oh, darling, I don't know that I like – but still, here you are and it's lovely to see you. Let's make some tea and have a good old chat.'

4.00 p.m.

Andy kicked at an empty cola can and gazed out over the choppy sea. He had been an idiot. Fancy even thinking there was any point looking for his mother in a huge town like this. He had walked from the Peace

Memorial all the way along to Palace Pier and back, pushing his bike and scanning the crowds for the tall, elegant shape of his mum. Nothing.

He wondered how Jade was getting on. At least she knew her grandmother would be there, warm and welcoming and safe. He felt a lump come to his throat. At fourteen he shouldn't cry, especially in public. It was OK for Ricky – no one minded if a seven-year-old sobbed his heart out. There were times when Andy thought it must be very nice to be little.

4.15 p.m.
Heart to heart

'And so, you see, I really do want to come and live with you.'

Her grandmother picked up the teapot and calmly poured out another cup. 'Darling, that wouldn't do. It wouldn't do at all.'

Jade stared at her. 'What do you mean?' she gasped. 'I wouldn't be any trouble, honestly.'

Charlotte smiled. 'Darling, it's not that. For one thing, you need to be with young people your own age and, for another, I won't be here.'

Jade was aghast. 'What do you mean?' she cried.

Her grandmother took her hand. 'After your father died, I was devastated,' she said. 'That's why I went to stay with Alice in America – to escape the memories, to avoid seeing your house every day.'

Jade nodded. 'I saw it,' she said. 'It looks horrible.'

'Things change,' said her gran calmly. 'Anyway, in the States I had a great time. Oh, don't get me wrong – not a day went by without my thinking of Rob and Lizzie, and missing you – but I had so many new experiences. I even went white-water rafting,' she added smugly.

'At your age!' Jade exclaimed.

'Excuse me,' said her grandmother. 'Seventy-two may seem ancient to you but I'm not quite ready for the rocking chair and slippers yet.'

Jade laughed despite herself.

'I want to go back,' her gran said. 'Not for good – just for a few months each year. I can't afford to do that and live here, so I'm selling up and taking a one-bedroom flat in Hove. So you see, angel, there would be no room for you anyway.'

Jade looked crestfallen.

'And just think, you've got those lovely friends you wrote to me about – Holly, isn't it? And Cleo?'

Jade nodded. 'Yes, they're cool,' she admitted. 'It's Paula that's the problem. She won't talk about things. I mean, it's as if she's forgotten all about Mum. I thought they were really close.'

'Oh, they were,' agreed her gran. 'Paula really leaned on Lizzie. I think your auntie must be missing your mum terribly.'

'So why won't she talk about it?' persisted Jade.

'Maybe,' said her gran, 'she's scared to show how much it hurts. Maybe you have to make her talk.'

Jade nodded thoughtfully.

'I think,' said her gran, 'these might help.' She opened her bureau and took out a brown envelope. It was stuffed full of pictures. 'They were in your mum's cabinet,' she said.

Jade opened the envelope and took out a handful of photographs. There was one of her mum in a Guide uniform with Paula as a very shy-looking Brownie at her side, and another of Jade as a tiny baby, asleep in Paula's arms.

She touched them with her forefinger. 'Oh, Gran,' she breathed.

'Take them. They're yours. And they might just be what you need.'

4.40 p.m.

Andy stood at the corner of Western Road, tapping his foot and eyeing his watch anxiously. Where was Jade? If they didn't get moving soon, they'd be late back and then there really would be trouble.

What a wasted afternoon. He wished he had asked Tansy to come. Then he might not feel quite so alone.

4.45 p.m.
Time flies

Three slices of flapjack and a cream bun later, Jade glanced up at the clock. Four forty-five!

'Gran, I have to go!' she said, leaping to her feet. 'I'll miss the train.'

Her grandmother stood up. 'Come down soon, darling – for a whole weekend. I'll talk to Paula.'

Jade nodded and gave her a hug. 'I do love you. Gran,' she said.

'And I love you too. And remember, never forget the past but don't let it cloud the future. Bye, darling!'

4.48 p.m.
Missing property

Jade tore up to the bus shelter and stopped. She looked frantically from left to right.

The bike had gone.

It couldn't have! She slumped against the wall. What now? She couldn't go back to her grandmother and admit the truth. But how would she get back?

Then she remembered Andy, who must be wondering where she was. She could ride back to Downsview on the back of his bike. They wouldn't make it on time but maybe no one would notice.

Sending up a silent prayer that Beetle and Birdie wouldn't be on the ball tonight, and not daring even to contemplate how she would explain a missing bike, she flew down the hill.

4.50 p.m.
A face in the crowd

I'll give her five more minutes, thought Andy. And then I'll go. He glanced along the road to see if she was coming.

And that was when he saw her in the distance, pushing her way through the late-afternoon shoppers. Tall and elegant. In the sunflower-patterned dress that Ricky called her happy dress. His mum.

Heart racing, he grabbed his bike, leaped astride and began pedalling along the road. The woman turned to look in a department-store window.

'Mum! Mum!' he cried, his voice choking in his excitement. 'Wait! It's me!'

4.51 p.m.

Jade belted round the corner into Western Road and dashed up to the doorway where she and Andy had agreed to meet.

He wasn't there.

He must have got fed up with waiting and gone without her.

Now she was going to be found out. Not only would she be in trouble for bunking off, but she'd lost a valuable bicycle and you could bet your life the school would make Paula pay and then she'd like Jade even less.

She leaned against the shop window, suddenly feeling alone and scared and stupid. She'd have to go back to Gran's house and tell her the truth. Two tears trickled down her chin.

'My dear, what is it?' A tall woman in a dress covered with orange sunflowers looked down at her. 'Are you in trouble?'

Jade shook her head and sniffed. 'My bike was stolen,' she muttered. 'I'm OK.'

She was about to move away when she saw Andy belting up on his bike. He leaped off, totally ignoring her and grabbed the woman's arm. 'Mum!' he cried.

The woman turned, an astonished expression on her immaculately made-up features.

'Mum, it's . . . oh. Oh. Sorry. I thought you were someone else.'

4.53 p.m.
Back at base

'I don't understand it,' said Scott, as they queued at the drinks machine. 'I've cycled three times round each track and I can't find her anywhere.'

Holly frowned. 'I didn't see her either,' she said.

'Well,' said Cleo, 'that's hardly surprising since you spent the entire afternoon in pursuit of Paul. You wouldn't have noticed if the Queen had nipped out from behind a bush.'

Holly stuck her tongue out.

'I can't find Andy either,' said Tansy, pulling the ring off a can of orange. 'The instructor said he took a bike out – not that he told me.'

Holly grinned. 'Perhaps they are having a secret love affair,' she giggled. And stopped.

The expressions on Scott and Tansy's faces told her she wasn't being very funny.

4.56 p.m.
Trying to help

'I'm sorry,' Jade said for the fifth time. 'I wish it had been your mum.'

Andy shrugged. 'Well, it wasn't, and now you've lost a bike and we're going to be late and the whole day has been a disaster.' He tightened the strap on his safety helmet.

'I'll just have to climb on the back of your bike and we'll get home that way,' said Jade.

Andy nodded. 'Just pray that no one has noticed we are missing,' he said.

5.00 p.m.
Family input

Jade's grandmother decided she could dither no longer. She picked up the telephone and dialled Paula's number.

'Paula? Is that you? Charlotte here, dear. It was so lovely to see Jade today but I honestly don't feel that you should have let her come all this way on her own. You hear such terrible . . . I beg your pardon?'

As she listened to the conversation at the other end

of the phone, her mouth fell open and the colour drained from her face.

'But she told me she had a train to catch . . . Oh, my dear. . . Yes, yes, I think you should. Phone the centre right away. And let me know what happens.'

5.01 p.m.
Taking action

'I'm going to tell Miss Partridge,' declared Tansy. 'They might have been attacked, or had an accident and be lying in a ditch somewhere.'

Or Jade might be trying it on with my boyfriend, she thought. In which case we can't move fast enough.

'I think,' said Holly, 'we might be saved the bother. Here comes Birdie and she doesn't look happy.'

Miss Partridge strode up to them. 'Have any of you seen Andrew Richards or Jade Williams?'

They shook their heads.

'Right,' she said and bustled off again.

'I think,' said Holly, 'it's about to be all systems go.'

5.03 p.m.
Pedal power

'This is harder than I thought,' panted Andy, pulling into the side of the road and wiping the sweat from his brow. 'It's going to take ages.'

'Don't stop,' pleaded Jade. 'We're wasting time.'

They had gone a few hundred metres more when a car overtook them. A police car. It pulled in front of them, and the stop sign on the rear began flashing.

'Oh no,' breathed Andy.

An officer climbed out of the driving seat and walked over to them. 'Do you realise,' he said, 'just how dangerous it is to carry a pillion rider on a pedal cycle? And that cycling without a helmet is the height of stupidity, young lady?'

Jade tried to look innocent. 'My bike was stolen,' she said. 'And we have to get back to Downsview before they discover we're missing and . . .' She stopped as Andy's heel kicked her.

'I see,' said the officer. 'I think the three of us had better have a little chat, don't you?'

5.05 p.m.
Red alert

Paula slammed the phone down and put a hand to her forehead. This was all her fault. If she'd let Jade visit her gran as she had begged her to do she would never have run off. She'd have to phone the centre. And what were they going to think of her? Some rotten substitute parent she had turned out to be. She was just about to call the centre when the phone shrilled.

'Yes?' she said abruptly. 'Oh . . . Mr Grubb. Yes, I know. Her grandmother rang. She's gone there.'

The kitchen door opened and Allegra burst in. 'Who's on the phone?' she demanded.

Paula waved a hand and gestured to her to be quiet. 'A bicycle? Oh dear. But anything could happen . . . I see. Well, you will let me know, won't you? The minute you hear anything.' She put the phone down and began to cry.

'Mum! Mum, whatever is it?'

Paula sniffed. 'It's Jade,' she said. 'She's run away. And it's all my fault.'

5.30 p.m.
Reception committee

Miss Partridge and Mr Grubb were standing on the steps when the police car pulled up. There were faces at every window, and under different circumstances Jade might have felt quite important. Right now, she felt very sick and rather small.

'Thank you for phoning us, officer,' said Mr Grubb. 'We'll take over now.'

The policeman nodded. 'I've reported the bike stolen, sir,' he said. 'I'll let you know if we have any news. Not that I hold out much hope.'

Mr Grubb turned to Andy. 'Right, Andrew, come with me. Miss Partridge, I think you have something to say to Jade?'

Jade steeled herself for the ordeal to come.

5.35 p.m.

Miss Partridge led Jade into a small room and shut the door.

'There's the phone,' she said calmly. 'I suggest you ring your aunt. She's frantic with worry.'

'You didn't phone her?' gasped Jade.

'Of course, but she already knew. She'd spoken to your gran.'

I am as good as dead, thought Jade, reluctantly dialling the number. Now she really will hate me.

'Paula? It's me. I'm sorry.'

'Oh, darling, thank goodness you're all right. We've all been so worried. Nell's in tears, Allegra won't eat her supper – thank heavens you rang.'

Jade swallowed. 'I didn't mean to cause trouble. I just wanted to see Gran and to talk about things and – '

'I know, darling. Just come home safely and we'll talk. We'll talk all you want. And Jade?'

'Yes?'

'Please try not to hate me too much.'

Jade bit her lip. 'I don't hate you,' she said. 'Honestly I don't.' And to her surprise, she realised she meant it.

7.30 p.m.
Reunions

When Jade got back to the girls' room, Holly, Tansy and Cleo were rushing around in their underwear getting ready for the disco. They all clamoured for news at the same time.

'Jade! You're back! What happened? Did you get a real rollicking? Where did you go?'

'Did you go off with Andy?' demanded Tansy.

Jade grinned. 'Not off as in off,' she assured her. 'I wanted to see Gran, and he hoped he'd find his mum – oh, can we talk about it all later? I feel a total idiot.'

Cleo smiled. 'Scott will be pleased to see you,' she said. 'He didn't have seconds of anything for supper. And if that isn't a sign of love, I don't know what is.'

For some reason that made Jade feel happier than she had done all day.

8.30 p.m.

An hour later, she discovered she was wrong. She was getting happier by the minute. She was dancing with Scott and they were having a whispered conversation.

'I'm sorry I was such a jerk,' he said. 'Going on and on about wanting you to be happy all the time. Just as long as you still – well, you know.'

'Still what?' urged Jade wickedly.

'Love me,' whispered Scott.

Jade's heart swelled till she thought it would burst through her chest.

'I do,' she whispered back. 'I really do.'

369

8.45 p.m.

Andy was treading on Tansy's toes with great regularity. Dancing was not his strongest point.

'I should have told you what I was planning to do,' he said. 'You'd have stopped me. You're so sensible.'

Tansy frowned. Sophisticated, hopefully. But sensible? Boring or what?

'I think what you did was really go-getty,' she said. 'And one day we will find your mum.'

'We?' asked Andy with a small smile.

'Yes,' said Tansy very firmly. 'We.'

9.00 p.m.
Ego-boosting

'You know,' said Cleo to Trig as they sat on the sidelines sharing a can of ginger beer, 'I would never have had the guts to do what Jade and Andy did. I'm such a wimp.'

Trig shook his head. 'No you're not – why do you always put yourself down?'

Cleo shrugged.

'You had a go at everything even though you were scared – that's being really brave.'

Cleo smiled.

'You're lovely,' said Trig. And kissed her.

Cleo decided that this was the best activity she had engaged in all weekend.

9.10 p.m.

Paul tapped Holly on the shoulder. 'Dance?' he asked.

Holly nodded in what she hoped was a coolly offhand manner.

'I was wondering,' said Paul, 'whether you'd like me to teach you to sail. Properly. On Dunchester Lake.'

He's asking me out, thought Holly joyfully. We'll be an item. Briefly she pictured herself in a small yacht, her hair blowing in the breeze, Paul staring at her adoringly.

She took a deep breath. 'I really don't think I want to sail.'

Paul looked at her quizzically.

'I was terrified,' she admitted. 'I've had it with trying to be something I'm not.'

Paul looked downcast. 'So you don't want to go out with me?' he said.

'I'd love to,' she said, laughing. 'As long as you promise it will be on dry land.'

SUNDAY

1.00 p.m.
Home again

Paula drove into the school car park and manoeuvred her Metro into the last available space. The coach wasn't due back for another ten minutes but already a cluster of parents was gathering by the gate.

'Excuse me, but are you Jade Williams's guardian?' A tall, thickset man with greying hair and red cheeks approached Paula anxiously.

'Yes, I am,' she replied, puzzled that she didn't recognise the guy.

'I'm Allan Richards,' he said. 'Andy's father. I want to apologise. I think it was my son's fault that Jade was in trouble yesterday.'

Paula smiled and shook her head. 'On the contrary,' she said, 'I gather that it was all Jade's idea. She misses her mother so.'

Allan nodded. 'But at least she has you – I try to be mum and dad to my boy and get it wrong every time. I'm sorry – I shouldn't be talking like this.'

Paula smiled. 'Oh, please,' she said, 'don't apologise. It's comforting to know I'm not the only one who messes up on a regular basis.'

1.05 p.m.

Cleo clambered off the bus, closely followed by Trig and the others. Her mum was standing by the car, deep in conversation with Holly's mother.

'. . . and so I said to him, you just give me the knickers and leave the rest to me,' Diana was enthusing.

'Indeed?' Mrs Vine murmured. 'How fascinating. Oh, look, here are the girls.'

'Darling!' Diana threw open her arms and hugged Cleo. 'Did you have the greatest fun? Was it all too exhausting?'

Cleo cringed. Whenever her mother was in work, she turned all actressy and gushy which was hugely embarrassing, especially since all her friends had normal mothers.

'Mum! Don't!' she hissed.

'Darling, I got the job,' Diana gushed. 'I am so thrilled. I want to tell you all about it.'

Not here you don't, thought Cleo. 'Mum?'

'Yes, treasure?'

'Get in the car. Now.'

1.12 p.m.

Jade had been expecting Paula to totally flip but instead she had given her a quick hug, bundled her into the car and driven off. Halfway home, she turned the car into Beckets Park and turned off the engine.

'Let's walk,' she said.

Here it comes, thought Jade. I might as well get in first.

'Paula, I'm sorry. Really. I know I shouldn't have gone off like that. I was just in such a muddle.'

Paula squeezed her hand. 'What you did was crazy,' she said. 'And we've still to talk about paying for that bicycle. But first, there are more important things to talk about. Like your mum. Like Lizzie.'

Jade gazed at her.

'You do want to talk, don't you?' questioned Paula.

'Oh yes,' said Jade. 'Yes, I do.'

'We'd had a row, you see,' said Paula with a catch in her voice. 'Just three days before the . . . before she died.'

'A row?' Jade was astonished. Her mum and Paula were always all over one another when they met.

Paula nodded. 'She said I was being unfair on Nell.' She sighed. 'I'd told her about how I sometimes wished that I hadn't had her, how I wasn't getting any younger . . .'

Jade gasped involuntarily. She remembered the words she had heard behind the closed doors of David's study earlier that week. 'Nell? It was Nell you wished you hadn't had? Not me!'

Paula stared at her. 'You? Of course not, darling. And, of course, I love Nell to bits and pieces too. It's just that she is so shy and timid and whines all the time. She's so unlike Allegra was at the same age, I sometimes don't know how to handle her.'

Jade started thinking.

'Anyway,' Paula continued, 'I shouted at Lizzie and

told her that she had it easy, that anyone could cope with one child and she should try having three to deal with. I don't know what made me do it – she always wanted another baby after you but it just didn't happen. I was so horrid to her. And that was the last time we spoke.'

Jade saw that her aunt's eyes were wet with tears.

'Mum would have understood,' she said gently. 'Everyone fights sometimes.'

Paula nodded. 'But Lizzie was always there for me. Always,' she said. 'When our mum died, she took charge of me. When I was bullied at school for being so thin and weedy, she stood up for me. And now she's gone too.'

She paused, and Jade noticed that her shoulders were shaking. Shyly she took her hand. 'Come back to the car,' she said. 'I've got something to show you.'

1.20 p.m.

'Oh, I remember that!' exclaimed Paula with a grin, picking up another photograph. 'Lizzie dressed up as a nurse and made me be the patient. Only she stuck the plaster over my mouth because she said I talked too much for a sick person!'

Jade burst out laughing.

'And will you look at this!' cried Paula. Those platform heels! I thought I was so trendy.' She turned to Jade. 'You know,' she said, 'I've never taken out my photo albums since the day of the accident. I couldn't face them. Now I think I can. Let's go home.'

'Wait.' Jade lay a hand on her arm. 'About Nell . . .'

'Oh, darling, take no notice. She'll sort herself out.'

Jade shook her head. 'No, she won't,' she declared firmly. 'We have to do that. You and me.'

1.35 p.m.

When they got home, Allegra was standing in the doorway. Jade fully expected snide remarks and comments about how juvenile she was and how much trouble she had caused everyone, so she was very surprised when her cousin grinned and gave her a hug.

'I'll kill you for frightening us all like that!' she said, but there was a note of teasing in her voice. 'Did you really get arrested?'

'Hardly!' laughed Jade. 'I'll tell you all about it later. Wheres Nell?'

1.40 p.m.

'You went away,' said Nell accusingly.

'Well, I'm back now,' said Jade. 'And I've been thinking.'

'What?'

'Well, you haven't told me that some nasty kids at school are bullying you, have you?'

Nell shook her head furiously.

'And you didn't say that they asked you for money, did you?'

More frantic headshaking.

'And you didn't tell me that it was Amanda and Jane and Susie . . .' Jade tried frantically to think of the names of more of Nell's friends.

'It wasn't them, silly! It was Emily and Rebecca in Year Four.' She stopped and clamped her hand over her mouth.

'That's it, of course,' said Jade. 'But you didn't tell me that.'

Nell eyed her. 'I didn't tell you that they called me Nellie the Elephant cos I'm fat and horrible, did I?'

Jade shook her head. How could anyone be so horrid? 'They'll cut off my hair if you tell,' she said. 'Then I'll look all funny like you.'

Jade laughed. 'Oh, Nell,' she said, 'I do love you.'

'I love you too,' said Nell. 'Will it all come right?'

Jade hugged her. 'It will,' she said, 'I promise. And from now on, I shall call you by your real name. And so must you. That will shut them up.'

Nell looked impressed. 'Helen Veronica Madeleine Webb,' she said.

'Helen will do just fine,' Jade said, laughing. 'Have you ever heard of an elephant called Helen?'

1.50 p.m.

Paula and David sat side by side on the sofa.

'How could we have been so blind?' said David for the

third time. 'All that asking for money and crying at night – we should have guessed.'

'I should have known,' said Paula. 'After all, I was teased at school and it was Lizzie who put a stop to it. Yet I couldn't see it in my own child. It took Jade to make us see what was happening under our noses.'

'Thank heavens for you, Jade,' said David. 'I was all set to be mad at you for running off like that but I don't seem to have the energy now! It's just good to have you back.'

Jade grinned. 'It's nice to be back,' she said.

Allegra looked up from the floor where she was building a Lego castle with her sister. 'Oh, please,' she said. 'Can we finish with all this sentimental twaddle and have something to eat? I've got some serious flirting to attend to this evening.'

2.10 p.m.

They were demolishing cheese pie when the phone rang.

'Hi, Jade, it's me – Cleo. Is everything OK?'

'Fine,' said Jade. 'What about you?'

'Don't ask,' said Cleo. 'Portia is locked in the bathroom because Gareth dumped her, Lettie's howling because the goldfish died, and to cap it all my mother is due to appear on national TV in her underwear.'

Jade burst out laughing. 'Well,' she said, 'look on the bright side. It's better than appearing without her underwear.'

'Honestly,' said Cleo, 'they're all manic. Families! Who'd have them? Oh, sorry, Jade, I forgot you haven't got one.'

Jade glanced at the table. Josh was reading *Insect Weekly* and telling his father that he simply had to acquire a pet scorpion, Allegra was picking bits of onion out of her pie and telling her mother that she had put them there purely to give her bad breath for Hugo, and Helen was spelling out her new name in French fries.

'Yes, I have,' she said. 'I have a perfectly manic one of my own.'

If you would like more information about
books available from Piccadilly Press
and how to order them, please visit
our website at:

www.piccadillypress.co.uk